THE FUTURE
THE PAST

Gilbert Parrell

TotalRecall Publications, Inc.
1103 Middlecreek
Friendswood, Texas 77546
281-992-3131 TL
www.totalrecallpress.com

© Copyright 2020, by Gilbert Parrell
Book Cover Design: Bruce Moran

ISBN: 9781648830280
UPC: 643977402806
Library of Congress Control Number: 2020942552

Printed in the United States of America with simultaneous printings in Australia, Canada, and United Kingdom.
FIRST EDITION
1   2   3   4   5   6   7   8   9   10

Dedicated to my wife, Jean, for her love, confidence, dedication and guidance. Without you, this book would still be stuck in my head or device somewhere.

To Mom and Dad,

Rest in Peace.

Love, your son.

About the Book

Steve Johnson, a forty-year-old Special Operations Sergeant Major, is badly wounded while on Operations. He leans back against the stone wall, knowing that this time out will probably be his last. Just as he begins to feel himself slipping away, he is astonished to see a brilliant light opening and hands reaching out, dragging him into the light itself. Only snippets of memory remain, pain, of course, and the sound of people talking. He vaguely hears, "he's going to make it" before he falls into a deep sleep, full of odd learning sessions and confusing dreams. Two years later, Steve is brought out of his sleep, completely healed, and his body regenerated into that of his twenty-year-old self. Most shocking, however, is that he finds himself in an alternate universe, on a planet called Midgard.

Johnson discovers that Midgard needs him to return to Earth to help a young woman whose invention will benefit both worlds. There are obstacles he must overcome to succeed. Midgard Rebels are determined to take this machine and will send their people to try and stop him. Earth's time is also moving much faster than Midgard. Twenty years have now gone by on Earth since his disappearance. His family has mourned his passing and has now moved on with their lives. He can go back, but his life can never be the same.

INTRODUCTION

They had always known that other worlds and dimensions were out there. They just needed a way to get to them. They understood that energy could be used as transport, but the mechanics of the procedure eluded them. It was no use sending someone or something through to another world only to have them end up a jumbled mass of meat, quivering its last gasps far from home and planet. Finally, one day, a day no different than any of the rest, they hit the right combination. A complex mix of energy, weight, and distance that would transport a person or thing anywhere they wanted. The first and most important step had been accomplished. Now it was time to see exactly how far this knowledge would take them.

CHAPTER 1

JUST ANOTHER COUNTRY

The F18 took off well before the sun lifted itself into the sky. The pilot hit the afterburners, and the combination of speed and technology hurled the aircraft into the air. The flight would be two hours out and two hours back over some restricted airspace, but that didn't matter if they didn't know the aircraft was there. He banked up to the supertanker and located the long hoses extending into a small cone. Connecting his plane to the hose, he watched the gauges patiently as the fuel forced its way into his tanks. Disconnecting from the tanker, he dropped back down onto his intended flight path. Fifteen minutes out from the rendezvous, he broke radio silence.

"Spartan 2, this is Lightning 5. Radio check, over."

"Lightning 5, this is Spartan 2. We've got you loud and clear. What's your ETA, over?"

"Lightning 5. ETA is fifteen minutes out from your location, over."

"Spartan 2, roger that. I'll have splash on the target in two mikes, over."

"Lightning 5, I'll confirm once splash is identified and code is good, over."

The heat was searing on the desert floor, with temperatures well over 110 degrees. Even under the packed earth they had dug out the night before the day was warm. Ten heavily armed men had started walking from the border three nights before and were now holed up well into the new country. It was a free zone, ten kilometres wide along the border, where they had let terrorist groups do whatever they wanted. Until now.

The Joint Special Operations Command (JSOC) had picked the Canadian Special Operations Team to carry out a rare daylight hit. It was time to send a message to these groups and the neighbouring country that they would take no more. The Intelligence, Surveillance and Reconnaissance, or ISR, had tracked the insurgents back to their training compound after they had watched them place IEDs along the road. When the country refused to do anything about the enemy camp, the coalition forces decided it was time to look after it themselves. The Canadians happened to be the next in rotation, and now four men were in a hole with eyes on the compound. By training standards, they only needed two people to run the equipment. Still, if they needed to fight their way back, the other two would provide additional insurance. The soldier turned on the machine, and it went through its self-check mode. After a minute, a green light came on, indicating all was operational. He aimed the laser intensifier at the target and said softly to the Section Commander, "Target acquired. Codes are identified."

The Section Commander pushed the talk button on his vest and relayed the information. "Rear Security, this is Spartan 2. We have eyes on and contact with Lightning 5. Get ready for some noise."

"Rear Security. Roger that. All's quiet back here. Let's get this thing done." The six men that comprised the group tapped each other, letting the other know it was showtime.

Back just over the border, the rest of the team was distributed into six CH-147 helicopters in a loiter position, flying racetrack circles in the sky. The Commander of the Operation heard the call from Spartan 2, and he broke his radio silence. "All call signs Spartan, this Spartan 1. We are five minutes to target." As the men in the birds stirred about, doing one last equipment check, the CH-147s turned east, starting their final run into the target.

The pilot of the F18 held at 20,000 feet and looked at his head-ups display, telling him his bomb codes were identified and locked in. The aircraft then released the deadly cargo, gaining altitude as the bombs fell away from the jet. The two one-thousand- pound bombs were guided by an invisible beam to their target. Sliding out of the sky, they steered left and then right, adjusting to the air pressure and wind. They hit their mark with a deafening roar, and it disappeared into a ball of fire and smoke.

"Lightning Five, this is Spartan 2. Target destroyed. We need your overwatch while we wait for extraction, over." The Team Leader turned to his men. "Pack this shit up, and let's get out of here."

"Spartan 2, roger. Will loiter till extraction complete. Be advised, assault force is twenty seconds out, coming in over your six. Out."

The target was destroyed, and the men cleared the bunker, leaving behind four pounds of C4 plastic explosives on a timer. This would give them thirty minutes to get well away from the location before the charge blew up and destroyed all evidence of their presence. The Team Leader turned his head as he entered the Rear Security position just in time to see the assault force land and hit what was left of the compound. Once complete, the ten men made their way to the extraction point.

The war had been raging for the past five years, with the terror groups gaining ground in strategic areas in the country. They'd pushed the government forces out to the fringes, leaving them barely hanging on. The nightly news continued to show abuse of civilians at the hands of the terrorists, and they were finally getting the attention of world leaders. But the leaders and their countries were tired with what they'd been through in recent conflicts. Pumping hundreds of millions of dollars, as well as having their soldiers killed in another country far from home, wasn't conducive to reelection. They needed these countries to solve their own problems, with only a little help from them. Unfortunately, it always came down to the same two choices: Turn their backs, let the country fall and put up with the terrorists or take control of the country and sort out the whole mess for them. It was the latter the West had decided to do. That's when everything changed, with all the major countries deciding to step in. Instead of sending in large, expensive ground forces to engage, they sent in their Special Operation Forces or SOF. They could work in conjunction with the country's government forces, conducting pinpoint strategic hits that would cripple the terrorists more effectively.

The SOF teams had been making good headway in the last six months, taking back control of facilities, airports, main highway routes and media centres. Once an area was back under their control, they would turn it over to the government forces, who were good at looking after the day-to-day running and security. It was only the offence they were crap at.

Steve Johnson was the Sergeant Major of the Canadian SOF team. At forty years old, he stood just under six feet tall and sported a receding hairline. He weighed slightly over two hundred pounds, all of it toned muscle and bone. His hardened, weathered face reflected his no-bullshit attitude toward his work. As some Commanders would say, "He ain't pretty, but he can get the job done." That's why they liked him. That's why he had countless deployments under his belt. Some were longer than others, but all were in shitholes around the world. It was in these places he had fine-tuned his job and set his standards. If the Officers and Noncommissioned Officers (NCOs) working with him were competent and understood their duties, no problem. If they didn't, good luck. Despite Johnson's hard-working and hard-charging good points, many disliked him. It was what he said, how he said it, and what he believed. For Johnson, it was about getting the job done, period. No whining, no bitching, get it done and do your best to bring everyone home. So, to say he had more enemies than friends was an understatement, and he knew that. His motto to himself was, "Don't trust anyone" — DTA. The team had been in the country for about three months, with at least another four to go. The rumours were they were pulling out early and were needed somewhere else. Johnson didn't like what he was hearing. They were still required here to hunt and hit the enemy hard.

Besides these rumours, HQ had changed plans again. They'd flown in over ten hummers, a four-wheeled hybrid between a beefed-up jeep and a light half-ton truck. It could usually carry six people, depending on the weapons platform, mission and configuration. HQ was again deciding how the Squadron would conduct business when they were thousands of kilometres away. Getting these new vehicles left the Officer Commanding (OC) and Johnson wondering how they were going to utilize them.

Johnson stood in the compound, mulling over possible uses for the hummers when he noticed the OC walking toward him. A bit shorter and stockier than Johnson, Major Tom Layton, was a much younger, thirty-year-old man with clear, ebony skin. His intelligence and ability to get things done allowed the two men to work exceptionally well together. As the OC got closer, the look on his face said it all and his words confirmed it.

"Sergeant Major, what the fuck are we going to do with these?"

Johnson just laughed and said, "Nice weapons' platform if you could get it into action."

"HQ wants us trained up on them ASAP, so the unit can justify the money spent to send them over."

"No problem, OC. My take on it is we take them out, do a few overnighters to say we tried them out. Then everyone's happy, everyone saves face, and the money's justified."

"Sounds good, but if shit goes sideways, you and I will answer for it, not them."

"I know. We've always answered for it, good or bad — that's what we get paid for."

"Yeah...pay. That's another story. I don't want to be a Major all my life."

"I got it. It'll all be fine. Once we have the vehicles outfitted and prepped, I'll come and get you for the final look."

"Do that," the OC said and walked back to the HQ building.

The teams worked on the vehicles throughout the day, packing and unpacking, seeing what would fit and what wouldn't.

"Sergeant Major," was the call that brought Johnson's head up. A Communications NCO was walking over to him with a piece of paper in his hand. "Sergeant Major, the OC needs you. We got a ping on target 357."

Johnson read the paper and said, "I'll be right there. Tell the OC I'm passing on the Warning Order to the Warrants. They can get their guys moving." He looked again at the note and thought, *Looks like we're working tonight.*

CHAPTER 2

*T*arget 357 was one of many compounds the coalition forces had under listening surveillance. It was a small village, surrounded by a twenty-foot high mud and straw wall. Inside the wall were various buildings of different sizes and purposes, from housing livestock to family units. The enemy had set themselves up within this compound and had begun conducting offensive operations.

Walking into the Ops Centre, Johnson saw the OC. "Warning Order is being passed now. What do we have?"

The OC looked at him from a large screen displaying a satellite image of the compound marked 357 and replied, "They picked up communication and want us to engage the target tonight. We'll lift off at last light. Flying time is about an hour. Hit the target, do a search, see what we can find. Then depart before first light. Hopefully, we'll be back here at sunup in time for breakfast. Time is now 1200 hours. I'll give orders at 1400. Rehearsals just after that, eat, rest, then fly out."

"Good. I'll pass that on. You need a hand with anything?"

"No, not at this time. Everything is Standard Operating Procedure. Let's keep things simple."

"See you at 1400," Johnson said. He exited the building and gathered the second in commands of the platoons. They had been alerted with the warning order and had passed the information on to their men. Johnson made things quick, confirming the timings and what was needed for special equipment.

Once the briefings were completed, Johnson headed back to his quarters and passed by the telephone line. He stopped and looked at the long row of empty phones and decided to give a quick call home. He punched the sequence of numbers slowly into the pad. His experience was that if you did it too fast, the line wouldn't work — something to do with connecting to the satellite, the techs had said. The line on the other end hesitated momentarily and then rang. After a few moments, a sleepy female voice picked up the line.

"Hello," she said.

Hearing his wife Elly, visibly released the tension mirrored in his face. He raked his hand over his thinning hairline, pulling the sweat-filled strands of hair away from his face. "Baby, it's me. Sorry to wake you."

"Oh, hon, it's okay. I always love hearing your voice. What time is it?"

"Over here? Just after 1230 hours. Must be about 0200 your time."

She paused for a second. "Yup. Two o'clock in the morning. Just checked the clock. Are you okay?"

"I'm okay. I just miss you. This op has been a long haul."

"The news said an SF team went over the border and took out a training facility. Their news is saying it was a hospital."

"No, it wasn't us," he lied with a twinge of remorse. He had never enjoyed keeping the truth from his wife. "But I doubt that it was a hospital. There are no hospitals here." Wanting to change the subject, he added, "So what's new? How's the new job and the boss?" Elly was a grade five teacher at a local elementary school in Ontario.

"Oh, the job's great. We're busy with the school year winding down. Report cards and assessments are due. It makes the days go by quickly. It's only the nights that are lonely." Elly's passion for her job and the children she taught spilled through her words as she began talking to him. They had never had children of their own. Johnson only half-listened to her words as she continued to talk about her day. Instead, he recreated in his mind the picture of his beautiful wife. Despite her being nearly forty years of age, she had maintained a slim, athletic build. He closed his eyes and painted a picture of her face and long blonde hair.

She suddenly yawned deep into the telephone and said, "Oh, sorry."

Her comment brought him back. "No, I'm sorry for waking you." Although he didn't want the conversation to end, he said, "I'll let you get back to sleep."

She paused for a second. "Steve, are you sure you're okay?"

"Baby, all's fine, just another boring day in the sandbox," Johnson said.

"Okay." She hesitated and then continued. "I love you, and I miss you. Look after yourself and come home to me."

"I will," he said. "I love you, too. Get some sleep and kick ass at the job."

"Always," she said. "Thanks for calling, babe. Love you."

"Bye for now. Talk to you soon."

The line went dead. Johnson stared at the phone, already missing their connection. Sighing, he softly hung the phone back up and walked away.

By 1700, all the battle preparations had been completed. By 1900, after one last question and answer, the Squadron moved to the hummers. Once all fifty-five personnel were loaded, they moved to the flight line. As they drove out to the helicopters, Johnson looked at the OC with a grin and said, "I told you we'd use them."

The man rolled his eyes and replied, "I think HQ wanted more than just a two-kilometre drive to the flight line."

"They never specified," he snorted. They both barked a short laugh.

As they got closer to the helicopters, Johnson could see the crew from the aviation unit prepping the birds. The pilots and their crew were rushing around, opening panels, checking tires and blades. As they off-loaded the hummers, the airmen signalled for the team to move in behind their assigned birds. The men strained under their heavy loads, forming into files twenty metres behind the ramps.

Johnson moved to his position, then stood looking west across the desert landscape. The air had started to cool, and the sun was slowly going down. The dust in the still air reflected the sunset's brilliant colours, turning the otherwise brown, bleak desert into a vibrant kaleidoscope of reds, blues and yellows. He turned his head back and gave his equipment one last check. His attention was drawn to the ticking of the igniters along with the smell of jet fuel burning. The whine of the engines started, quietly at first, then picking up to an ear-shattering roar as they came up to a slow idle. The word finally passing on to load up, the men made their way onto the ramps and into the black openings.

They sat down on the floor of the helicopter, with their backs up against the wall. The pitch of the rotors changed as the machine sped up. Finally, the aircraft started to move forward, picking up speed, then lifting smoothly into the air. Johnson hit the button on his watch, illuminating its face. *One hour to go*, he thought, closing his eyes as they rose into the dark night.

A kick to his leg and someone screaming into his earpiece brought him around. "Fifteen minutes to insertion," a dark form in front of him hollered. Johnson grabbed the man next to him, repeating the same words in his ear. He made sure the man was moving and had passed on the order. He did another equipment check by feel and then ran the Operation sequence through his mind one more time.

A tap and another scream came into his ear. "Five minutes." It signalled they'd be on the ground soon, so he turned on his night vision goggle (NVG). Flipping their NVGs down, he and the rest of the team stood and braced themselves. The descent came quickly, with the pitch of the rotors deepening. The jolt of the landing signalled their arrival, and they spilled out into a black rush of movement, pushing into the hurricane blast from the rotors and the darkness of the night. Moving straight beyond the rotor wash, Johnson could see the infrared laser pointer from the Gunship. It had picked out the teams' entry point, helping the men get oriented and moving toward the target. The first element sprinted to the mud wall, placed explosives on it, and blew an entry hole directly into the compound. The OC and Johnson listened to the team's progress over the radios as they picked up and started moving forward.

Stepping through the entry point and into the compound, they moved down an alley, staying tight to the mud walls. Johnson watched through his NVG as the details of the area were revealed. The ambient light was good. Looking down the alley, he could see the lead man signalling a four-way intersection ahead. The group silently stepped into the void, crossing the junction. As Johnson stepped up, ready to move, heavy fire started from the right. He watched, narrow-eyed, as the enemy's green tracers and the team's red tracers were either going straight and hitting something or skipping and flying off into space. The confining view provided by the NVG added further confusion to the battle scenario. They tried to get around the enemy, looking for other avenues of approach to possibly flank or find a weak point. Johnson knew the enemy was trying to do the same thing to them. The advantage was given to the enemy; this was their terrain. The enemy's first bit of fire was to test the team, hit them lightly, to see what they had. With a better picture, they would decide to either fight now or leave it for another day. They had this option; his team didn't.

The team went full-on, striking hard and winning the firefight. The men got the automatics moving, firing their 220 rounds a minute. After the first maneuver, Johnson could see the OC wanted them to come in from the right, then toward what appeared to be an old cattle corral. After securing that position, they could advance through an alley to the enemy's HQ, hit it, secure it and search it for Intel.

The team moved hard and fast, seamlessly working through the problem. They had gone through these situations many times before. As the firebase increased its rate of fire, the assault team moved in while the enemy's heads were down. Moving up to the corral area, a mix of fresh cow shit with an underlying odour of rotting decay hit him. They stopped, caught their breath and then sprinted to the far side of the corral. Johnson looked around, breathing hard. He could see the rest of HQ was with him. Off to his left, they had finally made a breach and were flowing from the corral into an alleyway. With the firefight starting to die down, the enemy was pulling back to better positions, possibly to get the team into a kill zone.

The gunship flying above them was giving real-time situation reports on where the enemy was. This worked well in the daytime, but at night, it sometimes added more confusion to the fight. Hearing what their observers saw from the aircraft and trying to integrate it with what they were actually looking at was difficult. Combining all that with their restrictive night vision and a hidden enemy trying to kill you compounded the difficulty.

The men flowed into the narrow alley and along its sides, using what little cover they had. Pushing forward and staying low, they could hear the enemy's rising panic. They had begun shooting at shadows, giving their positions away and providing the team with the advantage. The end of the alley opened into a clearing, where the team pushed along its sides, keeping up their rate of fire. Johnson glanced to his left and noted the OC with the radio operator, directing teams and managing situation reports.

Once secure, they pushed across the open area, taking up positions at a low wall on the far side. Johnson sensed, and then saw, the enemy to his left and shouted, "Movement on the left!" He gave a fire control order and joined the fight, firing steadily and rapidly toward the threat. The OC was now on his left and shooting beside him as Johnson hollered, "They're moving to our rear!" The forward team had already pushed through the area, leaving them and the Rear Section to deal with the problem.

Johnson kept up a steady rate of fire at the enemy's muzzle

flashes. Simultaneously shooting and moving to his left and right, he heard screams that confirmed he had hit his targets. As they secured the flank, he could see their Rear Section coming up, ready to push through.

The OC yelled at Johnson, "Stay with the Rear Section for communication." Johnson acknowledged and fell into an extended line formed by the section as the OC pulled back to coordinate the rest of the fight. It was a ballsy move by the enemy, trying to surround the team, sucking them into a kill zone. They'd have succeeded, Johnson thought, if they'd been quiet and taken their time. But they jumped the gun and showed their hand. The team, he realized, now had the advantage.

Johnson, with the Rear Section, pushed up the left flank. They were mainly comprised of medics and explosives personnel. If they came under contact, the men could hold their line for a short time but not for long. Hopefully, it wouldn't be the latter. The gunship, still scanning, could see no further activity or movement and passed on the good news to the Squadron.

Johnson pushed the Rear Section farther to the left and stopped them, giving the men time to shake themselves out. Taking a deep breath, he paused and wiped the perspiration from his face. The sweat had combined with the desert dust, leaving a thick layer of mud over his uniform. Off to his right, he saw a housing complex surrounded by a rock wall with a locked gate. He yelled, "Hold, we need to search the area." A Fire Base was put in place, acting as overwatch while Johnson and the section climbed over the wall and pushed forward. A quick cursory search was conducted, and the area seemed to be clear. He suddenly realized that the rear was getting too far from the main party, which could cause a deadly break in contact. Immediately, he informed the OC and was told to move forward ASAP.

Withdrawing, Johnson began to walk back to the wall, turning for one last look behind him. A flash of movement at ground level caught his attention, making him react instinctively.

"Tunnel complex!" he screamed as the man emerging from the ground pulled up his weapon and aimed it at Johnson. He wasted no time engaging with the man and thought, *This is going to get ugly*. The taking of a life was never easy, but Johnson had little remorse for those who were threatening his life or the lives of his men.

The rest of the section was already over the wall, and he needed to move fast, clear it and get over to the other side. The enemy now started to pour out from the ground and return fire, their faces showing a fierce, desperate determination. They were dressed in their traditional gear, baggy trousers, loose-fitting tops and turbans. All carried an AK-47 with magazine pouches of ammo across their chests. Clawing up out of the opening, the muted colours of their garments blended into their surroundings. They swarmed upward, firing their weapons indiscriminately on fully automatic. Johnson moved as fast as he could, feeling the bullets ricocheting off the wall beside him. Seeing some cover a few metres to his right, he dove for it, tucking himself in beside it. Returning fire, he heard the rear section behind him, getting up on the wall and doing the same, only to hear the enemy respond in kind.

He began screaming at his men, "Push right, push right!" hoping they would get some fire laid down. All he needed was a few seconds to get over the wall. A sudden momentary lull in the fighting gave Johnson his chance. "Move now," he muttered to himself, getting up only to feel the shock of bullets tearing into his shoulder and legs. Heaving heavily against the wall, he felt himself falling back down into the dirt. Taking only enough time for a shallow, pain-filled breath, he pulled himself back to a position against the gate. A quick inventory of damages done ascertained that he could still control some of his movements. He grimaced and wryly thought, *Nice try, buddy*.

Reeling with pain, he tried to reach for bandages in his first aid pouch to stop the flow of blood. It was steadily running from one of the wounds in his leg, *running*, he thought, *like it was happy to be free of his body.* He suddenly realized that his left arm wouldn't move. Dropping his weapon, he used his right hand to reach for the kit but had only enough energy to pull out the bandages and drop them onto his lap. His head was beginning to feel light from the loss of blood, and his vision was starting to blur. Through his earpiece, he could hear his team calling for the medic. Johnson furiously fought to hold himself together, tensing himself against the searing pain to maintain control as he began to feel his world whirl around him. *I've gotta fight this, get out of here. I've gotta keep going, keep trying. It can't just be over!*

Straining to keep his head and shoulders upright, Johnson again heard voices through his earpiece reporting, "The Sergeant Major's hit bad." The team pushed forward to retrieve him, but the enemy responded in full force, firing RPGs in their direction. He could feel the vibrations as his body was lifted off the ground from the repeated impacts, hitting him again and again with shrapnel. He vaguely became aware that there was a loud and low drone above him. Blinking his eyes rapidly, trying to focus through the blood, he realized it was their gunship. It was laying down suppressive fire, finally providing the team with a respite from the enemy. He thought *We'll be all right. I'll be all right… if I can just hang on.*

Shock had started to set in, and he was getting cold. He tasted the metallic tang of blood boiling up in the back of his throat. Oblivious to the fight around him, he asked himself, *Is this my time? Is it over? No. Hold on. Fight.*

With the support of the gunship, the team was finally beating back the enemy assault. Not able to hold his head up, it rolled back with the weight of his helmet, and he could only helplessly watch the tracer fire ripping over his head. Johnson tried to call out, but he couldn't speak. Through his earpiece, he heard the men pull back and regroup. *That's it*, he thought. They wouldn't be able to get to him in time. His head sagged to the left, and he tried to lift it again, but his body had stopped obeying him.

As he gradually felt his remaining will to stay conscious leave him, he saw what looked like a lightning bolt ripping open a gaping hole beside him. The light emanating from the sphere was so bright he had to close his eyes, and he wondered for a moment if it was perhaps the sun coming up at dawn. *No, that wasn't right,* he worried. *It's too bright, and it's not time yet. What is this?*

The illumination increased in intensity, and the gaping hole became all-encompassing. Johnson could feel a warm breeze coming from the light. A pair of arms grabbed him hard around his chest, and he heard words whispering into his ear, "You're needed somewhere else." He felt himself being dragged backward and, looking back, briefly glimpsed the black night of the compound. As quickly as it had opened, the hole closed. There was no sound, and everything became utterly still. His eyes closed, and he knew no more.

CHAPTER 3

*E*ric Stanton was the Commanding Officer of the Government Intelligence Agency or GIA. He was a tall man, forty-five years old, with quick brown eyes and shortly cropped hair. The lean muscles in his arms, back and legs gave confirmation of the hours spent keeping himself in top physical and mental form. He was very focused and driven in his pursuit of perfection and expected no less from his subordinates. Now, his fingers tapped impatiently on the desk in front of him. He had just been informed by the Traveller that they had potentially found a window of time in which to gather Steve Johnson. Johnson was a POI, a person of interest, that they had had their eyes on for some time. They had tried to predict the right time for extraction, but for some reason, they hadn't been able to pinpoint an exact time on him until now. The combat situation he was in had a high probability of his being seriously injured. The opportunity to take him had finally presented itself.

Fortunately, the GIA didn't need him immediately. His injuries would heal, and they could now take the time to perfect their system, a system that had the potential to save their world. He leaned back in his chair with a smirk on his face, remembering why they had picked Johnson. He wasn't the smartest, quickest or most skilled person they'd been keeping their eye on. But he was the most consistent, self-sufficient subject they had found, and he was relentless in completing a mission. They needed this man. They needed continual access to Earth because their bodies were only able to sustain short periods of time on the planet. A human from Earth could go back and forth without difficulty. He opened Johnson's file, looking further into it. *It sounds to me like you could change the world all by yourself.* He smiled. *All you'd need is a baseball bat and your attitude, so I've got a job for you. Sleep tight and heal. You're all mine now.*

Through his eyelids, Johnson began to sense bright lights that flickered overhead. The cold air of the room moved against his skin, and he could smell the harsh mix of antiseptic and blood. He tried to open his eyes, but they wouldn't obey; they were being held down by something. He could feel the movement of people all around him, hands probing and pushing at him, pulling him onto a platform of some sort. The world swirled around him. Johnson felt sharp, deep pain emanating from the wounds in his body, then clothes being ripped off and pressure being applied. He struggled to remain conscious while his mind tried to comprehend what was happening. Did I pass out? Did the guys get me out? Was I in the medical tent? Am I with the enemy? A flash of hard insight came to him as he realized the answer to that one question. He hadn't been captured. The enemy would have shot him in the head and stripped anything of value off him.

So where was he, and why couldn't he wake up? *Maybe it's purgatory*, he thought, *limbo, where you're judged on what you'd accomplished in life.* He vaguely recalled the small, vicious nuns that had so diligently supervised his education and threatened him with hell at every perceived transgression. *I wonder what the verdict will be,* he thought hazily. Just before drifting back into unconsciousness, he heard someone in the distance say, "He's going to make it."

"The Operation is almost complete." John Alexander spoke briskly and professionally. He was the Head Doctor at the Medical Centre, a tall, trim man with a ready smile, sharp blue eyes and a head of thick, unruly hair. At thirty-eight years old, John was the youngest doctor to ever hold that position. He possessed a brilliant, analytical mind and was respected by his employees because of his work ethic and ability to lead by example.

These attributes made him perfect for this rush job. It was a highly unusual, unprecedented event. But here he was and not a minute too soon; his patient had only just pulled through. *I wonder why they wanted him, and what makes him so unique?* John thought as he was finishing up.

Sarah Rhodes and Mark Countryman were John's two assistant medical physicians, along with an array of nurses and other medical staff. Sarah was the more spontaneous of the two. At only twenty-nine years of age, she was a small and vivacious woman who loved her work.

Mark was the steadying factor in the duo. He was thirty-three years of age, a tall, thin man whose professional, calm and quiet manner enhanced the team's performance. Together, they were unbeatable. They were now working quickly and efficiently, doing the essential vitals checks, wrapping up the final dressings and disconnecting intravenous tubes that were no longer required.

"John, it looks as if his BP is down again. How much longer?" Sarah asked.

"BP will stabilize in a minute. This one's a fighter. Just a bit more," John said coolly as he finished his last wraps. "Okay, that's it. We'll place him in a thermal envelope, initiate coma induction and let him heal. He should be fine."

After a few minutes, Sarah looked at John, smiling slightly. "You were right," she said, "BP is stable."

John nodded back at her. "Hook up the feeding tube and connect the electrical therapy unit to his muscles. We'll do one final check on them to ensure the pulses are operational and are keeping his muscles fluid."

Half an hour later, Mark looked down at their finished product. "Nice job, John. Looks like you put him back together."

"We'll see. Johnson's not out of the woods yet, but the prognosis for now is good. Once the wounds have stabilized, we'll put him into deep sleep recovery and healing for as long as it takes."

One of the nurses gently reminded John, "Doctor, one last piece. The wrist coder."

"Thank you," John said. "Don't want to forget that." He reached onto the table, grabbed the narrow, silver band and slid it onto Johnson's arm. "Sarah, can you look at the screen and confirm it's functioning, please?"

"Let's see," she said, looking over and manipulating a few icons. "Confirmed, Doctor. Heart rate, blood pressure, GPS tracking. Everything is good."

John looked down at the patient, lying so still, wrapped in bandages from head to toe and enveloped in the thermal blanket. He was stable, all the holes were patched and sealed, and anything disconnected had been reconnected. Medical advancements had significantly improved, but there was still only so much that could be done. The man had been gravely wounded and had not been pulled out of combat until the very last moment. John looked down at him and then to the hologram. "You're going to make it. I know you will." He glanced at Mark and Sarah and said, "Let's roll him out. Time for lunch."

It was well past dawn and hours since the soldiers had taken over the compound. Prisoners had been flown out, and any useful information had been sent back to HQ. More land forces had been flown in to secure the location as the special operations team began to make their way back to camp. The OC stayed with one of the platoons as the CH147 landed in the field. The helicopter's rotors slowed down to a stop as the engines died, and the Commanding Officer (CO) walked off the back ramp. He looked up and, seeing the OC standing in the middle of the dirt field, said briskly, "Tom, why can't we find Johnson?"

The OC, clearly frustrated, replied, "Sir, I don't know. We've been over this area a dozen times. We even had the dog handlers searching, but the dogs keep returning to the spot where he was wounded. If he'd been blown to bits, we'd still have found a trace. Even the RPGs they used would've left something."

"Follow me," the CO said. The two men turned and walked up the ramp of the CH147. Inside, he reached for a laptop. "Watch this video from the Gunship."

Tom stepped closer to the screen, and they both scrutinized the video as it played. It showed the compound, the men moving and the ensuing firefight. They could see Johnson, with his back up against the wall, trying to make it over but then falling back down. Without warning, the screen erupted with a blinding white light, the entire area completely obscured. A second later, the light disappeared and, with it, Johnson. The video stopped playing, and the two men sat without speaking. The CO finally closed the laptop and placed it back into the webbed seating of the helicopter.

Tom shook his head and said quietly, "What the hell was that? One of the prisoners said he saw Johnson get pulled into a light. I didn't believe him, but if someone had dragged him off, the dogs would've followed the scent." He stood up and contemplated quietly before taking a deep audible breath. Without looking at the CO, he said, "Sir, we've been all over this place, even taken the dogs out along the blood paths leading away from here, but there's nothing." He shook his head in defeat and returned his gaze to the CO. "I can't explain what we've just seen, and I don't know where he is."

The CO nodded and replied evenly, "I know you've done your best, but we need to take one last look. We've brought in some new dogs, anything that's going to give us a possible different result." The group walked the compound again with the different dogs. As each of the animals took the scent, they did the same thing. They zigzagged around the enclosed space on their long leashes and then came to rest on the last spot Johnson had been seen.

The day stretched into late afternoon as the search ground to an end. The men assembled themselves on the dirt field they used as a Landing Zone and watched patiently as the distant specks of helicopters became larger with each passing second. As they landed, the men made their way onto the birds. Tom was the last to load. Coming up onto the ramp of his helicopter, he stopped, turned and saluted toward the compound. "I don't know what happened to you, buddy. I'm sorry I couldn't find you and bring you home." Wearily he turned, walked into the helicopter's belly and sat down. The pitch of the rotors changed, and dust flew about the field, darkening the sky. Lifting off, they hovered for an instant and then shifted to forward flight. The chopper quickly gained speed and altitude as the compound they left behind slowly became only an abandoned speck in the desert.

CHAPTER 4

Johnson was dreaming strange, disjointed dreams. At times he was still in the compound, still fighting, still feeling the bullets and shrapnel ripping into his body. He tried to scream in agony, but his voice failed him. Hands were reaching for him. He tried to fend them off, but they kept moving forward, kept clawing at him. At other times, he was in a large, darkened room with people in white lab coats, drawing close, poking and prodding his body and saying, "He's coming along fine." The dreams came and went as he drifted from scenario to scenario.

Sometimes he was home, laughing and holding his wife; at other times, he felt he was back in college. Mathematics, chemistry, physics and a barrage of different subjects were reintroduced and updated into his mind and then new information flooded into him. Computer systems, electromagnetic energy, lethal weaponry and an array of other topics he could barely comprehend. He was learning about a new culture, not unlike Earth, but still very different. He could hear a kind voice encouraging him to keep his brain working, to keep learning and felt gentle hands calming him. His body was being manipulated, being moved. He sensed electrical impulses that contracted and then relaxed his arms and legs. The pulses were intense and, in his dreams, transitioning into long runs and hard physical workouts. He could sense the weights as he wrapped his hands around them and lifted them above his head. He felt the sweat dripping from his brow and could see the rolling wheat fields of his native prairie homeland as he ran through them. The physicality of the dreams was so lifelike he could smell the grass under his feet and the breeze against his face.

TWO YEARS LATER

The nurses guided the four beds down the hallway to the Recovery Room, talking randomly as they went. Each bed had a patient on them and levitated above the floor, moving silently and effortlessly with just a slight touch of their hand. As they approached the Recovery Room, a scanner picked up the patients' identification, and the door slid open. They directed the patients into a large, well-lit room big enough to hold twenty people. The nurses stopped in front of a Control panel and punched a stabilizer button to hold each bed in place. In turn, the room's computer automatically picked up and identified each patient, displaying a hologram of their body, with vitals and other pertinent information above their heads.

John, Sarah and Mark walked into the room immediately behind their staff, moving to a position behind the Control panel. They looked out at the four patients as the nurses went through their routine protocol and reported to John individually. As the last nurse nodded and gave him a thumbs-up, he said, "So remind me, who are we waking today?"

Sarah brought up her screen and pointed to each hologram above the patients. "We have three residents, two men and a woman. We also have one non-resident man. On the left, we have a man named Agar, thirty years old, who has been under for three months. He was badly wounded in a raid but has healed nicely. Next is Sanchez, twenty-four years old, who has been under six months. He was hurt in a training accident. Next to him is a woman named Hanson, thirty years old, injured in the same raid as Agar. She's been under three months as well. Lastly, we have the non-resident, Johnson. He's been an anomaly; we've never seen anything like this before. At the time of recovery, he was forty years old. His spontaneous regeneration now has him at approximately twenty-two years old. He's been under for two years, the longest we've ever had anyone in Stasis. You remember him. He was our last-minute job for the GIA."

John nodded and said, "Yes, I remember this one. We had to include an extensive learning protocol. It's time he came around. Anything else?"

Sarah spoke, "Three of the patients were taken from combat situations. We should be ready once they start to wake up. They may still think they're in the fight."

"I assume the nurses are prepared?"

"Yes, sir. We have sedation ready, but I don't want to use it if we don't have to. The other concern I have is patient number two." She handed John the patient's screen. "As you are aware, we had problems with him during recovery."

John looked at the screen, frowned and replied, "His injuries have healed, but I see a neurological flaw. He looked over at Mark. "What's your opinion?"

Mark replied, "I've been all over his screens and can't pinpoint a fix. Five months ago, I thought he may have had an infection, but his scans and fluid work are all clear. I'm not sure we have a solution, but I recommend we bring him out and see what happens. If we leave him under too long, it could get more complicated."

John agreed and said, "Good, all four will be coming out of Stasis." He glanced at the clock. "Looks like we still have about ten minutes." The three doctors continued their observations with each of the patients, finally stopping at Johnson.

Sarah reviewed his screen. "I've been here five years and have never observed a non-resident brought out before."

John replied, "Sarah, I've been here a lot longer, and I've never seen one, either." He glanced again at the clock and said, "It's time." The three doctors walked behind the Control panel, and John nodded to Mark. "It's your show now."

Mark directed his next comments to the nurses standing quietly beside each patient. "All the scans look good. Be ready for any malfunctions. Commencing Stasis recovery now." He punched in commands, initiating a protocol designed to stimulate a waking process. The individual control panels began steadily pulsing each patient's neurotransmitters, gently at first and then increasing in intensity. The patients started their transition from a controlled deep sleep into a slow, waking process. There had been problems in the past, so each residing nurse could override the procedure from the bedside. Mark said to Sarah, "Could you assist with Johnson? They may need another hand there."

"I can do that," she said and moved from behind the panel to take up a place on Johnson's right.

Mark called out, "Halfway there." The patients were beginning to rouse while the nurses placed reassuring hands on them, speaking soft words of encouragement. Slowly, one by one, they opened their eyes and came out of the deep sleep.

Johnson felt himself floating up as if he were coming up out of a long, dark tunnel. Groggy and disoriented, he desperately willed himself to keep moving forward. Open your eyes, he urged himself, but his eyes resisted, heavy and unwilling to cooperate. Fighting back, Johnson shouted the command again in his head, this time feeling a twitch on one eyelid. Angry at his body, he called out once more, "Open your fucking eyes." Reluctantly, as if in protest, his eyes slowly cracked open and then raised all the way. It took a few long moments for the scene to come into focus, and he found himself gazing up at a ceiling that glowed with a soft, clear light. There were unfamiliar, concerned faces looking at him, and he tried to focus on them. Then came a voice. "Steven, can you hear me?" It was coming from a woman who was holding his hand and looking down at him.

Squinting his eyes, Johnson focused his energy into his voice and managed a harsh, raspy reply. "Call me Steve," was all he could get out.

Sarah nodded to the nurse. "Looks good. He's responding to us. You can tilt him up."

The bed moved from a fully prone to a half propped up position. Johnson could now make out two men standing behind a control panel. One of them suddenly rushed to a bed over to his right. Johnson was able to follow the man with his eyes and saw three other people in beds beside him. Two of the patients had been propped up, but another man was still in a prone position. He watched and tried to listen in, but the sounds were muffled, and his brain was having a hard time making sense of the scene. A few seconds later, he noted a man quietly shaking his head. In response, the nurse silently covered the patient's head and guided him out of the room.

Johnson could now begin to feel his body waking. Cautiously, he started moving his hands and then his feet and legs. He felt stiff and awkward, but there was no pain. Still confused, Johnson recalled his last moments and the memory of the bullets that had ripped into his body. *But the excruciating pain was gone*, he thought, relieved.

The nurse standing beside him said, "I'm going to run a few tests on you. I want to see how your pupils react, and I'll be shining a light in your eyes. I'll be checking your extremities by squeezing them, and you can tell me if you feel it or not. Are you okay with that?"

Johnson, still helpless and exhausted, could only stare quietly at the nurse. Understanding his inability to answer, she reassured him before shining a light in one eye and then the other. Satisfied with the result, she performed pressure tests, methodically starting at his head and working down to his feet. The tests finally complete, she turned toward the people behind the panel. "Johnson's fine."

Johnson turned his head slightly, seeing a hologram of his body floating in the air. Reaching out tentatively to touch it, his hand slid through the image, and he heard a voice say, "You can't touch or feel it."

He looked farther to his right. It was a woman on the bed next to him. She smiled and spoke again. "I said you can't touch or feel it."

Johnson returned her smile and replied haltingly, "Never seen one before."

Her face became slightly confused and questioning. "Never seen one before? You must've been under for a long time."

John looked out from behind the panel and said firmly, "Save the talk until your vocal cords have had the chance to recover a bit more. You'll have plenty of time to get acquainted later." The woman sighed resolutely at the doctor and turned her attention to her nurse.

"We'll be adjusting these beds now," advised Johnson's nurse as she unstrapped the belt securing his waist. To his astonishment, the bed moved down smoothly until he was in a sitting position, feet on the floor. He glanced down to look under the bed but could see no visible means of support. Confused, he asked, "Am I awake or still asleep?"

She smiled and replied, "You're very much awake. Let me undo this belt first, and then you can give me your hands. We're going to get you on your feet."

As Johnson held out his hands, the nurse took them and pulled him up. The room began to spin as blood flooded to his core. He wobbled momentarily but regained his balance once the rush of blood stabilized. Swaying slightly, he asked, "Where am I?"

"You're in the hospital. We've just taken three of you out of Stasis. Now, we need to get those legs moving. Try to take a step with me." She pulled slightly on his hands, and his body responded sluggishly. Willing his feet to move, he picked up one foot and placed it in front of him. Finding his balance, he adjusted his weight and then dragged his other foot forward.

"That's excellent. Keep going."

"I was wounded. I thought I was going to die. I can remember a bright light and a man pulling me into it."

She began guiding him around the bed now, one slow step at a time, and replied, "Yes, you were hurt quite badly. Everything seems to be in good working order now, though. A bright light and a man? I'm sorry. I don't know anything about that. How's your balance?"

"I'm off a bit," he said. "Let me try again." Exhausted but determined, he pulled his hands away from hers and supported himself on the bed for a moment. Taking a deep breath, he turned back to her and took another step. Walking this time on his own, he saw the other two patients doing the same thing. He appeared to be alive and whole, he thought. *The only thing that matters now is where the hell am I?*

CHAPTER 5

*J*ohn moved from behind the panel out to the three patients. *"My name is Dr. John Alexander.* I'm the Head Doctor here at the Medical Centre. These are my assistants, Dr. Sarah Rhodes and Dr. Mark Countryman. It looks like everyone here has successfully made it through their operations and Stasis procedures. Agar and Hanson, you'll be moved to the GIA wing and housed there until you're fit. After that, you'll be brought back to duty. I want the three of you to remember to take it easy for the first few days. Keep your movements slow." He walked to the panel, stopped and turned back to them. "I almost forgot — you'll also be given ample opportunity to contact your families. Any questions?"

Hanson lifted her chin toward Johnson and asked, "Where's he going?"

"Miss Hanson, that's our business, but I'm sure you'll see one another again."

Johnson had watched and listened to the conversation. "Hanson," he called, looking at her, "I'm Steve Johnson."

Hanson smiled. "Hi, Steve. I'm Asta. Pleased to meet you."

John cut them off abruptly. "Time to move. Let's get you settled."

The three patients obediently returned to their beds and were guided out of the room by their nurses. From there, Agar and Hanson were taken to the right, and Johnson's nurse steered him left, following the three doctors. As he travelled through the corridor, his mind raced back, trying to recall his last conscious moments. He remembered the gritty smell of battle, the dirt that was stuck in his nostrils and seeped into his pores. Nothing was left; it was all gone. The reverberating explosions of incoming rounds, the screams of the wounded men and the frantic battle commands were nonexistent. *I was hit*, he thought. *Not once, not twice, more.* He remembered the pain, the heat, the confusion. *The light. I remember arms pulling me into the light.*

His gaze shifted down to himself. He was wearing a sleek, tan coloured outfit made of an unidentifiable material that felt warm to the touch. The top was opened slightly, and he lifted it to examine his upper torso and arms. What had happened to his wounds? The wounds that had been so raw and bloodied were healed entirely, with only faintly lined scars remaining. He discovered an unfamiliar silver coder on his wrist and scrutinized it carefully, wondering what its purpose was. Reaching down, he pulled his pants up to look at his legs. Both showed faint scarring but felt healthy and whole and only slightly stiff from lack of movement.

The nurse guiding his bed stopped at the end of a corridor, where there was a set of closed doors in front of them marked "Special Access." She reached a calming hand to his, wished him luck and returned down the corridor. Sarah took over, guiding the bed through the now opened doors. The new hallway was almost sixty metres long, with doors running off either side and a large window at the end. They had nearly reached the end of the hall before John spoke.

"Welcome to your new home. This won't be permanent. We want you to get adjusted here, and we'll move you when you're ready."

They slowed, then stopped outside a door. A light turned from red to green, and the door slid open as a screen beside it, once blank, now showed his image. He stared at it, slightly confused. The picture appeared to have been taken at least twenty years ago. Sarah guided his bed into the room, secured it and raised him into a sitting position. "I hope this meets your approval," Sarah said. "Now, I need you to get up again. We have to show you something."

Johnson gingerly placed his feet onto the floor, and Sarah

assisted him in standing. "Walk this way, please," she said, guiding him by an elbow to a sink and mirror. He walked slowly but steadily toward it, gaining confidence with every forward step. When he reached the mirror, he lifted his head, saw his image and jolted to a stop. He stretched a hand out to the mirror, then jerked it back and brought it to his face. Looking at his reflection, he ran his hand over his nose and lips. The image in front of him was a much younger version of the man he had come to know. The picture on the outside door was now the same as the face looking back at him. His hairline, once receding, was again thick and full, and his hair was a rich, dark brown. His face was smooth, unlined, and the skin pulled tight across high cheekbones. His eyes were no longer faded but rather a bright blue. No laugh lines emanated from them, and he realized that he no longer needed glasses for detail. "What did you do?" he asked tersely, his hands now tightly gripping the edge of the sink.

Sarah leaned forward and joined him in the mirror. "I'll explain everything once you're ready."

"I'm ready now," Johnson spit out, an edge of steel in his voice. "What happened?"

Ann Petrov confidently walked down the long corridor, her hollow heels clipping steadily as they met the floor. At 5'11", with smooth, olive skin, she carried herself with athletic grace. She kept her straight, brunette hair short and easy to maintain. Her sharp, dark brown eyes missed nothing. It was for that reason that at only twenty-eight years of age, she had been placed in charge of Special Projects, a sub-unit within the GIA. She arrived at the Intelligence briefing and spoke briskly to the two Commanders awaiting her. "Are the teams ready?"

"Yes ma'am, we're all loaded. Just waiting for the order to roll," the man said. The men were in command of two of the eight teams of thirty-six attached to Special Projects. Their job was simple. Wait for the nod from Intelligence, move out and hit the

Rebels.

The Intelligence officer looked over at Ann. "Ma'am, all protocols have been met. You are clear to proceed."

With a calm demeanour that hid the excitement starting to pump into her system, she turned to the two men. "It's a go. Good luck." They nodded simultaneously to her, turned and walked out the door.

Sarah stepped toward Johnson with a screen in her hand. "Steve, I hope this will answer some of your questions." She placed the screen on a table, initiated a command, and a hologram image of Johnson in his uniform appeared. He looked severely injured and was being carried by three men dressed just as the doctors were now. They brought him directly into an operating room. Johnson's face was bloodied and torn. His arms, shoulders and legs were sporting gaping wounds that were turning grey with blood loss. His body armour and uniform were ripped to shreds, and blood ran slowly from both legs and arms. Despite his critical condition, there was no panic among the medical staff. There was no running or shouting. Instead, they immediately began a practised, calm protocol, stripping off his uniform, attaching intravenous lines, staunching wounds and inserting a breathing tube. A machine immediately began forcing air into his lungs and pulling it out again, breathing for him.

Sarah stopped the projection and began a brief explanation of what he was watching. "You arrived here in critical condition, so we needed to operate immediately. To complete the healing process, directly after the Operation, you were placed in Stasis for almost two years. You've seen your reflection in the mirror. The process we started in Stasis helped you recover from your injuries. The spinoff effect, however, is that it revitalized the rest of your system as well, effectively reversing your ageing process. It doesn't work that way for us on this planet, but your body functions are slightly different than ours. We've never seen this before. Even we were surprised by the results."

Johnson attempted to calmly digest the implausible information he had just heard. He folded his arms in front of him, using them as a shield before he asked his next question. "You said, this planet. I'm not on Earth?"

Sarah's face revealed that there was much more to this story. She spoke softly. "I'm sorry."

Johnson's mind was whirling, but he betrayed no emotion, deciding to let her continue without comment.

"Please understand. If we'd waited another thirty seconds, you wouldn't have survived. The injuries were far too serious."

Johnson, shocked at the events unfolding before him, finally managed to ask, "So tell me, where am I?"

Sarah glanced at John for confirmation before she spoke. He nodded slightly, and she continued. "You're on a planet called Midgard."

Unsure why he was familiar with the name and frustrated, he asked, "Why am I here?"

John interceded. "We can only conclude that the Government Intelligence Agency had been watching you. They brought you here when they realized you had been critically injured. I think that once you get on your feet, an agency representative will contact you."

Johnson shuffled slowly back to his bed and sat down, trying to process the information. He needed more answers. "I was asleep for two years?"

Sarah said, "Yes, about two years. Your injuries were severe."

"How old am I now?"

"We've estimated that your body has reverted to an approximate age of twenty-two years old."

Johnson was furiously trying to process the information. Being in Stasis for two years, regenerating to a twenty-two-year-old man and a mysterious "agency" that wanted him. Everything they were saying was screaming in his mind as impossible.

Sarah continued. "There's a lot more for you to understand here. Are you all right to continue?" Johnson nodded wordlessly, and she turned back to the hologram and changed the image. It provided full details of his injuries, and Sarah went through each of them individually. His legs and shoulder had received the most damage, and he had sustained head injuries, a severe concussion and deep lacerations. The enemy's rounds had almost torn off his left shoulder and his right upper thigh. They had replaced the unrepairable areas by regenerating bones, tissue and nerves in situ. No metal plates, no artificial replacement parts. He was whole. Understanding the condition he had been in, Johnson was inundated with a mixture of relief and bewilderment but said nothing. He would let them continue to explain.

Sarah turned over the screen to Mark. He explained the processes used to keep Johnson's body in shape. The combination of regeneration and electrical stimulation resulted in his muscles not only retaining their functionality but also rejuvenating them.

"This doesn't mean that you'll be feeling 100 percent yet," Mark said. "You'll have to do that the old-fashioned way, building your body up through physical training and exertion. In essence, however, your body has been brought back to the same physical state it was when you were in your twenties."

"I can remember someone talking to me, teaching me. Was that part of the program?"

"It was. We were continually running you through a series of procedures and tests to keep your brain functioning. We look at the brain as a muscle. It needs to be worked and stimulated. If you don't continually use it, it atrophies. We also provided you with the information you will need to function on this planet, which should help with your adjustment to Midgard. The Stasis program fluctuated between deep sleep and just below the surface of sleep. Your mind and body had to understand that you were not going to be in that state forever."

His explanation finally made sense to Johnson. "When I woke

in the Recovery Room, I thought I recognized the voices around me. That fluctuation would explain why."

Mark nodded. "That's right. We talk around our patients all the time, hoping they'll hear us and understand what's going on. It doesn't always work, and I'm glad it did with you."

John checked Johnson's vitals. "I think you've had enough for today. It's been a long couple of hours. We can continue with more tomorrow. For the rest of today, we'll get you set up with the basics, show you around a bit and get you something to eat."

At this point, Johnson was sure of only one thing. Without this place, without these people, he would be dead. Retraining his mind could have resulted in their brainwashing him; however, he had no choice but to set aside his doubts for now. Always a pragmatic man, he dealt with the situations he found himself in a focused, direct manner. *One thing at a time*, Johnson thought firmly. "The guy who came through the light and pulled me out, is he here?"

John replied, "No, but you may be able to meet him some other time. I think that's enough for today, we can continue tomorrow. Sarah will take you around and show you the facility. You've been on liquids for some time. Remember to go slow on the solid food until your stomach is used to it again, understand?"

"Solids. Watch the solids. Yes, sir."

John said, "Sarah, you've got him now." He walked over to Johnson, placing his hand on his shoulder and looked down at him. "Steve, it's good to see you up and about. We'll continue to monitor you, of course, but if you need anything, just contact one of us. Sarah will show you the ropes." With that, John and Mark turned and walked from the room.

Sarah waited until the two men had left and then picked up the screen. "I'll take a few minutes to show you the layout of our facility. Then we can go for a walk. It won't take long for you to get your legs under you."

Johnson watched and listened as Sarah opened the hologram

again, showing him the Medical Centre and how it was set up. The exterior was a large, sleek, one-storied complex that was basically a central hub holding the administrative staff and six separate wings emanating from its centre. One was utilized as the surgical ward, containing numerous operating and recovery rooms. Another was used for Stasis and three separate wings housed patients. The last wing was the one Johnson was most interested in now. It contained the gym, which he noted with satisfaction, but it also included the kitchen. He had just realized he was hungry.

A knock on the door interrupted the briefing, and he turned his head to it. The door slid open, and an older woman dressed in a grey uniform walked in. She was pushing a small hovering platform. On it was a large mug of coffee, utensils, condiments and a covered plate. Sarah looked at her quizzically and said, "Hi, Betty, what can I do for you?"

Betty was a tiny woman of indeterminate years. Her hair was white and neatly trimmed into a short, stylish bob. She had deep blue, piercing eyes that appeared to see through any nonsense. Her face held laugh lines and wrinkles that did not deter but instead enhanced the fact that Betty had lived a life full of adventure. No one really knew what she'd done in her younger years, only that she had a family that was grown, and she was now working as a medical assistant.

"I heard our patient has finally woken up, so I thought I'd bring him some breakfast."

"I was just showing Steve how the centre was laid out, and then we were going on a short tour. You're welcome to come with us if you want," Sarah replied.

Johnson could smell the food and began eyeing the cart with interest. The savoury smells emanating from under a white cover made his stomach growl.

"You've more important work than this," Betty smiled. "I can do the tour for you. I'll make sure he eats, then take him around to see everything. Once we're done, I'll bring him back here."

"He's just come out of Stasis and needs to take it easy on the solid foods, Betty. A full meal is not a good idea."

"You let me worry about that. By the look on this man's face, I don't think he'll have a problem. We'll just take it nice and slow."

Sarah smiled, turning back to Johnson. "Steve, this is Betty. She's been working here for a while, so I'll leave you in her capable hands. Do you have any questions for me?"

"I'm still trying to process what I've been told. There's a lot to take in, and a lot of it is pretty unbelievable," he replied honestly.

"I couldn't even imagine how I'd be handling things if I were in your position. We'll take things slowly. When you're ready, any questions you have, we'll try to answer. Right now, we'll only concentrate on getting your feet back under you. We'll take things one day at a time." She turned back to Betty, saying, "Thank you. I didn't know you had clearance for this area."

Betty only smiled as she slid the platform in front of Johnson and then held up her wrist. "Well, someone must have cleared me, dear. The light went green as soon as I approached."

Sarah observed the coder without comment and said, "I'll see you again tomorrow, Steve." She picked up the screen and left the room.

CHAPTER 6

*B*etty *levelled curious eyes on Johnson, studying him carefully. "You might not be aware, but I've known you a while now.* I used to come by while you were in Stasis to check up on you and talk. It's nice to finally meet you." With that, she held out her hand, gripping his with surprising strength and shook it. She continued talking, arranging his bed so he could eat from the platform. "The main meal is a softer one very similar in taste to your bacon and eggs, they say. You can eat it only if you think you're up to it. The soup, juice and yogourt are on the left. Your belly should be able to handle some of it."

Johnson lifted the cover off the plate. "I'll eat as much as I can and save the rest for later if that's okay?"

"That's fine. I'll leave you to it then. Take it slow, and don't overeat. We can't make the doctors unhappy. I'll be back in twenty minutes, and we'll take that tour." She turned, and before Johnson could make any sort of coherent reply, she walked out the door.

Johnson could smell the faintest scent of lavender soap emanating from her as she left. He realized that he remembered that same scent from when he was in Stasis. Her voice and touch were indeed familiar to him. She had been beside him on many occasions, reading and talking to him. Looking down at his tray of food, he picked up a piece of bread and, using it as a spoon, dipped it into the main meal. It resembled a soft, white porridge with meaty chunks. He tentatively put it in his mouth and chewed slowly.

Surprised at the flavour, his taste buds woke up immediately from their long drought, sending a delicious sensation to his brain. He picked up another spoonful and repeated the process.

His stomach, shrunken and unused to foods of any kind, quickly filled, and he realized it would take some time to get it back to normal. He suddenly spotted something that smelled like coffee. Taking a tentative sip, he immediately realized it wasn't the coffee he had envisioned. It was weak and watery and contained not a drop of the caffeine hit he had anticipated. Disappointed, he pushed the mug away after only a couple of sips. He laid his head back on the pillow, his appetite lost, and gazed up at the ceiling, trying to process everything he had gone through in the past few hours. His mind was suddenly overwhelmed with memories. Visions of home, friends and family flooded his brain. His wife. Where was she? What had happened to her? His head started to hurt. I'll find out all I need to know in due time. Patience is what I need now.

Eric Stanton's communicator lit up, indicating an incoming call. His assistant usually filtered them, but Stanton wanted to deal with this one himself. It was Troy Davis, the Chief Executive Officer (CEO) of the Agency hospital. "Stanton," he answered.

"Good morning, Eric. It's Troy Davis. How are you?"

"Troy. Nice to hear from you. I hope you've got good news for me?"

"I do," he said, pausing for effect. "Johnson woke up this morning, and the team has briefed him."

"That's good news, Troy. How is he?"

"He's doing fine. A little tired and shaky on his legs, but that's to be expected."

"I take it the doctors are with him now?"

"Yes. They'll be taking Johnson around so he can get acquainted with the place. I hope you're okay with that?"

"That's fine, Troy. How did he react to his reawakening?"

"He was obviously confused and had a lot of questions, but he appears to be handling it well so far."

They ended the call soon after that, and Eric leaned back in his chair with a smile of satisfaction. Plans were finally underway. Johnson had been pulled from Stasis not a moment too soon.

Johnson pushed his breakfast away and hauled himself to his feet, straightening up and forcing his spine to a vertical position. He pulled his shoulders back when he realized his head wanted to fall forward. The muscles in his neck were weak, not used to holding up the fifteen pounds of weight at the top of it. He tentatively moved his feet, shifting from one foot to another and turned. Once around and facing the door, he looked up and could see Betty on the screen, returning to his room. The door slid open, and she said approvingly, "You're moving well for someone who's been in Stasis for two years. How was your breakfast?"

"The eyes were bigger than the stomach," he admitted. "I managed to eat some of it but thought it best to leave the rest."

"Don't you worry. That belly of yours will come back to normal in no time. Are you steady enough on your feet to take a stroll?"

"I'll be fine," Johnson said. "My balance is off. I just have to concentrate on getting the equilibrium going again."

"That shouldn't take too long." She moved closer to him and said, "I recommend we keep your being from another planet between us two and the doctors for now. It will make things easier. Now then let's get you moving. Once you're familiar with the centre, you'll be free to move around any part of it. We'll extend that area as your health returns, and you become more accustomed to the place."

She placed her left hand on his right elbow and looked up at him. "Just to steady you a bit if you need it," she said. They walked out of the room and down the hall to a large window with a door beside it. The two stopped in front of the window, and Johnson looked out to see a large courtyard.

"The system will read the code from the coder on your wrist. If you're authorized to be in that area, the door light will turn from red to green, and the door will open. Let's see if you're online, shall we?" She motioned for him to walk to the door.

Johnson watched as the light changed to green, and the door opened. He was looking carefully for a locking device on either side but had seen none. Just the same panel on the wall as he'd seen in his room.

Betty caught him searching the doors. "You're not locked in," she said. "The coder is a confirmation of your identification, allowing you to enter the area and move about. It also communicates with all our social computing systems, money, and vehicle identification. Everything is encoded to it. Because you've just come out of Stasis, we've added additional monitoring of your vitals as well. We all have one." She held up her wrist, showing him her coder. "Our culture is completely automated. The coder is also linked into your DNA and other body identification systems so it can't be passed from one person to another." They walked back to the window as she continued. "We tried an implant, but people thought they were being monitored. So, we went with an open system...." She stopped when she saw the expression on his face.

Johnson, still and stiff, asked, "The Medical Centre knows where I'm at all the time and monitors everything I'm doing?"

"Well, yes." She paused for a moment. "You still may have a few medical concerns that need to be monitored for a short while. Once you've moved on, that function is no longer required, and we'll turn it off."

Johnson, with Betty still at his elbow, looked out the window at the quiet scene in front of him wordlessly. He didn't like being tracked by anything or anyone. Suspicious, he wondered if these people had trapped him, and he was being used. For what, Johnson did not know. He could only watch and learn everything he could about this new world.

Betty could feel the tension rolling off him. "Don't judge us just yet. I know you don't like being monitored. Give it some time. You're not a prisoner. You'll see the system has some great benefits."

They turned and walked down the hallway, back to the Stasis wards. As they walked, Johnson's steps gained confidence, and he could feel his stride lengthening. He observed the hospital staff's professional, calm demeanour. They all moved from one station to another, knowing what to do and when to do it. Beds, platforms and tables hovered beside them and could be moved or kept stationary with the touch of a button. In the Stasis Wing, he watched as machines were hooked up to people who were then run through a series of exercises. Others were propped upright in their beds, their hands moving in front of them as if completing a task. The other patients lay motionless, their bodies healing until one day they would be ready to climb up the ladder to recovery.

When they arrived at the kitchen, Betty gave a wave to the staff and introduced them to Johnson. She explained to him how the food was ordered and then made. He looked around and realized it looked almost like an army mess hall. *I guess you really can't improve on some things,* he thought wryly.

The gym was next. People were being directed by hologram fitness instructors running them through a series of exercises. Another area was cordoned off as the same images were training people in unarmed combat. He watched for a few minutes and said, "It's all good till you get that first punch in the face."

Betty laughed and replied, "You can set the program up to feel no pain, some pain or the real thing, depending on your level of expertise."

"Oh," Johnson said, surprised. "That's more like it." They continued to walk toward the weight room, which was laid out with machines rather than free weights. He spotted a set of heavy dumbbells in a corner and said, "Looks like these don't get used much."

"People seem to like and stick to the machines," Betty said.

"They don't know what they're missing. You need to get back to the basics occasionally. Pushing and pulling heavy weights will do that, and that'll be my plan over the next few weeks."

The tour complete, they walked out of the building to a path leading through the woods. The day was warm and bright. Johnson could feel the sun on his face, the warmth of it heating his body. He thought he could actually feel his strength coming back to him, and it felt good. He glanced down at Betty, who was still guiding his elbow and gently slid her hand away.

"I'm good now. I can handle this." His head lifted back, and his stride lengthened to match Betty's. He felt like a fighter, knocked down but rising to meet the challenge again, his hands up, facing his foe and ready to engage.

A two-metre-wide gravel path led into the woods, and when Johnson kicked at it, the dust rose from his feet. He inhaled deeply, appreciating the fresh, humid smell of the earth and cleansed his lungs of the antiseptic taste of the complex. He continued to walk, sometimes closing his eyes in concentration, trying to identify the different scents.

Betty smiled inwardly as she continued to walk beside him, content to watch. She had observed the regression in age during Stasis; it had been unprecedented within the clinic, and the results were astonishing. Now, the circle complete, he was physically transforming from a broken, comatose shell to a vibrant, healthy young man.

They broke through the woods and came to a small meadow with knee-high grass and wildflowers. A bench caught Johnson's eye, and he walked over to it, stretched out a bit and then sat down. Betty joined him, and with sympathy on her face and in her voice said, "I'm sorry we took you away from your wife and family."

Johnson avoided her eyes and instead continued to gaze steadily across the quiet meadow. Finally, he spoke. "I keep looking around, expecting to see her. I've been gone for two years. The Military would have declared me dead. What will she do? What will my family do?"

Betty turned her face away from him and was silent. "It's impossible for us to turn back time," she said after a minute. "I do understand how it feels to lose your partner. I can only say that as the days go by, time will lessen the pain." She stood up and said, "If you like, I can leave you here to make your way back to the complex. Please return by six o'clock for supper. Just stay on the path."

Johnson nodded his agreement, and with that, she turned and walked back the way they came. He watched her until she disappeared and then focused his gaze to the meadow and up into the sky. At first, it appeared to have the same blue atmosphere, even the same type of clouds as home. As he scanned the higher reaches, however, he could see two distinct, full, red moons opposite each other and a vast number of stars. The sun, smaller than home, appeared dimmer and, he speculated, possibly farther away. So far from home, he thought and lifted himself off the bench. He had no desire to see more. At that moment, he made a promise to himself. He would find out how, where, and why he had landed in this faraway world. He shook his legs, getting the blood moving through them again and made his way back to the centre and his room.

Johnson walked up to the sink and began washing his hands and face. Picking up a towel, he caught a glimpse of the young man in front of him. Leaning closer to the image, he studied every detail and ran his hand over his face one last time to confirm to himself that what he was seeing was real. Johnson swore softly and shook his head, still disbelieving. *This is real. It's not a dream,* he realized.

A few minutes later, he found himself in the kitchen. The centre seemed bigger and quieter now that the day was coming to an end. After picking up his meal, he glanced up to see Betty and the woman who had been in Stasis with him. Betty spotted him and waved him over.

"Good to see you made it back," Betty said with a smile.

"I did. Thanks for the walk. It was good to get outside," Johnson said and looked over at the other woman. "Asta, right?"

She grinned at him as he sat down. "That's right. It looks to me that your memory is working well enough. That's a good sign. And your name is Steve," Asta said confidently.

"Your memory seems to be running full steam ahead as well," Johnson replied. "So, how are you feeling?"

"I'm fine. Can't you tell by this plate of food I've been packing away?"

Johnson looked down at Asta's plate. It contained a heaping pile of chewed off bones. "Looks like you didn't have a problem with your stomach," he said, smiling at her.

"Gotta keep up my strength," she said, laughing. "Wouldn't want one of you youngsters taking my job."

Johnson blinked, not understanding and suddenly realized that, to her, he would indeed look like a younger man. "You're not looking a day over twenty-five," he replied. "I'm certain most of the men here would have a hard time keeping up with you."

"Hmmm. Good comeback," Asta said. "Now, are you going to eat or talk?"

Johnson laughed, picked up his fork and started to eat.

CHAPTER 7

*T*he air was hot and muggy for this time of year. Bill Lee walked down the crowded street, trying to avoid touching people but ended up continually bumping up against them. He had expected a few people out but not like this. He spotted an area where he could take a break and, pushing sideways through the crowd, made his way over to a wall and leaned his back up against it. The wall felt cold to the touch and, as his skin made contact, gave his body goosebumps. He looked in both directions before pulling out his screen and opened it to the daily news. Holding the screen lent the appearance that he was reading, but his eyes were focused elsewhere. Nonchalantly, he glanced again in all directions to ensure everything was normal. He rolled the screen up and shoved it deep into his pocket. Peering one last time over his shoulder, he made his way back in the direction that he'd come. The place looked clean, though crowded, but that was a good thing. Stopping one last time at a storefront, he looked back at the crowd behind him through the reflection in the glass. No one looked familiar, so unless they had twenty people tracking him, he was in the clear. His thoughts briefly hovered on what someone had once said to him. "You're too careful. You take too much time."

At forty years old, 5 feet 7 inches tall, balding, with a bit of a belly and short legs, he wasn't memorable. That's what he liked. He was able to walk into a room full of people, talk among them and walk out an hour later without anyone remembering him. He'd climbed up the ranks of the Rebels with cunning, drive and a determination to stop the agency. He was now in charge of eight states of Operators, a mid-level Commander.

Too careful, he thought scornfully, as he looked over his

shoulder again and then ahead at the market square. *All those assholes are either dead or had their minds erased by the GIA. Too careful. In this business, you can't be too careful*, he repeated to himself.

He headed to the outside of the market, turning right into an alley and entered it slowly, stopping to ensure it was clear before moving again. The foot traffic had dropped off substantially, and he walked to an intersection about fifty metres away. Marie, one of his top Operators, stepped out from around the corner. He walked cautiously up to her.

Recognizing him as well, she walked up confidently and stopped in front of him.

"Bill! How the fuck are you doing?" she said, smugly patting him on the head. Marie was just thirty-six years old, 5 feet 9 inches tall, with the hard, sinewy body of a Mu Tai fighter. Her long, dark brunette hair was hanging loosely around her shoulders, making her look younger than she was.

"Marie, I hate it when you fucking do that. Knock it off."

"Bill, you gotta lighten up or your heart's going to explode, and then they'll have to put me in charge, wouldn't they?" He shook his head as she put her arm firmly around his shoulder and said, "Shall we walk?"

As they moved down the alleyway, Bill slid out of her grasp, agitated, and placed his hands deep in his pockets. "You heard what happened?"

"Of course. Is that why you're all worked up? The GIA took that cell out because they were an easy target. We're not an easy target. We've always kept our security tight."

Bill shook his head and picked up his pace. "Perhaps," he said. "I just can't help wondering when it's going to be our turn. Suppose someone rolls over on us, and our front door comes crashing in. I can see that happening."

"Bill, you worry too much. Our people have proven their loyalty, and you run too tight of a ship for that shit to happen."

Bill stopped. "You can never be one hundred percent sure. All those assholes that I started with are gone now, done, locked up or had their brains re-wired. I don't want that to happen to us."

Marie started walking again and stated flatly, "And it won't. Think about it. We don't even know one another's last names, where we live, or what each person does. You had me do four different legs before I got here today. Four. You're worked up." Without breaking her stride, she continued. "You didn't drag me all this way for that. Something else is happening here, Bill. What's going on?"

Bill stopped and grabbed her arm, pulling her close, and said with agitation in his voice, "Word is Headquarters is going to try something big in the next month or so. I want our people to be the ones selected for the Operation. Not some half-assed dimwit from the other side of the world. Our people. You pass on the fucking word that if any protocol or security is broken in the slightest, they'll answer to you and me. You and me exclusively, got it?"

Marie had always understood his hair-trigger temper and knew how to deal with him now. Her expression turned from teasing to concern. "I've got this, Bill. Look, I know you're busy. If you need a hand with things, I can step it up. It'll take some of this pressure off you."

"No. I need you out here, directing ops, including the one for tonight. They've all got to go without a hitch. I need you kicking ass and taking names until we get this job. Pass on to your people that we've doubled up security. We don't need any breakdowns, and we can't afford to let the GIA get one up on us. No mistakes. Not one."

"Will do." Testing his resolve, she added, "I guess a quick beer is out of the question?"

"Get back to work. I'll see you again tonight," Bill retorted and walked away, turning off the alley and melting back into the busy street.

Marie watched him as he disappeared and then went back the way she came. *One day*, she thought, *that's going to be me.*

Johnson slept without dreams that night, exhausted by the physical and mental shock his body had gone through while coming out of Stasis. He had barely remembered showering and getting into bed.

"Rise and shine!"

Johnson bolted upright in the bed and looked around the room, trying to get his bearings. *Where the hell was he?*

Betty stood in front of his bed, with a tray of food smelling enticingly like pancakes. "Good morning," he managed. "How did you get in here?"

"It's good to see you had a solid night's sleep," she said, ignoring his question and cheerfully guiding the tray to the table. "John and the other two doctors will be here shortly, so you may want to get a move on."

"I'm moving," he said, throwing back the covers and making his way to the bathroom. When he returned, he found Betty had made herself at home, sitting by the table and helping herself to a cup of coffee.

"I've some good news," she said. "I read through your scans this morning. Everything looks normal."

"Did you expect anything else?"

"There was some concern because you'd been in Stasis for such a long time. Some patients with shorter Stasis periods have had complications. But as I said, it all looks good. How did you sleep?"

"I slept pretty solid. No bad dreams," Johnson grunted as he slowly dug into his meal. His stomach was still full from last night's supper. "This isn't going to happen every morning, is it? I mean, the breakfast."

"No, I just thought I'd give you a bit of a helping hand again today," she said.

Johnson finished up the meal in silence, with Betty calmly

sipping on her coffee, watching him. He heard a buzzer on the door with the screen beside it showing the three doctors standing outside his room. "Come on in," Johnson said, and the door slid open.

John was the first to walk in, followed closely by the other two. "How are you feeling this morning?" John asked.

"A bit fuzzy, I suppose," Johnson said, "but it's all coming around now." He picked up his coffee and took a deep gulp of the weak liquid.

"To be expected," John replied, looking down at his screen and checking Johnson's vitals. "Things are looking good, I must say."

Johnson decided to get right to the point with them. He needed answers. "I'd like to know a few details. I want to know why I'm here."

John shook his head. "Our job was to put you back together again for the GIA, and we did that. Unfortunately, we're not aware of anything beyond that."

"Who and what is the GIA?"

"It stands for our Government Intelligence Agency. The short answer is that under our government, we have several different organizations responsible for everything, from civil matters to Military factions. The GIA is one of these organizations. They answer directly to the President. One of their responsibilities is carrying out armed intervention against a Rebel Faction that is trying to retake our government. The GIA runs the hospital, along with other facilities in this world. As to why they brought you here? I'm sorry, I don't know."

"When am I going to meet these people?"

"They've been advised of your waking. If your recovery goes according to plan, I expect they'll contact you in a few weeks."

Sarah spoke now. "You need to allow your body to recover. That includes bringing back full function, both mentally and physically. We take care of those concerns exclusively. The GIA will step in then, not before. The quicker you come online, the quicker you get the answers from them."

Johnson looked carefully at the three doctors. He could usually tell when someone wasn't being straight up with him or held something back. It was in the responses they gave, the quick look away, a shifting of their body or a combination of all of them. People had involuntary muscle responses. Tells that were almost impossible to control. Most of the time, people didn't even know when they'd given an indication away. If they caught themselves and tried to cover it up, it just confirmed the deceit. But he didn't see anything that showed a lie.

"It appears I have little choice in the matter," he said, barely able to hide his frustration. "I'll use this time to get back into shape."

John continued with a look of some concern on his face. "This is our first time having a patient such as yourself here. We've conducted thousands of operations and Stasis awakenings. But this is the first time we've ever dealt with someone from another planet. Our physiology is very similar. However, we were never sure how you would react to our drugs or operations. For example, regeneration has never happened when our patients recover from rebuilding procedures. We'll continue to monitor you and pass on your results to the GIA. Hopefully, they'll like the results and come around as soon as possible. Betty will continue to work with you, although not exclusively, as she does have other duties. If we're not around and you need something, ask her. She'll get it for you."

Johnson realized that he was no further ahead now than he had been the day before.

He sat without comment as Mark took out his screen and sat down beside him, saying, "I suggest you start slowly. Just do some walking again today."

The doctors continued to discuss a short-term physical rehab plan with Johnson and then excused themselves from the room.

Betty, who had remained silent while the doctors had been

there, put her hand softly on his shoulder. "Don't worry about the GIA. They should be around in a few weeks. They'll be monitoring all your info, and once they're confident that you're strong enough, they'll make themselves known." Picking up the dishes, she said, "I'll take these back to the kitchen." She guided the food platform toward the door and stopped as Johnson pushed himself up to his feet. Betty turned to him and said, "I understand more than you know. I know where you've been and what you've gone through. It's in your eyes and your body language. The same telltale signs you were looking for in those three doctors to see if they were lying to you. I look at you and read those same signs like a book, and I like the book I'm reading. Now get out for that walk." She turned back to the door and started to step out.

Johnson was taken aback. He had not realized that he had been so transparent or that Betty had been that observant. "Betty," he called out softly. "Thank you."

She looked back in acknowledgement. "You're welcome, dear. We'll be working together for a long time, you and me."

Soon afterward, Johnson found himself walking smoothly down the path, trying to maintain a brisk rhythm and steady stride. He could feel sweat gathering on his brow and relished the feeling of exertion. There were others on the path who were patients in different stages of recovery. Although a few ignored him completely, the majority made eye contact and smiled, greeting him with a friendly "Good morning." He attempted to find some sort of physical difference between himself and the inhabitants of this planet but could find none. They were, for all intents and purposes, completely humanoid. How could that be possible? How could their societies be so similar?

CHAPTER 8

*T*wo weeks had passed since Johnson had come out of Stasis. The days were now starting to go by in a relatively routine manner, and visits by the medical staff dwindled. His progress was what they had hoped for, and he experienced no setbacks. As his health improved, the doctors shifted their attention to more important duties and other patients. Any questions he had about why he was there were still not answered. He kept to himself and spoke with the other patients and staff only when he had to. He felt as if they were running him through a constant loop, getting him ready for something that he couldn't see or understand.

The only constant was Betty. She would see him daily. Sometimes they would talk. Other times she just watched his workouts. The time of day didn't seem to matter. She always seemed to be around when he needed someone. She'd show up out of nowhere, with a smile on her face and something to eat and drink just when he needed it. He often wondered if she ever took time off and if she had a family somewhere.

Johnson woke early one morning, as was his custom. He rolled out of bed and automatically made it with Military precision, the bottom sheet extra tight, and the top sheet tucked in at the end. He liked it that way; crawling into it would feel like a fight, and then the whole system would cocoon around him. His next stops were the bathroom, the closet for some clothes and a cup of coffee from the kitchen. Making his way through the hallway, he stepped out to the courtyard, placed the coffee down and did a quick warmup. He jogged slowly back and forth across the still dew-covered lawn. Once a light sweat started, he stretched until his body was loose and then began to run. The pace was slow at first but increased to a steady, ground-eating lope. He leaned forward, letting his legs compensate for the loss of balance by pushing himself forward.

The further the lean, the faster the pace. Pushing into the fresh morning, a smile came across his face, and Johnson began to appreciate his younger, more resilient body. A run at this pace before would have left him breathless and achy for days afterward. A pond located five kilometres down the path was his halfway point. Some mornings he would turn around and race back. Today, he stopped and began a callisthenics routine, rotating through push-ups, sit-ups and burpees. Every time he finished, he expected something to hurt, but his body was young now and felt vibrant and energized by the exertion. He turned and headed back to the centre, focused on the path ahead and determined to maintain an even faster pace. His feet hit the ground in a smooth rhythm as his arms lifted and supported the cadence of his legs.

Johnson caught a glimpse of the centre about a kilometre ahead. He picked up his speed again, demanding even more from his body. Approaching the courtyard, he finally pulled back the pace. He came in, breathing deeply, bringing down his heart rate in a controlled manner. He was more than happy with the way he had responded to the training. Johnson had forgotten the physical endurance and speed he had had when he was younger and now revelled in his strength. The workout and cool down completed, he walked up and through the door to see Betty.

She greeted him and then asked, "How was it?"

"Good, really good," Johnson said, as he grabbed his towel and wiped his face.

"Have you eaten yet?"

"No, I was going to shower, then head down. Why?"

"How long will that take you?"

"About an hour," he replied.

"I'll meet you in an hour after breakfast, back here in your room," she said, as she began to walk away.

"What's up, Betty?" he asked quizzically.

"Sorry, no worries, dear. I've just received some information you might be interested in. Go ahead. It can wait until after breakfast."

Johnson scrubbed himself clean, ate breakfast and had just started back to his room when he spotted Betty.

"Come with me, please, Steve," she said. Johnson followed her through to the Secure Area, where Betty took his wrist and slid his coder off, placing it into a secured compartment just outside the door. "Nobody needs to know you're in here."

"What's this about?" Johnson asked as they entered the room.

"You want to know about our planet and why you're here, don't you?"

"I do."

"Then come in and sit down."

The room was empty except for a couple of chairs, and they settled themselves into them. Betty pulled out an electronic screen and ordered, "Briefing to Steve Johnson." The lighting immediately dimmed, and the space to their front lit up. Without looking at Johnson, she said, "John was correct when he said he didn't know why you were here. His job and the job of the centre are to put back together what the GIA breaks. The agency has asked that I provide you with the information you requested. This briefing is secret. The only three people authorized to discuss the information are Eric Stanton, Miss Petrov and myself. You will be meeting them when you're ready and the time is right."

"I understand," Johnson said. He had suspected that Betty had secrets of her own. She had displayed far more knowledge of the centre's goings-on than was usual. His interest piqued, he sat back, observing her carefully.

"Tell me about your last night on Earth."

Johnson tried to recall the details of that night, his mind wading through jumbled flashbacks, and he found he had to separate the real from the impossible. The truth was in there somewhere. He sorted and organized his thoughts until finally, a semblance of the events unfolded from the garble. He started to speak, the memory playing itself out clearly in front of his eyes. Betty watched him closely as he recalled the battle, the smells, the sounds, the cries of the men.

A few minutes later, Betty touched his arm lightly and said, "You can stop if you'd like."

Johnson glanced briefly at her but turned away when he saw the compassion in her eyes. He was still not ready for that. "No, I have to get through this. I remember the pain, the confusion, the hopelessness of not being able to fight my way out. I remember blood coming up in the back of my throat. I can still taste the metal. My vision started to shut down, cloudy at first, then fuzzy. I remember being tired, ready to close my eyes. That's when I saw a bright light in front of me. It expanded enough for a man to walk through it. He told me I was needed somewhere else and then pulled me into the light. I must have passed out after that, but then I remember being pulled into a bright space and people talking, pulling and prodding me. After that, there was nothing. Just silence." Johnson stopped, taking a deep breath and running his hands through his hair.

Betty nodded in satisfaction. "It's important for you to sort out the memories. We need you to be cognizant of what is real and what may not be real. You've come through this very well. You've been briefed on your recovery process. Let's get on with understanding where you are." Betty touched her screen, and a hologram appeared, displaying an infinite number of galaxies and stars. She zeroed onto a speck within that dense, vast amount of space. "This tiny speck is your galaxy and, within it, Earth. Now watch carefully." The image expanded and separated into two systems with a vast, empty split between them. She pointed up at a small galaxy cluster located on the opposite side of the screen. "This is where you are now, on Midgard. A very long way from home."

Betty explained the split and the vastness of space between the two systems. "The split between us has kept us billions of light-years apart. We're not sure why this happened. We have parallels, and, to be sure, those parallels are eerily familiar. Our physiology, our language, some of our customs are all similar. Even our planet's name, Midgard, is from your Viking mythology. There are several theories as to why, but the best our scientists have come up with is that the split created an alternative universe. Because we can map out the distance between our galaxies, we can confirm we are not on a parallel dimension. And are there more planets like us?" She shrugged, anticipating Johnson's question. "Possibly."

He stood up and walked directly into the image, looking at the model and then back at Betty. "That's a lot to take in. I was transported from there to here," pointing between the two systems.

"Yes."

Johnson tried to comprehend the enormity of the distance between the two planets and asked Betty, "How did you find me? How did you know where I was?"

"Years ago, we developed the technology to travel through the split to other planets.

We have people called Travellers. They move through space, knowing what we are looking for and what we need. If they find something or someone, they inform our people. A decision will be made, and if there is time and if it is necessary, we have the Travellers collect it. The system isn't perfect. Our physiology only allows us to stay on another planet for short periods. For example, if we stay over four weeks on Earth, we age very quickly."

Johnson's face hardened slightly. "So, you just take people?"

Betty smiled and said, "No, the agency has never taken anyone. We've been much more interested in acquiring knowledge and technology. You're the first. You were going to pass away, and nothing could have saved you. That was when the agency decided to act."

"You knew ahead of time what was going to happen to me?"

"With you, no. We can make predictions and assumptions with a person in a straight-forward life, with very few variables. But when you have a person interacting with an array of situations, people, machines and then opposing forces, the ability to predict is hit and miss. The Traveller kept a close eye on you, and, when the situation presented itself, they took advantage of it."

Johnson looked back at the hologram. "Why me?"

"I'm speculating that the GIA needs someone from Earth with your skillset. Why and what I haven't been told."

"Let me explain our political situation." Betty changed the image to their front, and Johnson sat back down. "A Rebel group has been operating against the government forces for the last thirty years. Initially a catalyst for change, they fought for the basics of life: food, clean water and medicine. World leaders got on board, and change began. They recognized an opportunity and stepped in. Positive transformations began, and peace was momentarily achieved. The Rebels, however, saw this as a power move to take them out, and rebellion began again. It was now a battle between their organization and world governments. Essentially, the Rebels want control."

"They went underground and went after the people they felt pushed them there. Leaders started going missing or showing up dead. Then they stole one of our destination machines, an earlier version," she said. "The Rebels don't have the additional technology to go outside our world yet, but I'm afraid it's only a matter of time before they do."

"They used the machine to raid government facilities, disrupting everything we had worked so hard to implement. Worse, they killed innocent people in their wake.

Our leaders finally had enough and began to retaliate. They placed a power bubble around essential facilities, making access to them impossible, then began tracking their transporter through power spikes. The Rebels figured out that strategy soon enough and moved to industrial areas where their power use could go undetected. That has made tracking them more difficult, but we can still find them."

Betty touched her screen, and the hologram changed again. "So, this is what we're up against. They have factions in every country within this world." She continued explaining the Rebel Chain of Command. The agency had encountered difficulties tracking them because they never used real names and limited their knowledge of the Chain of Command. The GIA could never find out who was in charge, what their numbers were or their primary base of Operation.

Betty pursed her lips together before speaking again. "This last portion of the briefing is going to be difficult. The time systems between Earth and Midgard are vastly different because of the distance and the split between our systems. As a result, our time here moves at a different rate than your planet." She opened a new file on the screen. "You asked about your family. I've received some information from the Traveller, but it's not good."

Johnson nodded grimly and said, "Let's hear it."

"After we took you, your unit remained as long as possible, looking for you. The gunship's video showed the light, but they assumed it was an explosion. They searched everywhere but found nothing. The Military listed you as Missing in Action. After a year and no new information, they changed your status to Killed in Action and held a memorial for you. Your headstone is now in Regina, Saskatchewan, your hometown, I believe."

"That's the protocol, it makes sense. What about Elly, my wife?"

Betty took a deep breath, then continued. "She loved you and had a hard time with your passing. She eventually needed to move on with her life. Elly met a man about two years after you left and has been living with him since then. She's happy and healthy. I'm sure there's still a void where you are concerned and questions that she wants to be answered. But in her and everyone else's mind, you're gone."

The screen flashed a video of Elly walking down the street that morphed into a holographic image. Betty said quietly, "Remember that I mentioned a time difference between our worlds? We've estimated there is a twenty-year time gap. Time moves at a faster rate on Earth."

Johnson, confused, looked at the older woman being shown and then closed his eyes, disbelieving. He got up and stepped toward the 3D image, raising his hand to her face. He observed her deepened laugh lines and silvered hair but said nothing. Time had done little to take away her beauty. He was still staring at the hologram when, from the pit of his stomach, he suddenly felt a lurch of fear as a realization came over him. He stepped back and said, "I think I know where the rest of this is going. My mom and dad are gone, aren't they?"

"Yes," Betty said, "your parents have both passed away."

He took in a deep breath and shook his head. He supposed it was the finality of hearing the words that made it real. He'd only ever pictured his mom and dad moving to a retirement community and vacationing someplace warm every winter. "How did they die?"

"Your mother had a stroke when she was seventy-six. She never regained consciousness and passed on the same day. Your father had a heart attack at seventy-nine. He never came out of surgery." She hesitated and then said, "I'm sorry, Steve."

Johnson sat back down in his chair. Everyone he had known and loved was gone. Too much time had passed on Earth, a lifetime in fact, and he could never get it back.

Shocked, he could only stare mutely at the floor, regret and sorrow flooding through him.

After a few moments, Betty broke into his thoughts, saying, "Your brother is still alive. He's a father of two and grandfather of four, all girls. His wife of thirty years passed away a few years back. He's still living in Regina."

Johnson blinked as he recalled his brother's two young girls. The revelation that they were now married and had children of their own seemed impossible to him. They were school-aged when he had last seen them. He shook his head incredulously and finally said, "I'm glad he's still there, but I must admit, this all feels like a horrible dream. A nightmare. I've missed so much, and I wish I could have been there for my parents during their last hours."

"I would be devastated in your position, Steve. We can continue to monitor your brother if you'd like. Our Traveller can check in on him whenever you wish."

"I'd like that," Johnson said.

Betty spoke sympathetically, "I hope you understand that everything that has happened to you and your family can't be fixed or replaced. We can't go back in time. We don't have the technology for that. I hope that you can grieve them and eventually, in your own time, move on."

Johnson found himself staring again at Elly's image. "Yeah, this sucks," he said softly. "Can you change the image, please?"

CHAPTER 9

*T*he sun was sinking down to the horizon, and a light breeze had begun to cool the air. Her shift was finally over, and she shivered slightly as she headed toward the vector that was her transport home. The woman walked, her head down and shoulders stooped, eyes staring resolutely at the ground. She was tired. The day had been a long one and the week even longer. Her coder flashed the vehicle to life, and the bubble over the top of it, protection against the elements and collisions, retracted. She lifted her leg over the vector's side, sat down and took a deep breath. The Control panel came to life. "All systems online," the mechanical voice began and then said, "Text message waiting." Her heart rate picked up, and her hand shook slightly as she touched the "read button."

She scanned the message silently and directed, "Vector, follow coordinates given in last message." The machine hummed slightly, initiating the startup procedure, and the voice spoke again. "Coordinates locked in. Ready for transport. Preparing safety protocols." The magnetic bubble enveloped the machine, and it rose silently into the air.

The detour she was taking was one she'd made a few times before. She didn't want to take it. She had to. The man wanted to see her again. An hour later, the vector silently approached a wooded area flying along the coordinates provided. She looked down through the trees but was unable to see her contact from the air. Her vehicle came to a parking area, slowed and landed smoothly. She stepped out, wrapped her coat protectively around her and began walking down a narrow gravel path. She followed it down a wooded hillside and into a scenic valley, walking briskly, eyes darting in every direction. *There would be no one here, not at this time of day*, she thought. *That's why he always picked this same spot, this same time.* The woman looked at the stream flowing through the woods and then to the path around the hill. The meeting place was close now. She wished silently that she could be here under different circumstances, perhaps with her family. But she wasn't.

Leah Evans was only thirty-five years old but looked older. Her eyes were always tired and sad. She had found her passion early in life as a trauma nurse and excelled in her field at one time. When the agency hospital called, it had been the opportunity of a lifetime to work for them. Now, however, she was burned out.

She had married early in her career and had two children, a boy and a girl. That was when reality crept in. A life of dirty diapers, unwashed clothes, unending housework, sick kids and the mundane routine of being married. Her husband was ten years older than her and worked for the local news agency. He was continually looking for the next move up the ladder but never found it. He was always being passed over by the younger face or the better connection.

The clandestine meetings, like today's, had begun five years ago. Five years since "the incident," as she referred to it. They had trapped her because of where she worked and what she had access to. They had recruited her, not with money but with blackmail. It had been a girls' night out and a stupid mistake. The next day, pictures of her and the man she had spent the night with appeared on her home computer. The photos were followed with a message: meet us, or these will show up on your husband's screen.

Leah, humiliated, had no choice if she wanted to save her marriage. *How could I have been so stupid?* She thought. Now she was here, handing over Intelligence to the Rebels. She stopped for a moment and fidgeted nervously. She hated these face-to-face meetings. Resolutely, she started walking again, turning left and following a path of beaten-down grass to a copse of trees, the meeting place. She approached slowly and, as she got closer, spotted the man waiting for her.

The man greeted her. "Leah, it's good to see you again."

She closed the distance, feeling awkward and embarrassed, not saying anything.

The man scanned her and once satisfied that she was not being tracked, took her arm in his and said, "Let's walk." They stepped out of the trees and began walking down the pathway. "What do you have for me today?"

Ignoring the question, she asked timidly, "How much longer do I have to do this?"

"Sweetheart!" he laughed, a false grin spreading across his face. "Only a few more times, I'm certain. Then we'll be out of your life forever."

"That's what you said two years ago," she said desperately.

"But won't you miss me?" he teased, an unreadable look in his eyes. "This time, it's the truth. Now, what do you have for me?"

She reached into her pocket, taking out an envelope and handing it to him. "There's a man that they've just taken out of Stasis. His name is Steve Johnson. He was under for two years, the longest I've ever seen, and they've finally woke him up."

The man looked at her quizzically and asked, "What makes him so special? It's a long time to be under, but they have people coming out of Stasis all the time."

"This guy is different. All we've been told is that he's a non-resident. There's an older woman, a medical assistant, that's been assigned to him. I'm so busy that I don't know her well, but she's with him all the time. The other day I saw them go into the Secure Area. That shouldn't have happened. She shouldn't have had clearance for that room."

"Interesting. Where does he come from? What's his history?"

"I was unable to access his files. I'm the head trauma nurse, and they never gave me access. That's another thing that doesn't make sense. I've also watched this man for two years while he was in Stasis. They may have been trying a new procedure with him because he began to look younger. Even the other staff were commenting on it. We asked the doctors, but they would never confirm anything."

"Strange. We may have to investigate this. Is there anything else?"

She paused and said, "No. He's a bit of a loner. Different, but I can't put my finger on why."

The man thought hard and then replied, "Thank you, Leah. I want you to get close to this man, get as much information on him as you can and get back to me. Talk to the old lady as well. Find out what she's up to. I'll give you a week."

"I'll try," Leah said. "Is that all?"

"Do more than try, and maybe I'll tell the boss your job is finished. That's all for now."

Emotionless, Leah could only force a small nod before she choked out a tight, "I'd appreciate that," and walked back to the parking area. Tears began sliding silently down her cheeks. *No,* she thought sadly, *he's not going to tell his boss anything of the sort.*

Leah walked to the vector and slid into the machine. *It's not every day you get to betray your country,* she thought ruefully. The fear of being reprogrammed and losing her family left her empty. There was no solution for her. She initiated the startup commands, and the automated voice asked, "Where to, Leah?"

"Home. Take me home." The vector obediently lifted off the ground, speeding into the setting sun.

CHAPTER 10

*J*ohnson *took his time as he made his way to supper because a late arrival at supper usually meant less of a lineup. He walked into the kitchen and grinned.* The line began and ended with him. He ordered his meal, and as it was placed in front of him, the cook commented, "Must've been working hard today. We got you on for another 1000 calories."

Johnson blinked in surprise before he realized that his coder had probably calculated his required food intake and relayed it to the kitchen. He was now able to eat full meals, and his younger metabolism demanded extra nutrition. "Yup, I was. Thanks," he said, as he turned and spotted Betty, who was alone at a table, eating her meal. Johnson made his way over to her. "Mind if I sit with you?"

"Of course not," she said. "As you can see, I'm here with all of my friends. Or better yet, all of the people I can trust." She waved her hand at the empty seats in front of her.

Johnson laughed. "Looks like the same crowd I hang with," he said, sitting down and digging into his meal.

Betty watched him shovel in his food and wanted to say, "You remind me of my husband." The thought made her inexplicably sad, and her face revealed the slightest touch of pain.

Johnson swallowed his food, sipped some water and glanced at her. "Sorry, did I say something wrong?"

Looking up, she said, "No, of course not. I was thinking about something else."

He cut another piece of meat, put it into his mouth and casually chewed. "Conversation," he said, once he had swallowed, "takes two people, unless you're crazy and the other person is in your head. Then you can have a conversation by yourself. I've done it a couple of times, but don't recommend it."

"Sorry," she said. "The news I gave you this morning, I wish it would've been better."

"I'd prepared myself for the worst. Still wasn't quite prepared for the truth of it. The time difference is a lot to take in."

Betty sipped on her water and then cleared her throat. "The news wasn't good, but you're alive." She paused and said, "The situation could've been a lot different."

"Of course," he replied. "Dead is dead, and there's no coming back from that. I appreciate the fact that I'm alive, young and healthy. But I've lost almost everyone I've known. And you still haven't explained what the agency wants me for."

"You're a valuable asset, Steve. As I said before, I have no idea what they want you for, but the GIA did select you because you're worth saving. Common sense, good instincts, experience, consistency and a will to succeed. A rare combination."

"I think you know a bit more than what a medical assistant is supposed to know about the agency business."

She looked at him without expression. "I'm old, Steve. I've done a few things."

Johnson's plate was clean, and he pushed back on the chair. He was willing to accept her less-than-forthcoming attitude for the moment. "Anything you want, Betty. It's not my place to say. Time to get moving, I suppose." He stood and picked his plate up.

Betty stood with him, and said, "By the way, I've put a box in your closet. It has everything in it that you had on when you came to us."

"I appreciate that. Thanks. I'll see you in the morning."

They said their goodbyes, and Betty watched Johnson until he turned the corner and disappeared. He walked, she noted with surprise, the same way her husband had. Like he always had someplace to go, somewhere to be. *The man has confidence*, she thought, *and that's good because he'll need it.*

Johnson walked into his room and headed straight for the box in the closet. He bent down and picked it up, feeling the weight of it in his arms. The memories in the old uniform weighed it down. Placing the box on the bed, he opened it and looked at the contents. The clothing had been thoroughly washed, cleaned and folded, with the Canada tag on the front, facing up. Taking out each item one at a time, he inspected it and placed it on the bed. His uniform and body armour had been torn to shreds, but of course, he had expected that. At the bottom of the box was a small package. Opening it, he found his personal items: his ID Card, ID Disc and lucky quarter. The quarter had been given to him by his grandmother when he was just a young boy. She'd found it on the day she'd met her husband and had kept it as a good luck charm ever since. "Hopefully, it will do the same for you," she had said. *I wonder if this new life is the luck Grandma was talking about,* he thought. *It could easily become a curse.*

Picking up his shirt, he looked under the left armpit for a seam he'd cut open previously. Pulling at the thread that held it together, it let go, and a piece of paper covered in plastic fell out. The opened seam and the plastic-covered paper had always been an integral piece of his personal routine. It contained his name, nationality and service number. This wasn't Military protocol, just self-preservation. If he was buried in an unmarked grave, he hoped that someone, somewhere, would find the paper and use it to ID him. He looked at his uniform again and pulled it to his nose, taking a deep breath. He'd hoped to smell something, anything from home, but there was nothing. Johnson looked at the items one last time and then packed everything up and pushed it under the bed.

John Alexander, Head Doctor at the Medical Centre, was sitting in his office when his communicator buzzed. "Dr. Alexander, this is Ann Petrov from Special Projects. How are you?"

"I'm fine. What can I do for you, ma'am?"

"I've spoken with Mr. Davis, your CEO, and he's given me permission to speak with you directly about a patient you have."

"No problem. What patient are we talking about?"

"Steve Johnson," she said.

"Yes, of course, the non-resident, in Stasis for two years."

"That's him. I understand he's progressing well since you woke him."

John leaned back in his chair, placing his feet on his desk and relaxing. He had been very pleased with Johnson's progress and was eager to discuss his patient. "Yes, he is. We're very pleased. I was concerned with how he'd react when he was woken, but his mental and physical state is much better than expected."

"Do you think we need to erase any memories and replace them?"

"No. Johnson's coming along very well and has already surpassed where we thought he'd be. I don't like erasing unless it's necessary. It can be problematic. You never know if it's just going to create another problem. We've had too many instances of patients becoming mentally unstable. Memories can't just be replaced. There are too many interlocking pieces to the puzzle."

"Thank you, Doctor. Is there anything else I should know before we sign off?"

"No, that's it for the moment. You can look at the progress reports anytime on the main data frame. There's a day-to-day record available, complete with staff observations."

"Doctor," she said firmly, "I'm aware of that, but I'd rather talk directly to the person who put him back together and sees him daily." She paused for a second and then continued, "So when I call, please indulge me."

"Of course, Miss Petrov, I understand. Any time you want to talk about Johnson, just call."

"Thank you, Doctor. We'll talk again."

CHAPTER 11

*S*pecial *Projects was the generic name the GIA gave Ann Petrov's department. The official story was that the complex housed a group of scientists developing specialized technologies. The truth was* known to only a few.

It had been built away from the prying eyes of the public, amongst the hills and valleys in the centre of the country. It had been chosen first for its quick and easy access to the major cities in case of Rebel attacks and second for its ability to include adverse and climactic conditions for training.

Special Projects S2 - Intelligence Commander was Dave Corbin. He was slim and compact in stature and unassuming in bearing. His demeanour was that of a kind and soft-spoken man, saying little and never asking questions. He simply preferred to watch and listen. In the early part of his career, his Commander was insulted because of Corbin's behaviour. Ordered to stay behind after a particularly long meeting, the Commander had said, "Corbin, I've been talking for the past hour, and you never took notes or asked any questions. Were you not interested in what was being discussed?"

Corbin stood up and walked to the front of the room, pausing before looking back at the Commander. "Sir, where would you like me to start?"

"Start? What do you mean 'Start?'" the Commander replied, furrowing his brow.

"I'll keep this brief, sir." With that, Corbin began an exact word for word rendition of the briefing, never pausing.

The Commander stopped him after a minute, waving his hands in surrender, asking, "Eidetic or photographic memory?"

"Both, sir. I can recall about 98% of what I see or hear,"

he replied.

The Commander had dismissed him without another word.

Corbin was now going over the reams of Intelligence information that had been collected over the last thirty days. Although his colleagues used a computer program for vetting, he preferred to use his mind. He looked for anomalies that had a human connection, not a mathematical percentage. His suspicions were suddenly aroused while scanning the report on an unusual energy spike within a communications signal from an industrial part of the city. It had been assigned to an office complex, and the amount of energy emitted was unusual for that area. Upon closer investigation, he found no physical evidence of a complex.

Ann was sitting at her desk when her communicator came to life.

"Miss Petrov," she answered.

"Ma'am, S2 here. We've got something in a town called Sturges. I'm sending you the information as we speak."

"I just got it," she said, scanning the document. "This looks promising. I'm alerting two teams now. If there's anything new, make sure I get it."

"Will do, ma'am."

As Ann scanned the screen, she could see why he had picked that location and why the programs had skipped over it. She walked down to the team briefing area and was met halfway by Corbin.

"We've pinpointed the location now, along with all schematics of the building."

"Good. Any Intelligence on the area?"

"No, ma'am. Not enough time."

"We'll go in without it," she said. "You must've gone through thousands of pieces of data. How did you find the target area?"

"I don't read everything, I just scan. My eye picks up on something and hones in on it. Nothing to it. Just a bit of practice."

Ann's mouth twisted into a friendly smirk. "Good eye."

The room was called to attention as they entered the briefing area.

"At ease," she said, walking to the front. "We have a target in Sturges about an hour's flight time, so we'll use Destination. Since there's a possibility of up to twenty insurgents, we'll transport everyone at the same time. Make sure you're in your fighting positions before departure. Drop off and pick up will be in the centre of the building. S2 Corbin will pass on any last-minute Intelligence. Operation commences in sixty minutes." She asked for questions and then walked to the back of the room. Her gaze shifted to the men and women as they made their preparations, momentarily envying their camaraderie. She thrived with the responsibility of leadership but often longed to be part of the assault team again.

Time passed quickly, and the team was soon ready, assembling into an assault formation. The two troop Commanders gave a thumbs-up to the man on the controls, who looked at Ann and said, "They're ready."

"Launch now."

He moved the power lever from zero to ten, activating the machine and sending the formation of soldiers to the location.

He had just picked up the last box and was about to move it to the transporter. The energy in the room suddenly fluctuated, and he felt the hairs on his arms lift, standing stiff. From the corner of his eye, he caught a glimpse of a swiftly growing sphere of brilliant white light. Without hesitating, he dropped the box and reached for his weapon. It was too late.

Ann watched quietly as her screen came to life, and the signal from the assault team's camera was received. Fifteen minutes later, the all-clear was given; the assault was over. She donned her gear, walked into the Destination Room and joined the team.

On her arrival, one of the Commanders immediately briefed her. "All secure; all friendly forces okay. It wasn't much of a fight. Five Rebels KIA. During the search, we found one man, unarmed and dead." He pointed to the body on the floor and went on, "Medics figure he was killed as we entered the area. We've run DNA on him. The system says he was one of ours. His name was Kevin Summers."

She walked over to the body and examined it. The man looked familiar, but she couldn't place him. *This was the fourth person they had found that had been kidnapped in the last four years,* Ann thought. She stood up and said, "Let's bring him home and notify the next of kin. I'll see you back at the compound."

Over the next few hours, Ann completed the After-Action Report (AAR) from the Operation. She forwarded it to Eric, also attaching the personnel file on Kevin Summers. She allowed five minutes to pass and then contacted him on his communicator.

"Hello, Ann. Thank you for the AAR," Eric said.

"No problem. The Operation went smoothly. Did you get the file on Summers as well?"

"Yes, I did. It's too bad. Summers is leaving a whole family behind."

"We're contacting his family now. Did you happen to note that he came out of Stasis a year ago?"

"I did," Eric started, hesitantly. "What are you thinking, Ann?"

"Sir, this is the fourth person in four years to be kidnapped by the Rebels. I've had Corbin go over the security system that protects our Operators. He says it's fine. No one appears to be hacking it, and there's been no unauthorized use. Both he and I believe that the weak link is in our hospital, specifically the Stasis Unit. Someone is leaking information and getting our people killed."

CHAPTER 12

*L*eah walked into the Stasis room, a small smile breaking over her *face. She loved its soft, ambient lighting and the warm, slightly humid temperature required to keep their patients comfortable.* Taking off her sweater, she glanced over the large room and the long lines of floating beds. They could max out at fifty people, but today it was only half full. Leah stopped at each patient, scanning their vitals. The state of each person was, for the most part, wholly monitored by the machinery. If the patient fell into trouble, the system alerted the standby staff.

She'd already checked her status screen and ensured that each of them had been physically attended to. All the staff, however, were very aware that attending to only the physical aspect of a medical condition was not sufficient to keep the human body alive. Leah never failed to give a caress when she thought it was needed or say a few soft words when she tucked the bedsheets under them. The power of human touch and interaction was necessary for the recovery process. This aspect of the job was the part that Leah loved the most.

She methodically made her way from bed to bed, talking gently as if they were awake, worrying over an incorrectly placed pillow and brushing back their hair. Finishing up, she stood back and briefly wondered what they were dreaming of, thinking of, and where they thought they were. Her reflections turned dark as she speculated what they would think of her if they knew she had given information about them to the Rebels. The shame and guilt she'd felt the other day at the meeting with her Handler overcame her in waves so intense she had to sit down. *Why was I so stupid?* She wondered, shaking her head in disbelief. After a moment, she regained her composure and glanced at her watch.

It was break time. She walked over to her sweater, pulled it over her shoulders and then looked back at the room. "Sleep tight," she said out loud, then signed off and walked down to the nurses' break room.

Leah's next shift was in the Physiotherapy Ward. Its atmosphere, unlike the Stasis Ward, was lively and energetic, filled with the voices of encouragement from both patients and medical staff. Almost every apparatus was utilized, and it was going to be a busy day. When she arrived, she found Sarah and Mark assessing two of the patients who were receiving physiotherapy. Sarah looked up as Leah walked in and said, "Leah, could you give me some help here, please?"

"Of course," she said, walking over to her. "What do you need?"

The two women worked quietly and efficiently together, assessing and measuring the damage to a patient's body. She was a member of one of the assault squadrons, seriously wounded a month ago. Beside them, Mark was assisting a young man who had fallen and received a compound fracture to his upper leg. The two doctors began a short conversation as they worked.

"What do you think about Johnson going out with Betty tomorrow?" Mark asked.

"I think it's good. It's about time for him to get out," Sarah replied and glanced at Leah. "Leah, you remember Steve Johnson, don't you?"

"Steve Johnson," she repeated slowly, feigning confusion. "Which one was he?" *Of course, she knew Johnson,* she thought. She'd cared for him for two years.

"Steve Johnson, big boy," Sarah reminded her. "He was in Stasis for two years. We pulled him out not long ago."

"Oh yes, of course, I remember now. You said something about him going out tomorrow? Is he ready to leave?"

Mark, still assessing his patient, replied with only a half glance toward her. "No, he's not ready to leave yet. Betty Sharpe is just taking him on a little ride through the countryside."

"Well, that's good, isn't it?" she said. "People need to get out after being under that long. All done here, Doctor. Do you need me anymore?"

"No, I think we're all done. Thanks for the help, Leah," Sarah said.

Leah walked away, tending to the rest of her rounds. The remainder of her shift went by without issue, the hum of the hospital quieting as the day ended and the night shift staff came in. She picked up her coat and was walking out of the building when she heard a voice.

"Leah! There you are! We're off to the pub for a drink. Would you like to join us?" It was one of the other nurses on her shift.

"No, not tonight. I'm bushed," Leah said. "Thanks for thinking about me." She climbed into her vector and silently sped off into the darkening sky. At the halfway point, she directed the vector to land. It slowed and came down in a town two hundred kilometres from the hospital. Her Handler had picked that location for unscheduled contacts because it was on her way home. If someone were to scan her records, there would be a plausible reason for her to be there. Stopping at a store would not be considered unusual.

The machine shut down, and the door slid open, allowing Leah to step clear of it. She walked into a park, spotting a bench in the distance and the form of a lone person sitting on it. Reluctant and resigned, keeping her coat pulled up well into her neck, Leah continued walking toward him. As she came up to the bench, the man looked up at her appreciatively and said, "Leah. So nice to see you again. Come sit down. We need to look like a couple."

She complied, and as their two bodies touched, she felt his arm move up and around her shoulders. She shuttered involuntarily and stared ahead, not saying a word.

"Just give me a second," he said, pulling out his screen and scanning her. "Now, what do you have for me?"

He listened intently as Leah explained to him her week at the hospital, the patients that were of interest, and how they were doing. When she was finished, she added what she had learned today.

"That guy, Steve Johnson, the one I said went to the Secure Area with the older lady? I don't think he's going to be of interest to you. The doctors said he was going out on a trip tomorrow and that she was taking him around, so he's not under any kind of special guard. She's only a medical assistant."

The Handler stopped her. "Who is this older lady again?"

"I don't have much contact with her. She keeps to herself. She doesn't talk much, except to the patients. Her first name is Betty, but the last name I can't remember. Starts with an S, I think."

The man stiffened slightly and ran the name through his head, his brain kicking out only one possible result.

He asked stiffly, "It wasn't by chance Betty Sharpe?"

Leah looked at him, surprised. "That's right. That's it. Betty Sharpe. Do you know her?"

The lie came effortlessly. "Not really. There was a Betty Sharpe working at the Central Hospital a couple of years ago. She helped a friend of mine. Just the same, I think it might be best to stay a good distance away from her. Watch her as much as you can and pick up anything of value from the other doctors and nurses. If you can, find out where they go tomorrow and keep track of how long they were gone. Then report back to me through our usual channels."

"Okay, sure," she said, although she was unable to imagine what possible interest they would have in Betty. Reluctantly, she added, "I'll do that."

They sat in silence for a moment before he asked sharply, "Now, what's the problem?"

Leah hesitated and then stammered, "You said you'd talk to your boss about how much longer I'd have to do this..."

"Yeah, yeah, I did," he replied, now impatient with her, but knowing he had to put up with her cowering a while longer. "They just need you around a few more months, that's it. Then all is forgotten."

She stood, feeling utterly defeated, shoulders slumped and head down.

Leah spoke quietly, in almost a whisper, as she looked at him. "A few more months then. Okay." She turned around and made her way back to her vector. Stepping into it, she pushed the home button on the screen. The machine came to life and lifted into the air. Recalling her last two meetings with the man, she suddenly realized that the "few more months" would never really end for her. *It's time for me to look after myself,* she thought.

The Handler had watched her walk away, and when he could no longer see her, he stood up and looked around. Digging his hands deep into his pockets, he tightened up the coat around his body, pushing out the cold chill trying to get in. He turned and walked in the opposite direction, thinking about two things. Leah was becoming desperate and desperate people will do desperate things. She'll need to be kept on a short leash. The other was the name Betty Sharpe, a name he hadn't heard in a long time. He had always wondered what had happened to her.

CHAPTER 13

When Mark and Betty arrived at the Head Doctor's office door, John let them in and gestured for them to have a seat. He asked, "What can I do for you?"

Mark replied, "I'd like to send Johnson out with Betty to her village tomorrow. It will allow him the opportunity to get out of a hospital setting."

John was unconcerned and immediately said, "That sounds like a good idea."

"I've given him full access to his screen, so if he wants to become familiar with something before departing, he can."

Betty commented, "Everything should work out fine, but please monitor him closely on the outing. If something were to go wrong, I'd like a team to come and take over."

"Of course," John said. "The possibility of him mentally or physically breaking is slim, but if he's going to, I want him to do it sooner than later. We'll have a chance to correct it immediately. What are your plans, and where will you take him?"

"I'll start slow. Use the vector to take him to my house for tea and a walk around. We should only be gone for about half of the day."

"It's a good start, I think, but I don't want his communication system open yet. We'll do that later. Anything else?" John asked. As the two of them shook their heads no, John continued. "All right, let's go with that. Betty, good luck tomorrow."

The next morning, Johnson saw an array of vehicles in all sizes, slowly coming into view as people arrived for work. All of them were designed to move through the air using an electromagnetic torque that formed an anti-gravity field around the vehicle. The system pushed the machine off the ground for takeoff and landing, and then, once airborne, transitioned the energy to forward flight. A force field formed around the vehicle to protect the occupants from accidents or loss of power. One offshoot from using this technology was light refraction from the energy field that made the vector invisible to the eye. As Betty approached the machine, it lit up, and a slight humming could be heard from its centre. She remarked, "It's another reason to wear your coder. The vector is linked to me so no one else can use it."

A voice from the vector said, "Betty, nice to see you again. Will there be two passengers?"

"Yes. Destination will be my residence, please."

"All systems are good. Weight calculations and time of flight will be calculated on departure."

The vector's dome opened, and they settled into their seats.

"Flight time will be fifteen minutes. Flight distance is one-hundred kilometres," the vector said.

Betty settled back and remarked, "Sit back, relax and enjoy the scenery."

The vector lifted off smoothly and rose into the air. They reached two-hundred metres above the ground and were then propelled forward. The only sound Johnson heard was a slight hum from the machine, and he set himself back against the comfortable seat as he looked down at the countryside. Below him was a thick, green forest, filled with vegetation that resembled the different varieties of deciduous trees on Earth. He caught glimpses of streams and ponds splitting open the woodlands beneath him. They transitioned into an agricultural area filled with freshly tilled fields and farms. Small, well-maintained roads crisscrossed the land, and Johnson watched as people on bicycles rode in groups through them. In the distance were rolling foothills and, beyond that, a range of vast, rugged and snow-covered mountains.

Betty pointed forward and said, "Ah, we're coming up to my

town now." Johnson watched as a town came into view below them. He felt the vehicle transitioning, slowing down as the computer announced, "Shifting to landing protocol. Forward thrust off. Descending now." A moment later, they felt a slight rocking as the machine settled on the ground in front of a home.

As they stepped out of the machine, Betty asked, "So how was your first ride in one of our vectors?"

"Not bad. I remember learning about these when I was in Stasis. Nothing compares to this on Earth. Quiet, fast. I like it," Johnson said, standing alongside the machine and looking it over.

Betty said, "It's a good mode of transport for local travel. This one is used for shorter commutes, within 400 km. The larger versions are for longer distances and greater loads. Come along now, and I'll show you my home."

"You live here?" he asked curiously.

"Yes, my husband and I raised our son here," she said as she gazed across the property. "He passed away a few years ago, and my son has moved on. Now it's just me, but I don't mind."

The boundary of her home was marked by a waist-high stone fence and a metal gate. She pushed it open and walked toward the front door on a stone walkway with lush, green grass on either side of it. The house was dome-shaped and had been painted taupe, blending seamlessly into its surroundings. Multi-coloured flowerbeds and lush green trees were scattered generously throughout the property. As they got closer, Johnson noticed that even the windows curved gracefully around the house, letting in as much natural light as possible. He stopped, looking up and down the street, and realized the other homes in the area were generally the same. Some were bigger and some smaller, but all were built in the same quaint style.

Betty watched him and said, "We try to use the natural contours of the land to support our roads, buildings and life. We want to capitalize on what nature has provided and not disrupt waterways, forests and landscapes. The concept makes sense for a village but doesn't always fit well in a large city environment. We had a population crisis 500 years ago."

"I remember learning about that."

"That's what led to the strict laws on family size to keep our population stable. They used to cram a thousand people into where there should have only been a hundred. The land was unable to support it, and the living conditions were inhumane." She paused a bit and then continued. "It took a long time to change, and there was a lot of pushback. Nothing happened overnight. The country still doesn't dictate an absolute on the number of children that you want or what kind of home you want. If you want something and the area can't support it, then you may have to move or be placed on a waiting list and be picked up later. Some people don't like it, but that's the way it has to be."

They stopped at the front door and, triggered by Betty's coder, the door unlocked, and the lights flickered on. Johnson followed her into the house, saying, "That must have been a real fight at one point. A change like that never comes without opposition."

Betty nodded. "The change wasn't gradual, which made it more difficult. And yes, there was a fight. Some thought it was easier to live in a flawed system. Finally, people realized they had no choice; it was either we change or disappear as a species. We could only lie to ourselves for so long. If you do the same thing repeatedly and expect a different outcome, you're only fooling yourself. Our world deteriorated to the point of no return, and people knew it was time to change. There were years of upheaval and rebellion, and a massive loss of life. But finally, the country and then the world changed."

They continued into the kitchen, and Betty made her way over to her food dispenser, ordering tea for the two of them. Handing Johnson one of the mugs, she said, "Let's go to the back yard."

The back yard was large, with natural gardens, a quaint pond and a greenhouse. He caught sight of strange-looking, exotic plants with large, bulbous pods on them. She identified them as a high protein bean pod used as a substitute for meat.

He asked, "Does the food dispenser also make your food?"

"Yes," she said, "we synthetically produce what we need. There's a database containing the genetic codes for fish, poultry and any other kind of meat. If I want a steak, I go to the protein printer, punch in the size and type and presto, there it is. I can cook it myself, or the printer will do it for me. It tastes the same, although sometimes I prefer to do my own cooking. I have a few old recipes that I still like using. Meat, poultry, fish and any other organically based creatures are still raised and can be purchased, but it honestly tastes no different. I believe that, as time goes by, the organic stock may eventually disappear."

Johnson deadpanned, "And here I thought microwaves were high tech."

Betty laughed. "We used something similar years ago. We've just had more time to refine things. The dispenser doesn't just replicate protein. I used it to make our tea. It works on the same principle and, depending on the ingredient, is either re-hydrated or replicated using plant DNA."

After tea and a walk around the back yard, they continued through the house. Betty was still talking and had opened the front door when she noticed Johnson wasn't with her. She turned back, searching for him and found him in front of a group of pictures on the wall. She looked over his shoulder to see which one had caught his eye.

"Is this you?" Johnson asked, pointing at one of the photos.

"Oh, yes," she said. "Now please understand, that picture was taken a long time ago. Goodness! I can't believe I was ever that young."

The photo showed Betty with two young, fit men, arms slung over each other and smiling into the camera. There was something in their stance, something in their bearing that made him take a harder look. Although they were smiling, there was a weariness to them. They seemed exhausted, and their eyes all held the same sharp edge, a wariness. With a sudden realization, he looked back at her and asked, "Were you in the Military here?"

She gazed quietly at the picture for a moment and then answered, "No, no. It was just a camping trip. We'd just finished a rather challenging hike. Now, let's get moving, and I'll walk you around the village."

She returned to the front door and called to Johnson, who was still studying the picture. "You coming?"

"I'm coming," Johnson said, following her obediently out the door. *That was no camping trip*, he thought.

As the two of them toured the small village, Johnson was surprised to see that although this world was highly technologically advanced, it had maintained a simplicity, a quaintness. On the one hand, it had incredible flying machines and devices that instantly made your food. On the other, people were still walking or on bicycles and had an easy-going openness to them. Everyone they passed had greeted Betty with a friendly smile and talked about day-to-day life. They were not that much different than any other village at home, he realized. He commented on the similarities between their two worlds but acknowledged Earth's technological shortcomings.

Betty said philosophically, "That will come soon enough."

Eventually, the two returned to Betty's home. "I think that's enough for one day," she said.

"Yeah, I think so too, although it was nice to get out. Thanks for inviting me."

The vector opened, the two of them stepped into it and flew back to the hospital without incident. Johnson thanked her again for the outing and headed for the weight room before supper.

Betty watched him leave, then turned and headed to John's office. She reached up and touched the entry screen, requesting permission to enter. John, at his desk, opened the door and greeted Betty when she came in.

"Betty, I've been monitoring the two of you today. Looks like things went well."

"Yes," she replied, "I think it all went very well. He's smart and learns quickly. Can you pass that on to Stanton or Petrov for me? It'll save me the call."

"Stanton or Petrov? I wasn't aware that you knew them," he said startled.

"John, I've known those two for a long time. As a matter of fact, I was an instructor on Petrov's course before she changed over to the agency. And Stanton, he's a good leader, smart and physically very adept."

John looked up into Betty's eyes. *Of course,* he thought, *it all makes sense now.* Someone had been placed here by the GIA to watch out for Johnson and guide him through.

"Got it. I'll say hello."

"Thank you," she said briskly and walked out the door.

He watched, speechless as the door closed behind her. *I should've known who she was. I was too busy to piece it all together,* he thought.

CHAPTER 14

*J*ohnson started his morning run earlier than usual the next day. His breathing became heavier as he pushed his body harder and harder. *Keep the pace,* he thought. *Keep pushing.* Sweat had begun to pour off his face, and the cadence of his feet quickened as he leaned farther forward. Johnson was fully aware of how his body was performing, and he was working to keep the momentum of the pace, moving through the pain that developed. A voice in his head began to protest and then plead with him to slow down. He ignored it and kept going, blocking out the distraction and picking up the pace. He focused solely on his deep inhalations of oxygen and the steady rhythm.

From behind him, he began to vaguely hear a runner rapidly closing in on him. Glancing over his shoulder, he was surprised to see a woman who was coming up fast. Within seconds, Asta Hanson appeared beside him and, with a teasing smile, said, "Morning, Steve! Come on, keep up!"

Johnson returned her smile and watched approvingly as she slowly pulled ahead of him. Accepting the challenge, he again leaned forward, coaxing as much as he could from his protesting body. Finally pulling up beside her, the two runners ran stride for stride for a few moments. With 400 metres to go, Johnson began a final sprint, pulling ahead of Asta and watching her shoulder disappear from his peripheral. His brain was now pounding, demanding more oxygen, and he felt the lactic acid in his legs, threatening to seize up.

Asta laughed to herself as she cruised a metre behind him. With 200 metres remaining, her pace quickened, and her stride lengthened. She closed the one-metre gap between them within seconds, now easily in control, and smoothly pushed past him.

Johnson could only watch as she pulled away from him. He wasn't happy, but there wasn't a damn thing he could do to keep up. Reaching the finish, she slowed and then brought herself into a walk. He joined her a few seconds later and said, "Nice pace, Asta."

She smiled at him, her face radiating health and extended a hand in welcome. "Good to see you again, stranger! I was wondering what happened to you."

Johnson took her hand and shook it, replying, "Looks like they're keeping me separate from the rest of you for the time being. I thought you were gone."

"No, but I leave tomorrow. How about you? When do you leave?"

"I don't know yet, but I'm sure it'll be soon. Can't wait to get back into something."

"I know how you feel. You stretching out?"

"I am," Johnson replied, walking with her to a level spot and beginning a stretching routine.

Midway through, Johnson asked, "So where do you go after this?"

"Right back to Special Projects."

Johnson did not want her to know he had no idea what exactly Special Projects was. "They'll keep you busy, I'm sure. How long have you been with them?"

"I completed selection five years ago," she said, moving gracefully into a balance pose on one leg.

"How'd you hurt the leg?" he asked curiously, observing the long but well-healed scar on her thigh.

"Took a high-velocity jolt from a Rebel weapon that almost tore the leg off. I was worried about bleeding out, but the team was able to stem the flow. They evacuated me, and I ended up in Stasis here for three months."

Johnson was impressed. Asta was made of stern stuff. She showed no side effects either psychologically or physically, and only the scar remained from the near-death experience. He'd seen people with much slighter injuries throw in the towel and give up. The two of them finished their cool down and began walking toward the Unarmed Combat Room, where the screen read their coders, and the door slid open for them.

The room was large and broken down into eight court areas for individuals or teams to spar in. Six were being used by an array of people. A light in an open court lit up, and Johnson indicated to it before saying, "That one is for us. I'll take the first scenario." He walked out to the centre of the court and then said, "Activate fight program, male 220 pounds, six foot four inches, full effects." The program went through the request, and a minute later, a hologram of a man bigger and taller than Johnson stood off to the side. Unlike standard holograms, its program extended the power field around the image, turning it into a solid energy form. When hit, it would feel substantial; when striking, the opponent would feel the impact.

Asta stood with her arms folded across each other and a skeptical look on her face before finally saying, "Are you sure you know what you're doing? The image is bigger than you, and it's on full effects. You're going to feel all the pain. How about you start with someone your size?"

Johnson shook his head, saying, "Nope. I've been working with this program for about a week now." He began a short warmup, shadow boxing up and down the side of the court. After a minute, he walked to the centre and said, "Start simulation."

The hologram, linked to Johnson's coder, moved in facing him, hands up, eyes locked on him. It closed the distance quickly, coming in first with straight kicks and feigning punches. Johnson swiped the first kick, then moved laterally to the side of the image, giving it a hard, straight left punch to the kidneys. He could feel the weight of the strike on his fist as the hologram reacted, twisting to its side. Johnson, seeing the image drop its hands slightly, tried to come in with a quick uppercut but was intercepted and pushed away. It stepped back slightly, regaining its balance and then stepped forward with a high kick, catching Johnson on his right side. The force of the blow knocked the air out of his lungs. The hologram immediately followed up with a straight left and then a right, which Johnson was only partially able to block.

The early morning run had been the warmup. This was the real workout. Sweat began to run down his face and into his eyes, but he managed to pull in the needed oxygen and replenish his muscles. Johnson now moved in tightly toward the image, grabbing it and trying to control the inside space of his opponent.

Asta studied Johnson carefully as he advanced around the court. This type of fighting and his tactics were new to her. As he continued, his fighting style attracted the attention of some of the others in the room, and they gathered beside Asta. They watched as he caught his breath and set up a vicious right elbow to the hologram's head, rocking it back. The blow was hard enough for the image to sway back slightly, dropping its hands. Seeing the opportunity, Johnson immediately responded with a high roundhouse kick, connecting to the side of its head. His opponent staggered back, its program trying to recover. He instinctively knew the image was hurt and continued to close in, throwing a right and then a left punch before it fell to its knees. He stepped back then, dropping his hands and said, "Stop program."

The kneeling image evaporated, and he walked back to the small group which had assembled. Asta asked him, "You had it. You should have finished it. Why didn't you?"

"It was down. It was out. No need to go any further. Your turn."

Asta shrugged, slipped off her running jacket and simply replied, "The Rebels won't be as sympathetic. Activate fight program five."

Johnson spent the next hour with some of the others who had gathered, discussing and demonstrating moves and techniques. After that, they gathered their gear and left to return to their rooms. As they turned a corner, Johnson spotted Betty walking down the hall, guiding a floating pallet.

"Betty," he called. "How are you?"

"I'm fine, thanks," Betty said, coming up to them. "Looks like the two of you have been out this morning."

Johnson laughed, "Asta here kicked my butt in a run and then showed me up in the Unarmed Combat Room."

Asta retorted, "Not the way I saw it. I've never seen his style before. It's deadly. Ma'am, nice seeing you again."

"I'm glad to see that nasty wound of yours has healed so well. I believe you'll be leaving here tomorrow?"

"Yes, ma'am. That's right. The doctors did a great job, I feel good and can't wait to get back to work."

"I hate to be rude but, if you don't mind, I need to talk with Steve for a few minutes alone."

"No, of course not. We've just finished," Asta said. She glanced at Johnson and said, "Thanks for the company this morning, Steve. Hope I'll see you in the future. Ma'am, if I don't see you again, take care."

"Thank you, dear. Good luck."

Johnson watched thoughtfully as Asta walked swiftly away from them and then turned to speak with Betty. "She stiffened up as soon as she met you."

"Oh, she's just polite, that's all," Betty said, and the two made their way down the hallway, stopping by the nurses' station to drop off the pallet. "Since you had no difficulties on our trip yesterday, why don't you take a walk down to the village this afternoon?"

"Just show me the way," Johnson said.

Betty pulled out her screen and brought up a map of the area. She pointed to a town close to the centre. "This is a nice little town called Jersey, about a twenty-minute walk from here. It has a few shops, a library and a cafe you can stop at on the way out. To purchase items, just scan your coder. The hospital has provided you with a sufficient number of credits to last for quite some time."

Johnson and Betty walked away from the nurses' station just as Leah Evans walked up from the opposite direction. She watched as the two of them disappeared down the hallway and then turned to the nurse behind the console.

"What did they want?" Leah asked.

The other nurse looked up from her screen and replied, "Who are you talking about, Leah?"

"The medical assistant and that patient. I think his name is Steve. He was the one in Stasis for such a long time," Leah said.

"She just dropped off our pallet. I overheard something about a walk he's going on this afternoon to Jersey."

Leah gave a short grunt of acknowledgement and quickly finished her tasks. She had other work to do.

The nurse behind the screen looked over at her and asked, "Are you okay? You seem a little uptight."

"I'm fine, just tired." Leah paused and then said, "I need to take an early lunch." Without waiting for confirmation, she turned and headed straight out to her vector. The machine took her to a town a hundred kilometres north of the centre. It landed, and Leah got out, bought a salad from a street vendor and found a secluded park bench. This was another place her Handler told her to use if she needed to get a hold of him on short notice. It was inconspicuous and not at all an unusual location to stop for lunch. She unrolled her screen and made the call.

He answered immediately. "Leah, good to hear from you."

She did not have time for social niceties. "Johnson," she said, "is going to Jersey by himself this afternoon. He may be on his way now."

"Such a nice surprise, Leah. Thanks. I'll pass that on. Is there anything else?"

"Yes," she said, steeling herself for what she felt she had to do. "This is the last time I'm dealing with you. I won't do this anymore." Without waiting for a reply, she shakily disconnected and looked over across the park, both relieved and scared. She could not afford to wonder whether or not it was the right thing to do. She only knew it felt right.

Leah got up from the bench and made her way back to the vector. The adrenaline that had propelled her was seeping out of her system, and her hands and legs felt weak. The door to the dome slid back as she approached the machine.

"Good afternoon, Leah. Where would you like to go?"

"Back to the hospital, please," she said, letting out a sigh as the vehicle took off. She leaned back into her seat, closing her eyes and hoping to get a few minutes sleep before landing. She wondered what she would do if her Handler called her again. What can I do, who could I go to, what would happen to me after I admitted that I was a traitor? Breaking the oaths that she had taken, to preserve life and to defend the government meant that if she were caught, it was off to a government facility for reprogramming. What would happen to her children and her husband? She worried. Everything she'd worked for, everyone she knew, would be gone.

The voice from the vehicle brought her back to reality. "Ten kilometres out. Starting landing protocol." A few seconds later, the machine announced again, "Five kilometres out. Two minutes till landing. GPS protocol overridden as requested. Removing protection field and body harness."

The words startled her out of her slumber, and a confused panic overwhelmed her. Leah screamed back at the vehicle. "Reinstate safety protocols. Reinstate safety protocols!"

The machine continued, ignoring her commands. "Override in progress. All safety protocols off."

She grabbed the Controller in front of her, trying to regain control and reconnect her harness at the same time. It rapidly dawned on her that someone else had command of the vehicle. Screaming with frustration and fear, she used both hands to try to pull up the steering lever. There was no response, and she could only watch in terror as the machine picked up speed and careened toward the ground. The vehicle hit with gut-wrenching force. Its momentum flipped the vector repeatedly before finally crashing against the side of a tree. Leah was thrown about wildly within the cabin, bashed and battered with every flip. She felt bones breaking and crushing until, mercifully, she lost consciousness.

The people standing outside the hospital did not see the crash but heard it and dispatched an ambulance toward the sound of the impact. The medics found her and immediately extracted her limp body from the crumpled machine. Placing her in the ambulance, they triaged the wounds and brought her to the hospital. The doctors worked frantically, but the internal damage was too severe. Her skull fracture had already initiated a fatal swelling when Leah opened her eyes. Taking a minute to stifle the searing pain and trying to focus on the scene around her, she spotted Betty and called for her. Surprised, the doctor motioned to Betty, who had been notified of the crash and was watching on the sidelines. She came quickly and leaned over Leah, reaching for her hand and holding it. She could see the woman's lips start to move and bent her ear closer to them.

Betty could barely hear the words Leah was forcing out with her last breath. "I told them Johnson was going to be alone in Jersey this afternoon." Betty lifted her head in surprise and then gazed at Leah with understanding and compassion. Their eyes locked on each other for a moment before Leah managed a small, laboured breath and whispered with regret, "I'm sorry."

The medical staff was now working frantically. "We're losing her," the doctor said. The last of her breath escaped Leah's lungs. Betty stayed with her and continued to watch Leah's eyes as the light in them died. Activity around them ceased as the doctor finally announced, "Time of death 1330 hours." Betty reached over to the dead woman's eyes, still open but now vacant and pain-free, and gently closed them.

CHAPTER 15

Ann Petrov prepared for the meeting and opened her screen one last time to ensure the agenda was in order. She closed it and then walked to the door, turning back for one last look. The sterility of the room and its barrenness were evident, and another person may have thought it cold and stark. It's simplicity, however, suited her needs and wants to a tee. *Just like my life,* she said to herself, conscientiously straightening her jacket one last time. *Clean and uncluttered, leaving nothing to chance and nothing to be compromised.* She walked out the door, and the dialogue in her head continued. *You don't need much when your whole life revolves around work — just a place to eat and sleep.* There were times when she had to get away and relax, but she knew that she was happier when the focus remained only on the job.

She'd tried to grow a garden years before because she thought it was expected of her, but that was an epic fail. Not that she didn't try. She had tilled the soil, fertilized it, strung out lines to keep the rows straight and added nameplates describing what was in the ground. The rows had been seeded, covered and watered lovingly, making sure the soil was damp but not saturated. A few weeks later, Ann watched in satisfaction when the plants had started to break the surface. That's when her job came calling like it always did. Work got all the attention, and soon the garden was overgrown with weeds. The same thing had happened to her marriage. Her husband had felt neglected for too long, and he finally said, "I'm sorry, but I give up, I can't compete with your job anymore." Since then, Ann had left the garden as a reminder of her failures in life, never weeding or replanting it. She had kept an old picture of her ex-husband hidden among her clothes for the same reason.

Ann stepped into the vector and flew to GIA Headquarters. Landing twenty minutes later, the dome door slid open, and she stepped out onto the parking lot, briefcase in hand. Ann straightened up, brushing any wrinkles from her suit and headed into the building. She was standing in line for the security scan when the Commander of the shift made eye contact with her. He waved her to him.

"Good day, ma'am. Sorry I didn't see you sooner. This will only take a second."

Ann replied, "That's fine. I could have waited with everyone else. There's no real hurry."

"Ma'am, I know. That's why we give you the VIP treatment," he said, smiling as he slid the scanner over her coder. "You're clear. Mr. Stanton is expecting you. I'll get one of the men to escort you down to his office."

"Thank you," she said and waited until a young soldier came around the corner and accompanied her down the labyrinth of corridors and turns. They arrived at Eric Stanton's office, and the door slid open quietly. She waited patiently by the door when she realized he was conducting a conference call with a dozen hologram images in place just above the desk. He turned when he heard Ann come into the room and motioned for her to sit down.

A few minutes later, he turned off his communicator, and the images disappeared. "Sorry about that, Ann. I had to discuss these reports with Higher. How was the trip?"

"Fine," she replied, "The skies were clear. No problems."

"Good. Now let's get on with this," Eric said. He looked down at his screen and scanned through it, touching the image button. A new hologram now appeared.

He picked up the Controller and flashed through the briefing to the start point.

"This was put together by my S2 cell. I've sent out a watered-down version to the other units, but I wanted to talk with you face-to-face. We've speculated for a few years now that our lines have been compromised by the Rebels. Someone has been giving away sensitive information and, as a result, some of our Operators have been murdered. I've had the S2 collate all the reports that have come in over the last twenty-four months. I wanted to see if there were any information leaks due to lack of security." He brought up a picture of Summers, the man that was murdered by the Rebels in their last raid. "We wouldn't have thought anything was awry if they hadn't hit Summers like they did. We would have missed the link."

Ann nodded in agreement and said, "But they got greedy."

"Yes. Yes, they did. Good for us, bad for them. My S2 went back sixty months. He scanned through all our casualties looking for possible links. The link he found was that all four people came out of Stasis at our hospital. They were smart. They selected only GIA mid-level commanders, all from different parts of the world, all to get a more in-depth picture of our organization. I'm recommending that we run a deep scan on every person working at the hospital to see what we come up with."

"I see what you're doing. It should flush something out. We have one soldier, a woman, coming out of the hospital tomorrow, who will need additional surveillance. And Johnson, what about him?"

Eric said, "Hopefully, this will be cleaned up in the next few days, and we won't have to worry about him. Until then, make sure he stays on the grounds."

"Hold on," he said, distracted by an incoming call. "I've got a communication I need to take, give me a moment." He answered the call and then stopped abruptly. "Ann, you need to hear this as well. I'm opening the line. It's Betty."

An image of Betty's face appeared over the desk, and Eric said, "Go ahead, Betty."

"I'm sorry for breaking in on you, but it's rather urgent. An ambulance was called out of the hospital at 1300 hours this afternoon. There was a vector accident. The person involved was Leah Evans, a nurse that worked the Stasis Unit. She was alive when they brought her in but passed away a few minutes later. I was with her when she went. Her last words were, 'I told them Johnson would be alone in Jersey this afternoon.'" Betty paused for a second. "I think we've found one of the people who was passing information to the Rebels."

Ann replied briskly, "Betty, are you in contact with Johnson?"

"No," Betty said, "he doesn't have a communicator. I'll make my way to Jersey once I'm done here. Ann, do you mind having a team on standby, please?"

"I'll do that and have them deployed covertly to the area. I'll also have the area contained, so no one gets in or out."

Betty said, "Yes on the team, no for the containment. I want to see how Johnson handles himself. Are you okay with that?"

"Looks good, Betty. We'll have the team locked onto you."

"Thanks. Out."

The communication terminated, and Eric remarked, "Test day for Johnson. I hope he's ready."

Ann smiled. "We'll see how he does in a few hours."

Johnson had made the Persons of Interest (POI) list in the Rebel HQ a few weeks prior. They hadn't figured out who or what he was yet. Still, Leah's information about Johnson's regeneration and Betty's sudden reappearance was enough to get him nominated. The POI list consisted of persons in or outside the GIA whom the Rebels deemed needed to be watched, captured or killed. Petrov herself had been near the top of that list for years. They just hadn't had the opportunity to get to her yet. When the Handler passed on that Johnson would be alone that afternoon, the decision was automatic.

The choice to terminate the informant was also made automatically. They had hacked into Leah's vector, turned off the safety protocols and driven her into the ground. At two hundred kilometres an hour, they'd hoped she'd have been killed on impact. But accidents are unpredictable, and the word was that she had survived but died shortly after being admitted to Emergency. Not perfect but good enough on short notice.

While they were driving Leah's vector into the ground, they were sending a message to Bill Lee. They preferred transmissions like this to be face-to-face, but time was short. Bill went over the on-line encrypted message. He deciphered it and, when he had its contents committed to memory, destroyed it by setting it on fire. Bill watched as the flames climbed the page and licked at his hand, then dropped the last remaining edge to the concrete floor, watching as it disappeared into ash. He picked up his boot and, with a short, harsh twist, rubbed it into dust, all evidence destroyed.

He ran his hands through his thinning black hair from front to back and began talking to himself. "Fucking short notice requests. No time to get the right people together." He mentally went through a list of available people that would be competent enough not to screw it up and finally settled on two that had been around for a while. The third member of the team was a newbie, a young woman who hadn't been tested yet but had shown promise. The two men would do the grunt work. Her role would only be a minor one. *Besides,* he thought, *with the scenario his Intel Section had spit out, the mission didn't look overly taxing.*

They could take Johnson down in one of three areas: while he was walking around town, shopping in a store or at the cafe. For Bill, the first two were nonstarters, but the last had potential. He wanted the kidnapping to be as discreet as possible, someplace hidden away, not in the open in front of a lot of people. The restaurant on Main Street would undoubtedly be his final stop before returning to the hospital. They could move in early and close it down, limiting the amount of traffic in and out, then take him however they wanted. The woman would be in place at the cafe, and the two men could observe Johnson from a distance. *It wouldn't be suspicious,* he thought. Johnson was new to the area, and people from a small town always checked out the newcomers. He nodded to himself. *I like this. It has possibilities.*

Fifteen minutes later, Bill stood in front of his three Operators and briefed them. When the briefing was finished, he added, "Remember, this is a quick and simple operation, with only a few moving parts. Don't make it complicated, get in, get Johnson and get the fuck out."

CHAPTER 16

Johnson stood in the centre of Jersey, looking up and down the Main Street. The place was tiny but surprisingly busy, with groups of people rushing to get their chores done during a lunch break. Trying his best to blend in, he discreetly looked in one direction and then turned and looked in the other. The town was small enough for him to see where it began and where it ended. *Not much here, but at least I'm out of the hospital again, and on my own,* he thought. He made the most of it, walking from one end of the town to the other, then zigzagging up and down the streets for no other reason than to walk. He made eye contact with the locals as they strolled by, smiling and saying hello. Most of them responded in kind, and he liked the fact that no one seemed any more interested in him than he in them.

The private houses and public buildings were the same basic dome design as in Betty's village but had many of the same features seen on Earth. Johnson had no difficulty recognizing the library, the town hall and the shops. He ended up back where he had started his stroll just sixty minutes later. Across the street was the cafe he'd seen earlier, and his stomach was telling him he'd missed lunch.

He glanced both ways and then stepped out into the street, making his way over to the entrance. It had long windows across the length of the front wall that allowed large amounts of sunlight to enter the room. Booths ran along the far wall to the right, and there were a few tables scattered through the centre. A long bar was to his left. It held floating stool tops for people to sit on. He mused that the checkerboard style floor was the same as you'd see in a fifty's diner on Earth. There was no sign about seating, and he was the only person in the place. *Unusual,* he thought, *but it was after lunch, and perhaps most of the people had gone back to work.* Sheer force of habit had him picking out a table that ensured his back was to a wall, and he had clear lines of sight to the front door. He'd acquired the habit years ago and had done it whenever he could. It put him at ease when he was able to see the whole room. Sitting down, he was surprised to see a menu light up on the surface of the table. He heard the kitchen door open and turned his head to the sound. A young woman he assumed was the waitress came out and began picking up dishes along the bar area.

Seeing him, she smiled and said, "Take your time. I'll bring the order out when it's ready."

Johnson scrolled through the menu options, checking off a beef sandwich, fries and a coffee. He waited only a minute or two before the kitchen door opened, and the waitress walked over to him with a tray.

"Beef sandwich, fries and coffee," she said, placing the tray in front of him.

"Thanks," he said. "Quiet day today?"

The girl hesitated as if having to roll through a hundred possible replies before answering and said, "It will be now. Lunch is over."

"You work here long?" he asked as he picked up a fry and ate it.

Nervously, she began shifting her weight from foot to foot, fidgeting with her hands. "Only been here about a month or so. I just need to scan your coder." She pulled a scanner from her pocket, held it close to his coder and watched as a green light lit up. She looked down at the readout. "Thank you, Mr. Johnson. If you need anything else, just order it off the menu." She returned the scanner to her pocket and started to walk back to the kitchen when the front door opened, and two men entered.

The waitress greeted both men with a nod and sat them at one of the tables before heading back into the kitchen.

Johnson ate quietly, glancing over the room and then at the other two customers. Something about their appearance was nagging him. From where he sat, their work attire, though worn and rough, showed no mud or dirt on the boots, and their hands looked perfectly clean. They didn't look like two guys that had just come in from a job site to get something to eat. In a few minutes, he had finished the last of his meal and downed the now lukewarm coffee. Sliding out of the booth, he walked past the men and confirmed that they were, indeed, too clean to be mistaken for construction workers. He stopped at the employee station as the waitress came out through the kitchen door.

"Can I get you anything else?" she asked.

"No, thanks. Do I owe you anything?"

"No, everything's been taken care of. Thanks for coming in."

Johnson heard movement to his rear, checked over his shoulder and then to the reflection in the window. He watched as the two men got up and moved in behind him. One stepped toward the door while the other reached his hand out to Johnson's shoulder. He felt the woman try to pull at his shirt, but he slammed her hand away. His instincts took over, and, moving smoothly, he turned, gripping the man's outreached hand with both of his. He swiftly twisted it and pushed it back into his forearm. The stranger grunted in pain, dropping like a stone while trying to stop his wrist from snapping.

Johnson added extra pressure to the man's wrist, gaining additional control and then looked for the other man. He was now closing the distance, and it was time to get rid of the extra baggage. Johnson pushed down hard on the locked wrist, feeling it snap and, in one swift motion, pulled hard on the broken arm. The man's head snapped forward into Johnson's right knee, slamming it with brutal force. Johnson felt the man's body go limp. He was out and no longer a threat. Johnson released his arm and watched dispassionately as he crumpled face-first onto the checkerboard floor.

He stepped to his left, away from the body to give himself more room. Johnson coldly locked eyes with the second man. "I'll let you walk out of here. It's not too late."

The second man moved in fast, saying, "You're coming with me," and spun quickly into a vicious kick.

Johnson's first thoughts were to get in fast, but the plan needed adjustment as he watched the kick come in at his head. With his arms held high, he absorbed most of the blow as the follow-through skimmed his forehead. The man's confidence was now up. "Maybe I'll let you live," he sneered, and moved in aggressively, mechanically throwing punches, knees and kicks. Johnson stepped back methodically, blocking and pushing the barrage of blows while waiting for his opening. It came when he stepped to his right, and the man threw a left jab followed by a hard right. Johnson side-stepped the combination, leaving a half-second opening with the man's hands down. He came in hard with a vicious right elbow, the man's chin taking the full impact. The last thing his opponent remembered was hearing a dull thump on the inside of his brain. Time slowed, and he struggled to regain control over his body. His knees finally collapsed, sending him crashing to the floor. His mind, hoping to minimize the damage, shut down, and it was lights out.

Johnson watched the waitress run back into the kitchen. *He'd deal with her later*, he thought grimly as he walked over and turned the first man onto his back. He slapped him hard across the face to bring him back to consciousness. *Not enough*, Johnson thought, when there was no response. Seeing the broken wrist, he stepped down on it with deliberate slowness. The weight ground the broken bones together and brought the man into consciousness, his eyes bulging as a deep scream uttered from his belly. Johnson looked down at him calmly as he continued to grind the broken wrist into the floor.

"What the fuck was that about, asshole?"

The man's lips started to move when a muffled voice outside

the door got his attention. "Stand back."

It meant one of two things. Someone was either blowing or shooting their way through the door. On either one of these occasions, he would need to find cover fast. Bending over, he grabbed his assailant by the chest and dropped to the floor, putting the man's back between him and the door. A human shield, he hoped, would absorb any shock waves or flying projectiles coming his way. The resounding blast blew the door inward and clipped the body in front of him. There was silence as the air around him filled with smoke and debris. The man's body had done what it was supposed to do, act as a cushion. A moment later, he rolled to his feet and moved quickly to the opening.

Betty slid around the corner at the same time. She stepped into the doorframe and calmly announced, "We need to get moving. Now."

He raised an eyebrow in surprise but gave a quick, "Give me a second." The man he'd used as a shield was unconscious again. He rolled him over and went through his pockets. Finding nothing, he went to the second man but found the same.

Betty now stood in the centre of the room. "Steve, we need to move."

"I know, just one more." He rushed to the kitchen door and kicked it open. In the kitchen, a man that Johnson assumed was the cafe owner lay unconscious on the floor. His eyes scanned the room and found the waitress standing in a corner, holding a kitchen knife in her hands. "That won't help you one bit, girl. Tell me who you are and what you want, or your day could get a lot worse."

The girl hit her emergency recall and spat back, "Fuck off."

Betty had followed Johnson into the kitchen doorway and eyed the young woman coldly. "We don't need her. We need to get going now, or this could get a lot worse."

Johnson took one last look at the girl, knowing he had to leave before they were sucked into the Rebel's recall bubble. "I've got a message for your boss. I'm coming to get every one of you fuckers."

"Leave them all. We have no use for them," Betty ordered. He nodded, turned, hoisted the café owner over his shoulder and followed Betty out the front door. A hundred metres up the street, she stopped and scanned the area in front and behind her. "Control, it looks clear, but keep an eye on us." Johnson transferred the unconscious man to an awaiting team of GIA medics and walked up to her. "You did well in there," she said, smiling.

"You think so? I thought I was rusty."

Betty chuckled and then continued, "There's nothing like a little incident to get the blood going again. Keep today's activities between us. Control knows, but the hospital doesn't need to."

"Sure, but the hospital will see my coder output."

Betty shook her head. "No, they won't. They'll see a blank spot. Let them think it was a malfunction."

"Sure," he said. "What was that all about? Why did they want me?"

They started walking again. "The Rebels had an informant in the hospital. She passed on to them that you'd be alone in Jersey this afternoon. They know about you, but why they want you can only be speculation."

"Why didn't you take them prisoner? You could have interrogated them."

"These were the hired help. They know nothing but the job. And besides, you gave her a message to pass along." Betty laughed.

"Are they so powerful that they can find out about a single person within the day and then attempt a daylight kidnapping? That's not a small organization."

Betty said, "I wouldn't go so far as to use the term 'powerful.' But they do have resources at their disposal and are ballsy. They weren't like this a few years ago, but I think it's because they've had a change in leadership."

Bill Lee watched as the Controller commenced an emergency recall from his console. The Controller glanced over to Bill. "I see only our people. Doesn't look like anyone else is with them."

"Are you sure?"

"I'm positive. It looks like the team never got the package," the Controller replied.

Bill's blood pressure started to rise. "Are they being followed?"

"No, I'm not picking up any energy bursts after them."

"Good. Send me in. I'll call when I want the cleanup crew and Medical."

"Will do," said the Controller and added power to the Destination Machine transporting Bill to the new location.

The two men and the girl had been in a Destination Machine before but never like this. The girl had initiated an emergency recall that had violently yanked them from one location to another. The two men lay on the cement floor, coughing. The girl staggered slightly, trying to keep her balance and held her hand to her mouth to stop her stomach from emptying its contents.

They'd been brought to an abandoned building with open, empty spaces and bare cement walls. It was illuminated with harsh incandescent lights that cast a cold grey pallor over their already pale faces. The two men struggled to their feet when they heard the sound of footsteps moving closer to them. Bill, his fists clenched, approached the two men, ignoring the girl. He stopped in front of them, furious and barely able to contain his anger. Clenching his teeth, he finally spat out, "I thought my orders were quite clear. You were to take Johnson out immediately upon entering the cafe. Did you not understand?"

The man with the broken wrist winced as he held the mangled

bones in place. "We were just going to grab a quick bite before we finished the job. I didn't think it would be a problem."

"Didn't think it would be a problem," Bill repeated slowly to the man and gestured to the broken wrist. "Wow, this looks bad. Must've been quite a blow."

"It was unexpected," the man mumbled.

Bill looked squarely into his face and reached out, supporting the arm gently with both of his hands. "We'll have to get that fixed now, won't we?" Before the man could answer, Bill locked both of his hands onto the break and twisted it in opposite directions. The man tried to move away but collapsed to his knees, screaming in agony. Bill turned the broken bones harder, feeling them grinding together. He gritted his teeth tightly as he spoke. "Are you going to follow my fucking instructions to the tee next time?"

The man's screams were the only answer Bill received, and he finally released his arm. The other two looked on numbly, too shocked to say a word and too horrified to think that they might be next.

"I take that as a yes," said Bill and, ignoring the others, took out his screen, unrolled it and called for the cleanup and medical crews.

A minute later, Bill heard the teams walking toward them and glanced at the lone woman following behind. Marie confidently walked up to Bill and said, "I told you to send me as the waitress. These two couldn't find their asses with both hands."

Bill watched her, his face stiff and tight. "Marie, I don't need your bullshit right now. You know I couldn't send you. That old bitch Sharpe knows you too well. Besides, these three should've been able to finish it."

She watched as the medics patched up the two men and took them away. "What are you going to do with her?" she said, motioning to the girl.

Bill said, "Her cover is fucked, so we'll have to alter her face."

"Maybe keep the alteration subtle. Then give her to me. I can retrain her."

"Once they're done, you can have her."

Marie brightened. "Hey, thanks," she said and walked over to the young girl. "You did good for a first mission, but you're going to get better. Come with me."

Bill silently watched them disappear into the darkness, then turned and walked in the opposite direction. A barely perceptible crack of light started to open. As he walked into it, he thought, *Who the fuck is this Johnson guy anyway?* And disappeared into the light.

CHAPTER 17

The Agency had dug deep into Leah Evans' background to try and unravel who she was and why she had begun to work for the Rebels. They took apart her life one piece at a time but couldn't find anything. They had interviewed her husband and talked with the children, even running a deep scan through all three but found no deception from them.

Next were the people she worked with at the hospital. They questioned her bosses and coworkers. Her friendships in the workplace were the most telling to the investigators. Four years ago, she had led a very social, outgoing life with a big circle of friends. They had all agreed that around that time, something had changed, and she slowly drifted from them. For a while, they had tried to salvage their relationships with her, but it appeared that the more they tried, the more she pushed them away. Her closest friend, Jan, who had gone through training with her, finally gave them a hint as to what could have happened.

They had gone to an end-of-shift party and had ended up at a crowded dance club. After a few drinks, most of the nurses went home: but she and Leah had stayed. They had ended the evening dancing with two men they met. Jan decided that she had enough and announced that she wanted to go home. Leah was not ready to leave and told Jan that she'd be fine and would see her at work in a few days. The next time they saw each other, Leah confided that she had ended up at the man's place and stayed the night. Her husband was away, and a babysitter was with the kids. She changed after that. She wouldn't go out anymore. She was very quiet and suppressed most of the time. Jan asked her to come out again after that, but she refused. Two years ago, Jan tried to follow and was surprised to find she hadn't gone directly home. Leah veered off and met a man in the park. Jan watched the scene unfold with surprise. At first, she thought Leah might be having an affair, but she hadn't recognized him from their night out. They also didn't appear to have a close physical relationship. There had been no touching, and, at one point, he seemed to be angry with her. Jan was embarrassed she had followed Leah and never spoke to her about what she had seen.

The more they analyzed the situation, the more they were sure that Leah was being blackmailed, and the person she had been meeting up with was, in fact, her Handler.

It had been two days since Johnson's incident in Jersey, and he'd heard all about the Stasis nurse, putting the two episodes together. Rumour was she had been passing classified information, so running into the two goons and the girl could not have been a coincidence; it had been planned. Rolling over in his bed, he stared at the ceiling. This world portrayed a sophisticated, well-organized society on the outside. On the inside, however, it had the makings of something very dark and disturbing. A sinister side that would target and hunt him with no remorse. It didn't bother him. If they wanted him, they could come and get it and may the best person win. He was sometimes worried about his lack of remorse. He had walked away from the Jersey incident and headed straight into the mess hall to get something to eat as if nothing had happened. His answer to himself had always been — they started it, I finished it. He knew that the next time the Rebels would be more prepared, meaning he could never let his guard down. He would always have to be ready.

Johnson got up, walked over to the window and thought about the picture he had seen in Betty's house. *What did she say again?* He thought. *Oh yes, a camping trip.* He knew there was more to this story. She'd been and was still involved with some government agency. Which agency was undetermined, but she was on his side, and that's all that counted. He changed into his PT clothing and commenced his daily ritual. Before yesterday, PT was only for his rehabilitation. Now it had a purpose. That purpose was to prepare for a fight.

Two hours later, he was contacted and asked if he could meet with Mr. Davis in the Secure Area. Fifteen minutes later, he joined Troy Davis and Betty. A door slid open, and Ann Petrov walked in. She greeted them briskly. "Good to see you again, Troy, Betty." Turning to Johnson, she held out her hand. "You're Steve Johnson. I'm Ann Petrov, head of Special Projects. Pleased to finally meet you."

Johnson grasped her hand firmly in his. "Ann, nice to meet you, too." He wanted to say more but couldn't think of anything intelligent. She had somehow put his mind in neutral, and his mouth was full of marbles until he forced himself to regain control. She was a stunning woman, tall, slender. Most importantly to him, however, were the keen, assessing eyes that missed nothing and the confidence with which she carried herself.

Ann caught his gaze squarely as they considered each other before she turned back, a slight smile on her face. They continued into the briefing room, where Eric Stanton was waiting for them. "Good morning, all," he said. "Steve, I'm pleased to finally meet you. I'm Eric Stanton, Commanding Officer of the Government Intelligence Agency, GIA for short."

"Pleased to meet you, Eric," Johnson replied, shaking his hand.

"Everyone take a seat, please. We'll start this briefing immediately. We have a security video from the cafe that we'd like to go through."

They played the video in its entirety before Eric stopped the image. "Steve, did you have any clue as to what was about to happen?"

Johnson replayed the scene in his mind and replied, "There were two things that alerted me. The first was the server's hesitation, and the second the men's appearance. Both looked like labourers, but neither had dirty boots, and their hands were too clean. I thought something could be up, but I didn't want to jump to conclusions. That was my mistake. I didn't listen to my instincts. Next time, I will."

Eric turned his attention to Davis. "Troy, you had no knowledge of this. I needed you to see for yourself the immediate danger our people are in. Four of them have been killed since Leah was recruited. Steve could have been number five. The next time we see the scanning program not up to date, you'll be replaced."

Davis' face reddened, and he protested. "We've tightened up security since the other day."

"As you should have," he said, "but it was too little, too late. That's all for now. You can go." Eric waited until Davis had left the room and then said to Johnson, "Steve, you were brought to Midgard under my orders. My Traveller warned me of a situation developing on your planet that would require monitoring and intervention. I had him look for suitable candidates that could assist us because, as you are aware, we cannot stay on Earth for extended periods. We'll discuss details on what exactly is happening a little later. Suffice to say, we believe that without intervention, your planet will not have the opportunity to grow and develop in the manner that it should. In any case, we needed a man with very particular qualities. You were located, evaluated and placed on a shortlist. When it became apparent that your demise was certain, I gave the order to bring you here."

"We want you to understand what's required of you, but we certainly can't and don't want to force you into anything you don't want to do. If you agree, we can provide you with training and bring you in on the first possible mission against the Rebels.

You'll learn our tactics and procedures, although it appears that they're not entirely different than yours. It will give you a chance to look at us and give us a chance to look at you. When you've completed the training, we can both reassess and decide which direction to take." Eric stopped for a moment and then said, "Would you be willing to work with us?"

Johnson asked, "Why are you interested in Earth?"

"There's a possibility that someone there will be developing an important energy source. We may be able to shorten the timeline for its development with your help. We can't do this. Only someone from Earth can."

"I understand."

"I have to be completely upfront with you. We do have our own reasons for promoting this development. Once the energy source has been fully developed, we can use it here as well."

"What kind of a timeline for training are we looking at?"

Ann joined the conversation. "Two weeks of training should get you sorted out."

Johnson didn't waste too much time in making a decision. The choice was simple for him. Hang around the hospital or take a chance on the GIA. The GIA won. He would be able to find out why they were so interested in his planet, and there was always the possibility he could get back home. He accepted the offer with a nod of agreement.

Eric was pleased with Johnson's decision and shook his hand firmly. "Welcome aboard. Ann, we need to get going. Betty, we'll send the required authorizations if you could expedite things on this end."

"I'll get everything in tonight and expect everything to be in place by tomorrow morning," Betty replied.

Johnson gathered up what little belongings he had that night, packing them into a duffle bag Betty had dropped off earlier. He took one last look in the closet at the box that contained his uniform and closed the door, leaving it behind. Betty walked him out to the parking lot, and as the vector landed, he said, "I suppose this is goodbye, Betty. Thanks for helping me out."

"My pleasure," she said, "but just to let you know, I never say goodbye anymore, only that we'll see each other again."

"I hope so," Johnson said as he hugged the woman and kissed her goodbye on the cheek.

He settled into the vector and watched quietly as it glided away from the hospital. For the first time in a very long while, he felt butterflies of anticipation. It was the thought of going somewhere new, doing something he knew how to do very well. He was getting back to what he did best, being a soldier.

CHAPTER 18

S tian Anthony was a Traveller, one of an elite group of operatives. They possessed extraordinary traits that allowed them to persevere under extremes of conditions. He had been handpicked and trained by the GIA twenty years prior. Stian was forty years old, of average height and build, wore glasses and had prematurely white hair as a result of an unavoidable extended stay on Earth. His appearance and bearing were unassuming, and he was able to blend into any group without notice.

Stian had been born and raised in the outer fringes of the country. He had been recruited because of his hard upbringing and intelligence. Trained to blend into different worlds, he knew the nuances, languages, customs and living conditions of each place. His mission was to follow without being seen, talk without being heard and report everything back to the GIA Commanding Officer. Their entire race was curious, thirsty for knowledge and interested in the different technologies they had found on the other humanoid planets. So the job came naturally to him. The long days by himself, away from everything and everyone he knew, could take their toll and others had broken before him. The life of living a lie, he often mused, could work on the best of minds. But the best found a way to cope, like any professional. And Stian was a pro, a superstar in the world of Travellers.

He had only recently returned from a trip when he received notification that Eric Stanton wished to meet with him again. Stian had discovered Johnson, and he was the one that had watched him. When Johnson was about to expire, he had contacted Eric for authorization to extract.

Stian walked out to his vector and, once airborne, opened his screen. He suspected that Eric wished to discuss the Earth POIs they had earmarked. He looked over the names and people he'd been assigned to. Flipping through each one individually, he confirmed to himself that there was currently no one that piqued his interest.

An hour later, he walked into Stanton's office and said, "How can I be of service, sir?"

"Straight to the point, as always," Eric said. "Nice to see you. Please sit down."

Stian settled himself while Eric produced a hologram of a woman named Sally Reilly. Stian recognized her immediately. He had been monitoring her progress for some time, and her face was as familiar to him as family.

"I need you to go back and get a detailed, up-to-date package on Sally Reilly."

Stian was surprised. He was unaware of anything that had changed in Sally's life since his last visit, and a requirement to return was unexpected. Eric continued. "There have been some changes since you last saw her. I need to find out why she stopped developing the machine she was working on. We need a new, detailed report from you as soon as possible for Higher."

Stian was puzzled because his last report had been only two months prior. "What's happened since my last report?"

Eric explained. "We predicted earlier that she was going to lead the change. When we conducted our update on People of Interest, we found that it is no longer her future. That change is now predicted to be initiated by her great-great-granddaughter, which means a huge delay in their progress. I need to know why Sally stopped what she was doing. She's living in a different locale now and is no longer conducting her research. We need you to find out what led to the change and see if we still have an opportunity to get her back on the right track."

"The change of residence is telling me that she's running away," Stian said slowly. "Abandoning her goals is saying the same thing. Her father is one of the top men in fossil fuels in

North America, and there's no doubt that he could have played some part in her changing her mind and running. There's been friction between them for some time, but it's obvious that I missed its true depth. When do you want me to leave, and how long do I have?"

"We'd like you out as soon as you can. Check with Futures for the latest update before you go and then take as long as you need to prepare."

"I don't think this will take very long. I'll be ready to go tomorrow."

"We'll be set up and prepped for you."

The next day, Stian stood on the side of a road, looking at the address in his hand. He was in Edmonton, Alberta, Canada. He had returned to where Sally and her research team were working to find out what had happened. The lot to the front of him was empty. It had been bulldozed flat, but you could still tell where the buildings once stood. The steel fence that secured the area was missing in places, and the gate was gone. Scorch marks on the cement foundation floor pointed to a fire and a hot one at that.

Stian looked up and down the road. The other lots housed everything from trucking companies to car wreckers and a mom and pop restaurant. No other businesses appeared to have been affected. He walked over and into the restaurant. There were only three customers inside and an older woman behind the counter. Stian sat down on a stool and ordered a coffee.

She poured him a cup and said, "I noticed you across the street. Are you looking at rebuilding?"

"No, I must have been given an old address."

"Let's see what you have," she replied, and Stian pulled out the paper and showed it to her. "That's the right place, just the wrong time. It burned to the ground a year ago. No one knows how or why."

"Who was in there?" He asked encouragingly.

She racked her memory for a moment before answering. "I

think her name was Sally. Yes, Sally and a few others. They were working on something to do with alternate fuels, I think. They were a nice bunch of young people, hard-working, ate here all of the time."

"So, it burned down a year ago? Where did they move to?"

"I don't know," she said. "It was strange. They just up and disappeared after it all happened. Went their separate ways. I think she went to California, but I don't know about her friends." She hesitated for an instant and then muttered, "Now, if the investigators would've asked me, which they didn't, I think her father burned the place to the ground."

"Her father? Why would her father do something like that?" Stian said in a disbelieving way.

"Her old man is one of the richest guys in the oil business. He makes himself out to be really important. That group," she said, as she pointed to the empty lot, "I heard they were making good headway. We had all sorts of people coming here, looking at what they could do. I know that because they all ate here. There were Russians, Americans, Germans, Brits. You name it, they came through here."

"And one night, the place just went up in flames?"

"Yep. My security camera was working that night. You could see they just barely made it out with their lives. I think it scared them so bad they quit, thinking it wasn't worth their lives."

Stian spoke with her for a few more minutes, then finished his coffee and got the waitress to call him a cab. He thanked her and pulled out his phone to dig up everything he could on Sally and the fire. Everything the waitress had told him was confirmed. The only explanation ever given for the fire was faulty wiring, with no mention of the possibility of arson. He knew that Sally had not gone to California. In all probability, she had used that lie to cover her tracks. The Predictions Section had determined that she had headed east to Regina.

The next morning, Stian was in Regina at the cafe where Sally worked, sipping his coffee when she walked in to start her shift. He finished his mug and walked to the counter.

Sally turned, and seeing the empty mug, said, "Good morning, would you like a refill?"

"Yes, please, in a takeaway cup," he replied, placing the empty mug on the counter.

"I can do that," she said, then took a second glance at the man when she thought he wasn't looking. She'd seen him somewhere before, she puzzled, but decided to drop it.

"Thank you," Stian said, then paid her and sat back down, thinking, *Looks like this girl ran off and abandoned everything. Such potential wasted.* Five minutes later, he walked out the door and down the street, taking one last sip of coffee before dumping it in the trash. He drank it to fit in, not because he liked it. Their reliance on caffeine puzzled him.

The next day, he was back outside Eric Stanton's office, waiting for the door to open. When the door slid back, Stian made his way over to the conference table, where several others were waiting for him. An hour later, the briefing on his last mission completed, he looked over at the group and asked, "Do you have any questions?"

"I've got a question," Ann Petrov said. "Do you think we can persuade her to go back to her research?"

Stian was puzzled. He knew they usually relied heavily on their computer technology, not instinct, to form probability decisions. "You've already run this through the Futures Program, haven't you? I know they said there's a chance."

Ann never took her eyes off Stian. "Mr. Anthony, I'm asking you because you were on the ground, and you've had actual eyes on Sally. What is your opinion? If we send someone in, do you think we can be successful in getting her to start her research again?"

Stian carefully mulled the question over in his mind and finally said, "Do I think there's a chance for this to work? Yes. But whoever is going in must be able to protect her and her colleagues. I expect conflict, and with that, a good possibility of a loss of life. You do understand, Miss Petrov, that if we take even one person's life in that world, at that time, it could change their entire future? Our very presence will undoubtedly influence it in one way or another. You have to be prepared, and you have to be very careful."

"I understand completely," she said, satisfied with his answer.

Eric cut in. "Stian, thank you. Your input has been invaluable, as usual. If I need more, I'll be in contact." Requiring no further suggestion, Stian acknowledged his dismissal and left the room.

Eric turned to the others. "I want Johnson to do this job. Our priority is to get Futures to see what the prognosis for his return means. Let's get this done now. You're dismissed."

CHAPTER 19

*I*t was early morning as Sally walked across the street to the park. The sun was just above the horizon, warming the air from the previous night. She breathed in deeply, her senses awakening, then held her breath and let it out. Sally loved her time alone in the morning, and a day as fresh as this one could not be ignored. She started her walk around the park at a brisk pace, waving to the usual regulars as they joined her for their morning exercise. An hour later, she found a quiet, flat area where she started a light stretching routine.

Sally's long, blonde hair was perpetually knotted into a loose bun, the style accentuating her sharp cheekbones and striking light blue eyes. At 5′ 8″ tall, she maintained her slim build with regular, strenuous aerobic exercise. Sally was just under thirty years old. Twenty-eight years, to be exact, and the more she thought about the encroaching birthday, the more her heart would sink. Time was moving too quickly, and all the things she had wanted to achieve had been torn from her. Propelled by a desire to excel, Sally threw all her energy into her education, finishing university at the top of her class. She possessed a sharp, innovative mind and, much to her family's chagrin, challenged their authority and beliefs at every turn. When she was welcomed to one of the top engineering firms in the world, her father believed that the work would keep her "entertained" until an appropriate mate was found. Unfortunately, the firm did not agree with her innovative ideas and designing other people's dreams would have destroyed her if she had stayed. She resigned six months after she was hired, possessed with soaring goals of her own and disgusted with their lack of insight.

Her father was one of the wealthiest men in North America.

Shawn Reilly was born in Manchester, England. His family had come to Canada in 1954, shortly after he was born. He tried his best in school, but it was difficult for the young man. He made it as far as grade 10, dropped out and joined the oil industry as a rig hand. He worked himself to the top from the bottom with sheer grit. It was tough, and it was hard, but the lessons he learned he would never forget. One rule he lived by daily was to show no mercy. Friend or foe, the treatment was the same. It was also how he ran his family, making sure everyone under his roof abided by his rules and his way of thinking. Sally's two sisters and her mother hated it but had realized early on that if they wanted to live in luxury, they had to live by the rules. Sally had never been seduced by the money and chaffed under a life dictated by her father. His last actions had cemented her hatred and fear of the man.

Sally walked back across the park and in through the front door of her apartment building. It wasn't the newest in the area, but it had charm. Built back in the late fifties, it boasted a brick facade and had its name cemented above the door. She checked the time and found herself with two hours to burn before work. Sally trotted up the stairs, using it as a final workout and entered her apartment. Her gaze went immediately to the opened box on the coffee table in the living room and the scattered papers surrounding it. She knew she had to forget her past, but re-living the fire that had reshaped her life seemed to be a nightly ritual. Sighing, she picked up the newspaper clippings and began returning them to the box. Shuffling through them, she read the headlines for the 100th time.

The machine had been a prototype that Sally had thought of years ago while she was in university. The concept, with all its needed calculations and plans, had developed slowly into drawings, schematics and preliminary designs. She had worked hard, wanting an end state of lessening the planet's reliance on fossil fuels and nuclear energy. Her calculations said she was still fifty years out, but the numbers also promised that the world's power needs could be met by her machine. They would start with small versions, but in time, she knew, they would be capable of running entire cities. Her last calculations promised an even more exciting result that would double and then triple the power output.

That's when Sally had taken the project public. She shopped around, found the funding and three brilliant people that were willing to work with her to develop a prototype. They set up a company, and they were on their way. Or they were, she thought, until the fire. "But," she said out loud, "we did get out with our lives."

She continued to stare at the clippings, not seeing them, but the fire. The blaze had started in her office. She'd tried to return, with the thought of saving her files, but was thrown back by the heat. The flames had climbed the walls and swiftly moved up and across the ceiling and the roof, burning furiously as it reached the wooden tresses. Another fire was set off in the design shop, where an explosion had destroyed their prototype. The smell of the smoke, the heat and the confusion as they ran for their lives was something she would never forget. She was still plagued with nightmares. Sally ached with despair for the loss of her life's work but could only be relieved that they had all made it out safely.

The next day, the fire department allowed them to enter the yard and rummage through the ashes. The nauseating smell of burnt plastics tingled her nose and lungs while she stepped over the blackened, bent and twisted metal frame of the building. Her computers had been destroyed. Years of research were gone. Her eyes fell on the filing cabinet. She placed her hand on the outside of the box, which was still warm. Her inner voice told her it was no use, but she unlocked the cabinet and opened each drawer one by one, looking for something, anything. Only ashes and melted plastic remained. The last drawer held all her hard copy research notes. By then, she knew what she would find, and she reached into the drawer, scooped out some of the ashes and placed them in a zip-lock bag. *This would be a reminder to never let this happen again,* she thought grimly, sealing the bag and putting it into her pocket.

The fire inspector spoke to her at length. "You were lucky," he said. "I was surprised no one died." They had first suspected arson, but nothing was definitive. The building's wiring revealed a potentially dangerous mixture of copper and aluminum. The explosion was explained away with the prototype itself, despite the protestations of her partners. "You wouldn't be able to prove a thing," the inspector insisted. "Can you prove that anyone would want to hurt you or your business?"

The question had gotten her attention.

Her eyes were still fixed, looking across the front room, the palms of her hands now breaking out with nervous sweat. The words kept repeating themselves in her mind. "Can you prove that anyone would want to hurt you or your business?" Sally couldn't think of anyone that would want to hurt her but did know of someone that wanted to hurt the business.

After the fire, her partners found work elsewhere. They all said, "If you want to do this again, we're in." But Sally's heart wasn't in it. They had worked hard on the project and were on the verge of a breakthrough, but lost it all. Besides, the money was gone.

Her mother almost convinced her to move back when she made the mistake of coming home for supper one evening shortly after the fire. Her father's questions were like an interrogation. She thought he'd perhaps show some compassion, a little bit of heart, but of course, she should have known better. He asked nothing about what had happened, and there was no sign of sympathy from him. Instead, she was reminded of her faults, her failings and given only threats and demands of obedience. He was ruthless in belittling her and scrutinizing her colleagues. His last words as she left that night were, "Alternate power is all bullshit. It'll never fly. Don't you forget that, little girl."

The next morning, she packed up her apartment, taking what she could in the car and giving the rest to Goodwill. She headed south along the Yellowhead Highway. Her bank account would give her a bit of respite, but she would need a job in about a month, even if she watched her spending. She could take a position with an engineering firm, buy a new suit and shoes, maybe get a haircut, but that wasn't her way. She was desperate to get out of her father's sights. Six hours later, she found herself in Regina and was filling up with gas when she spotted a coffee shop on the side street. She walked over to the shop, sat down at a table with her coffee and looked at the bulletin board that said, "Help Wanted." Sally had not hesitated. This could be a place for her to find herself again. She took the sign off the board and walked to the front counter. "I'd like the job," she said to the lady behind the counter and got it on the spot.

Sally looked up at the clock and realized she now had only thirty minutes to get to work, and she still had to shower. She grabbed the newspaper clippings and tossed them in the box. Fifteen minutes later, she was showered, dressed and out the door. *How can I ever get to where I want to be?* She wondered. Arriving at the coffee shop, she pushed open the door and stepped inside. She had no idea that someone had been watching her for a long time. And they were going to push her to get her to where she needed to be.

CHAPTER 20

*T*he streets were packed with people, and the crowd was moving as a single mass along the sidewalk. Gritting his teeth, Bill Lee shoved his way through the people to the outside. He hated getting this close to people, hated the claustrophobic crowds and despised their mindlessness. Bill firmly believed that they had caved to the demands of their society like cattle. Finally free, he breathed in deeply and ran his sleeve across his face to wipe off the nervous sweat on his brow. He watched the throng of people walking in front of him. *How can people be so naive?* He thought. The movement was supposed to have freed them, not created another box for them to crawl into. He had been contacted by his HQ and asked to meet with a representative from the Rebel Eastern Intelligence section. He knew the man well. Hassan was someone that he had worked with on countless occasions in the past, and he trusted him completely. Bill was very interested in why HQ had sent him to this location.

He pulled the screen from his pocket, opened it and rechecked his location. For security reasons, he never met his friend in the same place. He confirmed his direction of travel and then folded the screen back up and returned it to his pocket, having some distance to cover. He started walking again, this time away from the centre of the city. Thirty minutes later, he came to a tiny, rundown hotel. He sighed inwardly, disappointed. He always assumed that the people from Intelligence would have better, perhaps even, he mused, more refined tastes when it came to business dealings. Pulling on the door, Bill entered the foyer and stilled while his eyes adjusted from the bright sunlight to the dim lighting within the entrance. The reception desk for the hotel was off to his left and was presently unmanned. There was a small snack shop to his right, where he could make out mismatched tables and chairs with only a few people sitting down, eating a meal.

Bill recognized the man immediately; he was sitting in one of the darkened corners of the room, facing the door. Bill made his way to him and greeted him warmly.

"Hassan! It's so good to finally meet again! You look well."

"Bill! My god, man, you've gotten old! Good to see you also," Hassan said. "How was the trip?"

Bill and Hassan sat and ordered two drinks before lowering their voices. Hassan was brief and to the point. He leaned his head toward Bill. "In the last year, we've lost a number of our Operators and compromised our Operations all because the GIA can track our energy flow. If there was a way for us to mask that energy, our odds of being tracked during Operations would go down considerably." He paused and then continued. "Are you with me?"

Bill nodded. The Rebels had gone to great lengths to stay hidden, always in the shadows. The GIA appeared to have an uncanny method of hunting them down whenever they were launching an Operation. If they could develop a way to mask the energy they used when using the Destination Machine, the agency would never find them.

"We've picked up transmissions between Eric Stanton and a Traveller by the name of Stian Anthony. They've been sending him to a place called Earth to watch a woman named Sally Reilly. From the messages we've intercepted, she's possibly developing some sort of machine that can take a minuscule amount of energy and magnify it. They're saying the bump-up could be 500 percent. If we could get to that planet, track Reilly and get the machine, we could use it to mask our power output. Our Operations would no longer be tracked."

Bill raised an eyebrow and said softly, "Hassan, you've got my attention. What do you need from us?"

"Let's get out of here. I have something to show you," Hassan said. The two of them left their untouched drinks and walked out of the hotel. Fifteen minutes later, they walked into an old apartment building and proceeded down a set of steps, stopping at two steel locked doors. Hassan slipped his hand into the reader, and the doors slid open.

The entire room had been converted to an Operations Centre. Bill was shocked but schooled his features to show no reaction whatsoever. He had never been privy to any information about another Operations Centre. He was very aware that his being allowed a glimpse of it marked a sharp departure in protocol.

"We like to hide in plain sight," Hassan began. "I know this is dangerous for you, but I had to bring you here."

Bill hesitated at the door. "This puts me in jeopardy and could make me a prime target for the GIA."

"We're aware. But you need to see this so you can act on it."

Fuck, Bill thought. His inner voice warned him to turn around and go back. If he were ever about to be captured by the GIA, the Rebels would terminate him. Unfortunately for him, his ego prevailed, and he simply replied, "Lead the way."

They walked through to an open area filled with workstations and people, then stopped at an office door where the light went from red to green. When the door opened, they walked in, and Hassan went behind a wooden table, pulling up a chair. He motioned for Bill to join him on the other side. Hassan opened a screen, and a holographic image of Eric Stanton and Stian Anthony appeared above the table.

"Of course, nothing is easy, and things appear to have gotten complicated," he said.

"A few weeks ago, we picked up another conversation between Stanton and his Traveller. He asked the Traveller to go back to Earth and check up on Sally Reilly again. They're concerned that she's at a standstill for developing her prototype machine. Turns out her research facility, and all her work was burned to the ground. She quit right after that, gave up."

Bill looked at Hassan, puzzled. "All of the research and work is gone?"

"Everything."

"If it's gone," he paused, "that means there's nothing left, and we can't use it. What do you want us to do?"

Hassan brought up the next image with an unreadable look on his face. "There's more. Steve Johnson. You remember him, I suppose?"

Bill reddened slightly as he tried to suppress his anger. "Yeah. We tried to pick him up."

Hassan smiled sourly and retorted, "But you didn't. I found out a bit more about his background. Two years ago, a Traveller brought him here from Earth. We found out that he was a soldier, badly injured in combat. The agency repaired him and put him in Stasis for two years. His body reacted differently to the procedure, and he regenerated in age. Now they want him to go back to Earth, help Reilly get back on her feet and get the project up and running again."

Bill looked up sharply. It all came into focus now, why Rebel HQ wanted Johnson and why he had been treated differently at the hospital. "Our Headquarters will want those plans before the GIA get them."

Hassan nodded. "They want the prototype and plans. We can reverse engineer it, make it better than it was in the first place. The easiest solution would be to kidnap Reilly and bring her here. Unfortunately, our destination machine was never designed for people other then Midgardians, not like the current model the GIA is using. They've gathered DNA from Earth and programmed it into their machines. Ours will never be able to do that. We'll be able to modify it to travel between Earth and here, but that's all. The only option is to get Reilly's plans as soon as they're ready."

"That turns a short in-and-out mission into a possibly very

long one, especially if we have to wait until she's finished building a prototype," Bill observed.

"It will be worth it. Plus, we'll get a chance to see what kind of resources Earth may have for us. One last thing. We also want Johnson terminated when the job is done. He's a wild card, too dangerous." Hassan stood up and paced around the room.

Bill leaned back on his chair, studying Hassan carefully. "When will our machine be ready?"

"Soon. We've started trials now, and a team will be sent once they're complete. Did you want to be part of the team?"

Bill shook his head. He knew the possibility of his leading the team were slim; he'd screwed up one too many times. The possibility of having his people selected, however, would be favourable to him.

Hassan shrugged, unconcerned. "One last point. We expect Johnson to depart within the month. Our destination machine should be ready shortly after that."

"That should work for us."

Hassan turned away from Bill, hands behind his back, and said, "It's too bad, what happened to Leah Evans. She was an excellent source for you."

Bill said nothing. Hassan's warning to his friend was not subtle.

The briefing complete, the tactical details were transferred from Hassan's computer into Bill's, and he was escorted back onto the street. He was already preparing his brief to HQ. Bill held on to a faint hope of leading the team and began his long walk back to the hotel. *There will be no mercy for anyone on my team if they fuck up again,* he thought. *Just as there will be no mercy for me.*

CHAPTER 21

*J*ohnson *completed his two-week refresher training without incident, assisted by what he had learned during Stasis. He relished returning to his roots, honing old skills and learning new ones.* The weapons, instead of being projectile-driven, were energy-based. The function of the weaponry, however, was almost the same. Sights, safeties, triggers and grips were common to both worlds. Tactics, he discovered, were similar as well. There were only so many ways in which to enter a room. He'd arrived at Special Projects two weeks previously and was now comfortably settled into a more vigorous routine.

He walked into the Training Section Team room and was immediately called over by two of the trainers. They were responsible for keeping the eight teams of fifty Operators each, up to date on all operational procedures and techniques.

"Johnson!" one of them barked while throwing on his assault gear. "You're needed at Miss Petrov's office this morning. Two teams are getting spooled up for a mission."

"Any specifics?"

"Petrov will brief you," he stated. "Grab your gear before you leave. You'll be going directly."

Johnson slung on his equipment, gathered his weapons and walked up to Ann's office. The door slid open, and he saw her sitting at the conference table, waiting for him. Ann, dismissing any kind of greeting, acknowledged his presence with a nod and began speaking the moment he was seated. "Our S2, Dave Corbin, found a cell of twenty-five Rebels. It appears to be in a large depot about one hour's flight time from here, so we'll be using heavy-lift vectors. We're going in with two operational teams. They'll be the first in. You and I will follow up as

Command and Control. The teams are giving their detailed orders now. Are you ready?"

"I am," he replied and, with that, followed Petrov to the team briefing room.

Ann proceeded to the front of the room to address the teams gathered there. "You've got the latest Intel, and you know what you're up against. I want you to hit this faction hard. They'll have no qualms about sending you home in a bag. If they point a weapon at you or your people, you are authorized to use deadly force. I expect you to carry out this mission to the fullest extent of your ability." She paused, eyes running over every operator gathered there. "Remember the basics — shoot, move and communicate with each other and your Commanders. I'll be in the C and C vector along with Steve Johnson." Johnson walked up to the front of the room and stopped beside Ann. She continued once he arrived. "Get to know him. You'll be seeing a lot of him in the next while. Good luck and watch your back. I want everyone to come home."

Johnson could feel the team's suspicious eyes on him, assessing and evaluating. He was aware that his youthful appearance was the reason for their judgement. Youth had a perception of inexperience, and it was never a positive attribute to leadership. He needed this mission to prove himself and gain their trust. Johnson laughed ruefully to himself. He had been in their position before and knew it wouldn't be easy.

The teams got to their feet, assembled into chalks and loaded themselves into the transport. Ann briefed Johnson as they walked up the ramp of the C and C vector. "We're going to cut their power usage so they can't use the Destination Machine and disappear. On five minutes out, we'll place a bubble over the area, letting us in and keeping them from getting out. We'll land when the first part of the building is in our possession. Hopefully, most of the fighting will be over by that time. We'll wait for the Commander's order to hold and reorg. Once the area is secured, we'll do a search and hopefully find something."

Johnson looked back evenly at her. "Plans only survive until first contact."

"Understood," she replied, "but we'll stick with it for now."

The Team Commanders radioed to Ann that all the chalks were ready. She pushed the button on her communicator to Operations. "Operations, are you ready?"

The Operations Officer replied, "We're set, Ma'am."

"All call signs, this is Petrov. All protocols have been met. Clear to commence Operation."

The vectors lifted off and vanished immediately. Johnson sat quietly as the machine flew smoothly to their objective. He listened to the sporadic chatter of the teams over the communication system and mentally reviewed their mission again. Their procedures were not that different from what he had initially been trained to do on Earth. However, even minuscule variables could mean the difference between life and death. Sixty minutes later, he could see the wavy image of the vectors reappearing and landing next to the objective. The troops disembarked swiftly and silently, placing explosives on the outside of the building. Fifteen seconds later, the explosives violently ignited, blowing holes into the walls that the Operators then poured through. He could see that they had contact as soon as the teams moved forward, and bodies started to drop. Johnson reported the action to Ann. "They've met resistance. When we get on the ground, I'll take the lead for security. You just look after commanding the Operation." Ann nodded, and they both did their final checks.

Two minutes later, their vector landed, and the back ramp dropped down. Taking the lead position, Johnson doubled out of the carrier and across the open terrain to the middle entry point, weapon at the ready. Ann and the entourage of medics, comms and others followed closely behind. Looking through the entry point, Johnson located Rear Security and made contact. Entering the room, he shouted at them, "Which way?"

The soldier said, "This area's clear. We've pushed through, forcing them to the outer building. They know we've got a bubble covering the place, and there's no way out."

The medical team set to work on the wounded as the communications team set up a rear link with HQ. A minute later, a hologram illuminated the middle of the room, indicating that the connection had been established. Ann walked over to it, looking closely to see where the teams were.

Johnson walked over to her, and she said, "It looks like they need the Rear Section. We'll move forward with them."

Johnson hollered, "Rear Section, get ready to move."

Ann opened her communicator and told the troop Commanders they were moving forward and to alert the security teams.

"Are we ready?" Johnson asked her.

"Let's go."

Johnson led the way, following the path of destruction left behind by the team's assault.

The closer they got to the front, the more the rate of fire picked up. Ten minutes later, with smoke and the chaos of battle all around them, they cleared the last entry hole and Johnson contacted one of their Commanders for his update.

The lightning-fast assault had taken the Rebels by surprise. They fought hard at first but took such losses they had to fall back, hoping an extraction would come. It never did. They were pushed to the last corner of their domain as the agency's Assault Commander asked them to surrender. They answered back with automatic weapons fire, the energy bursts haphazardly blazing across the room.

Ann stepped forward and listened while the Commander grimly advised her of their next course of action. "Ma'am, I'll reorganize with new troops. They'll push forward on the main assault."

Ann confirmed his plan. "We'll stay here and move forward once the assault has pushed from this location." Without another word, the Commander turned and disappeared to take up his position.

Johnson said to Ann, "I'm going with them" and fell in line behind one of the soldiers. The soldier turned her head and assessed him quickly before a grin appeared on her face. "Hey there. I saw you with the Boss. You've progressed through the ranks rather quickly, haven't you?"

"Asta," Johnson flashed a genuine smile at seeing a familiar face. "I'm glad to see you're in front of me. I'll try to keep up."

"You wish."

Three successive explosions rocked the cement walls, and the overpressure reverberated through the air. Entry points were now forced open for the assault force to push through. Immediately the soldiers filed into the gaps and weapons fire erupted from all directions. Johnson walked behind Asta, his left hand on her left shoulder and his eyes looking forward over her right shoulder. Holding his weapon at a forty-five-degree angle, Johnson stepped through the entry point. Asta moved left, and Johnson stepped right, bringing his weapon up. His back was to the wall, and he faced forward, looking into the large room in front of him. Fire came his way well above his head, indicating the Rebels were firing blind. Johnson and Asta returned the fire harder than they were receiving, chewing up the barricade to their front until there was silence. The team, now well spread out, cleared the corners and then pushed forward into an extended line.

The three explosions had scattered all sorts of debris toward the Rebels' last defendable position. Moments before, they had been behind cover, an organized unit concentrating on defending their position. Now their world had been upturned, and they were wildly disoriented; those still able to react were quickly overwhelmed by the assaulting forces' firepower. Their

Commander, in a last-ditch attempt, was screaming at the remaining fighters when weapons' fire hit him in the chest, splaying it wide open. He crumpled to the floor without a sound into a rapidly widening puddle of blood.

Johnson continued to move forward, hearing fire to his left and right. Sensing movement to his front, he automatically slid the weapon up, aligned the sight and fired twice. The weapon, once sighted, automatically determined the type of target, the amount of energy required and then activated. The sound of shots being fired automatically ceased. Its silence was only broken when Johnson began to hear the shouts of his teammates yelling, "All clear," as areas were secured.

Tapping Asta, who was standing next to him, Johnson said, "Cover me." She turned and watched him move forward, jumping over the barrier he'd taken the fire from, weapon up, butt tight into his shoulder. Sprawled out on the floor were two Rebel soldiers. Johnson kicked the weapons away from their hands. He looked closer at the bodies to see a small neat hole in both of their heads. He reported back to his teammates, "All clear. Two dead."

The fight over, the Team Commanders secured the prisoners, cleaned up the wounded and gathered the dead. Johnson and Ann were making their way back to their initial entry point when she told Johnson, "I'm taking a look at the prisoners before we leave." They stopped and stood back, watching as the wounded were evacuated first. Five prisoners in restraints were then brought in, halted and forced to face the wall, head down. Ann walked over to the lineup, ordering the guard to turn them around. As he did, she spotted two women and walked over to them. She lifted their heads, looking into each of their faces and then turned back to Johnson. She never had the opportunity to get any words out.

A man next to one of the women had slipped loose from his restraints. As she turned, he grabbed Ann from behind, his left forearm across her windpipe, cruelly cutting off her air supply. He pressed her body tightly against his, immobilizing her completely. His right hand groped for and then gripped her weapon, unholstering it, and pressed it hard against the side of her head.

Ann was starting to slip away. The blood and air had been cut off to her brain, but the coolness of the sidearm felt alarmingly good. The man gripped her throat even tighter, and she found herself helplessly gasping for even a mouthful of air. She could hear the pulse from her carotid artery banging in her eardrums and felt the man's chest heaving as he breathed. She could feel the vibration of his voice as he spoke but couldn't decipher the actual words. Her eyes could only watch as Johnson moved forward, sidearm drawn and up, and she couldn't understand why he was pointing the weapon at her.

Ann's vision began to cloud until only a narrow central spot was clear. She finally felt herself start to lose consciousness, her knees slowly buckling under themselves. Johnson's eyes were locked on the man, his hands firmly wrapped around the grip of his weapon, his breathing calm and regular. He could see three-quarters of the man's head on Ann's right side.

"Drop it. Let her go. It's over," Johnson said calmly.

The prisoner answered, "You'll let us go, or I'm putting a hole through her head. You've got five seconds."

Johnson looked down the sightline of the weapon to a point just below the man's right eye. He focused on his front sight, waiting for the prisoner to start his countdown. When the man reached a count of two, Johnson slowly pulled the trigger, activating the firing mechanism. The weapon bounced up only slightly in his hand as the man's head jolted back. A small, neat hole suddenly appeared under his eye, and the back of his head exploded into a spray of blood and human flesh. He dropped to the floor like a stone.

Ann, now unconscious, had begun to fall limply from the

man's grasp. Johnson reached her just as her knees hit the floor and gently guided her down to the cold cement. Moving forward, he picked up her weapon and placed it in his belt before addressing the four remaining prisoners. "Anyone else?" he asked. Johnson walked over to the biggest man, who was standing stock still, a dribble of blood from his dead partner running down his cheek. "How about you?" Johnson asked coolly. The man, speechless, was unable to make eye contact and gave Johnson only a quiet shake of his head. The other three, stunned and covered with gore, watched with undisguised horror as Johnson returned Ann's weapon to her holster and said, "I didn't think so."

He watched impassively as the medics came forward, placing an oxygen mask over Ann's mouth and nose and fitting her with a neck splint. He could already see her colour coming back but never took his eyes off her until she was loaded into the evacuation vector.

The Team Leader responsible for collecting the prisoners walked over to Johnson.

"You needed to talk that guy down, not blow his head off. We wanted him for interrogation."

Johnson, unimpressed, only looked at the young Commander and then down to the piece of meat on the floor. "Well, I guess he's not talking now," he drawled. "Your men should have secured him properly. And I never give in to demands." He turned and walked away from the man, who only stood there, wordless. Johnson continued to walk past the prisoners and to the vector. He was just passing a group of soldiers who were waiting to re-deploy when he heard his name being called.

"Johnson!" It was Asta, who had witnessed what had happened and was now making her way to him. He turned and waited for her to come up to him. She came in close, leaning into him and said, "I noticed you've taken my advice and learned to finish things."

Johnson nodded and tapped her firmly on the shoulder. "I learned from the best," he said, honestly. "It was great working with you, Asta."

"You, too," Asta replied, before watching him walk away. She had never met anyone as young as Johnson that had the presence and maturity of someone so much older. *He'll go far*, she thought.

When the Command and Control vector was ready for departure, he walked up and settled himself into a seat. A young soldier sitting across from him mouthed the words, "Nice shot." Johnsons's mouth twitched slightly in response, and he pulled his helmet over his eyes, leaned back and fell asleep.

A light kick at his feet brought Johnson around, and he heard a voice calling out, "We're home. Let's go." Gathering his gear, he walked off the vector and headed straight to Medical. The first person he saw was Eric, who was standing at the nursing station.

"How is she?" Johnson asked.

"She's fine. Here she comes now," Eric said, looking behind him.

Johnson turned and watched Ann coming toward them, speaking with one of the doctors. She looked up and, seeing the two of them, let a wry smile creep across her face before commenting, "Should have known you two would be here."

Johnson, quick with his retort, said, "Hey, gotta make sure the boss is good. Otherwise, I wouldn't get paid, and the kitchen won't feed me."

Ann let out a hoarse laugh and said, "I see your stomach rules your brain."

"Man gotta eat," he replied. "But seriously, how are you?"

"I'm fine. Just been given the green light to go back to work," Ann said. The three of them headed out of Medical as she continued. "Throat's a bit sore, and I have a headache, but it could've been worse."

Eric joined the conversation. "I've watched the video, and we ran his face through Intelligence. He was one of their top

Operators. He would have done what he said he was going to do."

"I owe you thanks, Steve," said Ann.

"Just doing what I'm paid to do. You ready for supper?"

Eric shook his head in mock disbelief as Ann let out another hoarse laugh.

Johnson grinned and said, "It's good to see you up and about, Ann. I'll see you later."

He left them to store his gear and pick up something to eat. For him, the day was done. But for Eric and Ann, there would be reams of Intelligence and After-Action Reports to complete.

Johnson finished his supper, ordered a plate for Ann and walked it to her office, activating the door. The light indicated she was inside, but the door remained closed. He shifted the plate over to his left hand, rapping his knuckles on the door and waited patiently until it finally slid open. Ann was leaning up against the door frame, arms crossed over her chest. The lights in her office were down, and a hologram video of the afternoon's encounter was still playing above the conference table.

Johnson held up the plate of food. "I brought you something to eat."

She turned away from the door with a quiet, "Thanks" and let him in.

He placed the food on the table and, without looking at her, said, "I know what you're doing. You're rehashing what happened today. What you did right, what you did wrong, what you should've done." He pulled up a chair and sat down on it, facing her. "You need to only think of one thing. We won today, and they lost."

Ann rubbed her hands over her cheeks and looked away from him, taking a deep breath. Quietly, she said, "I could've got you killed."

"That wouldn't have happened," Johnson said, shaking his head. "I had him. He sealed his fate the minute he grabbed you. I just ended it."

Ann shook her head in denial as she walked to the table. "I'll play the scene for you," she said, reaching for her screen.

Johnson reached for her hand and stopped her. "I don't need to see a replay. I know how the movie ends." He turned off the hologram and moved the plate in front of her. "Sit. Eat," he ordered.

Ann sat down and began to pick at her plate while Johnson watched. He'd been in her situation a few times and understood the adrenaline rush, the panic and pain that she had gone through. After a few minutes, she gave up on the meal, pushing the plate aside and said, "I guess I'm just not that hungry. I need to get back to work now."

"No chance. We're going for a light run, and then we'll hit the gym. Take my word, everything will look different when we're done."

"I honestly can't," she protested. "I need to get this report out."

"Ma'am, I'll be back here in ten minutes. If you aren't ready to go, I'll drag your ass out wearing the kit you have on now. Got it?"

Ann sighed and realized she would never win this argument with him. A run, she thought, would probably clear her mind, so she finally said, "Okay, okay. Ten minutes."

An hour later, the two of them had finished their run and, drenched in sweat, were stretching outside the gym. He thought that she looked much better now, despite the bruising around her neck. The run had flushed Ann's face, and she was smiling again. They walked back to her office, and Johnson said, "I'm not saying I don't let things bother me. I do. At times I've even had to fight to stop those emotions from overwhelming me. When it happens, I can't undo what's been done. The sun is going down tonight, and tomorrow it will come up again. That means a new day. A new day to start over again, a new day where it's great to be alive."

They reached her office, and when they stopped outside it, Ann said, "Thanks. I needed someone to hit my reset button."

"We all need that every once in a while." He turned away and began walking before shouting over his shoulder at her, "And get that paperwork in, ma'am. You're late."

CHAPTER 22

*E*ric Stanton watched the video of the raid and then looked through the information in the After-Action Reports. Hearing a slight rap on the door, he looked up as the S2 came in and sat down.

"Sir," the S2 began, "we've picked up some important information after scanning the prisoners. There's a vague thread that keeps reappearing, something to do with moving to other planets."

Eric was startled. "Bring it up on the screen."

The S2 pulled up the information. "These quotes about jumping don't mean much on their own. But we've got something interesting from one of the women. She's the same one that was at the restaurant the day they tried to take Johnson. She went through plastic surgery right after the attack. When she was in the Recovery Room after her surgery, she overheard a conversation about travel outside our system."

"The scan can pick that up? What exactly was said?"

"As long as it's lodged into their consciousness, we can pick it up. She overheard two doctors talking about transporting people outside the solar system. From the others, we found the words jumping, rips and then a reference to a jump to another world."

Eric studied the hologram and said, "Yes, I see it. What's the date on that last comment?"

The S2 checked his screen. "It was a few days ago. As a matter of fact, that coincides with the other references to jumping."

Eric stood up and then went to his desk, flipping through his screen. Finding the file, he transmitted it to the hologram. "This is from quite a few years back after the Rebels stole one of the Destination programs from us."

He continued scrolling down the text. "But what got my

attention were the words that the scientist that worked for us used. Look in the text here. Jumps. Rips. The Rebels are using the same terminology as he did. It's possible that he passed information to them. The man is dead now; otherwise, I'd have a few questions for him." Eric stopped and looked away from the hologram. "We need to take a harder look at all of our people again and step up surveillance on the power grid for spikes. I want you to go over everything from two weeks ago to the present. If you find nothing, go deeper, all the way back to when they stole Destination." He paused and then slowly added, "By the looks of things, I think they now have the technology to travel outside our system."

The S2 nodded and confirmed, "We can do that, but it'll take a while. There's a massive amount of detail to look into."

"Make it your first priority and call in Corbin to assist. He has an eye for this," Eric said. "I think we may be on to something. I've already got a call into the Secretary, and I'll be briefing her this evening. The President will be notified shortly after that. I'm expecting to get the word from him to launch, so we need to be proactive. I'll pass this on to the S3, and I know he won't be happy. He'll want more time to get Johnson and the mission up and running, but we need to be there before the Rebels decide to go. We have no time. Johnson will have to be launched five days from tomorrow."

The S2 was startled. "Five days?"

Eric repeated the order. "Five days. I don't know how long it will take the Rebels to find out about Earth and Sally Reilly. We need to be pro-active. Get the Travellers' reports together and give them to the S3. That should help them a bit. Any questions?"

The S2, his mind calculating the myriad of things to be accomplished, said, "I'll open everything up for the Operations crew. Five days will be tough to make, but we'll do our best."

"We have to do better than our best. Even if the Rebels can't stay there long, if they get to Earth, it will change everything in this world and that one."

Ann was at lunch when she got the message to report to Stanton's office with Johnson. She called him and asked him to meet her in the parking lot.

"So, where are we going?" Johnson asked when he arrived.

"Eric wants to talk with us."

He looked at her quizzically. "Can't we do that electronically?"

"No, there's been a bump-up on security. It's best if what we discuss stays off any electronic media," she said, climbing into the vector. "It won't take long. Ready?"

"Ready," Johnson said, settling into his seat.

"Let's go."

When they arrived at Eric's office, the S2 and S3 were already seated and waiting for them. Eric started the meeting by saying, "My apologies for the short notice, but we need to get on this immediately. I briefed the Secretary last night, and she's passed it on to the President. This morning she contacted me and authorized us to deal with the situation as soon as possible."

"Steve," Eric continued, "Back on your world, Sally Reilly, the daughter of the petroleum billionaire, Shawn Reilly, has invented a prototype machine. This machine is capable of taking a small amount of power and multiplying it a hundredfold. She was doing well before her research facility burned to the ground, destroying everything. We were hoping that she would see this as a minor setback. Unfortunately, the situation was traumatic for her, and she abandoned the project. Earth needs this machine, and we need it as well. I want you to go back, persuade her to get her team together and carry on with her research. Once she's on track, we can run the Futures. If all looks good, we'll bring you back, and our Traveller can look after everything else."

Johnson knew there was a lot more to the story. "Why do you need me? What's the catch?"

"There are three things for you to be aware of. First, we suspect the Rebels can now travel between planets using their Destination Machine. The machine they stole years ago was one of our first models and was only capable of travelling through Midgard. We think that they've modified it and can move from one planet to another as we do. It will never have pinpoint accuracy; a failsafe system is manufactured into every model, but it could get them within a general area. Since the Leah Evans fiasco, we can assume there are informants in our organization. If so, we're also assuming they know about Sally and her work. If they were able to get her machine and bring it back here, it means our number one method of tracking them is gone. That brings us to number two. We suspect that your time there will be interrupted by a visit or two from them. You can't let them have that machine. Number three is Sally's father. We believe he was responsible for setting the fire in the research facility. His livelihood depends on the fossil fuel industry. I'm sure he'll have something to say about her starting over again. Coming from Earth, you have the skills needed to stop them. You're familiar with the area — you know the minute intricacies of the people there. Not to mention the fact that the time needed to accomplish this isn't something our bodies can handle. That's why we need you there."

Johnson's interest had been piqued right from the start. He had to admit to himself that going home, regardless of the time that had passed, was something he wanted to do. "How long do I have?"

"You'll have five days for prep on this end and approximately two months to get the job done, although an end-date can't be firmly established. You'll be going to Regina, Saskatchewan, your hometown, so orientation shouldn't be a problem. Your cover story is that you're there to attend university in the fall, and you're in early to get set up."

Eric was utterly upfront now. "We understand that being in

your hometown may create a problem, but I'm sure you can work around it. You'll have comms with us at all times. The S2 and S3 will give you all the details on the tasking."

Johnson felt a spark of anticipation when he realized he would be going home but revealed no emotion to them. He only observed, "The timings are tight."

"Tight but necessary," Eric agreed.

Over the next hour, the S2 gave Johnson the Intelligence picture. He then covered what had happened at the facility, how close Sally had been to a working prototype and the fire. He was shown her initial concept, which gave him a general idea of what the final design would look like and the principles behind it. They still had years of tweaks to go on the process itself, but when completed, it could be as large or small as needed, depending on what it was going to power. Johnson eyed the machine, thinking of its possibilities. It had been clear to him before what it was capable of, but seeing the schematics made him realize its implications for use. It was clear now why the Rebels wanted the machine and why her father wanted to destroy it.

Ann joined them, and both she and the S2 went over training, insertion, weapons, communications, money, living and finally, extraction. Johnson got up after the last briefing and stretched, glancing at Ann. "I'm going for a coffee. Want one?"

"Yes, please, with cream and sugar," she said.

He walked down the hallway, thinking to himself that briefings were tedious, but they had to be done. The details of an Operation were essential for a successful result. More important, however, was that ground rules had to be set. People had to know what was expected of them and what outcome could deem the mission a success. He walked back into the room, setting Ann's coffee in front of her and was surprised to see another man with them, someone he had never seen before.

"Sorry! If I had known, I would have brought another coffee," Johnson offered.

"Quite alright," the man replied formally. "Can't abide the stuff, truthfully."

Ann introduced him. "Steve, I'd like you to meet Sally's Traveller, Stian Anthony. He was also assigned to you and was the man that brought you to Midgard."

Johnson stuck out his hand and said, "Nice to finally meet you. Thanks for pulling me out of that mess when you did."

Stian clasped Johnson's hand with a firm grip and said, "You're welcome. The timeframe on that was tight. Glad you made it through, and it all worked out. I've sent information to your screen. Please open it now and go through it with us."

Johnson was surprised by Stian's remoteness. He appeared to be rather cold and clinical, and not inclined to social graces. Without comment, Johnson obligingly opened his screen to look over the notes that Stian had provided for him. The Traveller started by saying, "I was assigned to Sally Reilly since she was first identified."

From there, Stian and Johnson began a long discussion about Sally's life, her upbringing and relationships with family, jobs, friends and colleagues. They discussed possible ways for Johnson to introduce himself and, most importantly, how they could approach her about getting back onto the prototype project. All this information would be essential, Johnson knew. Knowing a person's past and present could help him predict what they might do in a given circumstance.

Stian continued. "Sally knows what has to happen, but her situation doesn't allow her to pursue it. She has the strength and conviction, but since the burning of her research facility, her will has been broken. She's frightened. You're going to have to work with her. Learn what she's thinking, get rid of roadblocks and give her the courage to take the lead." He paused for a moment and sighed, "I see her father as the real problem. He's powerful, influential and has clout, both physically and monetarily. You'll have to be ready. The man doesn't appear to operate completely above the law."

The briefing finished, Stian stood up from the table and shut down his screen. "Good luck," he said to Johnson.

Before Stian could leave, Johnson asked, "You've been in Regina, observing Sally, right?"

"That's correct."

"Would you have seen my brother, as well?"

Stian looked to Ann, received her approval and said, "I have, Steve. He's doing well." He nodded to Ann and said, "It's always good to see you," and left the room.

Johnson was momentarily relieved and leaned back in his chair. "He's difficult to read, seems rather emotionless."

"It's in their nature. That's why he's a Traveller."

Over the next few days, the training staff ran Johnson through different scenarios, making sure that he understood exactly what he could and couldn't do. It was essential for him to understand the fine line that he would be treading with regards to possibly altering the future of Earth. He had to ensure Sally would pick up her project again, but his presence had to be invisible. He could leave no footprint that would possibly alter future events in irrevocable ways.

On the third day of training, Ann dropped by to watch and asked, "How are things going?"

"No problems," he replied. "They've run me through a bunch of scenarios, and I'm confident I've got it down."

"Eric will be here in about an hour. He wants to meet with us."

"At your office, I take it?"

"Yes."

Johnson tipped his head toward her and said, "You keep longer hours than I do. Must be tough on the family."

Ann motioned for him to join her as they walked to her office. "It is tough. My marriage imploded because of it. I find it easier now that's it's just me and the job. This is my life, and I like it that way."

"Sorry, I didn't mean to pry."

"Don't be sorry, I'm not. Let's get moving."

Johnson and Ann entered the office to find Eric waiting for them.

"I hope you're ready," he said evenly. "Our Intelligence has confirmed that the Rebels can travel to Earth and will be going after Sally's machine."

CHAPTER 23

Bill made his way down to the gym to speak with Marie. She was not expecting him, but he was too impatient to wait for her to come to him. It had been a week since his return, and he had not heard a word from Higher. Why hadn't they gotten back to him? Everything was prepared, his Operators had their cover stories, the timeline had been finalized.

He came into the gym and found Marie, where she was working out on a heavy bag. Marie saw him immediately. She laughed to herself as she watched Bill's agitated form coming toward her. She could tell he was frustrated.

"I wasn't expecting you," she said. "What's going on?"

"I had to get out."

"Bill, relax. You're headed for a heart attack."

Bill stopped in front of the bag and slammed his fists into it, working several different combinations before stopping.

"Hey, you've still got some moves there!"

"When I was a kid, my dad brought me into the ring. Old school boxing every night. Taught me to look after myself."

"So why are you here? You didn't tell me you were coming. You never do that."

"I had to get out. It's been a week since I've handed in my report to Higher, and they haven't gotten back to me yet."

"It takes some time, Bill."

"I had everything outlined for them. Three separate courses of action planned and readied for the Operation. The first scenario, the simplest, was to get to Earth, get the prototype, the paperwork and come home. The second scenario involved scanning Reilly on Earth for all the information and bringing it to Midgard. The third scenario was to infiltrate her group, help build the machine and bring it back."

"The simplest solution would be for us to bring her back to Midgard and force the information from her," Marie commented.

"We can't. Our machine doesn't have the DNA match capability. We're ready. What the hell are they waiting for?" Bill said, frustration showing in his voice.

"Maybe our last couple of ops haven't been that successful?"

"We've had two screw-ups in the last two months," he agreed, begrudgingly. "First the fuck-up in the cafe, when we should've had Johnson and now this. Because we didn't get him, the GIA took out the entire depot! And to add insult to injury, it was Johnson who took out one of our best Operators. Can you fucking believe it!" His attempt at remaining calm was now thrown to the wind.

"Bill, relax, there are other people here. If you want, I'll go with you to see them. They'll listen to me."

Bill did not need a subordinate to do his work. He was about to lose his temper with her when his communicator suddenly beeped. He looked down at the text and then up at her. "I'd really love to continue this discussion," he said dryly, "but I have to go."

"I'll tell you one last time, Bill," she drawled. "I'll go with you or by myself. Your choice."

Marie watched as he walked away without speaking again. *I hope this works out soon*, she thought, *I need some action.*

That night Bill sat solemnly on a bench overlooking the lake, deep in thought. He was calmer now, not like earlier. He had been so wound up when he left Marie that a schoolboy could have tracked him. A voice startled him, bringing him back to the moment. "Bill, nice to see you. Let's walk." He stood up, joined his contact and began a leisurely stroll along the hardened path that formed a dark rim around the lake.

The man talked first. "It's been a tough couple of months for your people."

"Yes, sir, a couple of hiccups, but we're over it now. Things will get better," Bill said.

"We know. But this doesn't look good on you, old boy. The cafe incident should've been easy. But we've talked about that before, haven't we? Now, an entire depot has been obliterated. Not to mention the loss of one of our best Operators, who was taken out by none other than Johnson, who you should've had in the first place." He paused for a few uncomfortable seconds, letting his last words sink in. "Bill, do you understand what we see at HQ? Put yourself in my place. What would you do?"

"I said, I'm working on it. I'll sort it out," he replied, trying to disguise the agitation in his voice.

"We need to talk with Marie. Can you send her tomorrow?"

Bill thought one thing but said another. "I'll pass that on to her." The acid in his stomach boiled up, hitting the back of his throat. He realized now if he did not get the job. He would be left behind.

The man stopped walking and placed his hand firmly on Bill's shoulder. "I know you'll sort out the mess you've got down there. Start looking after yourself a little bit better. We want to win every battle, but understand we can't. When we lose, we need calm heads to be able to take us to the next phase, so we don't lose again. You have a lot of work to do, so get things under control. Understand?"

Bill felt the power in the man's hand on his shoulder and could only nod his head in frustrated agreement. The dressing-down was a constant reminder of his shortcomings. He just needed more time to sort this mess out.

"I want you to take a few days off, get away from here and relax." He released his hold on Bill's shoulder. "Thanks for meeting me. I'm serious when I say it's good to see you again." He turned and walked silently away.

Bill stood with his hands in his pockets, watching the man walk off. Marie would be getting another high profile job while he would be stuck here, babysitting and watching from the sidelines. *Fuck*, he screamed silently to himself.

CHAPTER 24

*J*ohnson had twenty-four hours before his insertion. He walked down *the hallway and entered the Destination Facility.* The technician sitting behind the Control panel lifted his head and greeted him, "Steve Johnson?"

Johnson said, "That's me."

The man got out of his chair and came up to him, shaking his hand. "I take it this is your first time in the machine?"

"Second time, I suppose. Although I can't really remember much about the first time."

"Well then, I'll talk you through the process. The trip itself should take no more than thirty seconds. The plan is to insert you into a wooded park not far from the apartment that's been set up for you. We'll be sending you in during daylight hours so that the light produced by the tear won't be as noticeable. Has Operations inserted your tracker?"

"Got it inserted just the other day."

"Good. Between your tracker and your communicator, we'll be able to hone in on your location at any time. Once you're in, we need you to activate your communicator and let us know you've arrived at the right place and time. Travellers keep it low key. They usually send just a headline from a newspaper. You can follow that protocol if you want."

"I'll do that," Johnson said.

Lastly, the technician pointed through a glass window to the rectangular enclosed room on the other side. The interior held a perforated metal platform that was surrounded by what appeared to be a highly reflective metal. "That's where the tear opens."

"So the tear opens, I walk into it, and from that time on, I'm just along for the ride?"

The technician nodded and continued. "Everything you're taking with you must be attached to you, not loose. Once you've set down and the tear is gone, you may want to sit for a while. We don't have any problems if the travel is local, but the longer the distance, the more the disorientation. Earth is a long way off. Dizziness and nausea are to be expected. Only Travellers become accustomed to it."

"Will do," Johnson said, looking across the Control panel. He spent the next half hour with the technician, who pointed out some of the technical aspects of the tear. Finally, the man said, "That's all I have. Any more questions?"

"I'm good for now. Thanks for the tour. I'll see you tomorrow."

Johnson proceeded down to Operations for his last meeting with Ann. "You wanted to see me for some last-minute points?" he asked.

"Yes, I did. We've prepared your communicator, and I want to give you a preliminary briefing on it, as well as a few other items." Ann picked up the wallet first, saying, "This is how we'll be communicating. It looks like a normal wallet, with your money, credit card and ID inside it. This portion, however," she said, unfolding a light metallic flap from the wallet, "is for transmissions. Paper messages are placed under this fold, and when the wallet is closed, it sends it back to us. For anything larger than one slip of paper, we're sending you in with a backpack that has the same technology, a separate section designed for transmissions that go both ways, to and from Midgard."

Johnson picked up the wallet from the table and emptied it. Scrutinizing everything, he picked up each piece of ID, the money and credit cards. Once he was satisfied, he placed everything back in the wallet, then wrote a quick message on a lined notepad and stuck it under the flap of the wallet. When he closed it, he could feel a slight vibration in his hand and saw a faint light emanating from it. He opened it, and asked, "Where do these messages go?"

Ann said, "The Destination Facility. They have a direct link to Ops."

Johnson tucked the wallet into his back pocket and asked, "If I get into a jam and need something right away, can I get it?"

"We'll have everything set up in the Control Office. Inanimate transmissions are faster and easier to send. They can be sent almost instantaneously."

Johnson was relieved. Someone would be on the other end in case of an emergency. He added, "I need you to know that I'll be seeing my family while I'm back there."

"I thought you would. My concern is the Rebels. If they start surveillance on you, they could use your family against you. It would put them in jeopardy."

"I'm not worried about my brother. He's a police detective."

"He used to be a detective. He's retired now. Twenty years have passed, and circumstances have changed. Be considerate," she said cautiously.

Johnson knew she was also referring to his wife. "I'll be careful," he said. "One last thing. It's my last night here for a while. Would you like to have supper with me?"

Her eyes scanned her desk for a moment. "I have some things to finish up, but yes, since it's your last evening with us, I'd like to join you. See you in the parking lot at 1830 hours?"

"Excellent," he said with a smile and headed out of the office.

The next morning, Johnson got up early, skipped his workout and went to breakfast. He ate and then returned to his room, running the mission through his head. His biggest problem, he knew, would be trying to get Sally on board. Convincing her would undoubtedly take solid communication skills. He also had no preconceived ideas about the possibility of interference from her father and the Rebels. He knew it was coming, but he also had to ensure there would be no consequences to Earth's future. The Rebels would be dealt with as he had dealt with any other Military opposition. When he found them, he would take them out one by one and then send them home. With her father and the men on his payroll, Johnson decided that he would have to let them make the first move. Depending on the circumstances, he'd then decide what to do. Claiming the life of someone who could be critical to the planet's survival would be a catastrophe.

He looked up when he heard his door buzzer and, recognizing Ann at the door, let her in.

"Good morning. I hope I didn't catch you at a bad time."

"Not at all. I'm just running some details through my head, making sure I've got everything down."

"Good," she said, coming up to him and seating herself on the couch. "This is a big day for all of us."

Johnson noticed she was dressed in casual workout gear, and her face held a flush of healthy colour. "You must've been outside already," he said.

"Just a short run. I'll see you off, and then I've got a meeting this afternoon." She sat quietly for a moment as if waiting for him to say something.

Obliging her, he asked, "You okay?"

"I'm fine. Thanks again for supper last night. It's been a long time since I've been out for a social evening."

"You were always looking at your watch. I thought maybe it was my company."

"Not at all. You're fun to be with, and I enjoyed the evening immensely. I was just concerned about getting you home too late." She paused and then said with a slight grin, "I do want you to come back. Life around here is certainly more interesting with you."

"I promise I'll be back," he said, then stood up and lifted her to her feet. They looked at each other for a moment before he pulled her in close, kissing her gently. Her body felt warm as she moulded herself into him. She smelled of fresh air and some delicate perfume he could not identify. The kiss deepened now, each of them asking, demanding more.

The sound of her communicator jolted them. Ann looked down at it and glanced at Johnson. "Sorry, I have to take this," she said, stepping away from him and then out of the room. She never returned.

Ten minutes later, Johnson walked into the Operations Centre, which was busy but not frenzied. It was just another day for them and just another launch. He heard his name being called and made his way over to a technician. The man was standing by an array of articles, including a small energy weapon and a few sets of clothing.

"Here is your backpack. You can put all these items into it. If you want to use it to send anything back to us, place the item into this inner pocket and close it up. Simple as that. You already have your ID and credit cards. Everything's been legitimized by a Traveller, and we've confirmed you're in the system. You've got enough money to last you for the duration of the mission. If you need more, just let us know. The apartment and the safe house have been prepped. You have the addresses, directions and here are the keys. Do you have any questions?"

"No, I think you've covered everything," he said.

"You've got one hour before insertion. Mr. Stanton wants to see you before you go."

Johnson walked down to the office and sat down in front of Eric.

"I'm not going to give you a long speech," Eric began. "You understand how important this mission is for us."

"I do. That's why I agreed to it."

"This mission will be a trial for us. If it goes well, we can set up future endeavours over a wide range of worlds. It won't just help us establish a bigger footprint — it will also help each world we deal with. We're looking for a favourable outcome."

"I'm aware of that," Johnson said, dismissing Eric's statement in his mind. His only concern was the immediate task ahead of him. He was very aware of political ambitions and underlying plots he was not privy to; he was not interested in the game being played.

"The Rebels will take no pity on you. You are an immediate threat to them. We are one hundred percent certain that one of their first priorities will be to eliminate you. If you ID them, you have complete authority to take them out as quickly and as cleanly as you can.

"I got it," Johnson said.

"That's it, then. Good luck," Eric said, standing up and shaking Johnson's hand, "and safe travels."

Johnson walked to the Destination Facility, threw on his backpack and ensured everything he had was firmly secured to his body. He was only vaguely aware that the opportunity to go home had filled him with anticipation. Adrenaline seeped into his system as he tried to imagine what it would feel like when he stepped into the tear. A technician passed him a pair of dark glasses and said, "We're ready for you now. You can move to the platform."

Johnson slipped the glasses on and stepped through the doorway to the other side of the enclosure. He could see the countdown clock registering five minutes remaining. Johnson tugged again at the backpack's shoulder straps. *The last few minutes before engagement to any Operation were always filled with nervous tension,* he thought. At the one-minute mark, he heard the hum of the equipment as it gained in strength and power. The energy was intensifying and moved thickly through him. A tight, whirlwind of spinning bright light appeared, and he watched and waited as it grew steadily larger.

The tear's energy levels finally stabilized, and a dazzling white light now spread into a six-foot circle. "Fifteen seconds," he heard over the intercom. The light was no longer a whirling tornado, and its resulting brilliance was both intense and consistent. Even with the dark glasses, he could barely look into it. "Insert in five, four, three, two, one. Clear to insert."

Johnson glanced back to see Ann standing behind the Control panel. He nodded to her, silently mouthed, "Watch my back" and walked into the tear. The light disappeared instantly, and the platform was empty. "Insertion complete," came the announcement from the technician. Eric looked around to everyone in the room and said, "Good job." Turning to Ann, he simply said, "Look after our boy."

CHAPTER 25

*T*he instant Johnson stepped into the tear, his body was pulled forward into a vacuum of sound, heat and movement. He could feel pressure all around him, pushing into him as he struggled to take a breath. His body felt as if it were propelling itself faster and faster through the darkness toward a constellation of lights far in the distance. The pressure increased, but his breathing became steadier, even as his speed grew faster. He was in a protective bubble, and that bubble was pushing him toward a light that was getting larger every moment. Flashes of movement began to spin around him; his body felt as if it were slowing down, the pressure easing up. The light in front of him now began to open, transforming itself into deep greens and browns. In front of him, those colours now formed into distinct trees and shrubbery, and he realized that what he was looking at was a secluded, wooded park. He took a step onto the grass-covered ground and was immediately overwhelmed with nausea.

Johnson bent forward at the waist, dry retching violently and clenching his stomach. Weakly, he lifted his head up, watching for any perceived danger as he began breathing deeply in and out. A few moments later, nausea subsided, he straightened up, supporting himself by leaning heavily against a tree. Johnson rallied his protesting body and surveyed his surroundings. He determined that he'd been successfully inserted, and the area was clear. Johnson took a bottle of water out of his pack and took a long drink. Feeling somewhat revived and much steadier on his feet, he straightened his backpack and slowly began to make his way out of the park. *What a ride,* Johnson thought. He was thankful again for his younger, more resilient body. His forty-year-old self would not have recovered as quickly.

Coming to a stop at a street, he looked around and then headed to a convenience store. A bell rang out from the top of the store's door as he pushed it open. Johnson eyed a newsstand just beside the door and picked up a copy of the local paper. The top of it read, "The Prairie Post, Monday 1 June 2014, Regina, Saskatchewan." He had left Earth in 1994. *Well,* he thought, *I'm home, better late than never, and I managed to hit the right time and place.* He tucked the paper under his arm and headed up to the cashier.

"Got everything ya need?"

Johnson checked the side rack and located maps of the city. "I do now," he replied, pulling out a map and putting it on the counter with the paper.

The man picked up the items one by one, tallied the total and put them in a bag. "That will be $7.35, please."

Johnson slid his debit card into the machine and punched in his code, tensing slightly as he wondered if the transaction would go through. The register pushed out his receipt, and the clerk tore it off, handing it to him. *The debit card works,* he thought. *One less item to worry about.*

He sat down on a bench just outside the store, ripped off the date from the top of the newspaper and placed it in his wallet. He had just put the wallet back into his pocket when he felt a slight vibration emanating from it. *This is where I am, folks,* he thought and then reached into the bag for the map. Unfolding it, he oriented himself to where he was and where he wanted to be, a twenty-minute walk away.

Finding himself back in Regina was surreal. Johnson had always had a soft spot for the place, as it was where he had grown up. It was the largest and brightest city he had known until he joined the Military. It wasn't until years later when he was home on leave and driving down the main artery, that it hit him. The city he had once thought to be big and bright was nothing but one long strip mall through the prairies.

The Operations Centre waited patiently for Johnson's confirmation that he was in place. Finally, one of the technicians said, "We've got some movement." He got up, walked into the launch area and picked up the transmitted piece of paper before looking back at Ann. "He's where he's supposed to be, ma'am."

Twenty-five minutes later, Johnson walked up to the old apartment building from the rear alleyway. "Guess this is home," he said aloud, and then looked up and down the lane. He walked up to the back entrance and unlocked it with his key. The building was an old school 1940s brick four-story, with centrally placed doors in the front and rear of the structure. Fire escapes were at either end and led to hallways joined in the centre with a large staircase. There were no elevators, and he began ascending the centre steps, taking two at a time, pulling out his key again when he reached the second floor. He walked down the hallway to apartment number 25 and had just unlocked the door when he heard a door opening behind him and to his right. Leaving their apartment was a couple in their fifties. "Good afternoon," Johnson said, as they walked up to him.

"Good afternoon," replied the man. "We were wondering when the new tenant was going to move in. The place has been vacant for a while now."

"I've only just arrived," Johnson said. "Hopefully, it won't take me too long to get myself settled in."

"If you're not familiar with the area, there's a store one block north of here where you can pick up groceries. It's not bad for prices. I'm Jim, by the way, and this is my wife, Diane."

Johnson smiled and shook Jim's hand. "I'm Steve. Nice to meet you both, and thanks for the directions."

Diane nodded a greeting at Johnson and then tugged on Jim's arm, saying, "We have to get going now, dear."

"You're right. The show will be starting soon. Welcome to the neighbourhood, Steve. If you need anything, feel free to ask," Jim said, before turning and heading down the hallway with Diane on his arm.

Johnson unlocked the door and looked around his apartment. It was nothing fancy, a simple one bedroom with a living room, kitchen and bathroom, all painted in a light shade of blue. It faced the street with two windows in the main living area and one in the bedroom. He looked out the front window. If he had to make the drop to the ground, it would jar him, but he could do it. He unpacked his bag, placing his weapon under his pillow in the bedroom. Satisfied, he walked out of the apartment and made his way to the grocery store Jim had told him about.

CHAPTER 26

*I*t *was night. A light rain that had fallen earlier left the streets smelling fresh and clean.* Jack stood alone in the darkness and watched as the outline of a lone woman walked toward him. *Not bad looking,* he thought. *Could have been a lot worse coming from Bill.* He was six feet tall, with faded blonde hair and cold, judgemental brown eyes. His fingers itched for a cigarette, but he knew that the light would give away his position. Jack was Bill's boss, a high-level commander with the Rebels. At only 38 years of age, he had moved up quickly within the organization, not because of his skill but by using back door politics and influential contacts. Unfortunately, Jack had now reached the peak of his progression. He knew this, and that knowledge made him furious. He wanted more, and this operation could very well be the key.

She was walking in the shadows, making sure to stay away from the light emanating from the streetlights. *This will be fun,* he thought and signalled to the people standing across from him. Two big men, with heavy jackets and hands in their pockets, stepped into the street. They closed the distance quickly, walking side by side and headed toward the woman.

Marie continued down the dark street, in a city she didn't recognize and couldn't have cared less for. *I've been at this all day,* she thought. *When I'm in charge, things will be different. No more hiding in the shadows.* She immediately spotted the two men stepping out from the darkness. She slowed her pace and took in two deep breaths as she watched the men come nearer. Both were heavyset, with lumbering steps. *How obvious,* she said to herself, disgusted by what she considered to be a blatantly amateur attempt at intimidation. She watched as they slid their hands from their coat pockets. One man held a pipe, the other a rope.

When they were five metres from her, she stopped and said sharply, "Can I help you?"

The two men slowed, one taking the lead and the other slipping in behind him. The man in front announced with a smirk, "We're here to help you."

She took a few steps backward as the men continued forward, her eyes narrowing. The men had slowed slightly, amused when they saw her rummaging in her pocket, then gathering her hair and tying it back into a ponytail. Marie's brain had automatically calculated the situation, telling her how and when to react. Her breathing became focused and deep; she could feel her heart rate steadily picking up. She would not allow them the opportunity to strike first. She would be the attacker.

In a flurry, she lunged at the first man, catching him by surprise. Her arm struck out in a straight punch to his throat, burying her fist deep into the soft flesh. The man, caught completely unaware, gasped loudly for air, eyes bulging from their sockets. The pipe in his hand dropped, clattering loudly as his knees bent, and he fell into a kneeling position onto the road. Marie stepped in, snatching the pipe off the ground. The other man had stopped moving and took a few steps back to reassess the situation.

Marie smiled. The pipe in her hand felt good, like an extension of her arm. It spun slowly in her right hand as she said to the second man, "You missed your opportunity. You should've come in directly after him." Raising the pipe, she swung it like a baseball bat across the kneeling man's face. The man's head was flung backward, his body collapsing as he sprawled, arms outstretched, onto his back. Marie then came up to the second man, blood raging through her veins. She pointed the pipe at him and said, "That was a lovely warmup. When you wake up, you can thank him for me." She was about to swing the pipe again when the man from the shadows stepped out.

"Marie, that's enough," he barked, stopping her in her tracks.

She looked over at the voice, seeing a man that fit the description Bill had given her. "We done? Did I pass your test?"

"With flying colours," he said. "We've got to go now. Come with me."

The next morning, Marie was up early. She walked out of her bedroom and into the kitchen for a coffee. She took the cup with her as she stepped out the front door and looked at her surroundings. Marie hadn't been able to see much last night when they arrived but soon realized they were in the middle of nowhere. The heavily wooded countryside around them appeared to be vast and completely uninhabited. The complex was surrounded by hedge trees on the outside and tall coniferous trees on the inside. Five inconspicuous domed buildings were tucked into the area, with an open space at its centre. *No one would ever find them here,* she thought, making her way back to the house for breakfast and some answers.

Stepping through the doorway of the kitchen, she glanced over to see three people engaged in light conversation around the table. She walked over to the machine, got another cup of coffee and leaned up against the cupboard. She recognized the man at the end of the table; he was the same man who had orchestrated her "test" the evening before. He had not bothered to introduce himself and, she knew, would eventually only give her a pseudonym. The other man and woman she didn't have a clue about, nor did she care.

The man looked up at her, smiling, and said, "Good morning, Marie. Did you sleep well?"

She raised an eyebrow at him but did not reply as she studied the three of them, quietly sipping her hot coffee.

Not at all bothered by her lack of response, he continued without a pause, "Still a little pissed about last night? I had to confirm to myself that you were as good as Bill said you were."

She took another sip of her coffee and placed the cup onto the countertop before she spoke. "What's the job?"

"We can discuss that later. For now, let's just get something to eat," the man said calmly, picking up his fork.

Marie kept her eyes locked on him. "I'm asking nicely one last time. What's the job, and why am I here?"

The man dropped his fork, and the other two, feeling the tension, slowly pushed their chairs away from the table.

"Marie," he said, eyes glinting with something Marie could not decipher, "relax. I know your background and what you can do. But you don't have a clue as to who I am, so I'll tell you just once. I've buried people with twice your experience and twice your skills. Save your breath and, like I said, relax."

Marie said nothing but studied his demeanour and his words. She would accept his bravado and façade for the moment. There was something in his actions that told her he once could have backed up his words, but that was years ago, not now. His practiced, smooth motions set her senses to high alert. *This man was nothing like Bill,* she thought. She would never trust him.

The man turned to the other two and said, "Where were we? Ah, yes, breakfast. Dig in people. Help yourselves. There's plenty, so let's eat. Marie, sit down. Eat."

Warily, Marie obliged, and the four of them began to eat their meal. Not another word was spoken until the man finally dropped his fork and wiped his mouth with a napkin.

"Well," he said, looking around the table, "now doesn't that feel a bit more civilized? Let me introduce the three of you. Marie, this is Ivan and Sonia." The three of them nodded in acknowledgement as he continued, "You can call me Jack."

Ivan was just under six feet tall, with a medium build and a full head of shoulder-length brown hair. His selection for this job surprised Marie, as his demeanour appeared to be submissive to the others. *Out of all the Operators,* she thought, *why would they pick him?*

Sonia was just over five and a half feet tall, with straight blonde hair cut just below her ears. She appeared to be the opposite of Ivan, as her demeanour was outgoing, confident and direct. Marie would later learn that she was able to break into a place with her hands but preferred to do it with a smile and a handshake. Marie herself had always leaned toward the former course of action because it saved time and energy. Which meant she never had to pretend to be friends with anyone.

Jack finally began his briefing with them. "General shit first. You've all been selected for your skills and the task at hand. We have an opportunity to procure a machine from a planet called Earth that has the potential to put the Rebels in control. Our latest Intel says that while the machine was under development, it was destroyed, along with the prototype and lab work. The person who developed it, Sally Reilly, decided not to pursue the research. You have been tasked to go to Earth and bring back information on how to build the machine. We've now gained the technology to move Midgardians from planet to planet. It's not as pinpoint as the GIAs and needs a bit of work, but we are still able to travel."

He continued. "The GIA is sending a man named Steve Johnson to help her get the program back on track. Johnson is from Earth and was picked up a few years ago by the agency. We think they want the machine for use here on Midgard, and we won't let that happen. We need it. We'll let Johnson be until he gets Reilly back on her feet, and the program is restarted. Once that's complete, you step in, steal the prototype, the lab work and the plans and bring it all back here to Midgard. Your secondary tasking is to gather as much information on Earth as you can. Natural resources, climate, the people, anything you think will be useful to us. Our GIA contact has given us enough to get you started, we need you to fill in the blanks. The last part of the plan is to convince Reilly not to develop something like this again. I don't want you to kill her. She may be of some use to us later."

Marie asked, "And Johnson?"

Jack's response was hard and fast. "Wait until Sally's up and running. Then kill him."

Marie showed no emotion. "No problem."

"Ivan and Marie will act as a married couple, Sonia as a single person."

Marie interrupted immediately. "You can change that now. I'll be single. These two can act as the married couple. As a matter of fact, you can just send me. These two will only slow me down."

Jack barked out a short laugh and said, "I don't give a fuck who's married to who. All three of you are going. I'll make the change with Ivan and Sonia. Marie, you can be single."

Marie shook her head in mock disappointment. "I'm just trying to save you some time. When do we leave?"

"At this point, it's looking like three days. You'll be given a crash course on what we know about life on the planet."

Ivan said, "Three days. That's a bit of a condensed training plan for an Operation like this."

Jack turned his head smoothly and stared at Ivan. "Are you saying you can't do it?"

"No, sir," Ivan quickly stuttered.

Jack looked carefully at Ivan, silently judging him before going on. "If there are any problems, you'll have to work through them yourselves. You're on your own for accommodation, but we'll give you everything you need for ID, clothing and currency. Our agency contact has been very resourceful. I expect you to get along."

CHAPTER 27

Back from the grocery store, Johnson looked at his watch. He knew Sally wasn't working, but he wanted to head out to the coffee shop and get a general feel of the area. After that, if he had time, he would walk past where she lived. Johnson walked east on 13th Avenue, surprised to be feeling awkward and out of place in a city that was once so familiar to him. Glancing around, he noted that the area had changed from hard-working Italian families with immaculately kept shops and restaurants to rundown cafes and tarot card readers. Ten minutes later, he looked ahead to see a sixties-style neon sign flashing on and off, announcing itself as Donuts and Things.

Pushing on the old wooden door, the squeak of rusty hinges announced his arrival. The shop was bigger than it appeared from the outside. He continued in and walked past a bulletin board on the wall, crammed with local advertisements, garage sale announcements and a list of names of people signing up for Burning Man.

His first order of business was to down a cup of coffee, something with the kick of real caffeine; he had been looking forward to this moment. Johnson ordered a coffee at the counter and immediately took a sip, sighing inwardly with satisfaction. Making his way over to one of the side tables, he took a seat and noticed a collage of employee pictures. He recognized Sally immediately. You could tell she was something special. It was the way she held herself: her smile, the intelligence in her eyes.

He savoured the last drop of his coffee and then walked the empty cup to the front counter and slipped out the door. Sally's place was a bit out of the way, but he wanted to scope it out and get to know the lay of the land before calling it a day. Pulling out his map, he studied his route and soon found himself standing in the park across from her apartment.

He looked at the building carefully, noting its entrances and exits. Her place was older than the apartment he was staying in. The only modern addition was a security buzzer at the front door. He knew it would not be enough to protect her from unwanted visitors, should they arrive. He looked through the park and spotted a few places that could be used for observation if needed. Not particularly satisfied, he had no choice but to accept it and return to his apartment, a meal and a good night's sleep.

Johnson woke the next morning and, out of sheer habit, walked over to the window facing the street, making a mental note of the cars and a general description of the people walking by. His plan this morning was to meet Sally at the cafe, but he needed a few items first. After a shower, he headed out for the day and soon found himself walking down one of the main streets. The stores were just opening when he stopped in front of one of them and looked in through the storefront window. It was called "To Be Worn Again" and was a second-hand store. Johnson walked in and headed directly for the T-shirts and jeans, finding clothes that would suit him and let him blend in. He paid for them, stuffed them into a bag and made his way down to the cafe where Sally worked.

He walked into Donuts and Things and up to the register. There was a short menu pasted on the counter beside the till, and he had just begun going over each item when he heard a voice say, "Can I help you?"

"Yeees," he drawled, lingering on the menu, going through it item by item.

A few seconds passed, and he heard, "Do you need more time?"

"Nope. All set," he finally announced, this time looking toward the voice. Sally stood in front of him behind the counter, awaiting his order, a calm, patient expression on her face. She had had her blonde hair cut since the last briefing photo on Midgard, but her blue eyes, bright and alert, were exactly what the pictures from Midgard had captured.

"Sorry," he said with a grin. "I'll have a coffee, black. No room for cream, please."

"All that reading for a black coffee," she said, returning his smile.

"I really wanted a donut, but I don't need the extra sugar, so every time I walk into a place like this, I go through a procedure to talk myself out of overindulging. Sometimes I think I go through a menu just to torture myself."

She laughed, pouring Johnson's coffee and placed it in front of him. "You're probably not the only one that wages that kind of silent battle. Is this your first time here?"

"Yup. It seems like a nice spot."

"It's a very nice spot, indeed. Welcome to Donuts and Things. We've got today's newspapers and magazines to read if you like," she said and motioned to the far wall with her head.

"Thanks," he replied and took the coffee to a spot by the big front window. Setting the coffee down, he walked over to where the morning papers were and brought it back to his table. Sitting down, he opened it, his eyes skimming through the headlines. The only thing that interested him was talking with Sally, but he knew he had to be patient. This wasn't going to be a hundred-metre dash; it was going to be a marathon. After fifteen minutes, he finished his coffee and walked the empty cup up to the counter.

Sally watched as he came up to her and said, "Thanks for bringing up your cup."

"No problem, you're welcome," Johnson replied, placing the cup into a tub.

"Off and doing anything important today?"

"Just taking the bus out to the university, signing myself in and then checking into the library," Johnson replied.

"Ah, off to university. Good for you. Well then, good luck to you."

"Thanks. I'll probably see you tomorrow if you're here," he said over his shoulder while making his way to the door.

"I'll be here all week."

Johnson walked up to Broad Street and caught a bus to the university. He found it ironic that, as a teenager, he had studiously avoided the higher echelons of education. Yet here he was, voluntarily signing into classes. The afternoon flew by, and, after picking up two books on the environment at the library, he took the bus back to his apartment. Johnson walked in with a slight smile on his face. The first contact had been made, and it had been successful, albeit uneventful. Pulling out his wallet, a piece of paper and a pen, he sent a situation report to Midgard. It was now 3 June 2014.

CHAPTER 28

*T*hree *days later, Marie and her team, their training complete, watched as a group of cleaners swept through the compound, clearing equipment and wiping everything down. Marie looked over at Sonia and Ivan and said, "That's it.* We leave for the departure area tonight, and transport is scheduled for tomorrow. Do either of you have any questions?"

Over the last three days, Sonia had learned very rapidly, although reluctantly, to go along with Marie. She thought of herself as more like a surgical tool, someone to be used for delicate operations, whereas Marie was a battering ram. Great if you needed a door smashed in but useless when it came to anything requiring technique. Marie's head-on approach had already been aimed at Ivan during training. Sonia's method of dealing with her would have to involve tact and timing.

"Nothing from me," she replied.

"There never is," Marie said sarcastically. "How about you, Ivan?"

"I already brought this up two days ago. We still need more time. Three days isn't enough time for us to get all the info we need on Earth or Reilly. They've admitted there's a strong possibility the prototype and documents have all been destroyed. So even if she gets her shit together and puts everything back in order, it'll be at least a few months before anything happens. We could use that time to get a better sense of how we want to run the mission and how to deal with Johnson. Then there are the issues with the Destination Machine. We know their accuracy is out. They haven't told us what to expect after travelling millions of fucking kilometres to this place," he sighed. "We should know how far from the target Destination will be inserting us."

Marie had listened, arms folded in front of her. She had been impressed by Ivan's performance but not with his whiney attitude. She congratulated herself on her restraint and self-control before she continued. "If Command needed us in a month, we would have been given the time, but the mission is short notice. We're on this timeline for a reason, and Destination will have smart people behind the controls shooting for an offset. That will compensate and hopefully get us near the city, not in the middle of a lake somewhere."

"We leave tomorrow morning. If you think you need more time, say so, and we'll leave without you." Marie turned and walked back to the house. She grudgingly conceded that his concerns were somewhat warranted and, inwardly, she had some of the same misgivings. She also knew her people would get them onto Earth, maybe close to the target, perhaps thousands of kilometres away. Her reasoning said that was why they were going in early, in case they needed the time to get to Regina. But she couldn't bother explaining that to Ivan.

She walked into the kitchen just as Jack was going through his screen. "Any problems?" he asked her.

Although she usually didn't single her people out, she was ruthless enough to let him know Ivan's concerns, in the hopes that she could do this mission on her own. "Yeah," she said, "Ivan thinks we need more training."

"What do you think?"

"I do agree, to a point. But you brought us here on short notice for a reason. I think that if you had a longer timeframe, you would have given us more time. But then again, if there was more time, I may never have been selected for the job."

Jack stood up and stretched. He had been sitting too long. "Every Commander wishes they had more time. But time is a commodity we don't have now, especially with this mission. You need to get in there with your people and establish yourselves. You're going to be at a disadvantage because we could only give you limited knowledge about the planet. Take the time and find out as much as you can, keep track of Reilly and watch Johnson. We never said it would be easy," he finished.

"It never is, but it'll get done," Marie answered.

At 0100, the vectors arrived to pick them up, coming in at twenty-minute intervals. Marie was the last to depart, settling into the vector and watching impassively as the machine flew quietly to their destination. The vector slowed just before landing. Stepping out of it and into an open lot, she spotted Jack and walked over to meet him.

Jack did not waste time. "You're the last in. I'll take you to the others." He led her into an old warehouse building a couple of hundred metres from where they had landed. A door opened, and they entered a Receiving Room, where they were scanned for weapons and communication devices. Once cleared, a door to the front slid open, and the two walked into a larger area, where they were met by Ivan and Sonia.

Jack gave his instructions in his usual curt manner. "You'll be leaving in an hour from that location," he said, pointing to a glass enclosure a few metres from them. "Our contact in the agency has been most useful. The Tech will set you up with ID, money and cards for credit. We're also implanting transponders in each of you. They're locator devices. If something happens, we can find you and bring you back at any time. Marie, you'll have a communicator. I want one message shortly after you arrive, then once every three days after that. I'm hoping the mission will be no more than six weeks. See you back here in an hour." With that, he turned them over to the technician who had been waiting for them.

Fifteen minutes before insertion, the three walked to the glass box and watched as coordinate calculations were finalized. As they waited, a stray cat had wandered into the room, curving itself first around Ivan's and then Sonia's legs, asking for attention. She absently bent down and gave it's back a soothing stroke. "You shouldn't be here," she said. "It's not a safe place for cats."

"Get that thing out of here," Marie said sharply. "It's probably got some kind of disease."

Sonia was quick to comply with the demand, in case Marie's method of disposal involved violence. She picked up the cat and moved it carefully onto one of the side shelves, where it settled itself. Marie ignored her when she returned and asked the Tech, "How close can you get us?"

He answered confidently, "I've got it pinpointed to just outside a city called Regina. It shouldn't be too far out. You got five minutes till departure."

Marie turned and looked for Sonia, spotting her talking quietly with Jack. She frowned. The conversation between the two of them looked intimate, not something Marie would have expected to exist between a boss and a subordinate. Jack looked up and saw her eyeing them. Marie watched as Jack said something, and Sonia returned to the group.

"What was that all about?" Marie asked.

"Nothing. Just saying good luck," Sonia replied casually. Marie did not believe her but pulled the two in close. "Let's not fuck this up."

Jack called out, "We're ready," and the three of them walked into the glass enclosure.

One of the technicians gave a countdown as the rip began to appear, flooding the area with its blinding light. When the portal had extended to two metres, he ordered, "Step through now." They strode into the light and were immediately swallowed up by it. A second later, the portal disappeared, and the energy dissipated.

Jack knew the agency would be able to detect the enormous energy spike they had just generated. There was no time to celebrate their success. He barked out his next order. "We've got fifteen minutes to get out of here. Tear it all down. Now. Move!"

The agency's sensors were monitoring the country's energy fluctuations, recording the levels being used and every detail as to what they were being used for. Ninety-nine percent of the activities were legitimate businesses, working through the night or just starting up a new day. Only one percent had been attributed to criminal activity. The system picked up the spike early that morning, along with hundreds more. It wasn't the time of day that gained the attention of the operator but rather the level of the power spike. The operator immediately double-checked the anomaly and zeroed in on its location before contacting the S3.

Ann was sitting behind her desk when the call came, saying that an operator had detected an unusually high power spike early that morning on the fringe of the country. She studied the power graph and then asked, "It's coming from a manufacturing area. Are you sure it wasn't a company just starting up early?"

"No ma'am, it wasn't. And the power spike was too huge for any plant in the area. Besides, that building is sandwiched between two large plants. It's rented, but it wasn't supposed to be in use."

Moments later, she had contacted two teams, and in twenty minutes, they were at the site via Destination. She walked into the building a few minutes after the teams' arrival to find her S2, Dave Corbin, already there.

Ann asked, "Any idea what happened?"

The S2 walked her away from the others. "The Rebels used their Destination Machine from here this morning."

"Any indication as to where they went?"

"From the amount of energy that was used, I'd say they went to Earth."

"Shit," Ann muttered. "I want every stitch of Intelligence they left behind taken back with us. Nothing stays behind. And don't forget the cat." She pointed to the stray sitting atop one of the shelves, then turned on her screen and contacted Eric. "Sir, we conducted a hit this morning. There's a strong possibility the Rebels are now on Earth."

Stanton asked, "What's your plan of action?"

"I'll contact Johnson and pass on the information."

"Agreed. Anything else?"

"I'd like to activate Sharpe and send her to help him."

"Sharpe?"

"I know what you're thinking, but she's right for the job, and she'll blend nicely. Besides, she knows the Rebels' tactics and operational procedures better than anyone."

"All right, but we never had this conversation."

"I understand. Betty will be there in the next forty-eight hours."

"Like I said, we never had this conversation."

Ann ended the connection before Eric could say anything more and then immediately contacted Betty. "Betty, it's Ann. How would you like to go on a little trip?"

CHAPTER 29

*S*ally's shift didn't start until 1300, and Johnson had the entire morning to himself. He dressed in PT gear and headed out for a run. The weather was cold, and the air fresh. He began jogging slowly at first and then picked up the pace as his body warmed. His route would be to the large park that surrounded the parliament buildings, once around and then head back home. As he ran, he put his plan together for that afternoon. He'd go to the coffee shop after lunch when the rush was over, and the cleanup was complete. Once he had ordered a coffee, he would lay out the books that he'd taken out from the library on the table. Hopefully, Sally would recognize them and start a conversation, any kind of conversation. It wasn't much of an idea, but it could be an introduction and, with luck, a start to something. Forty minutes later, satisfied with both the run and his plan of action, he found himself back where he started, then cooled down and walked back up to his apartment.

Walking through the door, he poured a glass of water and caught a glimpse of his wallet on the table, a dim light emanating from it. Opening it, he found a message that had been sent from Special Projects. It read:

"*Raid has been conducted on Rebel warehouse this AM. We have confirmed their use of Destination to travel to your location. Your mission has possibly been compromised. Their mission and numbers are not readily known. Betty Sharpe will be sent to your location in the next forty-eight hours. Sharpe's participation is for your eyes only. All previously discussed orders remain the same. Proceed with caution.*"

Johnson reread the message one last time, destroyed it, and wrote back to Special Projects, confirming he had received the message. There wasn't anything more he could do now. His plans and actions would remain the same. He would just have to be on the lookout for people that looked like they didn't belong. Johnson was surprised and suspicious about Betty's arrival but then remembered the picture on her wall. Obviously, there was much more to her story than what he had been told. He hoped that she would level with him and tell him the truth about what was going on with her.

He still had a few hours before meeting Sally and decided to pick up a few extra items he would need. His first stop was the second-hand store again. This time, he picked up a comfortable shirt, a pair of dress pants and a jacket before he headed for the cashier. He dropped off the clothes at the dry cleaners, where the clerk said they would be ready by the end of the day. His last stop was the hardware store, where he purchased door stops, cellophane tape, duct tape, two broom handles, a screwdriver and pliers.

Returning to his apartment, he opened the door and, just as he stepped into the room, heard a familiar voice say, "You're rusty. You should've checked the corner of the room."

Initially startled, then both relieved and embarrassed, he said, "Betty, you scared the shit outta me."

"You're lucky you've only been scared. Did you get the message from GIA?" she asked.

"I did. HQ said you wouldn't be in for another forty-eight hours."

"I pulled a few strings and got inserted early with their skeleton staff. That was quite the trip, by the way. I still need some time to recover. In any case, I've cut down the number of people who know I'm here. I never liked people knowing where I'm going or what I'm doing. The agency has gotten too big, and information tends to get out."

"How did you get in here?"

"Stian gave me a key. He also found me a place to stay not far from here."

"Do you trust him?"

"Yes, I do. I scanned him quite a few years ago. I looked into every nook and cranny of his brain and found no deception. Some time ago, his mother and father were kidnapped. I went in with an unsanctioned crew and got them out. He owes me," Betty smiled.

Johnson didn't want to know any more. He asked, "Where are you staying?"

"Two blocks north of here," she said and gave him the address. She looked at his parcels and then around the room before stating, "Looks like you're putting in a few early warning devices."

"I am," Johnson said, "but first, tell me why they sent you, Betty. Come clean with me."

"Let's sit. Do you have any tea?"

Johnson obligingly made two mugs of tea and sat down beside her as she began to tell her story.

"I was recruited by the agency as a very young woman at a time when the Rebels were starting up another revolt. We almost lost that battle, and times were tough. We fought hard, month after month, year after year before we gained some control and life returned to near normal. I learned more about the Rebels and how they operated than any of the Operators working now. I met my husband at the agency. We managed to have a family, and our lives were good for a very long time. Then I lost him. My son has grown and works on the other side of Midgard, so I decided to return to something I knew with the agency, doing side projects, like working with you."

"Out of all the Operators within the agency, why did they send you?"

"My experience, I suppose. I can pick em out, and I can terminate them."

"You've come a long way to do that, and Earth is dangerous for you. You can't stay for more than a month, or you'll start to age."

"Let me worry about that," she replied, dismissing his concern.

Johnson was unconvinced but merely shook his head and said, "We can talk more while you give me a hand to set up."

Betty got up and began to help him unpack, Johnson peppering her with questions, most of which Betty ignored. An hour later, they had placed wooden stops on all the windows, allowing them to only open a couple of inches. Broom handles were measured and cut to act as jams for the door handles, and the triangular doorstops were set up. A strip of cellophane tape was placed on the outside of the door between the door and frame. If it were broken, it would indicate that someone had tried to open it. Lastly, Johnson worked on his bedroom door, cleaning the grease and oil from the hinges and then soaking them down with saltwater. In a few days, the hinges would be as noisy as an old gate.

Betty sat down with a tired sigh and said, "Let's keep our link-up to ourselves for now. Give it a couple of days before you let them know I'm here."

Johnson looked at his watch and, seeing the time said, "Betty, I need to get going. You can stay here if you want."

"No, I'm done here. I need some rest."

"Thanks for the talk. Nice to have a partner."

After Betty left the apartment, Johnson picked up the books he'd signed out the day before and headed out the door. Twenty minutes later, he was in the coffee shop. Only a few people were sitting at different tables throughout the room. He made his way to the counter and placed the books down, looking for Sally, but she was nowhere in sight. An older lady walked up to him, asking, "What can I get you?"

"A medium coffee, black. No room for cream, please."

"Medium black," the lady repeated, pouring the coffee and handing it to him. Johnson paid and made his way to a table. He placed the books and coffee down and settled himself in a chair.

I can only wait, Johnson thought and looked around the room. He picked up one of the books and opened it, then heard someone kicking at the door. Looking up, he saw Sally with two armloads of groceries, struggling to open the door and bring in her bags at the same time. Johnson got up, held the door open for her and took one of the bags.

Sally heaved a sigh of relief and said, "Thanks," smiling at him. "Your name is Steve, isn't it?"

"That's right," Johnson said, walking the bag to the front counter. "And your name is Sally."

"Yes, it is," she said. "Thanks again for the help." She took the bags and disappeared into the back kitchen.

Johnson sat back down and opened the book again, paging through it. A few minutes later, Sally appeared beside him with a fresh cup of coffee and placed it on the table.

"On the house. I see you've brought your own reading material."

"When I signed in for classes the other day, they gave me a list of material to read, plus a short assignment," he replied, pointing to the books.

She looked down at them and picked one off the table, paging through it. "I've read this one. It's got some good information in it."

"You're interested in environmental issues?"

"I am. It used to be a bit of a passion for me."

"Do you have a few minutes to explain this chapter?" He asked, pointing to a particularly obscure chapter on climatic considerations.

"A few," she replied and settled herself in beside him before picking up the book. They spoke for a few minutes, Sally immediately diving into the intricacies of the subject.

A voice interrupted them from the counter. "Excuse me, can we pay up?"

"I'll be right there," she answered. "Time to get back to work."

She got up and left him to attend to the customers.

Finishing his coffee a few minutes later, he walked the empty cups to the counter. He asked Sally, "Can we continue to talk about this book some time?"

She warned him, "If I start, I may not stop."

"I need to have a paper completed by day one. If you're willing to talk about your ideas, I'm willing to listen."

"I'm busy for the rest of today but free tomorrow evening after work. Is that convenient for you?"

"It is. Can I take you out for a drink afterwards as payment?"

"You're on. I'll meet you here at about seven o'clock outside the shop. We can go to the library."

Johnson nodded. "I'll be here, and thanks." He gave a slight wave and left the cafe, making his way over to the Records Department at City Hall.

He had placed a tightly closed box around his need for closure with his family until now. Today he had the time and the opportunity to open it. Johnson needed to find out where his brother lived and where his parents were interred. Within minutes, the clerk behind the counter handed him a slip of paper. His parents were buried in the old cemetery just off Broad Street, and his brother lived a few kilometres south of his current apartment. *That was enough for now,* he thought, as he jumped onto a northbound bus heading away from downtown. The streets moved past the window, waking memories that had long lay dormant for him: the high school football games, the icy cold winters. Growing up here felt like a lifetime ago. He had left the city immediately after finishing high school and joined the army. His time in the Light Infantry had changed him, hardening his outlook, teaching him that life was neither simple nor easy. Learning how to survive, fight and kill, had made any commonalities he had left with this place only a distant memory.

He immediately recognized his old street and got off at the next stop, walking up the sidewalk to what was once his family home. The house looked almost the same, although the young sapling in the front yard had grown into a large and healthy tree whose branches engulfed the entire yard. The house had been well looked after, and the siding, front steps and windows had been replaced. As his eyes scanned the front yard, he felt as if he could look back in time. He remembered the first time he backed his dad's car out of the driveway, his father's voice of encouragement, the crack of hockey sticks on the road, his brother's laugh. The only thing missing was the scent of his mother's apple pie.

Johnson walked the rest of the street and could recognize where new residents had moved in after the old neighbours had moved on. It was a self-sustaining and rejuvenating project, replacing the old with the new, the cycle in constant motion. He made his way to the bus and found a seat before the vehicle started to move. As he looked out the window, he was reminded that the old saying was true. You could always go home, but you could never really go back.

CHAPTER 30

Marie led them out of the tear and into the middle of nowhere. They had arrived at nightfall, and the cloud cover gave them limited visibility. Unsure of their surroundings, they immediately flattened themselves onto the cold, damp ground, peering through the darkness for signs of trouble. All three were exhausted and nauseous, so they took a few minutes to gain control of their bodies before shakily pulling themselves up to a sitting position. They'd used Destination before throughout Midgard; this trip was like nothing they had experienced before. *At least we're not in the middle of a lake*, Marie thought.

"Where do you suppose we are?" Sonia asked after a few minutes.

"By the looks of things, on the outskirts of a major city," Marie said, pointing to a distant skyline on the horizon. "We can only hope what we see there is Regina."

"You think they could've placed us a bit closer," Ivan sulked.

Marie glanced at him and said, "Really? Millions of light-years away and you're complaining? It could have been a lot worse."

"The walk is going to suck," he muttered as he tried to get on his feet. He wobbled for a second and immediately sat back down. "I feel like crap. How about you two?" His face suddenly drained of colour, and, turning to one side, he began throwing up.

The two women could only watch as he heaved the contents of his stomach onto the grass, doing their best to hold theirs in. Sonia spoke shakily, "I was okay until you did that."

Ivan wiped his face on his sleeve and said with a half grimace, "I've never had problems like this before." Giving in to his body's queasiness, he lay down on the grass, holding his stomach and moaning.

Marie managed a snort of disgust but said nothing for a few minutes. Finally, rousing her protesting body, she forced herself up into a standing position. "Get up," she ordered. "We'll head to the centre of the city, then determine where to go from there."

They had indeed arrived just outside the city limits. Their walk was long and uneventful, although they were shocked at the utter flatness and seeming desolation of the prairie around them. Their first night was spent in a hotel, and, over the next couple of days, Marie confirmed Sally's location and found two separate apartments nearby. Marie wanted the three of them to be close to each other but not close enough for anyone to make a connection between them. They purchased food and clothing and then worked on the nuances of basic everyday life. Although they were briefed before, they were surprised and relieved by the direct similarities between their world and this one. It would be straightforward for them to assimilate into the population. At the end of the second day, all three met for a meeting.

Marie told them, "Tomorrow we start watching Sally. We'll start with her movements. I want to know where she goes, what she does and who she sees. Hopefully, over the next few days, we'll have an outline of her basic movements. Over the next week, I want something more solid, with all the details filled in. Once that's complete, I want to see where she is in her previous research. We may have to dig deep to find anything. That means actual contact with her and a look around her apartment. If you see Johnson, hang back and don't make your presence known. Watch him only as a secondary target. He needs to do our work for us, convince her to get her research up and running again. If he does convince her, I'll let it go until she's back on track, probably in a few weeks. Then we can take him down."

"Sonia, you and I will split up shift timings between 0600 to 1800. Ivan, you've got her from 1800 until she goes to bed. If she goes out for a night, Sonia, you and I will split that up. Any questions?"

Johnson was eating supper when a vibration from his wallet interrupted him. Taking the grid references provided on the message, he opened his map of the city, laid it flat on the table, and confirmed an exact location. He placed his finger where the two lines intersected and studied it carefully. It was in the middle of a field outside the city, with the nearest road 500 metres away. He destroyed the message, grabbed a flashlight, plastic bag and coat and stuffed it all into his backpack. Shortly after, he made his way over to the shopping centre and hailed a cab.

"Where to?" the driver asked.

Johnson unfolded the map and pointed to the spot he'd located earlier. "Can you take me there?"

The driver was silent for a second, the wrinkles on his face made deeper by the setting sun. "Okay," he said reluctantly, "but it'll cost you an extra twenty bucks. It's a fair way out of the city."

"That'll be just fine. And I'll throw in another twenty for your trouble," Johnson said.

The driver's eyebrows raised in surprise at the unexpected windfall, and he immediately started the engine, put the car into drive and pulled away from the curb. He glanced at Johnson through his rear-view mirror. "You look'n for that UFO?"

Johnson asked him, quizzically, "UFO?"

"Yeah, they say the other night, there were bright lights spotted in that area. Some people were sayin' UFO. Don't believe in that, myself. I say they're crazy." He stared again at Johnson, trying to determine if Johnson himself was one of the crazy ones. Johnson did not bother to reply. The less he engaged, the less chance there was of repercussions.

Thirty minutes later, Johnson stood on a gravel road looking back to the city as the taxi pulled away. The driver called out a "thanks," waved, and then floored the vehicle, spitting rocks and gravel at him. He turned his back to the cab and surveyed the field with a thoughtful expression. The area, once all grass, had been trampled to the ground where people had walked. The cab driver provided him with a heads-up; there had been people here looking for something. He hoped that they hadn't found anything before he did. The location he received from Special Projects was exact, but his map wasn't. It was made for city streets, not a spot in a field. Still, someone with experience could line up the location, make a few adjustments and find the exact area without too much difficulty. He oriented the map to a building in the distance that would keep him on the right path. He estimated the point to be 500 metres to the left of where he stood and folded the map up, placed it into his back pocket and began to walk. He counted off his paces, the ground changing from beaten down to standing grass. *A promising sign,* he thought. *No one has searched this area.*

Fifteen minutes later, as the sun was going down and with little daylight left, he found it. A small area in the long grass in front of him appeared to have been flattened. Standing off to the side, he could see where tracks went out but did not return. *This is where they inserted,* he said to himself, moving in for a closer look. The footprints told him what he wanted to know. Comparing the outlines and indentations, he knew that one man and two women had been inserted. He pulled the flashlight from his pack, turned it on and swept it slowly over the area. A reflection off the ground caught his attention, and he moved closer, kneeling beside it. *Someone has a weak stomach,* he said to himself. He pulled out a plastic bag, placing a bit of the vomit into it and tucked it in his backpack. Seeing nothing more of interest, he pointed the flashlight at the ground and slowly walked counter-clockwise around the site. At each complete revolution, he made the circle wider and wider, finally confirming he'd left nothing behind. His gaze shifted south as he watched the streetlights of the city slowly start to sparkle on. *Nothing more to do here.* He picked up the faint tracks the three Rebels had left behind and followed their path out of the field and into the city.

By the next morning, Johnson had sent his findings back to the agency for their analysis. He then gathered his backpack and headed to the university library to meet up with Betty. Through Stian, she had secured a volunteer position as a librarian there. It would provide Johnson and her with a safe and comfortable place to meet. She was standing at the front counter as Johnson walked up to her. "Good morning," he said. "I was wondering if you could help me out."

"And what exactly do you need?" she asked, a friendly expression on her face.

"The private areas in the back. I was wondering if you could show them to me. I may want to use one for a presentation and would like to see if it will suit my needs."

She looked over at the woman working with her. "Agnes, I'll be gone for a few minutes." To Johnson, she said, "Please follow me" and stepped out from behind the counter, walking down the aisle to the back of the room. Johnson followed Betty until they came to a door. Betty opened it and entered a private room, Johnson following close behind her.

He closed the door behind them and asked, "How are you holding out?"

"Libraries are boring, Steve. How about you?"

He barked out a short, soft laugh and said, "I received a message from the agency. They've verified that a Rebel crew was inserted. The assumption that the Rebels are going after the machine has been confirmed."

Betty's face changed instantly. No longer bored, she said, "Now you've got my attention. Go on."

"It was a field north of the city. It caused a bit of a stir. Even the taxi driver knew about it. He said there were rumours of a UFO being spotted out there."

Betty's eyebrows furrowed together. "The light, people saw it? Did they go to the area?"

"Yes, they did, but they were looking in the wrong spot. I

found the right one. From what I could figure out, there were two women and a man that came in. One of them threw up. By the hand and knee indentations beside the vomit, I'm guessing it was the man. I've sent it back to Special Projects for analysis. They might be able to get something off it."

Betty nodded briskly. "Good job. We'll just have to wait for their results."

"Since we've confirmed there are others here, we'll need to watch ourselves," Johnson said. "They may not have identified us yet, and they sure as hell don't know about you. We'll have to stay apart and meet only in isolated spots."

Betty agreed. "That'll work fine. Just be careful. I've been flying below the radar for years now, but I'll still work on my appearance, so they won't get me on the first look."

They left the room and walked back to the front counter. "Thanks for your time, but the area isn't suitable for what I need. I'll look elsewhere for my presentation," Johnson said courteously when they arrived.

"That's fine," Betty said. "If you need a hand with anything else, please drop by." Johnson walked away, and as she watched him disappear through the doors, she could not help feeling a thrill of excitement. She had always hated the mundane.

CHAPTER 31

The next day, Johnson was standing outside a twenty-four-hour convenience store across from the coffee shop. He surmised from what the agency had told him and the evidence he'd gathered that the Rebels would assume surveillance as their priority. He predicted they'd be watching Sally to establish her routine and decide how to conduct their operations.

Without knowing their mission, Johnson could only put himself in the Rebel's position to stop them. He'd conduct surveillance first, get to understand the target, where they lived, their routine, likes and dislikes. He'd place the women on during the day. They could blend in without difficulty, and the questions that they'd ask would be less conspicuous. The man would probably take the night shift as there would be fewer chances for conversation and more watching. All three would collate their information daily and come out with a picture of her life.

He assumed they already knew where she worked and lived, so he stayed outside the convenience store, scanning the area in front of him. Not knowing who or what he was looking for, he went back to the basics of Surveillance 101. Look for the unusual, the out of place, sizes and shapes of people, something different. Or look for the person interested in you. All of this was to be committed to memory and be recalled when needed.

Satisfied that nothing seemed out of the ordinary, at seven o'clock, he left and walked into the coffee shop. Sally had just put on her jacket and grinned when she saw him. "Hi," she said. "Are you ready for a wild night at the library?"

"As ready as I can be. Are you sure you're still up to this? You've just done a full day of work," he replied, opening the door for her.

"It's fine. If I didn't want to do it, I wouldn't have volunteered. Besides, the topic is a passion of mine, and if I can do anything to help, then I will." With the decision made, they left the coffee shop and made their way to the city library.

Johnson, hands tucked into his pockets as they walked, asked her, "What made you such an advocate for the environment?"

Her response held traces of the born teacher that she was. "You're the one writing the paper. What made you decide to go into the field?"

"Well," he confessed, "I can honestly say that I wasn't until about a year ago. Up until that time, my thoughts on saving the whales consisted of killing them all and stop worrying about them."

She winced. "Ouch. Brutal."

"I know, I'm just being honest here. Then one day, I literally woke up and thought there's got to be a better way to do things. We've lived on this planet for thousands of years, side by side, with all living things. But in the past two hundred years, we've contributed to making more species of animals extinct than any Ice Age. We've pumped pollution into our air and oceans, cut down most of the great forests, and piled landfills with garbage that'll still be there in a thousand years. And I still haven't talked about fossil fuels, overpopulation or anything nuke. Something must be done, but I still want to flick on the light switch, turn on the stove and use transportation to get around. We need to start talking about this now before it's too late."

Sally listened without comment as Johnson spoke, never showing if she agreed or disagreed. It was always comforting to hear someone that cared as much as she did. She finally said, "The best fighters are the ones that learn the reason why they're fighting."

They continued down the street without talking and finally arrived at the steps to the front doors of the library. Sally jogged quickly up the stairs beside Johnson, and he opened the door for both of them. They found an empty table in the back of the large main room and sat down. Johnson took out the books from his pack, along with his laptop. "Okay, I'm set."

Sally looked at the two books laid out in front of her, picking one up and paging through it for a moment before beginning. For the next few hours, the two of them spoke ardently and passionately, heads bent close to each other, alternately discussing and arguing. The time went by unnoticed until the librarian put a stop to the evening, approaching them and clearing her throat. "The library is closing in ten minutes and will open tomorrow at nine o'clock. Please make your way to the exit," she said.

Johnson, surprised by the time, scanned his notes and said, "Wow, I've got a lot here. Thank you. I think I may have had enough information after the first thirty minutes but didn't want to stop you."

"Sorry. I get carried away. When I get started, I can't stop."

"Don't apologize. I may have enough material here for the whole semester." They were still laughing as Johnson picked up the books, and they made their way out of the building. As they walked down the front steps, Johnson stopped and said, "I owe you a drink. Where would you like to go?"

"Follow me," she said and led the way across the street and into a secluded park. The evening air was refreshing as they strolled past others who were either walking or seated on benches. Johnson noticed an outline he'd seen earlier. It wasn't the man's shape or size that he recognized, but his head. More specifically, it was his hair. The man was sitting, hands deep in his coat pockets, looking up at the trees. Johnson managed one last glance at the man as they passed. Although his face was unfamiliar, it was the long hair he recognized. Johnson had seen it earlier, in a car while waiting for Sally. *Unusual*, he remembered saying to himself.

CHAPTER 32

*T*he place was quaint. The music was old school Motown, and the patrons were neither young nor old but rather in that sweet spot right in the centre. The speakers were purring out Gladys Knight and the Pips "Midnight Train to Georgia," and they could both feel a mellow mood seeping from the walls. Johnson ordered two beers, handing one to Sally. "Cheers," he said, smiling.

"Thanks," Sally said. "I can't stay long. It's been a long day, and I've got to work tomorrow."

"No problem. I'll walk you home whenever you're ready."

They sat back for a while, talking, taking in the atmosphere and enjoying the music until they had finished their drinks and reluctantly walked out of the bar. The night had cooled significantly, and they walked briskly to Sally's apartment. When they finally arrived, Johnson said, "Thanks again for all your help, Sally." She half laughed and said, "It's my kryptonite. I really don't mind."

"I plan on having this completed in a couple of days. Can I ask you to have a look at it as a second set of eyes?"

"Sure," she said, surprised. "There's a lot of information there. You could give yourself more time than just a couple of days."

"It's all right. I like to hit it while it's still fresh, and I don't forget anything," he said, holding the lobby door for her as she brushed past him.

She took a pen from her purse. "Here's my number. Call me. If I don't answer, just leave a message."

"Thanks," Johnson said, and then watched her disappear up the stairs. He put the telephone number in his pocket and proceeded across the street, turning left down the sidewalk. He slipped into the park and made his way deep into it, beyond the ambient light produced by the streetlights.

Johnson slowly made his way back toward Sally's, watching to his front and sides. He stayed parallel to her street, where the vehicles were parked only on the right side. The left had been designated as no parking. Spotting a large tree that could hide his outline and his shadow, he came up to it and sat down, placing his back against the cool bark. The spot wasn't the best for surveillance; he was too deep for any facial identification, but he could stay out of sight. *Patience,* he thought, *just have some patience.*

The night had been successful for him. He had followed Johnson and Sally without detection and watched as Johnson left her at the door. The scene in front of him had not changed as he sat bored but motionless in an older Honda Element. If a car drove by, he would slide himself down ever so slightly behind the wheel. He hated the night shift.

By the second hour, Johnson's eyes were starting to get heavy. Fighting the urge to close them, he tightened and relaxed the muscles in his arms and then his legs, willing himself back into alertness. A light slam of a vehicle door got his attention. A man who had been sitting in a parked car left his vehicle, walked into the park and relieved himself. Johnson strained his eyes, trying to get facial recognition, but it was useless. He could only see the outline of the distinct hairstyle he'd seen earlier that evening.

The man was now finished and, zipping up his pants, stretched and walked back to the sidewalk past Sally's apartment. He slowed to look at the building and then moved on, stopping under a streetlight and looking at his watch before heading back to his vehicle. Back at the car, he took one last look up and down the street, got inside, started it up and departed. Johnson's patience had paid off. The illumination from the streetlight had given him a good look, and he was now sure it was the same man from the park. He stood, shaking the stiffness from his limbs and walked home.

The next day Johnson woke, dressed in PT gear, brushed his teeth, had a coffee and headed out the door. He jogged slowly down the alley, then zigzagged through the streets, eventually ending up at Betty's house. He walked through the back gate to the door and rang the buzzer, catching the slight movement of curtains before the door opened, and Betty appeared.

"Come on in."

Johnson reflexively turned around, checking in case anyone had followed him. Seeing nothing, he turned and stepped furtively through the doorway.

"Do you want coffee?" Betty asked as she made her way into the kitchen.

"That'd be great."

The two sat at the table as Johnson explained what he had seen the night before. Betty listened until the coffeemaker signalled that it was ready. She got up and poured them both a cup, placing the coffee in front of him. "Are you sure the man isn't just an old boyfriend?"

"If he'd been an old boyfriend, I would've seen a reaction from Sally when she passed him in the park." He picked up the coffee and took a sip.

"Did you get a decent look at the guy's face?"

"Not good enough for a police lineup, but if I saw him walking by, I know I could ID him."

"What's a police lineup?"

"I'll explain later."

"Maybe this will help," Betty said, walking over to the sink and opening the cupboard below. She stuck her hand up and inside it to take out a small package. Betty pulled out the contents and patiently began going through several photos. "There you are," she said and placed a picture in front of Johnson. "Is this the man?"

He looked down at the picture. The hair was different, but the shape of the head, nose and cheekbones were the same. Johnson looked at the image a bit longer, closed his eyes and thought back to the person he saw the night before. When he opened them again, he looked at the picture and put all the facial features in place. "That's him," he confirmed. "The DNA must have matched. Did the agency send that to you?"

Betty took the picture from him, placed it back in the package and tucked it into the cupboard. She didn't reply immediately and stalled by tightening her robe before sitting down at the table and reaching for her cup of coffee.

"I've got a contact. The agency will be sending you your copy shortly. What are we planning on doing?"

Johnson wasn't happy that Betty had received the information before him. He had, however, worked with and was well aware of how the "old boy" network operated. They looked after each other.

Betty made her way to the convenience store across from the coffee shop that Sally worked in. She stopped, faced the large window and looked at her reflection, her hands lifting to fuss with her hair, but her gaze was elsewhere. She'd picked out the Honda Element immediately. Johnson was right. The shape of the vehicle wasn't hard to miss. It had changed locations, and a man was now behind the wheel, not a woman. Betty made her way into the store, and a few minutes later was back outside with the daily paper in her hand. Stepping from the sidewalk to the road, she made her way over to the car on its front passenger side. The vehicle's windows were halfway down, and the doors locked. She slid her hand to the inside, pulled up on the lock, opened the door and slid into the vehicle. The man beside her, shocked, could only sputter, "Lady, you've got the wrong car!"

Betty's hand pulled out a compact weapon. Using the paper as a shield against onlookers, she levelled it at him and, without preamble, said, "You know what this is, don't you?"

Ivan's gaze went down and spotted the recognizable end of the weapon. His insides churned. It was from Midgard, he knew, easily concealable and totally silent. When the trigger was pulled, it would send out a pinpoint burst of energy and enter the body. From there, the charge would detect water and tissue and burst outward, turning his insides to a jellied mess, leaving the outer skin untouched. "I'm leaving," Ivan said without hesitation. "You can keep the car. Keys are in it."

Betty rammed the weapon into his ribs with her right hand. Her eyes narrowed, and her grip tightened. "I'd just as soon kill you here and now, but someone wants to talk to you. How about we go for a little drive, and I'll let you live?"

The car had been rumbling over the gravel roads west of the city for about ten kilometres. The two sat without speaking, other than Betty calmly giving directions when needed. Ivan's hands gripped the wheel tightly, the working end of the weapon Betty held still tightly rammed into his ribs. He took quick glances at the woman, trying to find a weakness he could exploit. There was none. Any chance of talking his way out of this was impossible. The car turned onto a dirt path that split a field into two halves. The vehicle went up a slight incline and then dropped into a gully. When they reached the bottom, Betty told Ivan, "Stop here." She took the keys from the ignition and unclipped his seatbelt.

No sooner was he released from the belt when his car door opened violently. A hand gripped the back of his shirt, yanking him from the driver's seat and into the wheat field. He caught a glimpse of a setting sun just before he felt an open hand whip across the side of his face. Instinctively, Ivan brought his hands up to the sides of his head to protect himself. The next time, the blow came from the front, and he fell onto his back. Ivan rolled to his side and was trying to get up when a boot connected firmly with his ribs. The blow knocked him back onto the ground, and he turned his head, trying to make sense of the two figures standing above him.

Johnson was looking down at him calmly. "Have I got your attention?"

Ivan stared at the two people, his mind racing, eyes locked wide open. He was sure his ribs were broken. Johnson bent over and wrenched him up by the collar of his shirt.

"I asked you a question. Do I have your attention?"

Ivan gasped out a painful, "Yes, yes."

Johnson stared at him for a silent moment and then released his grip, letting the man's body fall to the ground. In a slow, methodical voice, Johnson said, "Listen carefully. Don't move and just answer my questions. Who are you, and why are you following Sally?"

Ivan lay motionless on the ground, trying to breathe. He was about to bring his hand up to his face but remembered Johnson's command to remain still.

"I don't know what you're talking about," he finally said, spitting out blood as he spoke.

"Betty, I've had enough. Give me that thing. I'm going to turn his brain into jelly."

Ivan squirmed and managed to pull himself into a sitting position, his back against the vehicle, his brain slowly registering the name of the woman Johnson had called out to.

"Okay, okay," he said, shifting his gaze to Betty and staring at her, surprised. "You're younger than your pictures."

Betty's mouth twisted into a wry smile as she shook her head sadly from side to side. "My, my. Nice try," she said.

Ivan wiped at the blood on his face with his arm. "You're a bit of a legend."

Johnson put another piece of Betty's puzzle into place in his mind. Changing the subject, he repeated, "Answer my question. Why are you following Sally?"

When Ivan hesitated, Johnson immediately said, "You're

trying to run some bullshit answer through that head of yours." Johnson's foot lifted slightly and pressed itself squarely onto Ivan's hand. The man let out a scream as he felt the bones crushing.

"Last chance. Why are you following Sally?"

Johnson released his foot, and Ivan struggled to regain his composure as he pulled his hand back into his chest. He decided his life would be forfeit in any scenario and began to talk. Johnson asked the questions, and Betty pulled out a cellphone from her coat pocket to record the interrogation and take a picture of Ivan.

After all his questions had been answered, Johnson asked Betty, "You got anything to ask him?"

She shook her head. "No, we've got what we need. The agency will do a complete interrogation back home."

In front of them, a tear opened, and Johnson pulled Ivan to his feet.

Ivan, in a last desperate attempt, muttered, "One day, I'll find the two of you and gut you both like fish."

Johnson laughed and spat back, "I'll be waiting for you and anyone else they send. Have a nice trip." With that, he threw him into the brilliant tear, watching coolly as it swallowed him up.

"We can assume he's got some sort of tracker on him," Betty said. "The Rebels will know soon enough that he's back on Midgard."

"Then we'll have to move fast. Hey, look at this! We've got a ride now!" Johnson quipped when the tear had disappeared.

"Hmmm. Nothing fancy, but it'll do," Betty replied as they settled themselves into the car.

They had only gone about a kilometre before Johnson said, teasingly, "Hey legend, I'm hungry. How about you?"

Betty ignored the comment and looked out the window. She wasn't ready to provide Johnson with more details yet. The sun was almost down, she noted, and then said, "Yes, I am. Let's find somewhere to eat right after we check out these addresses."

"Chinese okay?"

"What's Chinese?"

Back at Special Projects, Ivan had arrived on all fours, dazed, hurt, and now, completely nauseous. He looked up around him, trying to focus. They could tell by his swollen, misshapen nose and face that he'd been beaten. Ann walked into the Destination area with the Security Detail. She stood back as they grabbed Ivan's arms and forced them behind his back, securing them with hand restraints. Ann stepped over to him, her arms folded across her chest as she locked eyes with him. "Ivan, nice to finally meet you. It appears you've run into a small problem while you were on Earth. It looks like their questioning techniques are a bit archaic."

Ivan cleared his throat and spit a lump of phlegm at her, hitting Ann's shirt between her breasts. It had barely landed when she responded with a fist to his jaw. Without missing a beat, she calmly said, "I also see you've learned some bad manners in your travels. We'll have to try and work those out of you. I think it's time for a quick scan to see where you've been and who you've been with. Don't worry. You won't feel a thing."

CHAPTER 33

Marie was in her apartment, putting the finishing touches on a plan for Sally. It was too bad they couldn't just kidnap the woman, everything would have been completed by now. They could have been home, and the Rebels would be extracting the information from her at this very moment. She was about to head out the door when her communicator pinged. Opening it, she read the message:

Urgent

A burst of Ivan's homing implant has been received on Midgard. Confirm his presence with you or relocate immediately. Suspect the agency may have detained him. Send SITREP when you can.

Marie calmly tore the message up and walked to the bathroom, flushing it down the toilet. She strolled to the window facing the front of the building and looked up and down the street. Not noticing anything out of the ordinary, she calmly walked back to the table, gathered up her belongings and then contacted Sonia.

"Move now," were the only words she needed to say. Marie then reached for a pencil, ripped a page from her notebook and wrote in block letters, "YOU'RE TOO LATE," before leaving the apartment.

Ann walked into the Interrogation I/C's office. "What did we get off of him?"

"His username is Ivan, but his real name is Richard Klein. Thirty years old, not married, no kids, no debt and was an average working-class guy. Raised in a middle-of-the-road family, no background in Rebel activity from his mother or father. He finished high school and got a job working textiles on the outer fringes. This is where we think he got recruited. He liked what the Rebels were about and joined them at age twenty-five. Nothing he has done or said is outstanding. As a matter of fact, he's a bit of a mama's boy, a real underachiever. I was rather disappointed when I read his report. I was hoping we'd have somebody we could go deep on, someone who's been involved in previous missions."

Ann was puzzled. "Why would they send him on a mission of this magnitude?"

"We're unsure, but I'm guessing this man was being used as a throwaway, someone they were willing for us to take. He doesn't know anything else," the interrogator replied. "Everything we've pulled from him is the usual lower echelon junk we already know. The two women on the mission are Marie and Sonia. Their boss was called Jack. Marie is in charge, and Sonia and Ivan were acting as a married couple." He then provided her with a description of Jack and both women. As Ann listened, she felt a chill go through her but did not react.

She leaned forward on his desk and asked, "Did we find the place they trained in?"

"Yes, ma'am, we did. We have overhead surveillance on it now."

"Good," she said, "make sure I get your full report ASAP. I have to let our man on the ground know all the immediate information."

"I will. I have to ask... is Betty Sharpe on the ground, on Earth? The scan says he was with her."

"I really have no idea, but I don't know how she could be," Ann said smoothly. "Go deeper on Ivan. You never know. Maybe we missed something."

"Will do, ma'am," he said as Ann turned and walked out of the office.

It was nightfall when Johnson and Betty closed in on the

two addresses that Ivan had given them during their interrogation. By then, however, both locations had been abandoned. Johnson immediately saw the note Marie had left and scanned the words quickly before tearing it up.

"Their Operations Centre must have picked up something when Ivan was returned and warned them," Johnson said.

"Sounds about right," Betty sighed. "I'm assuming that now they know how many of us from Midgard are here as well. They were probably watching when we came in through the door."

"Shit. They know there's only the two of us." Johnson thought for only a second before he turned to Betty. "We'll have to stay close. I've rented another apartment on the third floor of the building. I was using it as a safe house. You need to move in there. Tonight."

She nodded immediately. "I think that's a good idea."

They had no time to lose and immediately made their way out the door.

Ann sat behind her desk, just finishing up the results from the hits they had made on the Rebel's training and deployment area. Both places had been meticulously cleaned. Other than the DNA samples they had managed to retrieve from the cat, nothing significant had been found. She had an odd feeling that they were missing a few vital pieces of information, but it was late, and she needed to rest. She was about to shut down when her screen advised her of an incoming message from Johnson. "Display," she ordered, and the hologram in the centre of the table opened the message.

Ann,

Search for the other two Rebels has been unsuccessful. Their locales have been vacated and we are assuming they were aware of male's capture and return to Midgard. Possible compromise upon entering premises. To ensure her safety Betty will move closer to me.

All pertinent info gathered from Sally has been forwarded separately to Ops. Out.

She stared at the message, reading it a few times before closing it off.

Johnson hopped aboard the bus and was sitting in one of the rear seats, watching the streets fly by. There was something he had to do today before meeting Sally later. He reached up and pulled on the cord, signalling to the bus driver to let him off at the next stop. The bus braked to a halt, veering slightly to the left and then the right before stopping, passengers swaying in harmony with its movements. He stepped to the curb from the bus and looked at the boundary of the cemetery.

It was surrounded by a four-foot-high stone wall running to his front. The gate consisted of twisted wrought iron connected to two posts forming the entrance. The cemetery was marked by large, mature trees, indicating that it had been there a long time. Johnson walked through the gate and toward a stone building marked, "Grave Registry." He entered through the front door and was greeted by a short, older man who looked up from his desk and asked, "Can I help you?"

"Yes, I'm looking for the gravesites of Mr. and Mrs. Allan and Edna Johnson."

"Johnson, common name that. We've had a few of those. Let's see — Edna and Allan." He pulled open one of the drawers in the file cabinet that stood behind his desk and began looking through each record. "Right here," he said after a few moments. "Section O, Row 2. Wait, there appears to be another family member with them. Steve Johnson. Is that correct?"

Johnson, betraying nothing, simply replied, "That sounds about right."

The man continued, "They're at the very back of the cemetery. Go straight down the path that's outside this door. When you see section O, they'll be on your left. You'll find them easy enough."

Johnson followed the man's directions and, within a few moments, found himself standing in front of three tombstones placed beside each other. Standing at the foot of the graves, he regarded the dried flowers placed beside them and the names that were chiselled into the stone. He silently apologized for what had happened, and for the pain he must have caused them. Johnson shifted his gaze to the gravesite that was supposed to be his. The inscription read, "Gone from us, we know not where. We miss you." He could feel an unresolved, ignored emotion rising in his body and stifled it to maintain control. Walking over to his parents' tombstones, he bent over and touched the top of his father's stone. "I love you, Dad." He turned to his mother's stone and added, "I'm sorry I wasn't here for you when you passed. I'll come back soon." He stood back and spoke out loud. "I'm sorry I put you through all this." His head drooped, and he turned and left the cemetery.

Johnson walked to the coffee shop at six-thirty p.m., his completed assignment in hand for Sally to review. He had no difficulty finishing it. It had been sent off to Midgard, and they had done all of it, ensuring the contents were accurate and also tweaking her interest. He had felt not even a twinge of guilt. Making his way along 13th Avenue, he used his usual route. If the women were watching, they'd think he wasn't worried about being observed. He sat down on the bench outside the shop, picking up an old newspaper and perusing it while he waited for Sally.

At seven p.m., Sally walked out, turned and locked the door to the cafe. She saw Johnson sitting on the bench and said, "You're early. You must want to get this finished."

"Being early is just how I roll," Johnson replied with a grin. "I hate being late. Any idea where you'd like to go?"

"I thought we could walk up to the park and sit on one of the picnic tables by the pond."

"Sounds good. Have you had supper?" Johnson asked.

"No, but I have two sandwiches and two cans of soda with me," she said, holding up a bag.

"That's perfect. I'm glad you're not one of those women who never eat."

Sally laughed, "Are you kidding? The reason I work out is because I love to eat."

They headed up the street and found a seat at one of the picnic tables by the pond. They sat down, and Johnson handed her the proposed paper. She opened the report and started to read. It contained everything they had discussed. Her ideas on alternative energy sources were included, and he accurately voiced how the concept of wind and solar power was adequate but simplistic. He then described her idea of using electromagnetic torque for energy. As she read the final page, she looked at the bottom of the paper and found her name acknowledged as the contributor and concept person. She looked up at him with surprise. "This is very well presented, Steve. It has a maturity to it that I wasn't expecting and contains some intriguing arguments. Thanks for mentioning me. You don't have to do that."

"Thanks. But it was basically all your concepts and ideas. I haven't really had the time to develop my own," Johnson said, shrugging.

"Well, it's nice to be acknowledged for something," she said, digging into the bag. "Time for supper."

They sat in silence for a few moments, contentedly eating their sandwiches. Johnson finally turned to her and asked, "So how long have you been working at the coffee shop?"

"Oh, about a year and a bit now. It's not what I envisioned myself doing, but it's paying the bills for the moment."

"So why don't you do something else? Something that you want to do?"

She reflected before she spoke. "I would love to have pursued my previous work, but I've had some obstacles along the way that I haven't figured out how to deal with yet. When I moved here, I'd hoped things would have fallen into place, but they haven't moved in the direction I wanted. Now, time is slowly moving on, and I'm no further ahead than I was when I first came here."

"What kind of obstacles are you talking about?" Johnson asked.

"I don't really want to go into a lot of detail. Suffice to say there are a lot of organizations that would find themselves out of business if alternate sources of energy become the norm."

Johnson knew he was treading a thin line and had to bide his time before he asked any more questions. It was too soon to push her for more information, and he needed to gain her complete confidence. He simply replied by saying, "Companies have to learn that nothing stays the same and they have to change."

Switching the subject, as he suspected she would, she asked, "So why are you here? There are dozens of universities around the country, and you end up in Regina."

"Regina is a spot where I spent a bit of time growing up. I did one year of high school here before we moved, so I've always had a bit of a soft spot for the city. It has all the amenities, without the crush of crazy that happens in the larger places. The winter weather, though, leaves something to be desired."

Sally smiled. "I understand. The cold isn't for everyone."

"I still love the four seasons. I've spent some time in a few warmer climates and found I missed the changes. When the opportunity presented itself to come here and go to school, I took it. Mind you, as soon as winter comes blasting in, I just might regret that decision. We'll see how that turns out."

They ate in silence for a few moments, content to enjoy each other's company without forcing it. Sally fidgeted suddenly and then said quietly, "I should tell you. My family is in the oil business. It doesn't make good headlines when the daughter of the owner of the biggest oil company in Canada becomes an environmentalist."

"Well now, that might make for a very awkward Christmas dinner," he admitted.

"You have no idea," she laughed ruefully. "My father can get completely unhinged. I'd always hoped there could be a cooperative effort somewhere in the middle between us, but we've gone way past that now."

"Maybe not today or tomorrow but a few years down the road, Sally. I'm sure it'll work out for you."

"I suppose, but right now, the farther I stay away from him, the better I feel. You know, I could have gone along with my parents' plans for me, just live off their money until I find myself a man and get married. Then I'd be out of their way," she said.

"Is that what you wanted to do?" He asked with a surprised laugh.

"Never," she said grimly, looking away and shuddering slightly. "I could never compromise myself that much. I had to get away from what my father represents."

"You left the family?"

"Yup. I didn't just leave. I ran from the family, Steve," she admitted. "I had just enough savings to bring me to Regina and get a job at the coffee shop."

"You can do more. You've got the potential to do something big on your own. There's nothing wrong with working at a coffee shop. It's fine. But someday, when you're ready, you'll realize it's time to move on and do what needs to be done," Johnson said.

"Thanks. That's kind of you to say, but for now, it wouldn't be a good idea." She abruptly changed the subject by saying, "Let's finish up here and take a walk."

They finished their meal, packed everything up and continued walking through the park. As they spoke, Johnson could feel her opening. She talked about her upbringing as one of luxury and riches; private schools, exotic vacations and an overabundance of everything. He got the feeling that she felt ashamed of the extravagant lifestyle and of all the taking and no giving.

Sally and Johnson ended up outside a small English pub. Walking in, they settled themselves into a booth and ordered drinks. She appeared more comfortable in his company and he with her. Sally had skirted over the details of her life, but he already knew most of it from his briefings. Johnson also knew he had established common ground with his studies, and that was ninety percent of the battle. It was close to eleven o'clock before they decided to head for home. Stopping in front of her apartment, she pointed up and said, "I live in that apartment on the second floor." Johnson followed her arm and looked up at the balcony overlooking them as she said, "Thanks for the evening."

"Thanks for the picnic and for looking over my paper," he said, kissing her on the cheek. "I had a good time tonight. Can I see you again?"

She smiled. "I work mornings for the next week. I'll call you when I've reread the paper and made any corrections. Should only take me a day."

"Looking forward to your call." Johnson grinned. She walked into the building, and he waited until the lights turned on in her apartment before he turned and headed for home.

CHAPTER 34

TWENTY-FOUR HOURS PRIOR

The two women sat in the dark, binoculars around their necks, peering out of Marie's new apartment window watching the people coming and going. Marie had rented two separate apartments as an emergency measure. Her anticipation of complications had proven to be accurate. Her new accommodation provided an unobstructed view straight into the front door of her old place, and Sonia's was only a short distance away.

Marie stood up, stretched and looked cautiously out of the window, ensuring she would not be seen. The streetlights were finally on, illuminating the sidewalk. She had almost begun thinking that her plan was for naught when she caught sight of an old woman and young man making their way down the street. They paused momentarily in front of each building, looking hard at the house numbers. Marie moved her binoculars up to her eyes, focused on the two and urgently tapped Sonia's foot. "They're here."

Sonia brought her binoculars in line with Marie's and acknowledged, "I got them. Are you sure that's them? He looks too young."

"I got a firm description from the female agent at the cafe. She was surprised at how young he was too, but he knows the job and can handle himself. He took out three of our operators. Its got to be him."

They watched as Betty and Johnson walked up to the door, punched in the code and walked in. A few minutes later, a light came on in Marie's old apartment. Ten minutes later, the two had made their way back outside, Johnson's eyes searching up and down the street but finding nothing.

"Now we know what we're up against," Marie said. They continued to watch as Johnson cupped his hands over his eyes, blocking out the ambient light, and looked directly at their apartment. Despite knowing that they could not be seen, both women froze.

A moment passed before Sonia urgently whispered, "What do you think he's looking for?"

"You and me, sweetheart. These two are pretty good. They don't have the whole picture yet, and right now, they're angry. They feel like they've been had and are smart enough to assume they're being watched. Look at the way they're talking. See how Johnson just moved in front of the older lady? He's blocking any observer's view, so you can't see if she's looking for us."

Sonia asked, "Why would the agency send that old lady here?"

"I never thought I'd see her again," Marie suddenly said in astonishment. "Here's your history lesson for today. That old lady's name is Betty. She and her husband worked for the GIA and almost took down our whole organization over twenty years ago. We finally got the upper hand on one of my very first Operations. We sucked them into a kill zone and killed everyone, or so we thought. We looked through the dead, identified all of them, including her husband, but never found her. It was quiet for a while, but then, one-by-one, anyone involved in the ambush started going missing. In the end, there was no one left except the man that led the attack and me. One day we found him strapped to a chair with a noose around his neck. They say he was tortured before he died. She wasn't after information. She was after revenge. She was also sending a message, and that message was heard loud and clear throughout our organization. From that point on, that person you just called an old lady was and still is Number One on our hit list. She's still looking for me. That's how I learned to watch my back and cover my tracks."

Marie took a drink from her glass and continued. "We had

people follow her, but she turned it around and back-tracked them. She started showing up at their homes and their kids' schools. Soon nobody would touch her. She never seems to really care if she lives or dies and doesn't fear anything. In a way, I've grown to respect her — or at least her legend. Sure, she works for the GIA. But it's on her own terms, not theirs. She disappeared from our radar for quite some time. Years, in fact. And now, she's here. I wonder why."

Sonia watched as the two walked down the street and said, sarcastically, "Well, doesn't she sound terrific? I can't wait to meet her."

The two women exited the apartment and tracked Betty and Johnson from a distance. They then split up, Sonia staying well behind the two and Marie paralleling them one street over. Twenty minutes later, Sonia tucked herself down and watched as they entered a house through the front door, the light from the front room flickering on. Marie had continued for a short distance, staying in the shadows until she could move in behind a tall hedge.

Johnson had stood well back from the upstairs window, eyes scanning carefully out into the street. His eyes caught and fixed on the lone woman, and he smiled. Another piece of the puzzle had just been put into place. He waited until well after she'd left, set up a couple of lights on timers and then moved Betty over to his apartment. In a few days, he'd be back, checking the locks, doors and windows to see if anyone had entered.

On the walk back home, Sonia asked Marie, "So what's the plan now?"

"We'll lay low for the next few days but stay on track with our priority — Sally. Once we're sure they haven't detected us, you'll need to get close to her, make friends with her. Nothing pushy. I'll run some interference and look after the agency problem." The two women walked into the apartment and turned in for the night. Sonia would head for her new apartment in the morning.

Marie walked into her bedroom, stripped off her clothes and slid into bed but was unable to fall asleep for some time. Betty's presence had put a brand-new spin on this.

CHAPTER 35

*I*t *was now two days since Ivan's disappearance and night had fallen before Marie walked out of her apartment and down the back alley to Sonia's.* She wasn't happy about laying low, but experience had told her that, for now, it was the right thing to do. *Just a couple more days to let the heat cool down,* she thought. *Then we'll be back at it.*

A few blocks over, she walked up to the rear of a large apartment block. The back door had been left ajar for her, and she opened it, stepping through the entrance and taking the stairs to the second floor. She stopped at the fourth door on the left, listened for a moment and then tapped lightly on it. She heard a person approach and pause to look through the peephole on the other side. A moment later, the deadbolt clicked, and the door opened. Marie slipped inside the door quickly, Sonia closing and then locking it behind her. Making their way into the front room, Marie spotted an assortment of paper containers and plates of food on the coffee table.

"What have you been doing? What is all this?"

Sonia sat down on the sofa and picked up a plate of lasagna. "They don't have food duplicators here, and I'll be damned if I'm going to resort to learning how to cook. You can order it on the telephone, and they'll deliver it right to the door." She waved the plate at Marie. "They categorize their foods by ethnicity. This is Italian, not bad once you get by the smell of the garlic. There's lots. Do you want a plate?"

"No, it looks disgusting."

"Looks are deceiving. It's actually not bad."

Marie sat down on a side chair and commented, "You're watching television?"

"It's actually very entertaining. They seem to put a lot of emphasis on violence and comedy. Reality television is ridiculous. If people really act like that, it's no wonder they're so far behind. It does make the time go by rather quickly, though."

"I know it's been frustrating, waiting and hiding out. Two more days of this and then we'll be back out. We'll stick to the plan of you getting to know Sally. The other two, we just need to keep an eye on them. If they get in the way, we can deal with it at that time. I'm also working on another angle, but I have to put a few things in place first."

"Anything else?" Sonia asked.

"No, I just needed to get out, see how you're doing." She watched the television for a minute before commenting, "Looks like a lot of drivel."

"Oh, it is," Sonia replied. "Nothing but crap."

Marie got up and walked over to the door, Sonia following. As Marie unlocked the door, Sonia confirmed, "Just two more days?"

"Two more days."

It had been three days since Sally had gotten the paper from Johnson. She'd come home that night and placed it on the dining room table, and that's where it had sat. That evening, after supper and wiping the table clean, Sally finally picked up the folder. She had been oddly reluctant to start in on it. Her time with Steve, arguing and discussing options left her feeling guilty and envious about leaving her past and research behind. *How did he do this? Who is this guy?* He was so young and reminded her of when she had possessed that fire, that spark of ambition. She was still deathly afraid of her father, but her time with Steve made her realize where her real interests lay. And it wasn't working in a coffee shop for the rest of her life. She looked at the paper again and said, "Tonight, I get into this."

As she read, she couldn't help but think of her own research and what she'd given up. All the hard work and long hours that she and her colleagues had put in trying to invent something. Something that had the potential to change the way the world dealt with energy. Her mind drifted away from the paper. *It wouldn't have changed things that quickly. It would still be years before we gave up on anything fossil,* she argued with herself, making excuses. Another voice in her head cut in, saying, *At least you would have done something. Now someone else must take up the task. You're a quitter,* it finished bluntly.

She slid back in her chair, placing her hands over her face and looked up at the ceiling. Her father had terrified her when he burned down the old place, and she didn't think she could go through that again. Even now, she could clearly recall the flames leaping high into the air while heat tinged her skin. Resolutely breathing in, Sally sighed and sat back up, looking again at Johnson's paper, then picked it up and continued reading. She started slowly, reading line by line out loud. Sally's mind began working out the details and concepts Johnson had put forth. The paper was doing Steve's job for him, not changing everything at once, just slowly pulling her back to what she had always loved to do.

Johnson walked into the coffee shop and hung his jacket over a chair. He liked the spot because he could look out the front window and keep his back to the wall. Spotting Sally, he got up and walked over to the counter, smiling. "What's new with you?"

She reached down under the counter, taking out a folder and handing it to him. "You take good notes. I didn't change a thing."

"Glad you liked it. Could I get a coffee? Black, please?"

"I'll bring it to you. Save me a chair. I'm on my break in a minute."

Johnson paid for the coffee, then walked back to the table, picking up a paper along the way. A short while later, Sally came up and, setting down his coffee, said, "I've got an idea to float by you. Do you mind?"

"I'm listening," he said.

"I've been here for just over a year and a half. When I quit my research, I never wanted anything to do with it again. Then you came along, and we talk a bit, and you write this paper. It was when I was going over it that I realized I still need to be involved with developing something different. I think I might try holding a couple of community think tanks on alternate energy."

Johnson blinked in surprise. "Well, that's great! Do you have a plan yet?"

"My boss says I can use the shop on Thursday nights for talks to gather some interest. I'll advertise on the bulletin board, and the city paper offers free advertising for community events, so I'll place an ad in there as well. I have to tell you I've been through this before."

"I figured you'd had some experience," he said.

"I have, but there's a lot more to it." She hesitated before continuing. "I had a company that was experimenting in the field of power generation. We were developing power generators, and things were going well. The initial concept could potentially produce a massive amount of power with minimal resources."

Johnson said, "So what happened? Why did you stop?"

"I told you about my dad and his company. When I spoke with him about our initial success, I expected him to be happy for me, but he wasn't. He blew up. I think he viewed the empire he built from the ground up as being destroyed by his daughter. One day just after that, when we were still in the building, someone set fire to the place. Everything was destroyed, and the people that worked with me could have been killed. I can't prove he was involved, but I knew he was responsible. I warned everyone that I worked with, went home, packed a few items and ended up here."

"What do you think will happen when he finds out you've started again?"

"I don't really know, but I'm going to be concentrating only on renewable energy sources, specifically solar and wind for now. Raising awareness, that sort of thing. It's a start and one that has already been accepted into society. It's been a while now, and I've had no communication with either my mom or dad. Even if he finds out, he'll know I'm not experimenting with anything new, so I'm not worried. I still want to see this through." She fell silent and looked away, her mind elsewhere.

"I'll help."

She turned back to him. "Thank you! I'm going to get started right away with a few phone calls."

He nodded and watched as she went back to her job. It was the first step in the right direction.

Over the next week, he helped her organize the details for the first meeting. While they were at the newspaper office, a reporter happened to listen in when they were placing their ad. He found out who Sally was and had an impromptu interview with her before promising to attend.

After the deep scan on Ivan, the agency had pictures of the two women they found in his memory forwarded to Johnson. Both had long hair, one brunette, one blonde, both were in decent physical condition. They had no discerning physical marks, and everything was average, nondescript. Johnson slid the images over to Betty and said, "Recognize either of these two?"

She looked at Sonia's picture and shook her head no but hesitated on Marie, deciding not to tell Johnson who the woman was. "She looks familiar, but I'm not sure why." *There you are,* she thought grimly. *After all these years, I've finally found you.*

"At least now we have a good description," Johnson said.

Johnson was out in the morning again, trying to spot the two women. By noon, he stopped his search and determined that they could have quickly moved on, cut their hair and changed their appearance. He knew they hadn't totally disappeared.

Ivan's car had been left on the street, was ticketed and eventually towed away. Betty's old house had been searched, but Johnson couldn't tell if it was by the two women or the landlord. A few days after he had moved Betty, he walked past the house to check for break-ins but found the landlord instead. He had come by because the neighbours told him Betty was seen moving out. He found the house cleaned out and empty, with no forced entry. Johnson hit dry hole after dry hole, and it was evident that the two women had gone underground. He would have to be resigned to waiting. They would eventually have to surface if they wanted what Sally had.

CHAPTER 36

*M*arie and Sonia went gone back to Betty's house the next day and spotted a man inspecting it. The two asked if he was the landlord and if the place was for rent. He said yes, but they would have to wait until the end of July. He spoke freely, seizing the chance that these two might be potential renters for him. The previous tenant, he said, had paid in full until then. He handed the two women his card, telling them to call him in two weeks. They walked out through the back yard and into the alleyway.

Marie waited until they were well away from the yard and then said, "You know what this means?"

"I don't know. Maybe the old woman got recalled?"

"No. Johnson picked us up while we were following them," Marie said.

"How did they possibly see us? We were split up. I was so far back; I could hardly see them."

Marie continued, her mind running over the events of that night. "They picked something out."

"There were other people out walking about. It wasn't like we were the only ones," Sonia said, defensively.

"I think it's time for us to change our looks a bit. A haircut, new colour, clothes, everything. Completely opposite of what we are now." Sonia nodded, and the two split up, each going their own separate ways.

The next day, Marie sat in her kitchen, sipping a cup of tea. Her hair, once long and thick, was now gone. She'd cut it short, except for the spiked-up top, and it was dyed black. Her clothes, once a bit loose and flowing, were now more form-fitting, her blouse a little more revealing. The only thing she hadn't changed was her shoes. They had to stay the same. *Comfort over fashion,* she thought smugly.

She reached over and picked up a pen and paper; it was time to report in. She had no difficulty facing any kind of physical threat. She thrived in combat conditions and accepted any kind of challenge. Except for this. She dreaded explaining in words how the mission was going. She could have made the job easier by writing a little each day, but she couldn't do it. Instead, she always waited until the last minute of the last day a report was due. Her excuse for the delay in reporting was legitimate. Ivan's capture, the change in their living arrangements and discovering that Betty was involved allowed her little time for paperwork. But time had now run out, and she knew her HQ wanted an update on what was happening.

Taking in a deep breath, she gave in to the inevitable and started to write. She purged the information from her brain, her hand moving from line to line. When she finished, she reread the copy and, happy with the result, signed and sent it off. An hour later, her HQ sent their response.

Report received. Regrettable loss of team member. Damage done will be negligible if protocols are followed. Replacement team member not approved. Your mission will continue. Success is expected.

Jack

Marie reread the message, tore it to pieces, then disposed of it. It was apparent to her that Ivan was the throwaway. They had used him to try and bring Johnson, and whomever else was here, out in the open. It had worked, although a little sooner in the mission than expected. Now, however, augmentation of the team was denied, and she was a person down. She wanted to do the job on her own but realized that extra team members made the mission easier. *Perhaps,* she thought, *I can find someone here who could help me.*

Sonia sat reading the notes she had put together on Sally. Marie ordered her to get closer to the woman, and she could do that. She just needed to see what they had in common. Her eyes skimmed the pages in front of her. Every twenty-four-hour period of surveillance was recorded, written in a sequence of date, time and place. The idea came to her after a few moments of review. Sally worked out every morning in the park, and that would be her way in.

The next morning, Sonia warmed up and jogged to the park where Sally usually trained. Approaching it, she could see several groups moving about but went past them, heading to the one she knew Sally was in. She picked her out among the others and jogged over, asking, "Can I join in?"

Sally said, "Of course! The more, the merrier. Our instructor was just waiting for a few more people to arrive, and then we'll start."

"Thanks," Sonia said, finding a spot and stretching herself out while scanning through the group of people. She was looking for Johnson and was surprised when she didn't see him. Sonia was sure that he would have been close by.

The instructor moved to the front, getting the group's attention and began a warmup. For the next hour, he put them through a never-ending onslaught of bodyweight exercises combined with wind sprints. After the cooldown, Sonia made her way over to Sally and said, "Thanks for letting me join in. Do I owe any credits to anyone?"

Sally was puzzled. "Credits?"

"Sorry, I mean money."

"Anyone who has the energy to join can. No charge. The instructor shows up three times a week as a community service. On the off days, we alternate as leaders and run ourselves," Sally explained.

"Well, I'll be around for a while," Sonia answered. "If you need help with anything, I can do that."

"Thanks. I'm Sally, by the way. Any experience as a trainer? You look to be in great shape," she asked, holding out her hand

and shaking Sonia's.

"Janice," she said, using the first name that came into her head. "Thanks, I like to work out but not enough to train others. I've got a question...I've just come into Regina this week. Is there a decent coffee shop in this town?"

"You're asking the right person. I work in a coffee shop. In my humble opinion, we do a great job. Go straight down 13th Avenue till you hit Albert Street. We're on the left corner as you come down. We open at six in the morning and close at six-ish at night. Maybe I'll see you there?"

"Probably. Thanks, I'll have to try it out," Sonia replied and, waving a short goodbye, turned to thank the instructor.

Johnson walked down Broad Street, stopping outside the second-hand bookstore. He tried to look through the barrage of advertisements that plastered the window, one of them claiming, "If I don't have it, it can't be found." *Looks like I'm in the right place,* he said to himself, walking in through the door. He pulled a list of required textbooks from his pocket and gazed confusingly at the long lines of shelves and stacks of books crammed into every corner. *How am I going to find anything in here?* He thought.

A voice from behind the counter asked, "Can I help you?"

The man greeting him was in his mid-forties, balding, with glasses perched at the end of his nose. His plaid shirt was neatly tucked into a pair of faded jeans, his round belly straining the buttons of the shirt.

Johnson replied, "I've got uni classes this fall and thought I'd get the books now if I can." He handed the man his list.

The clerk moved his eyes down the paper, read the titles under his breath and then nodded. "I can help you with all of them. $150 bucks, cash only. You okay with that?"

"No problem," Johnson said.

The man continued, "Give me an hour. Remember, $150 cash."

"An hour," Johnson repeated and was about to turn away

before he spotted one of Sally's posters on the community bulletin board beside the counter. "What do you think of this?"

"I was on the fence, but my wife and one of my coworkers are going, so I'll come along. I heard she has some experience in that field, so we'll have to see how she makes out."

"It does sound promising," Johnson agreed. "Okay, see you in an hour." He walked out the door, found a bank and withdrew the money for the books. Finding an outdoor cafe, he purchased a drink and then passed the hour reading a newspaper someone had conveniently left behind.

Marie was watching him from a distance across the street. She had seen Johnson walk into the old bookstore and then over to the cafe, where he had sat for the last hour. *His life was boring,* she thought. A person needed to spice things up a bit, go out, have some fun and meet some people. She'd watched him the other day as he walked out of the coffee shop where Sally worked and then seen him again the next morning as he walked in for his morning coffee. Everything with this guy was routine. Where he sat, what he wore, how long he stayed and, of course, what he always ordered. *Routine, routine, routine,* she thought. *It'll get you killed you every time.*

It was just after six p.m. on 26 June, and Sally's first meeting would be starting soon. Johnson had arrived early, anticipating that she would need some help setting up.

"Well, hello," she said, as he walked through the door.

"Hi there. So, are you all set?"

"Yes and no. I've done this plenty of times before, but it's been a while. I suppose the nerves are a bit on edge," she admitted.

"What can I do for you?"

She handed him a floor plan and said, "Could you arrange the room for me?"

"Sure," he said, and got to work, organizing the chairs and tables.

Twenty minutes later, Sally walked over and said, "Looks good. Thanks."

Johnson found a seat at the back of the room and sat down. The creak of the door was constant now as people wandered into the coffee shop. The bookstore clerk came in with his companions, the reporter they had met when placing the ad in the paper, and then behind them a smaller woman. Walking over to Sally, the woman shook her hand in greeting as they began talking and then broke out into laughter. She took a seat near the front as people continued to enter, filling the room to capacity.

At seven o'clock, the meeting started. Sally welcomed everyone and then dived directly into the topics. She dealt explicitly with the need to continue to expand solar-powered energy. Her company, when it had first been developed, had experimented with several more efficient, effective methods of capturing that energy. She introduced the first speaker, a specialist on solar power who had developed a panel half the size of current models and could produce five times the amount of energy. The group grew animated, asking questions, voicing opinions and then examined a model of the new solar panel.

Johnson was pleased with the direction that the meeting had gone. It was an excellent start for Sally. She took the last spot of the night and, when she was finished, gave them the time and agenda for the next meeting, thanking her speakers and wishing them a good night. Johnson waited for the room to thin out and then began moving chairs and tables back to their original positions. Sally joined him after a few minutes, the two of them working quietly and efficiently. The woman he'd seen earlier with Sally walked over to them. Sally greeted her and called to Johnson. "Steve, I'd like you to meet Janice. Janice, Steve will be going to university here this year. His major will be in environmental science."

Janice stuck out her hand casually and said, "Nice to meet you, Steve. I heard you helped convince Sally to set up this meeting."

Johnson shook her hand and said, "Nice to meet you too. I can't take all the credit, honestly. Sally just needed to see how people like me were going to screw this world up real soon if we were handling it on our own. She had to jump back in before we messed it up. I'm sorry, it was very nice to meet you, but I need to finish up and be on my way."

He left the two of them to talk and took a moment to look back at Janice. She was attractive, with sharp cheekbones and large, almond-shaped brown eyes. She was average height, about 5 foot 6 inches, he estimated, with straight auburn hair that fell to just below her ears. She had a slim, athletic build that she tried to obscure with a bulky sweater but failed. Johnson thought back to the images they had retrieved from Ivan's memory and his recollection of the profile he had spotted outside Betty's house. When he looked at her, he could see the blurred lines of the image slowly fill into the face in front of him.

Janice was on her way out the door when she stopped and turned to Sally. "Will I see you tomorrow morning in the park?" he heard her ask.

"I'll be there," Sally said and waved a friendly goodbye.

Johnson began helping her straighten up her collection of leftover pamphlets and casually said, "I've never seen her before. You two been friends for a while?"

"No, I just met her a few days ago at one of our workout classes in the park. After class, she asked me if I knew of a good coffee shop, and I pointed her in our direction. Nice lady, funny as hell. I think she comes from a small town, though. She says the air here stinks and constantly comments on the noise."

The two finished reorganizing the shop and then locked up. Johnson walked her to her apartment. "Good job tonight, Sally. Next week will be even better."

"Yes, it will," she said. "Would you like to come up for a drink?"

He hesitated for a moment as he looked into her eyes but

knew it would be a mistake for both of them. Besides, although his body was younger, he was still a middle-aged man, and it felt wrong. "I would love to, but I've got an early morning tomorrow. Maybe next time."

Disappointment flashed briefly in her eyes, but she recovered and gave him a quick hug good night. She felt warm and fit snugly in his arms, but he kept the embrace short and friendly, only kissing her on the cheek before they parted, and he watched the door close behind her.

Back at his apartment, he opened the door and quietly walked into the room. He went into the kitchen and was about to turn on a light when he heard a short knock on his apartment door. Checking the peephole, he saw Betty standing in the hallway and opened the door to let her in.

"How did it go?" she asked as soon as the door closed.

"All according to plan," he said.

"Any new faces?"

Johnson walked over to the table, opened the drawer and took out the two pictures.

"I think I met this one tonight," he said as he handed her the picture of Sonia.

CHAPTER 37

*I*t was the First of July, and Johnson had been back on Earth for a month. Sally was on track and kept busy with endless meetings within the communities. She had also contacted solar and wind power companies and was actively pursuing them for investment. She still worked at the coffee shop because the rent had to be paid, and a woman had to eat.

Marie and Sonia were busy watching and wondering when a new alternative energy machine would be produced. Marie was angry and more than a little frustrated. From the meeting, she had determined there would be nothing worth taking for at least a couple of years. She was sure they had not come at the right time — there was never any kind of mention about a machine that could produce an alternate source of energy. If it was still in the preliminary stages of development, it would take at least two years for Sally to turn research into a working prototype.

It was Sunday morning, and Betty had nothing pressing to do. Once the breakfast dishes were cleared up, she leaned up against the counter, looked outside and sipped her coffee. It was going to be a good day. Regina was celebrating Canada Day, and all sorts of activities were planned throughout the city. Midgard had its own celebrations centred around the revolution's end, and she looked forward to comparing the two. Betty made her way to one of the kitchen drawers, taking out the photos of the two women and setting them down. Her eyes scanned them carefully, and she took in as much detail as she could. When she was finished, Betty picked them up and placed them back in the drawer. She would never forget the first woman. The other one, the one that Johnson thought he'd met at the cafe, was a stranger to her. Betty finished her coffee, threw on a light sweater and stuffed her weapon into her purse. The plan today was to first walk around Marie's old apartment to see what she could find.

Stepping out the back entrance of her apartment, Betty looked in all directions and then headed to the Rebel's old residence. She approached from the opposite direction this time and stopped a distance away to study the area before getting closer.

Both she and Johnson had known they'd been observed the night they entered the building, and she wanted to determine from where. The houses and other apartments that lined the street were automatically dismissed. They had too many trees out in front for proper observation. The other units were set at the wrong angle. It was the apartment across the street that drew her attention that night and did so again now. It was simple and something that she probably would have done herself. *Hide in plain sight and watch everyone looking for you*, she thought, laughing. *They must have had a great time watching us and then following us back home.*

Satisfied with her conclusions, she walked toward Sally's place, looking for the answers to three questions. How long would it take to walk there, what was the best route and where were the best observation points for the Rebels? Ivan said they'd used the park to watch Sally, either sitting in the car or on a bench. Betty walked to the park, finding a few vantage points and sat down at one, watching Sally's front door. She was hoping to catch sight of at least one of the women. Betty wanted to be close enough to see who the person was but far enough away to observe without being noticed. Thirty minutes later, with nothing to show for her efforts, she called it off. Betty began walking to the parade route on 13th Avenue, where more and more people started to join her. She found a high spot to stand in, a stairway leading up to a shop door with a landing at the top.

Betty walked up the steps and stopped, looking over the crowd to her front. Other spectators soon recognized the excellent vantage point and gathered around and below her. Soon the floats and fire trucks were passing by, the Shriners were on motorcycles, driving in circles and marching bands, all in step, were knocking out "Oh Canada" and Queen's "We Will Rock You."

The crowd was in constant flux, thinning out at times and then burgeoning to standing room only. Betty watched as the floats slowed to almost a stop and suddenly noticed a woman walk past her, stop and then walk back past her again. Out of all the people she had seen that day, this one stuck out. Physical descriptions may have provided more information, but hair length and colour could be changed. What couldn't be disguised was build and height, and Betty knew exactly who this was. She continued to watch as the woman mingled with the crowd, making small talk with a few people, then moving on.

Betty tapped the man to her front, said, "Excuse me," and made her way down the steps before moving into the crowd. She looked up to where she'd last seen the woman and spotted her immediately, walking perhaps ten metres ahead of her. Betty followed her, stopping when she stopped, moving when she moved. When the woman walked up to a street vendor, Betty closed the distance.

The vendor acknowledged the woman by asking, "What can I get you?"

"I'll have a sausage with onion and hot peppers and a Diet Coke," she answered.

Betty instantaneously recognized the voice. It was a voice that had been recorded and listened to a hundred, if not a thousand, times. It belonged to Marie, one of the Rebels in the raid that had killed her husband. The woman had left a recording for Betty years before, mocking her husband, Betty and the GIA. She slid into the cover of the crowd, four metres from Marie, and watched her as she was handed the food and paid for it, then sat down at a table set up beside the vendor. Her fury had started slowly at first, oozing out like tendrils of black smoke. Nothing alarming, nothing she couldn't control. Gradually, however, she began to feel her heart begin to beat faster, a burning rage inside her was building and bubbling like a cauldron. Betty reached into the purse, wrapping her hand around the pistol grip of the weapon. Her vision was focused on Marie's face as she chewed on the last piece of sausage and downed the Coke.

Filled with loathing and hate she had not felt for years, Betty slid the weapon out of her purse and under her shirt. The weapon would allow her to kill this excuse for a woman from where she was, without a sound and without discovery. Marie would simply fall face-first into the sidewalk. Betty levelled the weapon, waiting for a clear path. A moment later, there it was. She had just switched the safety off and tightened her grip on the trigger when a man suddenly stepped in front of her and blocked the clear shot.

Realizing she had blown her chance, she returned the weapon into her purse. The man took Marie's hand, pulling her to her feet, and Betty watched helplessly as the two walked off into the crowd. The last float passed by, and she was still standing, staring across the street. Her body was reluctant to let go of the adrenaline flowing through it, and Betty had to mentally calm herself down before beginning her walk home. In her mind, she could hear her husband's voice, "It's okay, baby. It's okay. Next time."

CHAPTER 38

That same day, Johnson left the apartment and walked up the street toward his brother's house. He'd put a lot of thought into this moment. He agonized between the need to see his family again and knowing that they could be in danger if the Rebels found out about them. Although his brother, Dave, had been a detective and was capable of handling himself in dangerous situations, it was still a risk that could be avoided. He weighed the consequences of watching from afar or actually meeting and talking with him. In the end, the need to see and reconnect with his family won. His next struggle was how he could meet Dave again and what he would say to him. Johnson had to find a way to convince Dave that he was, indeed, his brother. None of the solutions he had come up with seemed feasible. He knew nothing he could say would sound logical, so he decided to head over to his brother's house and just talk.

He walked up to the door, pressed the doorbell and waited patiently. He could hear the pulse of the bell on the inside, but there was no answer. Walking back down the steps from the front door, he spotted the neighbour. "Excuse me, sir, can you tell me if Mr. Johnson is around?"

The man rose slightly from his gardening, turned and glanced at Johnson. "And you are...?"

Johnson said, "I'm Steve. My father and Mr. Johnson were friends some time ago. I'm going to university here now and was stopping by to say hi."

"Nice to meet you, Steve. Where's the family now?"

"They settled in Calgary. I got in a few weeks ago, just getting settled before the fall semester," Johnson lied smoothly.

"Ahh, I hope your schooling goes well, then. You just missed

Dave. He goes to the cemetery every Sunday. If you miss him there, he stops in for a beer at the Jolly Roger, a bar fifteen minutes north of the cemetery. Do you know it?"

"I can find both places," Johnson replied. "Thanks."

He soon found himself walking down the familiar centre lane at the cemetery, heading to the back of the grounds. Getting closer to the family plot, he noticed a lone figure sitting on the bench, facing the tombstones. He slowed his walk and saw a fresh bouquet of flowers on each site. The man on the bench heard him coming and turned, watching him quietly for a moment before asking, "Can I help you?"

The man was older but had aged well, with only a slightly receding hairline, grey hair and laugh lines around his eyes and mouth. The faint scar above his eye was the giveaway as to who he was. Johnson knew it well. He had been there the day it happened. His thoughts ran in a hundred different directions. He suddenly realized how much he had missed his older brother, their talks and their friendship. He had lost all those years of life with him, he had missed becoming an uncle, he had missed his sage advice. But he couldn't tell him who he was right away. He didn't have the heart to do it. "No, sir, I was looking for someone else back here. Thought it might be them, but I guess not."

"It's a big place," Dave replied, "and easy to get turned around."

"It is that. Do you mind if I sit for a while?" Johnson asked.

"Sit yourself down, son," Dave said, as he patted the seat beside him before taking a long look at him. His face suddenly showed confusion and shock, and he pushed himself away from Johnson to look at him a little more closely. "Jesus," he said hesitantly, "you look familiar. My god, you look like my brother."

Johnson was unwilling to clarify his identity immediately and turned his attention to the tombstones. "Don't think so. I just got into town," Johnson said. He could feel Dave automatically revert into police mode, judging, calculating, observing his every move.

Not believing a word of what Johnson was saying, Dave simply replied, "Oh, I'm sorry." He shifted himself even farther away from Johnson, straightened his back and continued as if nothing were out of place. He tried to change the subject. "What are you in town for? Visiting anyone?"

Johnson knew that he could speak the truth. "Just visiting some relatives. How about you? Who are you visiting here?"

Dave hesitated. His cop instincts were now on high alert. He was unsure about speaking to someone who was obviously lying to him. In the end, he decided that by telling him, he would eventually find out more about this familiar stranger. "My mother and father, they passed a few years ago. My brother, too, although I guess technically, he isn't here."

Johnson asked, "Not here?"

"Well, we never got him back. As a matter of fact, they never found him. We placed some personal belongings in a box, had a funeral, said our good-byes and sent him off."

"Sorry to hear that," Johnson said, respectfully. "What happened?"

"He was in the Military, always away in some other country, trying to clean up messes other people started. They said they were out on a quick mission. They hit stronger resistance than anticipated, and some of his men got caught up in it. He went in to help and never made it back. Could be the enemy took him and dumped him somewhere. They looked everywhere, couldn't find a trace. Ain't that some crazy shit?"

Johnson looked down at the ground before agreeing, "That is crazy."

"Yup. And not a trace," Dave repeated softly before continuing, "but they also said it was over quickly for him. That was good for us to hear, but how could they be sure of that if they couldn't find him? There was even a report from one of the prisoners saying they'd seen a bright light and that he'd disappeared into it." He then pointed at Steve's gravesite. "That's him there."

Johnson turned his head, looking silently toward the site.

Dave continued reminiscing. "My mother and father had hoped he was still alive, but over the years, they came to accept the fact that he was gone. It was easier for my father to move on, but I think my mother never fully accepted it. It's hard when you lose something that was part of you, and children aren't supposed to die before their parents. But all that happened a long time ago." Looking silently at the stones for a few seconds, he finally said, "My name's Dave Johnson, by the way. And you are...?"

Johnson fought with himself before saying the words. He knew this would be a pivotal decision to make because once the words were spoken, there was no going back. He faltered for a moment, turned his head and looked directly into Dave's eyes. "My name is Steve, Steve Johnson."

Dave barked a short, harsh laugh. "Bullshit!" His gaze, however, sharpened on Johnson's features, and he looked at him again with a penetrating eye. He suddenly knew there was much more to all of this. His mind registered that this meeting had not been a coincidence. *What the hell is going on?* He thought.

Johnson knew exactly what his brother was thinking but continued with his story. "The man they captured told the truth when he said he saw me get pulled into a light. That's what happened. I'm your brother."

"I've had enough. Time to leave. I feel a scam coming on. What are you after? Money?"

Johnson could hear Dave's voice rising in anger. "No scam, just the truth," he replied calmly.

Dave stood up swiftly but then swayed slightly, struggling before regaining his balance and walking away. Johnson stood up with him and said, "Look, I understand. Just give me a few minutes of your time. If you want to leave after that and never talk to me again, fine, no problem, but please, just listen."

Dave halted. Johnson noted his brother's struggle for balance and was concerned, although the man's six-foot frame had aged little. He recognized the stubborn stance, the body language. Now was the time to provide Dave with the proof before his brother had the chance to respond by walking away. Dave answered with a stony expression. "I don't know why I should."

"There are a few things that only you and I know. That scar above your eye, for one. We were outside, and Mom and Dad were away. You were seventeen, and I was seven. We were playing street hockey. You took the ball away from me, and I high-sticked you in the face. There was blood everywhere, and we thought Mom would be pissed. You sat on the steps outside and told me to get you some ice and a towel. You placed it over the cut, told me to get your car keys, and we drove to Emergency. You had one hand on the wheel, one hand over the cut. I cried the whole way, and you told me it was okay. I remember you got nine stitches."

Dave's hand slowly went up to the scar on his face as his fingers ran the length of it, but he said nothing.

Johnson continued, "We had a crawl space under the house. I would go down and hide the toys that I wanted no one else to touch. I would pull them out of their box and play with them under the house. One day you found me down there. Do you remember what you said to me, Dave? You said, 'Your secret is good with me.'"

Dave looked confused. He didn't know if he could accept this. He knew the words were real. It had only been the two of them there a lifetime ago, but he still couldn't believe this young man was his baby brother. Things like this could never happen. It was impossible. "Your time's up. I need a beer. Be seeing ya."

Desperately now, Johnson said, "I've kept your secret about Allison."

Dave's mouth dropped open in surprise. He hadn't heard that name in years.

Johnson continued relentlessly. "You were supposed to be babysitting me for the night while mom and dad were out. You sent me to bed early, and I was pissed. I heard the back door open and snuck downstairs. You and Allison were on the couch, and I asked you what you were doing. You bribed me with a bag of chips and a coke and let me stay up to watch television downstairs until midnight. I had to promise never to say a word. I had to say *your secret is good with me*. Oh yeah, mom also told me you had to wear your shoes on the wrong feet until you were five because you were slightly pigeon-toed."

Dave was shocked by Johnson's words. He hadn't thought of that night in years. No one except Allison and his brother knew about that embarrassing incident. This man was confusing him and rightly so. Here was a guy claiming to be his brother, who knew some of his family and boyhood secrets, but could that really mean anything at all? Besides, it didn't make any sense. This young man was precisely that — young. The real Steve would have been in his sixties. But there was something authentic about him: the face, the voice, the mannerisms. It was all there, but how? The detective in him would not allow him to listen to anything more, but that same detective knew that there were truths to what this man was saying.

"It's time for me to go," Dave said roughly and began walking away. "I like a good story. You're welcome to join me if you like."

"Where to?"

"The Jolly Roger. It's a small bar just north of here. One beer, then home," he said.

"Sounds good."

They walked over to Dave's car and drove in silence to the Jolly Roger. The bar was adjoined to a hotel on what used to be the main thoroughfare in the city. It looked like it had been built a hundred years ago. The signage on the front needed a paint job, and the cement stucco was cracked and needed repair. It was the kind of place you stopped at after a long drive to sleep, eat and grab a beer. They walked in through the back door, Johnson's eyes taking a moment to adjust to the darkness after spending the day out in the sunshine. As they entered, he could smell the carpets, full of stale beer and whiskey and the odour of the wallpaper saturated with nicotine. They sat down at one of the round tables as the barmaid came over.

She was a woman in her fifties, Johnson guessed, with brassy blonde, chin-length hair and a generous bust line. She obviously knew Dave well, as she greeted him cheerfully. "Hi, Dave. What will it be?"

Dave smiled at her. "Hi, Becky. A couple of Blue, please."

"Coming right up," Becky responded, wiping down the table and then leaving to pick up their order.

Johnson scanned the clientele as he and Dave waited for their drinks. They were a quiet bunch. They didn't appear to care one way or another what you were up to, as long as you kept it to yourself. It was the type of place where you minded your own business because if you didn't, it could easily be beaten into you.

Becky returned, placing two foamy beer mugs on the table. Johnson paid for the drinks and gave her a hefty tip to go with it.

"I'm having a hard time believing what you told me, but for some reason, I'm willing to keep listening. How about you try to explain to me where you've been for over twenty years? What happened to you?"

Johnson took a long swig of the cold drink, wiped the foam from his top lip and began his story. He watched his brother's face go through a full range of emotions from disbelief and then wonder. Johnson started with how the Military Operation had gone down. He talked about being wounded, what happened when he was lifted into the light, and what he remembered learning in Stasis and at the Medical Centre.

Dave interrupted numerous times to get specific details and Johnson provided him with as much as he could. Dave decided to go along with everything he was being told to see if he could flesh out any inconsistencies. He asked Johnson when it was that he realized that he was on another world. Johnson recalled his first walk outside the Medical Centre, gazing up at a different coloured sun, the two moons and looking at the bright stars that shone even in daylight. Johnson continued, explaining the healing process that had left him young and healthy again. He consciously avoided any references to the exact reasons he had returned to Earth and said nothing about the GIA. Johnson fell silent then, embarrassed. Why would anyone believe a story like that? He certainly wouldn't.

Dave picked up his beer and took a long sip. Philosophically, he said, "I wish they had a medical facility like that here." He put down his mug and said, "I've just been diagnosed with cancer. It's in my brain, fairly aggressive. At first, the doctors thought they could remove the tumour, but now they say they can't. They figure I've got about six months left in me, only two of them will be good. The last few months, I imagine, will be ugly. I wanted to go out on my own terms, without pain."

Johnson was stunned and filled with grief at the news. Everything fell into place now as he remembered seeing Dave struggle with his balance upon standing. He recalled Ann telling him it wasn't advisable for him to visit with his family and now he understood why. The agency must have been aware that Dave was ill and chose not to tell him. Perhaps, he thought, because hearing it firsthand made his reaction a heartfelt reality, not a rehearsed response.

Dave appeared philosophical about his situation, having had time to deal with it. He continued with his questions. "If I believed everything you said is true, what are you doing back here? Government outfits don't do things just because they want to be nice. There's always a price tag at the end of it. What do they want?"

"I have to keep it to myself for now," Johnson explained. Dave accepted his answer with a nod, remembering that even when Johnson was with the Military, he had kept his Operations totally confidential.

They continued talking for over two hours, the one beer stretching into three, but it was now time for them to go. Johnson led the way as they were exiting the bar. Dave glanced up at the figure in front of him, and it occurred to him that this man was walking with the exact same gait as his father. The sight intrigued him. They waved a cheery goodbye to Becky and were soon out in the sunlight, squinting their eyes at the brightness of the day. They were almost at the car when they heard a voice from behind them.

"Hey! Spare us some change, will ya?" a voice demanded.

Johnson declined to answer but turned his head, looking over his left shoulder at the two men bearing down on them. In a glance, he'd sized them up. They were big but beefy, their clothing rough and hair dishevelled. No weapons were apparent, so there was nothing to be immediately alarmed about.

Dave spoke quietly to Johnson, saying, "The car's unlocked. Let's just get in and go."

Johnson ignored his brother and watched as the two men closed the distance to five metres. "I got a couple of bucks you can have," he called to them.

The lead man, the bigger of the two, came up to Johnson aggressively. "I'll take that, along with everything else you've got in your pockets." He suddenly lunged at him, coming in with a flailing right fist.

Johnson said nothing but knew this man would pay first. He slipped the punch, feeling the air rush by as the man's fist just missed his head. He stepped in close, grabbed the man's shirt and pulled him abruptly in. Johnson head-butted him across the bridge of his nose and smashed it into a red, wet mess. The man reeled back, dazed and in pain. Johnson brought his right hand across, pounding his fist into the right side of the man's jaw. His knees buckled, and he crumpled, unconscious, to the ground. Johnson's eyes now took in the second man, who had stopped in his tracks and was staring at his partner. "Your turn," Johnson said, motioning for the man to step forward. "Let's go." The second man, slack-jawed with surprise, abruptly turned and stumbled back to the bar. A groan from the first man alerted Johnson that he was coming to. The man, sputtering through his loosened teeth and blood, said, "You busted my fuck'n face, you asshole!"

Johnson reached down, grasped one of the man's wrists and pressed down, applying a hard, firm pressure on it before the man could react. He started screaming as the pressure built, Johnson watching him with a stony expression. He monitored the man carefully as he felt the joint slowly separating from its ligaments. Johnson only released the pressure ever so slightly just before the wrist reached its breaking point.

"Listen carefully," he said, maintaining a firm grip on the man. "I never want to see you or your buddy again. Do you understand?"

The man sputtered before managing to get out a pained, "Okay, I got it." He let out another howl as the pressure on his wrist suddenly increased.

Satisfied that he had made his point, he dropped the man to the ground and looked up to see a police car come around the corner and slowly turn into the parking lot. The car pulled up beside him and stopped. The officer got out of the vehicle and put on his hat.

"What do we have here?" he asked as he walked around the car.

Johnson looked levelly at the cop and said, "We were walking out of the bar when we found this guy lying here. Maybe his buddy over there can help you out."

The police officer glanced at both men, recognizing their faces. "We're well acquainted with these two. It looks like at least one of them has paid the price for being where he wasn't supposed to be. No need for a statement. I'll get an ambulance for that one. You two have yourself a nice day."

They got into the car without further comment and drove away in silence. Dave suddenly said, "You still got it, don't you?"

"The ability to fight? Yeah, you never really lose it."

"No," Dave replied, "that mean streak."

"I'm not going to make excuses. I had to do it. I hate bullies."

CHAPTER 39

Marie and Sonia met on the other side of the city. Marie, always suspicious, had made each of them go through complicated, indirect paths before reaching their destination. She was more like Bill than she wanted to admit. They entered a restaurant, sat down and ordered drinks. Marie glanced at Sonia and then looked closer. "Did you not get any sleep last night?"

"What are you talking about? I felt exhausted and went to bed at nine."

"You look like shit."

"Well, dear, have you looked in the mirror? You've got bags under your eyes."

Marie grew immediately defensive. She had noticed her face had looked tired but wasn't aware of any bags under her eyes. What the hell was going on here? "Forget about that. Anything new?"

Sonia waited until the waitress delivered their drinks and said, "I've got new information. We may not be here as long as we initially thought. I was with Sally at the cafe when an old colleague of hers came in. They appeared very happy to see each other again, and Sally told him what she's been up to. He'd heard where she was living and came to Regina specifically to find her. He wants her to restart work on their energy project."

"What makes you think he can convince her?"

"Money. He mentioned something about backers. Once they started talking, they didn't stop. I'm guessing they've kept research data so they can start work almost immediately."

Marie smiled thinly with the turn of events. Her frustration at the snail's pace everything had been moving, was lifted. Changing the subject, she asked, "Is Johnson aware of you?"

"We've been introduced," Sonia shrugged. "I think he may have his suspicions. He just doesn't have any definitive proof."

Marie said, "I've got a plan I've put together. Once I get it in place, we'll meet again. I don't want to get started on it with you until I'm sure everything can be done."

"That's fine. You know where to find me. Oh, how's the new boyfriend?" Sonia smiled thinly.

Marie smirked at her and said, "The way I like them. Young, nice looking, and easy. Something I can use and throw away."

Back at her apartment, Marie found the telephone number she'd previously written down and punched the numbers into her cell phone.

The receptionist answered, "Good morning, Reilly Industries. How can I help you?"

"Good morning. I need to speak with Shawn Reilly, please."

"Could I ask who's calling and the reason for your call?"

"It's Marie. The reason is confidential."

There was a pause before the receptionist said, "I don't see your name on the phone list for today or tomorrow. Is he expecting your call?"

"I'm not on any list. Something urgent and confidential has come up. I need to speak to him."

"I'm terribly sorry, but I can't put you through without an appointment. I can make one for you if you'd like, but you will have to provide me with the reason for your call. Mr. Reilly is a very busy man. If this is important, I'm sure he'll get back to you as soon as he can," she said.

Marie was silent for a moment, trying to rein in her temper but then gave way to it as only she could. "Listen, dear, I understand completely," she continued dryly. "Please pass this on to him. A few years back, there was a fire at his daughter's research facility. The team I work with is doing ground-breaking investigations into that type of incident. I've gathered evidence of arson, along with fingerprints that point to people in his employment. You have me on call display. I expect him to call me in one hour. If not, this goes to the evening news."

The line was deathly quiet as the receptionist tried to process the information and copy down Marie's cell number. Stuttering slightly, she finally said, "Thank you. I'll pass that on to him," and hung up.

Thirty minutes later, Marie's phone rang. She let three rings go by before she picked it up. "Hello," she said.

A male voice said, "I'd like to talk with Marie, please."

"This is she."

"I'm an associate of Mr. Reilly's. He's asked me to contact you. Could you give me a little more information about your so-called investigation?"

Marie listened until the man stopped talking and then snapped out, "I have no intention of speaking with anyone. Anyone," she repeated, "who is not Reilly. I'm going to make this really easy for you. He now has fifteen minutes left to call me, or everything I have goes to press, and the entire company goes down. I suggest that if you want to have a job tomorrow, you get your fucking boss on the line. Fifteen minutes." She ended the call with an angry jab of her finger and thought, *Well, that was fun. Let's see if that'll work.*

Ten minutes passed before her phone rang again. Marie let it go a few extra rings and then picked it up. "Hello," she said.

"Marie?" a deep male voice asked.

"Speaking."

"Okay, you've got my undivided attention."

"Were you aware that your daughter has started up her research on alternative energy again?"

She could almost hear the wheels spinning furiously in his head as he frantically searched for a plausible story to tell her. He finally replied, "I hadn't heard. Well, I suppose I should wish her the best of luck in her future endeavours. You understand, of course, that my company has also started a long-term research project of our own that has renewable energy as part of it. What concern is all of this to you?"

"Please don't take me for a fool, Reilly. We know what you did. And we know what will happen to your business enterprises when, not if, she develops this machine," Marie snapped. "Mr. Reilly, you might be able to fool the public and the press with a few windmills and solar panels, but really, let's not kid ourselves. We both know exactly why you burned down her place and what she was about to develop," Marie said smoothly. "You've got yourself a huge problem. And I think I can help."

Reilly was astonished at the woman's revelation and perception but was also furious at his vulnerability. Thinking quickly, he said as calmly as possible, "You seem to know a bit about my company and me, but I know nothing of you. Let me fly you to Edmonton so we can talk in person and discuss this whole matter face to face."

"No, you'll fly into Calgary. I'll meet you at the Renfrew Athletic Park off Highway 1. There's a baseball diamond in the back. You'll find me at third base. Seven o'clock tonight. Park out front and come alone," she said briskly and disconnected her cell.

Reilly heard the click and calmly disconnected as well. His hands gripped a pencil tightly, the only sign of his growing rage. He turned to his personal assistant and said, "The jet. Tell them to fuel it up and be ready in two hours. I'll be going to Calgary for a meeting." Without waiting for a response, Reilly abruptly got out of his chair and stalked out of the room. His assistant turned her head to look at his desk. The pencil had been snapped cleanly in half.

Marie stood waiting patiently for Reilly in the park. She was ninety minutes early but wanted to have a look around before the meeting. Marie walked from one end of the field to the other, found nothing suspicious and settled herself onto a bench. Ten minutes later, a car pulled into the parking lot, and a lone figure got out and walked toward her.

Despite his age, the man carried himself with the confidence of one who was accustomed to having things done the way he wanted them to be done. There was also, she thought, a lot of built-up anger in him. She could see it in his stride and in the set of his shoulders. "Well, this should be interesting," she muttered, standing up and making herself known.

"Marie, I take it," Reilly stated roughly.

She decided to play with him for a while. "You look older than your picture."

"Life tends to do that." *He was damned*, he thought, *if she thought he would rise to the bait she dangled in front of him.* "Before we start, I need to check something." He pulled out a small wand for detecting electronic devices. Marie obliged without a word but watched every motion as Reilly turned it on and ran it up and down her body. Finding her cellphone, he said, "Leave it on the bench." Obliging him without a word, she placed the phone on the bench. Once completed, he turned the wand off and tucked it back into his suit. "All right. Now talk. I assume this meeting is about my daughter and her damned energy machine."

"You assume correctly," she replied.

"What do you know about it? You've said she's started up again. How close is she to perfecting her machine?"

Marie confidently bluffed her way through the conversation. "A production model for consumer use is probably five years in the making. But that's not my worry. Anything can happen in that time. My concern is that her theory and principles are spot-on and important people are starting to listen. All she needs is a bit more backing, and that timeline I mentioned could easily be cut in half."

"Shit," he muttered, turning away from her, trying to hide his frustration.

"I assume that would not be of particular financial benefit to your company," she said smoothly. "In fact, it would be rather devastating to the entire industry, would it not?"

"If I have to stop her, I will," he said bluntly. "She's a selfish little bitch."

"I'm so glad you're concerned with your daughter's well-being," Marie drawled sarcastically before continuing. "I assume you're willing to risk going to jail, then? I would have no difficulties in bringing all our evidence to the proper authorities," she threatened.

He said nothing for a minute. Marie almost found herself smiling as she watched the conflicting emotions fly across the man's face. *This is so easy*, she thought.

"What are you proposing?"

"As I said, the people I work for are very interested in the research your daughter is doing. We are aware that you, on the other hand, are not at all interested. In fact, you would much prefer it if everything would just go away. Am I correct?"

"I would prefer that she no longer indulge in that area of research at all," he said carefully.

"I have a proposal for you, the result being something that would benefit both of us. All you have to do is help us receive all the completed research and working prototypes when your daughter completes them. Your life and your business go back to normal, and we won't infringe on anything your company is involved in."

"And what happens to my daughter? She could easily start all over again. How would you guarantee she won't do that?"

"Sally will be safe. She will not be starting her project here again," Marie said. She had purposely not mentioned that Sally would be taken to Midgard once their machine had the capability. "Your business will remain as profitable as it ever was, and nothing will ever be revealed about your involvement in any past incidents. Some of the people she works with may run into a few problems, but I can guarantee she'll be safe. I know if we do this, we can both get what we want, Reilly. We'll just need a bit of cooperation from you."

Reilly watched her carefully and then said, "You understand what's at stake here?"

"Oh, I understand completely. That's why I'm talking with you. I've got a plan. Do you want to listen?"

The day had been exhausting for Betty, and she was glad it was over. She made her way slowly up the two flights of stairs with an armful of groceries and opened the door to her apartment. *This volunteer crap is hard work,* she thought as she closed the door behind her. She placed the groceries onto the counter and began unpacking the bags, dividing everything up, setting the produce in the fridge and cans in the cupboard. She put the last of the groceries into place and then reached for the book that the GIA had given her for transmissions back to Midgard. A noise from behind her made her release the book. She stepped back slowly, closed the cupboard door, turned and peered into the front room. The sound she had heard was only a hint. The scent of the perfume was the dead giveaway. Betty moved slowly, using the corner of the wall for protection, looking in the direction she had heard the noise. She thought there was a chance that she could make it to the door and try to get some distance between herself and the intruder, but it was too late. The smell of the perfume was getting stronger. Betty placed her hands on the counter and leaned on them, whispering, "How could I have been so stupid?"

Sonia came around the corner, pointing a gun at Betty. "They said you were better than this. Guess they were wrong." She advanced slowly; the weapon now pointed at Betty's head.

Sonia reached into her pocket, pulled out a zip tie and threw it on the counter. "I found these. Handy little items. I might have to take a bag of them home. Now be a dear and slip your hands through the hole. Then pull the end tight with your teeth.

The older woman worked the tie through her hands and over her wrists and tightened it as Sonia walked around the counter.

"I've been waiting to meet you," she said. She suddenly threw a hard left to Betty's right side, the shock wave of the blow smashing against her liver.

Betty had only a moment to tense slightly, tightening her core just before the fist slammed into her side. The pain was automatic and overwhelming, and she collapsed, head crashing off the tile floor. Sonia walked forward, raised her knee and drove her foot hard onto Betty's head. Lights exploded and popped on and off in front of the woman's eyes. She rolled onto her back and looked up at the face above her. Betty tried to speak, but pain drove the "how-to" from her brain. Without warning, the toe of Sonia's foot connected with the side of Betty's ribs, breaking them immediately. Betty felt the crunch on the inside of her body as she tried to regain her breath. Forcing air into her lungs, she curled into a ball, protecting what vitals she had left. A hand grabbed her by the hair, and she felt her head lift up off the floor as hot breath came close to her face.

"So, I finally get to meet the old bitch that did so many of us in," Sonia said, as her fist came hard across Betty's chin, making a thudding sound in her ears. Betty drifted off into semi-consciousness. Her head fell back onto the floor again, and she looked up to see flashes of light above Sonia's head. She tried to move, ordering her legs to get up, but her body wouldn't obey.

The beating was finally winding down, and Sonia bent over, panting hard through her mouth. She spat into Betty's face and looked down at the old woman, who was now totally oblivious to her surroundings. "Time for round two," Sonia said, standing up, ready to bring her foot down on the woman's head again.

The door suddenly opened, and an accented male voice spoke sharply. "That's enough, bitch. Your boss wants her alive. Look how fucked up she is." The man wasn't happy. He gathered the woman up roughly and carried her out the door while Sonia stood back and watched with a satisfied smile. She pulled out the communicator that Jack had provided for her and sent back a message. *Jack. Bonus package for us. I've got Betty Sharpe. Do you want her?*

Betty's world drifted, then turned black. Her eyes were closed, her body shutting down to protect itself. She was dreaming, floating, watching herself as a young girl running through a field, the grass high, the sun on her face. The girl ran up to her with a butterfly in her cupped hands. Betty smiled back at herself, looking into the young Betty's eyes as the little girl spoke. "You know it's going to get a lot worse."

CHAPTER 40

Sally's second meeting was held at the community centre to accommodate the large crowd of over two hundred people. She had just raised her eyes to the front door when she noticed Johnson walking in. She greeted him fondly and said, "I have someone I want you to meet."

"I'm sorry I'm late. Who am I meeting?"

"A friend of mine," she said, turning and waving over a man. When he came up to them, she introduced him to Johnson. "Allen Wood, this is Steve Johnson. Steve, this is Allen. Steve is the man I've been telling you about. He's been great at getting me started up again. Allen is one of my old colleagues from Edmonton. He may have a handle on procuring funding for our project. If we get enough, we can keep going on the research we were doing in Edmonton."

Surprised and pleased at this turn of events, Johnson greeted him. "I'm glad to meet you. You came at exactly the right time." He shook Allen's hand, both men automatically assessing the other. Of Asian descent, Allen was a slightly built man who held himself confidently and intelligently. Johnson liked the man immediately.

"It's time to begin," Sally said, looking at her watch. "We've got to get this meeting going." With that, she turned and headed up to the podium.

The two men watched as Sally greeted the crowd and began her presentation. This evening was another surprise to Johnson. The first half of the meeting dealt with both wind and solar power applications. The entire second half dealt with her theories on alternative energy. She had designed the information to be as simple and straightforward as possible, keeping the scientific explanation short but expanding on its concept and uses. The audience was immediately able to understand the implications, and the room grew more and more animated as questions began to fly. Allen proved to be an equally talented speaker, with an in-depth understanding of the topic and an engaging manner with the crowd. The evening flew by and finally ended two hours later with an extended round of applause.

Sally stood by the entrance with Allen to thank people for dropping in. When the last of their guests had left, Allen gathered up his laptop and promised to meet with Sally the next day. He shook Johnson's hand firmly before he slipped out the door. "Thank you," he said softly to Johnson before leaving. "It's good to have her back."

Johnson nodded in reply and watched as Allen hopped into an awaiting cab. Turning to Sally, he said, "Seems like a good guy."

"He's been my right-hand man since I began this journey," Sally acknowledged. "We work well together. I'm able to focus on the math, the equations and the fine-tuning. He works on the physical engineering."

"Tonight was an excellent meeting. I wasn't expecting you to cover anything about alternative energy."

"I need to start looking at it again," she began, "because, to be honest, wind and solar are only a piece of the solution. Now that there's a possibility of funding, I can consider it again. Allen has been speaking with another company from Germany. They're interested in investing money for research and are flying in on Wednesday to talk. I'm a little worried about it and don't really have a plan set up yet," she confessed.

"Sally, just be yourself. Be as honest as you really are, as upfront as you really are, just like you've done here. They'll be more than happy to listen to you. Don't sell yourself short. I know this is going to be a difficult time for you, but you've got everything you need to make this a success," Johnson said.

The custodian interrupted by calling from across the room, "Time to go, folks. I have to lock up."

"Thank you very much," Sally said, waving goodbye to the man as they walked out the door. The wind had picked up, and lightning lit up the night. A storm was brewing. "Thanks for all the encouragement, Steve. I needed the extra boost. Guess I'll go home tonight and get that plan laid out for our potential investors."

Johnson kissed her on the cheek and said, "See you tomorrow. Good luck." He watched as she hopped into her cab and then headed home.

His cab drove through the wet streets with Johnson deep in thought. The mission was now starting to move ahead. On his next report back, he'd ask Ann to run the protocols. If they came out favourably, and the Rebels had been dispatched, they could be home in a week. The cab driver couldn't find a spot to park, so he let him out on the corner. *Nothing unusual,* Johnson thought absently. Everyone was home from work, and even the loading zone had a vehicle parked in it. The rain had finally tapered off into a light mist, and the air smelled fresh and clean as he approached the front door of his apartment block. His glance toward the loading zone had been quick. He hadn't noticed the man on the inside of the car, sitting and waiting. Johnson came to the front door as a large man was exiting the building. He greeted Johnson with a nod and held the door open for him. As Johnson reached the threshold, he heard the slam of a car door and the sound of running feet. His head swivelled to the noise. What he did not anticipate was the grip of a large hand on his shoulder. The only thing he could remember thinking after that was, *I'm in trouble.*

Betty could later recall only bits and pieces of what happened. Her next clear recollection was of opening her eyes but discerning only blackness and feeling the rumbling of a vehicle. She drifted in and out of consciousness, unable to determine the amount of time she had been travelling. After what seemed to be forever, she finally felt the vehicle slow to a stop. She thought she heard a garage door open and felt the car move forward again before finally coming to a halt. She could remember nothing else until she felt hands gripping her roughly and pulling her up, then hoisting her over a shoulder. She gasped involuntarily at the intense pain in her ribs as they made contact with the man's shoulder and again succumbed to a welcoming blackness.

She woke up with duct tape wrapped tightly across her arms and chest, pinning her tightly to a chair. Barely able to lift her head, she willed her eyes up and toward the sounds of two women speaking across the room.

"Well, you're finally awake," Marie said, observing Betty with an unreadable look. Betty desperately wanted to say something but found that she was unable to respond. Her body had reached the end of its limit.

"You won't be here alone for long. Johnson will be here shortly to join you. Oh, you remember me, don't you? Or should I introduce myself to you again? Perhaps I can jog your memory?"

Betty knew exactly who this woman was and, filled by rage, responded in a hoarse whisper, "You're the only one left for me to kill."

"That's right. But you never got that job done, did you? I'm in control now."

Marie had just pulled out a knife when the two women became aware of a garage door opening. A car was entering the abandoned building they had hidden in.

"Shit, they're back already," Sonia said.

"No time to finish this properly, I suppose," Marie said harshly. "We'll deal with her later."

Shawn Reilly entered the room just as Marie had sheathed her knife. He spotted the older woman who sat motionless on the chair and looked dispassionately at her before addressing Marie.

"Who is that, and what have you two been up to?"

Marie glanced smoothly over to Reilly. "No one of concern, just some personal business. Do you have him?"

"Yes, the boys are taking him out now."

When Johnson came to, he was lying on a concrete floor, cold and shivering, with a hood over his head. He could see a faint bit of light through the material but no shapes, people or movement. His wrists and ankles had been bound and tied with a rope that ran loosely along his back. His jaw was sore, and his head ached, but everything else seemed fine. He heard muffled voices, but they were coming from behind a door and were too far away to hear clearly. A few minutes later, he heard the door open, and the voices got louder as footsteps came his way.

"Give me a hand and help me lift him into this chair," someone said with an English accent. He felt two sets of strong hands gripping his arms, lifting him up and dropping him onto a chair. A rough hand grasped the top of the sack, and it was yanked off his head. He had barely registered what was happening when a large bucket of water was dumped over him. He spat the water from his lips, cleared it from his nose and, looking up, squinted his eyes at the lone, bright light that hung directly above him.

"Good to see you're awake, Mr. Johnson. I hope your nap was comfortable," the bigger of the two men said.

Johnson said nothing, his eyes measuring the entire room as he looked around it. He could see only the two men to his front. The room was large, and the concrete floor was bare. An old and empty office building, perhaps, he guessed. A few abandoned desks and chairs littered the area just beyond him, but, except for the one light above him, the rest was a wall of darkness.

Looking back at the bigger man, he asked, "How do you know my name?"

"A little bird told us, Stevie boy. Ah, here she comes now." Johnson heard footsteps approaching from his rear. He turned his head to see four figures coming out of the darkness. The first was an older man whom he recognized from pictures as Reilly and, after him, three women. The woman in the middle was barely able to stay on her feet, and it was only the other two women who kept her upright. As they got closer, he was shocked to find that he recognized her. It was Betty, her head lolling down, her upper body unresisting, and her legs barely able to support her. He looked up at the two men in front of him and said, "You beat up women. Aren't you real fucking heroes."

The bigger man laughed and said, "We didn't touch her, mate. It was one of the ladies that worked her over."

Marie watched Johnson's face with cruel satisfaction as he realized who they were dragging into the room and smirked. *That was well worth the effort,* she thought, as she let the woman's body slip to the floor in front of them.

Johnson could see that Betty was in dire condition. Her face had been severely beaten, and he watched in dread as blood dripped in slow motion from her mouth to the floor. Only semi-conscious, she tried to stand on her own, but her legs were unable to hold her. The two men ignored both Betty and Johnson, stepping toward Reilly to receive their next instructions. Momentarily distracted, they didn't notice that Johnson had forced himself up and off the chair. The rope still gripped, binding him to a half-crunched position as he hobbled forward to the closest man.

Hearing the noise, the man turned as Johnson thrust his head up, catching him under the chin with the top of his head. The two fell to the floor, with Johnson landing on top of him. The bigger man stepped back from Reilly and looked down at them. "Fucking heroes," he said, then stepped in and kicked Johnson squarely in the ribs, forcing him off the other man. Not content with one kick, he continued laying blows into Johnson's body until a final blow to his jaw knocked him back into unconsciousness. Reilly and the two women stood impassively throughout the entire beating.

Reilly looked down at Johnson, sighed and said, "I did want to find out what he and my daughter were up to, but I guess that won't be happening now."

The larger man said, "Sorry, boss. I got a bit carried away."

The two men grabbed Johnson and hoisted him up to a hook dangling from the ceiling, where they hung him up using the rope that bound his wrists and ankles. He swung there helplessly, legs, arms and shoulders pulled tight behind him and straining with the weight of his body.

"Let's discuss this in the office. You two come with me. That one won't be going anywhere," Reilly announced, lifting his chin at Johnson.

"I'm bringing her with us," Marie said. "I don't trust the two of them together." They forced Betty to her feet and began to make their way back to the office.

As the door closed behind them, Reilly admonished the two women. "Why did you bother with the old lady? Why did you need her?"

Sonia began to speak, but Marie stopped her. "This woman has some history with us that had to be addressed. We just got a bit ahead of ourselves."

Reilly shook his head and said, "Keep yourselves under control. Maintaining a tight rein on things is essential."

"This is our business and none of your concern."

"I'm here. And that makes it my business."

Reilly didn't want anything more to do with this. To the two men, he said, "You know what I want done. Just clean up after yourselves." He turned to Marie and said, "You and I are leaving now. I won't be anywhere near this." He turned and walked out of the building by way of the side door.

Marie turned reluctantly to Sonia and said, "Those two will

look after Johnson. You look after Sharpe. Do it as soon as I'm gone. Then meet me back at my apartment tomorrow morning."

Sonia allowed herself a thin smile and then quietly said, "I'm taking my time if you don't mind."

Marie walked over to the slumped figure and lifted Betty's chin up to look directly at her. Betty held Marie's gaze without flinching, despite the anguish and distress she was in.

Marie returned Betty's spite-filled stare without flinching. "Look at you," Marie spat cruelly. "You're not even worth my time. I'm done with you." Turning back to Sonia, she said, "Don't piss around. Just finish it." Without another word, she dropped her hand, turned and walked out the back door behind Reilly.

Johnson came to for the second time that night. The pain scale in his head had gone from bearable to excruciating. Opening his eyes, he watched the cement floor slowly sway back and forth one metre below him. The rope that connected his hands and feet put the weight of his body on every arm and leg joint, trying to rip them from their sockets. He moved slightly, twisting slowly and searching into the darkness for any sign of life, but everyone was gone.

Straining his arms and lifting himself slightly in his bindings, he found he could move a hand. The water they had thrown over his head and his added weight on the knots had stretched the rope. *This could work,* he thought, and a flicker of hope replaced the dread he had felt a few seconds before. He pulled and twisted his hands and wrists against the knot. The rope began to slide into the meaty part of his hands but tightened again. Johnson narrowed them, twisting and straining, feeling his broken ribs and gasping against the pain. Squeezing his eyes tightly shut, he persisted, the struggle producing only minuscule movements of the rope. A minute, then three passed, and still, he struggled until, finally, he felt one of his hands move. With one more pull from his aching shoulders, the rope let go, and both hands fell free. He had only a second to curl his head and shoulder into a half-roll as he smashed into the floor.

Both hands numb, he shook them vigorously for a few moments before the blood started circulating and then untied himself. Johnson searched into the darkness where he'd seen an outline of a desk earlier and staggered to it. Finding a pen and paper, he scribbled a quick message, "*Need weapon immediately,*" placed it inside his wallet and closed it. He caught sight of the extension cord powering the lone light and pulled it out of its socket. The entire area was plunged into darkness, and he moved haltingly back to the desk, crouching behind it.

From the far side of the room, he heard a door swing open, followed by footsteps and the voices of two men. As they exited the office, he heard one man say, "Let's get this done quick."

The other man said, "Shit, it looks like the light has gone on the blink again." A flashlight beam suddenly appeared and flashed from side to side in front of them, guiding them through a maze of desks and into the open area where they'd left Johnson. They stopped walking as soon as they caught sight of the hook hanging by itself and discovered the rope lying in a pile on the floor.

"He couldn't have gotten far," the other man said and began to follow the thick dust trail Johnson had inadvertently left behind.

"Control, don't let me down," Johnson muttered, and, as if they had heard him, a light suddenly flashed. He picked up the small weapon that came through and, in one motion, slipped the safety off. He ran his eyes down the top of it and pushed his arms to full extension. The sights aligned first on the man farthest in shadow, the same man who had kicked him in the ribs. Johnson squeezed the trigger, and the man fell, first to his knees and then face-first onto the ground, dead. As soon as he pulled the trigger and felt the energy charge leave his weapon, Johnson shifted his sight picture to the man with the flashlight. Again, he squeezed the trigger, and the man's head flew back from the impact, his flashlight clattering to the floor.

Johnson staggered up and walked around the desk, kicking both men to make sure they were down for good. Grimacing in pain, he bent over and picked up the flashlight. *Get your shit together*, he said to himself, breathing in deeply and trying to clear his head. Johnson switched the flashlight off and looked at the lit door the two had come from. Stumbling slightly toward it, he heard the distinct voices of two women, Betty and Sonia.

"From the sounds of things next door, it appears that your buddy has breathed his last. I have a change of plans for you. You're going back to Midgard."

Johnson was now at the office, standing back in the darkness, peering through the crack of the opened door. He could see Sonia standing a metre from Betty, who was slumped on a chair in front of her, but no one else.

Betty struggled to talk and finally whispered, "I definitely would've handed your ass to you if I were younger."

Sonia's mouth opened in surprise, and she suddenly laughed uproariously. "Whatever you say, you old bitch. It's the end of your era."

Betty raised her head and stared directly at Sonia for a moment before she said, "You're long-winded, aren't you? Let's get this over with."

Sonia moved forward as Betty tried to struggle to her feet, the younger woman coming down with a hard blow from her fist. Betty lifted her right arm instinctively and partially blocked it. Sonia came in quickly, reaching over and grabbing Betty's hair with her left hand. She brought her in close and said, "It'll all be over in a minute. I have my own people back in Midgard that want to talk with you, and Marie will be dead before she finds out you're gone." With that, she pulled a second transponder from her pocket and began to place it on Betty's arm.

At the same time, Johnson moved, opening the door fully as

he stepped through it. His weapon was up and levelled at Sonia's head, and her eyes widened in surprise when she caught sight of him. Helplessly, time slowed for her as she watched the slow recoil of the weapon. The narrow blast hit her between the eyes, her brain dissolved, and her body fell limply to the office floor.

Johnson ran to Betty and caught her just before she collapsed, helping her to a chair. She looked up at him and placed her hand on his arm. "I knew you wouldn't let me down. Take the transponder off my arm and send it back to the agency. They can use it."

He smiled back at her and replied, "I will."

Betty patted his arm once more and then collapsed, unconscious.

Johnson wrote another message back to the agency. He listed their injuries and informed them of the three bodies that were now cooling on the cement floor. Johnson assumed the woman was from the Rebel crew and the other two from Earth. He wanted all three of them to be sent back to Midgard to confirm their identities. *I have another plan for the two men*, he thought ruthlessly.

His reply came back immediately, along with medical supplies. The portal stayed open just long enough for him to heave the bodies through it, his sides ripping apart with every tug and pull. When the final body was thrown in, and the portal closed, he turned his attention to Betty. Johnson had thought very briefly about sending her back but knew that the trip was rough, even on a healthy body. She'd taken a hell of a beating, and he did not believe she could survive. Johnson unpacked the medical supplies. Both the head and torso braces were designed to not only support but to encourage healing by stimulation. He could only hope they worked as well as they promised.

He gently placed a head and torso brace on Betty and took the other torso brace for himself. Taking off his shirt, he put it on, zipped it up and activated it. The transformation was immediate, from intolerable pain at every breath to a tolerable ache. Betty groaned slightly, the head brace working its magic. To what extent, he would not be sure of until much later. He was very concerned about her. Johnson was convinced that her injuries would accelerate the advanced ageing her body was undoubtedly going through while she was on Earth.

He bent over and spoke softly into her ear, "Betty, we're moving now, I'm going to carry you." He placed his arms under her and carefully lifted her up and out the door. The fresh night air was a respite from the dusty building. He looked around and realized that they were in an industrial area of Regina but still well within the city. He carried Betty to a corner bus stop bench and laid her gently on it. Walking over to the corner pay phone, he made a quick call and returned to Betty just as she was regaining consciousness and trying to sit up. Putting his hand on her shoulder, he said softly, "Hey there, slugger. Take it easy and relax. We'll be out of here in a few minutes." She sighed, closed her eyes and laid her head back down.

He walked to the back of the bench and leaned up against it, scanning the area while he was waiting for help. He was disappointed. He'd let himself become complacent, and it had almost gotten the two of them killed. *Hard lessons,* he thought. *Why do I always need these hard lessons?*

Fifteen minutes later, the sound of tires splashing through rain puddles got his attention, and he saw the lights of a vehicle moving slowly down the street. Getting closer, the lights illuminated the two of them, and he turned sideways, reaching behind his back for the pistol. The car pulled ahead of them slightly, and when it stopped, he walked over to the passenger side.

His brother rolled down the window. "It's me. What can I do?"

"Thanks for coming," Johnson said. "I need a lift." He opened the back door, turned and gently transferred Betty from the bench to the back seat. He closed the door, took one last look around and eased himself into the passenger side, wincing as he did so.

"You're hurt," Dave observed. "Where to?"

"Your place, I hope. Would you mind having a roommate for a few days?"

His brother turned and looked at Betty lying on the back seat, flinching when he saw the condition she was in. "Shouldn't we be stopping at the hospital first?"

"No, I'll get more medical supplies when we get to the house."

Dave was reluctant but didn't say a word. He pulled smoothly away from the curb, careful to avoid jarring either of his passengers. He glanced at Johnson and added with a short laugh, "I knew you were going to be trouble."

"Stop. It hurts when I laugh."

At the house, Johnson and Dave placed Betty in the spare room and made sure she was comfortable.

"I need someone to watch her," Johnson said, ensuring the braces were secured correctly. "Give her some water and food if she wants it and introduce yourself when you get the chance."

Dave watched the woman lying motionless on the bed. "Those braces are going to fix what she's been through?"

"The braces are stabilizing her for now. I've got one around my ribs, and it seems to be dulling the pain."

The two men walked from the room and quietly closed the door behind them, moving down the hallway and into the kitchen.

Dave said, "Don't you worry about her. I can handle this."

"I need to send my plan for the next twenty-four hours back to my boss. Got a pen and paper I can borrow?" Johnson wrote down his intentions along with a few questions that needed to be answered and sent them back to Ann. "You got a gun?"

Dave nodded. "It's in the night table."

Johnson acknowledged, "Keep it handy. You might need it." He knew his brother would never be without a weapon. "I've got some business to tend to. The next twenty-four hours should be interesting. Thanks for everything, Dave."

"I don't know what you're doing, Steve, but be careful."

Johnson vaguely registered that Dave had used his name for the first time. He was home.

CHAPTER 41

*A*nn *was sitting behind the glass in the Destination area as the bodies appeared. The two dead men were identified as being from Earth, the woman from Midgard.* Their exact identities would have to be verified, and the Probabilities machine used to determine the consequences of the men's death. Orderlies arrived to lift the three bodies onto platforms and then guided them down the hallway. Ann opened her communicator. "Runa, I've got the woman coming to you now. How long for identification?"

Runa, one of their techs, had been waiting for Ann's call. "We're ready for her. Give me ten minutes. We should have something by then."

"Thanks," Ann said, closing off her communicator and picking up Sonia's two transponders. She'd turn them into Intelligence and have them analyzed. An hour later, Johnson's plan arrived. She glanced through the written notes, sending his questions to the specific departments. His last comments were about Betty, and his questions about her medical status troubled her. She asked the medical team to analyze the readouts Johnson had provided as soon as possible. It might mean that she wasn't responding, and the problem could be more serious.

Twenty minutes later, people from the various departments gathered in Ann's office. "Let get right to it. Futures, tell me about the two men."

"Ma'am," the man started, "this is just a quick prognosis. We ran the Probabilities. The first man, the bigger one, won't be missed. He disappeared from his family's life years ago, and future interactions indicated he would have been killed within the year. The second man was a violent one, family disputes, criminal gangs, you name it. Probabilities show that his death will be favourable to his family. We expanded that search and found nothing more than normal life progression, no presidents in the family tree. Sad to say, neither will be missed."

"Good. We were lucky this time," Ann said. "What about Shawn Reilly? What happens if Johnson terminates him?"

He answered, "That's a different story. Do you want every scenario we went over?"

Ann said, "Specifics only, please. If Johnson terminates him, does it have a residual effect?"

"It'll be nothing good. It looks like Sally abandons the whole project, blames herself for the problems of the family and moves on with her life in another direction."

Ann swore softly and then said, "I'll pass that on to him." She changed her focus to the IC of the Destination Room. "The two men we've got in the coolers, Johnson wants them back. Can we deliver them to an alternate location?"

He answered, "We just need to know where and when he wants them."

"Home in on him when he signals. I need you to be ready at a moment's notice. Thank you everyone for your work. You're excused. Medical, stay behind."

When everyone had left, and the door was closed behind them, Ann asked the doctor, "How bad is Betty?"

"She's bad. Her injuries are extensive, and she's not young anymore. The head and torso braces will heal her in time, but the damage they leave behind means she wouldn't survive the trip back."

Ann let his words sink in and turned away, folding her arms. "You're saying that if we bring her back, it will kill her?"

"Look, Ann," he said, "We can risk it, but there are no guarantees. My prognosis, from the information I received, is that the beating she sustained, along with her age, would compromise her transport. The pressure could easily rupture an artery, a blood vessel, an organ."

There was one basic rule Ann had never broken, and that was never to leave a person behind. There were times people were killed, but they all came home. Her mind made up, she told the doctor, "Send Johnson everything he needs for her. I'll tell him our prognosis, and he'll have to talk with Betty. The final decision will be hers."

"Ann, we have to talk about Johnson," he continued. "From the information we've received, he shouldn't even be walking. Now he wants to be transported somewhere. We can't do that."

She had already considered this and was blunt in her reply. "It's a shorter trip and won't be that hard on him. Besides, Johnson's a big boy and knows what he signed up for. Is there anything else?"

"I'll be sending the medical supplies as soon as we're done here," he replied, reluctantly agreeing.

"Thank you," she said. "Let's get this done."

He exited the office, and Ann picked up the communicator and called Eric Stanton. He needed to be advised about Johnson's plan and what had happened to Betty. He had, of course, been kept up-to-date on everything before this, but Ann had to let him know about her.

The hologram image of Eric's face hovered above Ann's desk. He was cautiously optimistic after hearing Ann's report. He said, "We've got positive results from Johnson so far, and that's good. I just hope he can pull off this plan of his."

He stopped and thought for a moment before continuing. "About Betty, I know it's tough, but she knew the possible consequences. She has her life, which has been longer than a lot of our Operators, and she can continue that life on Earth. We're allowing her to decide if she wants to stay or risk the travel back. It's as simple as that."

Ann's thoughts had echoed Eric's. "Thank you."

"That's done. Now let's keep our heads in the mission. You and your team are going to be busy with all the moving parts.

Make sure everyone is ready. Good luck."

"Thanks again, sir," Ann said, signing off.

Johnson walked around his brother's basement, stuffing the extra pillows from upstairs into the windows. The plan was to keep the light produced by Destination in the house. He finished the last window when he heard a noise and looked up the staircase to see Dave coming down. Johnson said, "Well, we're ready. They should be sending something soon."

Johnson had no sooner spoken the words when, without warning, a crack of light appeared in the corner of the basement. He said to Dave, "It gets pretty bright, so don't look into it." Dave turned his head just as the blinding, brilliant crack of light widened and, as quickly as it had appeared, disappeared, leaving a small number of supplies. Johnson dug through the pile and, finding an envelope, opened it and read.

Steve,

Deal with Shawn Reilly in any way you can, but regardless of what he does, do not kill him. I repeat, do not kill Reilly. Protocols would be highly unfavourable and could render the whole Operation ineffective. As requested, Traveller will locate and monitor Reilly to determine best time to transport you to his location.

The two male bodies are from Earth and will be sent back to the location of your preference and time.

The female you sent back is Rebel Operator Sigrid Thorne, confirmed through the Midgard Affinity Register. The female Rebel remaining is Marie. Picture is included. We advise you to use upmost vigilance when dealing with this person as she has been designated extremely dangerous. I'm asking you to take her alive if you can.

The medical team has determined that if Betty returns to Midgard, trip has a 95% probability of killing her. Her body will heal from injuries quickly, but age factors combined with compromised cardio system will make travel through Destination extremely hazardous for her. Please advise her on prognosis. Choice to return will remain with her. We ask

that she not make a decision until end of mission.
  Good Luck. Ann

Wordlessly, Johnson took the report and picked up the bundle of medical supplies, walking up the steps from the basement to Betty's room. There would be hard choices made today, he knew, but they had to be made. His brother walked behind him and, aware that the report was highly sensitive, left Steve to speak with Betty alone. She opened her eyes as soon as he entered the room. "They've sent more medical supplies," he said quietly. "They look a little more heavy-duty."

"I hope so. I have a headache from hell. Could you help me sit up, please?"

Johnson gently boosted her into a sitting position, propped up against the pillows in front of the headboard. He replaced the head and torso strappings with one large torso brace, activated the healing pulses and helped Betty lie back down.

"Much better," she sighed gratefully. "Thank you."

Johnson stowed the rest of the supplies beside her night table and then showed her the picture from the report. "I got this from Ann," he said. "I'm not sure how they got it, but it's definitely the other woman from the warehouse, although she's younger in the picture."

Betty scanned the page, an angry frown forming on her face, and said, "Yes, that's definitely her. She's the one I spotted the other day at the parade, the one I never got to tell you about. She was with Reilly and Sonia last night as well. Marie told Sonia to kill me straight away, but Sonia had other plans. I think she was trying to work a double-cross on Marie. Good for me, I guess." Betty's voice wavered slightly before she was able to speak again. "She's tough, so when you get the chance to take her down, do it. Don't hesitate. Promise me that."

"I would, but they want me to take her alive and send her back."

Betty's voice suddenly raised in anger. "Why? Why would they want her alive?"

"I can't answer that, Betty. I don't know."

"My husband's ambush, all those years ago. She was there. She was the last and the only one I never got. She's dangerous and has to be put down."

Johnson was surprised by the venom in her voice but understood her hatred completely.

"I should be going with you, I could cover your back," Betty argued.

"Betty, you're too busted up," he said honestly. "Besides, this is what I do." He leaned over, kissing her on the forehead. "I'll be back once this is all done."

"I know you will. She'll be hiding out in the apartment just across from their first locale. Westview Heights, apartment 205. I've been doing a little investigating on my own." A tight, forced smile on her face couldn't hide the concern in her eyes. She'd seen close-up what Marie could do to a seasoned operator, and she squeezed his arm hard. "Watch your ass and never underestimate her."

Johnson called to Dave, who came in with an extra blanket for Betty, and introduced them to each other.

Dave slid the blanket over her and promised to return in a few minutes. The two men walked back out to the living room. Johnson said grimly, "If I were you, I'd be sitting in Betty's room with that pistol of yours until I come back. Is it okay if I borrow your car? I shouldn't be that long — hopefully, no more than two hours."

"Not a problem," Dave said, tossing him the keys. "Don't worry about Betty. I'll take good care of her."

A few minutes later, Johnson drove back to the apartment Betty had directed him to. Parking the car a block away, he pulled out his weapon, made sure it was ready and tucked it back into his belt. He grabbed a crowbar from the trunk and slipped it into his jacket. Johnson stepped into the back alley and made his way down the block. Dawn was now beginning to break, and he could see a sliver of scarlet in the sky as the sun started to make its way through the night. Johnson would have to be careful not to be detected. As he got nearer to the apartment, he slid himself closer to the surrounding shrubbery, keeping low and staying to the edges. If his hunch was correct, all he had to do was wait. Johnson settled himself snugly beside a garbage bin shelter at the end of the alleyway. From this angle, he could watch the comings and goings of all the occupants from any door. He scanned the windows, looking for lights, but it was still too early for most of the residents to be rising.

Johnson's ribs were aching. Despite the medical respite he had been given, he knew that only time would heal them. He forced himself to focus on the apartment and not his pain, making himself as comfortable as he could while waiting. Within half an hour, his patience was rewarded. A slim, dark figure of a woman was making her way down the sidewalk. She walked quickly and confidently into the building. He watched closely now and was soon rewarded with a flicker of a light switch, revealing her location on the second floor.

Johnson was about to move but then hesitated, a cautious intuition that told him to be still for one moment longer. Not taking his eyes off the window, he was rewarded with a slight movement from the blinds covering it. Marie had revealed only a glimpse of her profile. It was enough for Johnson to confirm her identity in the growing morning light. Sliding silently from his hiding place, he walked to the side door fire escape and tested it. Sensing little or no resistance, he forced the lock open with the crowbar and came into a tight and dingy entry strewn with garbage and lit by a dim bulb. This would, Johnson thought, work to his advantage. It was the kind of place residents were hesitant about calling the law, and the police would probably take their time getting to. Johnson walked up the stairs to the second floor and moved silently down the hallway to the apartment.

He checked one last time to ensure there was no one there and then, with one fluid movement, pulled out the crowbar, rammed it into the door jam and split open the lock. He immediately shouldered himself into the entryway and closed the door behind him. The last thing he needed was a witness. Marie heard the noise and ran to the hallway from her bedroom, pistol raised. He slammed the crowbar across her arm, and the gun spun from her hands as she involuntarily cried out. Not allowing her even a moment of reaction, Johnson's fist connected with her jaw, and she was on the floor. He brought his foot down heavily on her throat, subduing her. "Good morning, Marie. Sorry, did I wake you?"

Marie was unable to reply, too busy trying to get a breath of air past the foot that was pressing down on her throat. For a second, Johnson thought everything was finished. Instead, she lifted her left leg up, swinging it around his waist and pulling him off balance. As he hit the ground, her right leg came up hard into his groin area, just missing the target. It didn't really matter though, as the push gave her enough space to throw her legs forward, kipping her up. Johnson reacted just as quickly, gathering his feet under him and pushing himself up to a standing position, ribs screaming in protest. Marie had shifted automatically into a fighting stance, her icy eyes glaring at him.

Johnson stepped back just as she came forward and twisted herself around, throwing a high roundhouse kick, aiming for his head. He could feel the breeze from her foot as it narrowly sliced past his face. She kept dancing forward, throwing two front kicks while trying desperately to maintain a space between them. Johnson squared off against her, sidestepping them. He brought his hands up high, lowered his shoulders and then launched himself forward, throwing his full weight into her. The full-on football tackle caught her just below the ribs and slammed her body hard against the wall. Marie's head snapped back, then forward, and he ran his left hand up and across her face, shoving it backward while trying to grip it in his palm.

Cocking his right arm back, he swung a hard right across her face, his fist searching for a jaw or temple but catching only air. Marie had outthought him and collapsed her legs, dropping to the floor. Her right leg kicked out, sweeping Johnson's feet from under him. He hit the floor hard, his ribs pulling even further apart as she leaped on top of him. Her first punch caught him on the left side of his face, her rings tearing into his cheek and leaving a long ripple of torn flesh and blood. The second punch was only a glancing blow to the right of his face as Johnson's instincts directed his hands up high to ward off the onslaught.

Marie could feel it. Victory, she knew, was close, and she renewed her efforts, her energy fuelled by rage. Only one more punch, her inner voice told her, just one punch away. Johnson could feel his defences starting to break and weaken. The night had been too long, and the beatings he'd taken, too harsh. He could sense her rhythm as her fists threw punch after punch, and he could feel her breathing getting heavier. It was time. Johnson moved his elbows out slightly, opening his defence and giving her a clear shot at his throat. Marie saw the opening and took an extra half-second to lean back. She hoped to get all her weight behind a final blow. Johnson, seeing her lean back, lifted both his feet up, wrapped them around her head and whipped her fiercely onto the floor. Exhausted, he rolled on top of her, grabbed a handful of hair and drove his fist into her face. The blow stunned her, giving him another moment to adjust, and a second fist came across her chin, knocking her out. Johnson collapsed forward onto the unconscious woman, gasping for air and reeling in pain.

He took a few moments to regain his composure and then staggered to his feet. Limping into the kitchen, he spotted two dish towels and used them to tie Marie's hands and feet together as tightly as he could. Finally finished, he sat down on the couch and wrote a message to the GIA. "The package is ready for pickup." Johnson slowly sat back on the sofa, wincing in pain, waiting for the portal to appear and observing her blankly as she lay on the floor.

Marie came back into consciousness slowly, but she could already feel the restraints on her wrists and ankles. She rolled onto her side and opened her mouth, moving her jaw gingerly. *Sore,* Marie thought, *but not broken.* She caught sight of Johnson, smirked and said, "Lucky punch." She continued speaking, deliberately turning her head away from him as if she were dismissing a subordinate. "The file I read on you was much more interesting than the real thing, kind of like when you see the movie after reading the book. I had expected so much more. Very disappointing."

"Seeing you in person is rather disappointing to me as well. I expected you to be younger, much younger. And you probably were a month ago. Obviously, your people forgot to tell you that Earth prematurely ages you." He had hit her in her weak spot — her own vanity.

Marie was shocked into silence. Everything suddenly fell into place. Sonia's looking older, her own facial features sagging. What the hell? She had to get off this planet. Now.

Marie twisted furiously back and forth on the floor, trying to weaken her bindings as Johnson watched without a word and waited impatiently for the portal to appear.

She spoke again, trying to change the subject. "They wasted my time here — they could've sent a first-year to look after you." She rolled onto her back, staring silently at the ceiling as a smile crept across her face. "How's Ann treating you these days? Did she ever mention she has a sister?" Marie broke out into laughter and then rolled back to her side, facing Johnson. "Let me introduce myself. The name is Petrov, and Ann and I are sisters. I'd like to shake hands with you, but I'm tied up at the moment."

She laughed again, but softly now. The joke really had been on her.

Sisters, Johnson thought. *I never would've known. I guess that's why Ann wanted her alive and maybe why Betty couldn't find her.* He looked down at his watch and realized impatiently that it had been ten minutes since he'd sent the message.

Marie continued, ignoring Johnson again. "Ann has a misguided idea that she was helping humanity by working with the GIA. I didn't agree and decided to work for the other side." She was quiet for a moment and then continued, "Do you ever wonder what happens if this all works out for the agency? Do you know what the next step will be?"

Johnson continued to stay silent, although he listened to her words. He knew she was trying to get into his head, and he wouldn't let her get there. The portal finally appeared, the glowing light mesmerizing and expanding slowly. He got to his feet and picked her up like a roped calf. She started to talk faster as he moved her closer into position.

"Johnson, this won't be the end of it. Don't you see once they have success here, they'll move on to other places? Killing what they don't want and taking whatever they need. This is just the beginning."

The portal had reached its final size, and Johnson finally spoke. "Say hi to Ann for me, and if you ever get out, tell your boss to send a man next time." He threw her into the tear, and she disappeared into it. The light emanating from all around him blinked out in a flash, and he stood still, allowing his eyes to adjust. He went to the kitchen sink, got a glass of water and downed it in one gulp. *Shit,* he thought. *She almost had me there.*

The IC looked on calmly as the Destination area flooded in light and then dimmed. The person sitting in the centre of the room moved her tied hands from behind her to her front in one smooth motion, bent over at her waist, untied her feet and slowly stood up. With her hands still bound, she wobbled slightly but stared defiantly through the glass window at the array of people assembled there. Three guards opened the door, moving on her with weapons drawn. She ignored them and continued to nonchalantly scan the group, finally finding the face she had been looking for. Marie smiled then, blood and spittle still running from her swollen lips. "Well, hi there, sis. Long time no see, bitch."

CHAPTER 42

*T*he Quick Reaction Team moved in on Marie, forcing her up against the wall. Two of the team members held her shoulders and arms back, while a third pushed on her forehead, forcing her head upright. Once she was secured and they determined she was no threat, another member moved in and placed a band around her right wrist.

Only then did they remove the towel Johnson had used to bind her wrists together. The security detail stepped back, and the Commander activated the band, which began emitting a steady, pulsing light. He asked her, "Do you know what this is?"

She looked at the band, rubbing her wrists where the towel had been. Without warning, she brought her hands up to strike him. Marie was immediately dropped to the floor by an electrical shock that collapsed her into a convulsive state, her body rigid, her chest so tight she couldn't breathe. A full thirty seconds went by before it ceased, and Marie was able to take a gulp of air. She stared up silently at the Commander, hatred flaring in her eyes.

"No lesson like a hard lesson," the Commander said with a tired expression. "Get her up."

Two guards stepped forward, reached down and hauled her up to her feet.

"Let me explain what that device on your wrist does. It picks up on any violent act and immediately generates an electrical shock. Your muscles will spasm until you are completely incapacitated. We're also able to operate it manually. Would you like a demonstration?"

Marie said, "I get the picture."

"Good. Your body functions go back to normal only once the brainwaves are at a preferred status. This places the onus on you, the prisoner, to comply and conform.

By the way, if you have a tracker embedded in you, it may have emitted a signal as you came into the facility. As of now, it's useless. You're in a black hole." He paused and began a slow, short pace back and forth before carrying on with his welcome speech. "Neither myself nor my personnel give a damn how you react or how your incarceration turns out. It can go hard, or it can go easy. The decision is yours. My suggestion is that we work together. It would benefit both parties."

Marie glared at the man. She wanted to fight, to resist, but knew it was useless. *Every system has a weakness,* she thought. *I'll just have to find this one.* She finally replied with a sarcastic, "I'll try my best to behave."

He said, "Welcome home," and then dismissively turned away from her.

Ann watched impassively as the episode unfolded itself and then told the Commander to take Marie to Interrogation. She glanced at the Control Room Technician. "Tell Johnson we've received the material. I'll send a detailed message later."

"Yes, ma'am. Sending now."

Marie was walked down to the Interrogation Centre, where they placed her on a chair in a half-sitting position. Her wrists, ankles, and waist were locked down on the chair, and there was a silicone cap on her head. She complied with everything that was being done. She knew what the procedure was and knew she couldn't do a thing about it. The machine was capable of reading and processing human thought. Nothing was sacred, no secrets could be withheld or hidden in her mind. It removed the need for repeated questioning, sleep deprivation, or physical interaction. All they had to do was hook you up and download every thought you ever had. It was that simple. Some people swore there was a way to beat the system by hurting yourself during interrogation or convincing yourself that you were somebody else. No one, however, had ever returned with a success story of how they beat it. *Let's just get this over with,* Marie thought as she watched Ann walk into the room.

Stepping up to the chair, Ann looked at the monitors and readouts before she shifted her gaze to Marie. "You had to do this, didn't you?" she sighed. "You have the talent, the smarts and could have gone far if you'd chosen to work with us."

"Ann, spare the speech for some kid who cares. You and your loving agency are so full of shit. Things would have been different if you had come with me. You could have done something right instead of meddling where you shouldn't, little sister."

Ann ignored the noise spewing from Marie's mouth and only shook her head.

Marie continued, malice in her tone. "And you fucking sent Sharpe after me. Are you that eager to get rid of me?"

"I'm done protecting you."

"You know our history. You know she wanted to kill me."

Ann continued without remorse. "I'm going to get my people to scan and download all the info in your head. Then when I'm done, I'm doing it again and again, until I have every detail and every stone rolled over. You've fucked up somewhere along the line, and your Command will be back to square one."

Marie only chuckled. "You'll get what you get. You'll also get what I don't know. You know that we work to keep things like this from pushing us back." She caught Ann's gaze and held it firmly before saying softly, for Ann's ears only, "I had him, you know. I thought of banging his guts out before beating the hell out of him. Fuck or fight. Hmmm, such a hard decision. He would have loved it. I always had a thing for younger men." She smirked then and finished with a mock kiss blown at her sister.

Ann stepped in closer to her and grabbed the restraints, tightening them until her sister winced in pain. She leaned in close and whispered into Marie's ear, "You hesitated, and he won. You think you're in control, but there's nothing you control now.

Let me remind you that you've aged at least fifteen years during your time on Earth. He wouldn't want an old lady." Ann laughed loudly at Marie's expression and then straightened. "I've tried to help you, but it stops today. As I said before, I'm going to get every drop of info in that bucket of yours. Then I'm going to send you to our most secure site for reorientation. If you're lucky, you'll be out in thirty years, crocheting cute little doilies for dollhouses." She paused for a moment as if considering her next words very carefully. "Oh, I forgot to tell you, Mom and Dad are doing well. Thanks for asking. I'll tell them you said hi." She smiled tightly at her sister, then turned and walked away before Marie could respond.

Eric had made the trip for this interrogation because he wanted to see firsthand what they could pull from Marie. He greeted Ann as she entered the area and said, "We did well by using Johnson. We've been looking for her for some time."

"Yes, he did," Ann replied, her gaze returning to the room that held Marie.

"Are you okay with this? I can take it from here if you prefer."

"I'm fine. I came to terms with this years ago when we took our separate paths. I always knew that one day it would come to this."

Eric nodded and turned to the technicians behind a panel of buttons. "Scan her."

The technicians began their sequence, the initial process taking only a few minutes. They would scan through her brain four more times, each additional scan confirming, enhancing, and providing further, subtle details. If any distinct anomalies showed up, they would rescan until everything aligned correctly. They could pinpoint a specific thought, what led to it, and if there was an outcome of any interest to the GIA. Over the next few weeks, they had planned to bring her in for updates, making sure they missed nothing.

Eric and Ann watched the screen as the system divided the

information, placing it in prearranged categories. The category they were specifically interested in was anything to do with the Rebels. All other information gathered would be put on her personal file, for the GIA's different departments to open and look through. This would complete the Intelligence picture against her and her organization.

"Done. The download was successful," the Tech behind the Control panel said after a few minutes.

"Thank you. We'll access it from my office," Ann said. She felt not a trace of remorse for what was being done to her sister. Actions have consequences. And her sister's actions had caused death and injury. Ann was adamant that Marie be stopped. "Make sure she gets into Holding."

They turned and walked away without giving Marie a second glance. A hologram image of her sister was waiting for them in Ann's office with a list of categories beside it. They opened the Training and Operations File to see who recruited her, when and where she had completed her basic training, who she knew and what missions she'd been on. If the material was recent, they could launch an Operation as soon as possible in the hope of catching the Rebels off guard. Unfortunately, there was nothing to be found. The Rebel protocol of limiting access had been successful, and they were unable to find any of the details they were looking for.

"Looks like we've got just the usual. Her group information we can act on. We'll send anything that can be useful to Johnson as soon as possible," said Ann.

Eric scanned the information, looking closer. "She's had to have contact with the upper echelon, and there's got to be a way to find it. Some thread that will lead us directly into it. What are we are missing?"

"I don't know, and I can't see anything yet." Ann pointed to the hologram and retraced the patterns. "We know where orders are given and executed, we know who works with her and their numbers, but it all stops at that level. Then at this point," she said, pointing to a line of text, "she's outside her group, and everything is done through voice alone. No contact, no liaison at a destination, and no names. We can see where she met that Jack fellow for their first meeting, but that's old news. We want to get above Jack to his bosses, something that can take us to the next level."

The two continued to search without speaking for a few minutes before Ann finally said, "One day we'll get there, sir. It just looks like it won't be today."

"You're right," Eric said, with a look of resignation on his face. "If there was any other type of communication besides verbal, we would have seen it here. I'll get my people to run the rest of this through their system and match it with the others we've scanned. Perhaps we can make a link." Eric stood up, frustrated with the temporary roadblock. "Pass on my thanks to the team and get back to me if anything new comes up. I'll send this on to Higher."

Ann watched as Eric left, and the door closed, then enabled the "do not disturb" icon on the office door. She needed some time alone. Gazing up at the 3D image of her sister hanging in midair, her mind returned to a time when they were just children, and Ann had followed after Marie wherever she went. Marie had been her hero and could do no wrong. How had this all changed? What had made her so jaded, so angry? It seemed like a lifetime ago. They had been on opposite sides now for a long time. A sense of deep sadness came over her. Her sister was right. Marie was the tough one, not her. A tear started in her eye, her emotions filling it to capacity before gravity tugged at it, setting it free to run down her cheek and drop to the table. Unable to recognize the strength she possessed, she pulled herself together with one deep breath, rubbed her eyes and got back to work. Closing the file on Marie, she blocked any lingering memories from her mind, readied the next SITREP and sent it to Johnson.

Marie lay in Holding, staring at the harsh light flooding her cell from the ceiling. The lights were so bright she could still see their sharp outlines plainly, even when she closed her eyes. The last twenty-four hours had taken a lot out of her, but that wasn't her worry. The worry was, what did they get and had she been able to hide it well enough? Had her father been right? The old nursery rhyme sung over and over through her mind until, exhausted, she slipped into a deep and dreamless sleep.

CHAPTER 43

Johnson walked out of Marie's apartment block, satisfied that his hunch was correct, and no one had cared about the noise emanating from the apartment. He hopped back into his brother's car and began driving down the quiet, deserted streets. The sun would be up soon, and Johnson thought that perhaps, with any luck, the elimination of the Rebel element would be the start of a new day for Sally as well. He needed to call his brother and let him know he was coming. Seeing a payphone booth at an all-night gas station, he pulled over, walked over to it and slid a quarter into the slot.

As soon as his brother answered, Johnson relayed his message. "I'm okay. See you in twenty minutes." Not bothering to wait for a reply, he drove back to his brother's home, parking in the rear. A short knock on the back door was all that was necessary for Dave to let him in.

"Coffee?"

"Hell, yes," Johnson said as he walked into the kitchen. "How's Betty?"

"She's sleeping now. She was up for a while, and we talked a little. She's a nice lady."

"She is that," Johnson said, sitting down to a fresh, hot mug of black coffee.

"I didn't think she'd make it through the night, but that vest and hood seemed to really help." Dave paused and looked quizzically at Johnson. "What happened to your face?"

"Just the hazards of the job."

The two drank their coffee without a word until Johnson finally said, "Betty may not be well enough for the trip home. Do you mind if she stays here until she gets her feet under her?"

"Sure, for as long as I'm able. I don't have much time, Steve.

My cancer will only get worse."

"I understand. Money, you don't have to worry about it. I'll take care of that. I'm hoping she'll be out on her own in no time." Johnson glanced sadly over to the counter where several pill bottles were lined up.

Dave saw his glance and said stoically, "They're for the headaches. They get bad. I try to hold out as long as I can, hoping I won't need them, but I do."

Johnson felt a frustrated helplessness in hearing those words from his brother and was momentarily speechless. He was saved from replying when he felt his wallet vibrate and took out a message from Ann, asking him if he was ready to take on Reilly. Stian, the traveller, had located him, and the protocols said now was the best time, as the man was alone in a condo in Vancouver. If he waited, it would be at least another week before Reilly would be alone again. "Sorry, Dave. No rest for the wicked. I've got to finish this now."

The two men walked down the steps to the basement, and Johnson slid a response into the wallet. "I'm hoping this will only take a few hours." He walked over to his brother's workbench and picked up a compact set of wire cutters. "Mind if I borrow these?"

"Go ahead. You plan on cutting your way into something?"

"You never know," Johnson said, as his wallet vibrated again. The message read

Reilly is not to be terminated. One minute to insertion. Johnson crumpled the paper and muttered, "Yeah, I got it."

The crack of bright light opened, and Johnson lightly gripped his brother's shoulder before saying, "I'll be back sooner than you think." He turned and walked into the light, its brilliance folding in on itself the moment he stepped through it.

The night was humid, but the breeze blowing in from the north was rapidly bringing a cooling touch to the air. Bill, hands in his pockets, casually strolled along the sidewalk to where the meeting was going to be held. He was hoping this was his last position change for the night; it had been a long one for him. Meandering through the streets, he frequently stopped to look around and ensure he wasn't being followed. Once he was convinced he was in the clear, he headed toward the meeting place. His mind drifted, and he wondered how much longer he could keep doing this. Bill stopped in front of a store window, automatically looking at the reflection and using the opportunity to see if anyone was behind him. His gaze shifted to his image. *I look like shit,* he thought, staring at the puffy cheeks, thinning hair, and dark circles under his eyes. He should just pick up and move away with the family, someplace obscure, and leave this all behind. A voice in his head interrupted his daydream. *You'll never* quit, it said. *The only way you're getting out is on a slab.* He shrugged and started walking again, checked the time and knew he was late. He couldn't have cared less and soon made his way up to a neon sign flashing the words, "Pinkerton Tavern."

The heavy door slid open, and he walked into a dimly lit bar. There were a few men at the bar, but all the tables, placed sporadically around the room, were empty. The only man that acknowledged him with a nod was the bartender, who was busy shining glasses behind the counter with an old rag. Bill stepped out of the doorway, took off his jacket, shook it and hung it up beside the door. He turned and walked to the far end of the room, where he could just make out Jack in the dim light. A few of Jack's men were strategically placed close by, in case things looked like they were going sideways. The bartender asked him, "Want anything?"

Bill turned and said, "Yeah, four blondes and a case of black mead."

The bartender smiled slightly, "If you're serious, I can find it."

"On second thought, that would probably be too expensive. I'll just take a glass of water."

The bartender reached under the counter, grabbed a glass, scooped some ice into it, filled it with water and placed it in front of him without comment.

Jack watched from the back of the room as Bill made his way over to him. He didn't like Bill, but they had to work together. The guy was too old-school for him. He never trusted anyone or anything. Everything had to be done his way, and that pissed Jack off. Whenever he complained, he was always told, "That's the reason Bill is still alive. You don't have to love him. Just work with him."

Bill walked up to the table, eyeing the muscle and asked, "What do these two do, hold your dick while you piss?"

Jack bristled and replied, "Fuck you, Bill. It's protocol."

"Still haven't learned to rely on yourself, hey?"

"Are you going to sit down or just stand there and flap your face all night?"

Bill pulled out a chair, skittered it across the floor and sat down with the two muscles in his peripheral. He placed his drink on the table, composing himself, and said, "Let's start over. It's nice to see you again."

"Yeah, sure, likewise," Jack replied automatically, leaving all conviction out of his voice. "Have you heard what's happened?"

"Yeah, I heard. And if anyone asks, you can say you heard it from me. That way, you guys can protect your cushy jobs and cover your collective asses. I'll start," he said, ignoring the angry emotion passing over Jack's face. Jack could easily intimidate others; Bill had worked with him too long and was immune. "It was your syndicate that was put in charge of gathering people and training them for the Operation. Marie had already been placed in charge by our Higher, so you had to find two others. Ivan was from a syndicate out in the West, and Sonia was from your area. Everything was fine until you decided to run a side Operation using Sonia."

Jack objected immediately and blurted out a harsh, "That's

bullshit! Wait just a minute."

Bill cut him off with a flicker of his hand. "Let me finish. It gets better. Marie sent all her plans back to me, so I knew she wanted to take out Sharpe and Johnson at the same time. I'm guessing something came up, and she left it for Sonia to finish." Bill paused, gazing around the room before casually sipping his water. "I've worked the scenario through my head a hundred times. Why didn't Sonia just whack those two and leave? Quick, efficient, and the job's done, right? I keep thinking about what reason Sonia would have to want to wait and risk everything. My guess, drum roll please, is that you wanted Sharpe to be sent back to your syndicate. Sonia was acting solely on behalf of your syndicate, not Headquarters."

Jack's jaw and hands visibly tensed as he shifted slightly in his seat. Bill leaned back, keeping his eyes trained on Jack's every move, ready to continue to talk or fight his way out of the bar. He knew now, based on the man's unrehearsed response, that his suspicions were confirmed. "You need to relax, Jack, and just keep listening. Now Sonia gets whacked, and Marie, one of my best Operators, gets taken and sent back to the agency. Your girl fucked this up for you."

Jack tensed, the vein along the right side of his neck pulsating. He took a deep breath as a calculating look came over his face. "This is all going to be on you, Bill. Marie belonged to your outfit and was in charge of the mission."

Bill's eyes looked unworried as he rested easy in the chair, spinning the water in his glass and then taking another sip. "Marie is mine. I'll eat my part of the shit sandwich. But your running a side-operation reeks of disloyalty. Now Marie is a prisoner in the agency's cells, getting scanned and drained of every detail of her life. Your people don't need to worry, but my people, the ones she had contact with, are running for their lives."

Jack eyed Bill carefully before replying. He hated this short, fat, bald man more now than the day they'd met twenty years before. "Is that it? Vague speculation on some kind of alternate plan? There's no proof of anything."

Bill stood up, shaking his head with a half-laugh that surprised Jack. "You can tell them that." He slid the chair back into the table. "You know, I was never a big fan of Marie's, never seen what HQ saw in her. As a matter of fact, she pissed me off more times than I can remember. Trying to take my job, telling me to retire and that I was too old. But she worked for me, and whether I like my people or not, I don't let them down and would never let them rot in some agency prison for thirty years. I'm going to get her back, Jack, somehow, some way. And when she finds out about the second op and the crisscross you had in place, I suggest you and anyone else in on this not be where she can find you. Yup, I almost feel sorry for you."

Bill suddenly imagined Marie taking her time, hitting the easy targets first, one-by-one before it would be Jack's turn. She'd wait until his guard was down, and it would be over before he knew it had begun. Bill let out a harsh bark of laughter. "I gotta be going now," he said, and walked to the bar, placing the glass beside the bartender. "Thanks for the water." He continued to the door, grabbed his jacket and stepped out into the cold night.

Jack remained stock still at the table, moving only to pick up his drink and throw it down his throat as Bill stepped out of the door. *Bullshit*, he thought. *What can one woman do?*

Johnson walked out of the rip and into the darkness of the room. He moved his head around, trying to see through the night but could only make out silhouettes. Breathing deeply and forcing his body to move despite the nausea he was feeling, his eyes finally adjusted. Laid out neatly beside each other in the living area were the two bodies of Reilly's men. It was an open concept condo, with a kitchen in one corner and a large couch and TV on the opposite side of the room. There was a long hallway that appeared to lead to the bedrooms. He took a few more minutes to get his legs back under him and then walked over to the floor-to-ceiling windows that ran along the outside walls. He gazed out at the sleeping city in front of him with the Lions Gate Bridge lit up in the background. *Nice place,* he thought.

He slipped quietly over to the long hallway and could see several opened doors, which he took to be bedrooms. There was one closed door at the end that he assumed was the master. Continuing down the hallway, he checked the rooms and confirmed they were bedrooms but, more importantly, that they were empty. Reaching the last room, he faced the closed door and placed his ear up against it. Hearing nothing, he turned the handle slowly, pushing the door quietly open.

A sliver of light from the large window inside passed through the opening and onto the wall beside him. Standing still, he could hear the faint sound of a person snoring. He stepped through the gap and into the room, making out the shape of a large man sleeping alone on a king-sized bed. He walked over to it and looked at the figure before reaching down and turning on the bedside lamp. The man stirred as the light hit his eyes, and he began to move slowly, bringing his hands up, trying to shield his eyes.

"Morning, Shawn," Johnson said softly. "Time to get up." With that, he hauled back his arm and brought the full force of his hand against Reilly's face.

The stunning slap and sharp sting on his skin brought the man to wakefulness with a gasp. His eyes opened wide with rage and disbelief. He looked up at Johnson, his mind not yet registering what was going on. "What? What's happening?" he stuttered.

Johnson stood silently over the man, his eyes emotionless. Not giving him a moment's reprieve, he grabbed a handful of Reilly's hair with his left hand and struck across his face with a solid connecting right.

Reilly's head shot back, and he gasped for air. "What do you want? Money? There's a safe," he managed to spit out.

"Money? You think this is about money?" He grabbed Reilly again by the hair and dragged him out of bed and into the bathroom. Hauled up by his underwear, Reilly found himself staring at the mirror with Johnson behind him, still holding him. "Look at me. Do you recognize me now, asshole?"

Riley squinted and then opened his eyes slowly as recognition dawned. In a low voice, he finally said, "It can't be. Fuck, no."

Johnson twisted the man around and threw him out the bathroom door and back into the bedroom. He rammed him solidly into a dresser, and Reilly collapsed onto the floor.

"Reilly, this is about payback," Johnson calmly said. He hauled the man up and tossed him back onto the edge of the bed. The man swayed dangerously back and forth, hands clenched to his chest, and his arms pressed tightly to his sides as he tried to staunch the pain. Johnson tapped the side of Reilly's face. "Reilly, wake up. I need your full attention."

The man managed to stutter out, "I'm awake. I'm awake. What do you want?"

"You're awake! Well, that's excellent. Now come with me. I want to show you something." Johnson grabbed the man by the back of the neck and half-lifted, half- carried him out to the living room. With a powerful heave, he threw him to the floor and then turned on a light.

Reilly found himself momentarily airborne before landing heavily onto his stomach, the wind knocked out of him. Gasping for air, he took a moment before lifting his head up. In front of him, not one metre from where Reilly lay, were the bodies of the men he had sent to help Marie. Struggling to his knees, eyes locked on the dead men, Reilly whispered, "I'll do anything. What do you want?"

"You sent these two dirtbags to kill my friend and me. You asked me what I want. I want to beat you as badly as you hurt my friend and then dump you. Unfortunately, my bosses won't let me," Johnson said with unnerving calm. "I'll let you live. For now."

He strode quickly over to Reilly, pulling back his fist. Reilly instinctively threw his hands up over his face, protecting himself. Just as suddenly as he had raised his fist, Johnson pulled the punch back. "You see," he said as if talking to a toddler, "fear is an excellent teacher. I walk over, cock my fist back, and you go into protection mode." He reached over and grabbed the man, throwing him into a chair beside a table directly facing the two bodies.

"This is the deal. You're going to write your daughter a letter and tell her how proud you are of her. You're going to tell her that you're never going to interfere with her work again, no matter how successful she becomes. Lastly, you'll let her know that if she ever needs anything, you will be there for her. Write it now."

Reilly only then realized that on the table lay a pad of paper and a pen. He shakily picked up the pen, and dutifully began to write. Johnson stood and watched every word as they were written. When Reilly finished, he signed the letter and looked up at Johnson, who silently took the paper and folded it.

"It's done. I've done everything you wanted. Can I go?"

"One last thing. In case you happen to think about going back on your word, I'm leaving you with a little reminder." Johnson threw the man to the floor, and Reilly reacted in horror when he realized he was face-to-face with one of the dead men. Before he had a chance to scream, Johnson dropped on top of him, his knees pinning the hapless man's body and head. Reaching for Reilly's right hand, he simultaneously pulled the wire cutters from his back pocket.

"What the fuck are you doing?" Reilly screamed at Johnson, trying to squirm free. Johnson applied more pressure to the side of Reilly's face, making it impossible for the man to make anything more than a muffled gag of protest. He despised this part of the job but knew that what he was about to do would be the only deterrent for the man.

He slid the wire cutter over Reilly's right-hand little finger, just past the first knuckle. "Take a deep breath," Johnson said as he clamped down on the handle and watched an inch of the man's finger fall to the floor.

Clean cut, he thought, wiping the blades on the back of Reilly's shirt and then sliding them back into his pocket. Johnson knew that Reilly needed a daily reminder of the consequences of going against his promise. He looked down and spoke quietly into the man's ear. "If you shut the fuck up, I'll get off you."

Reilly's body appeared to sag in on itself, and his struggling stilled. Johnson released the pressure on the man's jaw, hauled him to his feet and pushed him back into the chair. Reilly looked down at his hand and then at Johnson. "You're a fucking animal."

The beaten man sat quietly now, shoulders forward, head hanging down as he held his hand and tried to stop the bleeding. His face reflected the damage and pain Johnson had inflicted. It was clear to Johnson, however, that his morale had not yet been completely broken. Men like Reilly had difficulty keeping their inflated egos in check. Because of that, they had problems remembering the consequences of their actions. They would always be looking for an opportunity for revenge. Shaking his head, Johnson pulled out his wallet and notified Headquarters that he was ready to travel.

"Reilly, perhaps you don't really know how bad this could have turned out," Johnson said philosophically as he was waiting. He grabbed two napkins and threw one to the man to wrap his hand in. He used the other one to pick up the digit on the floor and placed it in his pocket. "Don't need anyone trying to sew that back on now, do we? The missing finger will be your daily reminder of our little meeting. If I ever hear of you hurting Sally, or disrupting her progress, I'll come back and relieve you of a few more appendages. Do you understand? Oh, and I'll let you decide what you want to do with the bodies." Reilly looked up and nodded mutely.

As soon as Johnson felt the air start to energize in front of him, he picked up Reilly by the back of his neck and shoved him away. "Now fuck off to your bedroom. I'm done with you," he ordered. The man staggered slightly and began walking, then running down the hallway away from him.

The light grew steadily brighter as Johnson heard Reilly push the door of the bedroom hard against the wall. He shook his head as he listened to the man opening and rummaging through a drawer. Johnson smiled grimly at the sound of the metallic clack of a pistol slide being pulled back and released. *Just another stupid man,* Johnson thought as he disappeared into the blinding light.

Reilly ran back to the front room of the condo, gripping the pistol in his bloody right hand, before stopping and looking around, confused. There was nothing around him but the dead silence of the two men lying before him.

Johnson stepped out of the crack of light and into his apartment. He walked over to the couch, collapsing slowly onto it and looked around the room. *What a night,* Johnson thought. This second transport had left him entirely spent, and he allowed himself several minutes for his injured body to adjust. He finally took a deep breath and stood up. His hand automatically went to his injured ribs, pushing and prodding. They were sore, but that was it. The brace had done its job. He walked over to the fridge, opened it and spotted the Pilsner beer he'd bought a few days prior. Grabbing three of them, he placed them on the counter, cracked the first one and downed it. He opened a second but stopped drinking at the halfway point and put it on a table.

Johnson took out Reilly's letter and sent it to Midgard for onward transmission into Sally's mailbox. She needed to receive it right away. It was now time to phone his brother. He punched the number into the phone and waited for the pickup.

A woman's voice answered, "Hello?"

"Betty?"

"It's me. How did the visit turn out?" Betty asked calmly.

Johnson was surprised. He hadn't expected her to be up. "Ahhh...what are you doing out of bed?"

"Are you my mother? Relax, I'm fine. Your brother is lying down now, so we'll keep this short."

"The visit went fine. I brought a little souvenir back as a reminder to Reilly."

"Hmmm, you'll have to tell me all about it later. You sound tired. You need some sleep."

"I'll lie down in a minute, but I need to tell you something first."

"Steve, I already know what you're going to say. I signed on knowing the risks of the job. I know how badly hurt I am and what you're about to ask. I'd rather stay here and live than die in transport back home. Did that just make your life easier?"

"There's more to this, Betty."

"Can't talk right now. Your brother is getting up. Talk to you later," she said briskly.

"We need to talk."

"Don't worry. We will."

Johnson walked over to the door and rammed his wedge tightly underneath it. He made his way back to the table, inhaled the remainder of his second bottle and cracked the third. He carried it around the apartment as he stripped off his clothing and had a shower. After drying himself off, Johnson reached over and drank the last of the beer before catching his reflection in the mirror. *Looks like I've been hit by a truck,* he thought, as his eyes scanned the bruises and welts over his body. Walking to the bed, he pulled back the sheets and climbed in, putting his head on the pillow and falling asleep an instant later.

CHAPTER 44

Ann had just gotten word from HQ that Johnson's last mission was a success. After his visit with Shawn Reilly, they had rerun the protocols. They determined that Reilly would now leave his daughter alone and not interfere with the project. Eric and his people would now only have to monitor the situation to ensure Sally continued with her work. Johnson would soon be able to wrap things up and return to Midgard.

She glanced at her screen when she entered her office and, noting that Eric had requested she contact him, sat down and initiated the call. "Mr. Stanton, I'm back in the office. You wanted to speak to me?"

Eric's face appeared on the screen. "Hello, Ann. I assume you've seen the protocols on Johnson's mission?"

"Yes, I did. I also read your people would be taking over the duties of monitoring the situation. Is that correct?"

"Yes. You can tell Johnson to start drawing down over the next few days."

"We'll do that," Ann said.

"I'd like to talk to you about Marie."

"What about?"

"The details on her primary Rebel cell were good, but the follow-up we conducted found nothing. Of course, they all scattered before we could round them up. I wanted to find more info on the Chain of Command, but we've gone over all the data and found nothing. It's highly unusual. It's either just not there, or she's managed to block it somehow. She may have developed a technique to fight our scanners using something we've never seen before."

Ann was puzzled. "I've only heard rumours of people being

able to resist. Our scanners go through the whole brain, piece by piece. How would that even work?"

"I think it's something very fundamental and simple that acts as a wall. The scan recognizes it as something back in a person's childhood, so moves over it. If you remember the first scans we did, there was a song that kept repeating. It comes from an ancient nursery rhyme, something about herbs for healing."

"I still can't see how or why the scanner would move around it."

"We don't understand it yet either, but they say there's a possibility. We did get some valuable information that I would like to exploit. Marie was moving up in her organization fast, and my prediction is they won't be cutting ties with her. They'll want her back, so I'm thinking — let's give her back."

"I don't understand. We've gone through all of this, and now we're going to let her go?"

"We're not just going to let her walk out the door or just hand her over. I'm thinking more along the lines of her breaking out of here and getting away. We track her and keep an eye on her to see what happens along the way."

"Sir, we know the Rebel Command won't just let her back into the fold."

"I agree," Eric replied. "I anticipate they won't take her back for a few years. They'll put her in the middle of nowhere and let the whole situation cool off for a while. She'll resurface in time."

"I understand. You're talking long term," Ann said.

"Yes, we are. Plant the seed, leave it alone and let it grow. We'll keep a close eye on her in the beginning, just to see what's happening. Once she's back in the organization, we keep steady track of her until we decide what we want to do."

"How would we track her? The first thing they'll do is scan every centimetre of her body."

"The techs have come up with what they think will be undetectable. It's not a device. It's a chemical that we'll inject into her. It acts exactly like blood does in our bodies, and when the chemical composition is examined, it looks the same. Its unique makeup allows us to follow it wherever it goes."

Involuntarily, Ann breathed a sigh of relief. Her sister's mind and memories would not be erased. As much as she hated Marie's actions, she was still her sister. Ann continued, "Sounds like it may work. Have they trialled it?"

"Yes, it's functioning well," Eric replied. "No one else is to know about this. We're taking all necessary precautions to ensure we don't have another informer. Tell your people only that we'll be running one last scan at your facility. My people will come in, inject the chemical and ensure it's working. At the same time, we'll swap out her band. The one we're going to give her has a faulty latch. We're hoping she'll discover it. The next day, I'll talk with her in one of the open exercise areas, where I suspect all she'll be thinking about is escaping. We then present an opportunity that she can't refuse, and once she's clear of our bubble, the Rebels should get her signal and pick her up."

"There's a lot of what-ifs and speculation in this plan. What if she decides not to run?"

"I'll be using my people and make it so she can't turn the escape down. That's why I want to use the open courtyard. She's going to be injured along the way, nothing life-threatening, just enough to sell it to her and the Rebels. A few non-lethal energy wounds."

"I can work with that. I'll have Marie ready for you. Is there anything else?"

"No, I'll see you tomorrow," Eric finished.

Marie was on the floor of her cell, pumping out push-up after push-up. On the last rep, arms shaking, she pushed up to full extension and then rolled onto her back. She regularly followed the same plan: repeats of sit-ups, burpees, and then body squats, all to complete failure. It wasn't meant to keep her in shape. It just kept her mind off the silence. That utter silence would make her days very long and the weeks even longer. Knowing those weeks had the possibility of turning into months and then years, she turned her thoughts back to escape. *I have to find a way to defeat this band,* she thought, *and get out of here as soon as possible.* Resolutely steeling herself, she got up and began to pace.

Ann contacted her people and advised them that HQ would be taking Marie through a few procedures over the next two days. A day later, Eric and his team were escorted to the Detention Centre. Ann met them at the entrance and said, "We're ready for you. All personnel have been advised that you'll be assuming responsibility for the prisoner. If you need me, I'm available."

"You can stay if you'd like," Eric replied.

"Thank you. I'll do that."

Just then, Marie walked around the corner, escorted by two guards. Ann observed her sister carefully. The lighting had emphasized the ageing that had occurred while she was on Earth. Ann almost felt sorry for her.

"Good morning, Marie," Eric said.

"So, what's on my agenda today?" Marie asked sourly.

"I've got a few pieces of information I need to confirm with you. It shouldn't take long," Eric replied. He turned to the guards and said, "Take her into room four, please and prepare her."

The guards escorted her into the room, strapping her down and then hooking her up to the probes. Eric initiated the scan, and Marie slid helplessly into an unconscious state.

"Are we ready?" Eric asked.

"Yes, sir," the tech replied.

"Let's get this done."

With that, they opened her mouth and administered an injection into the side of her cheek against the jawbone. They initiated the setup between the chemical and their tracking program, ensuring everything was functioning correctly. Once the link was established, Eric said, "That's it for today. We'll just replace her wristband and start phase two in the morning." A technician then disconnected Marie from the machine and ensured she was fully conscious before the guards returned her to her cell.

Once back in confinement, Marie faced another long, tedious day and night with no stimulation and no human contact. She paced back and forth for an hour, allowing her body the slightest physical release. Her mind was still restless, but she was careful not to show any outward signs of agitation. She would never give them the satisfaction of knowing that this incarceration was hell. Marie finally stopped and, lowering herself gracefully onto the cell floor, adopted a yoga lotus position, relaxing and slowing her breathing. Concentrating on the steady rhythm of her breath, she repeated a silent mantra over and over again. Her body was as still and quiet as a stone, her mind as far away from the prison as she could send it. She sat there for hours while the guards, bored and uninterested, watched her on their screens. Eventually, she started to move, stretching out her hands, arms and then her lower limbs. Marie stood up slowly, continuing to stretch her cramped muscles and then turned to face the wall. In this position, they were unable to observe her face as she knelt down and sat back on her heels. Moving her hands together, Marie slipped her little finger between the security band and her wrist, irritated by its presence. The band was tight, as usual, but she pushed at it hard when to her surprise, she felt the clasp loosen.

Maintaining a calm demeanour despite the excitement that rose in her, she continued to work at the clasp until it finally gave way and broke open. Her hand caught it before it could slip off her wrist, and she looked carefully down at the latch. It appeared that the clasp itself had worn slightly and given way under additional stress. She fixed it back into place on her wrist and once again locked it. Using the exact same motion as before, she watched with satisfaction as the band popped open again. Sitting back quietly for a moment, Marie allowed a small smile to form on her face before she snapped the latch shut one last time, raised herself up and went to bed.

The next morning, Marie moved under the covers and popped the band off and on again to ensure that she hadn't imagined it. She got out of bed and walked over to the toilet to relieve herself. Her face and eyes moved to the camera that observed her every action, invading every inch of her life. She mouthed "Fuck off" to the offending piece of machinery and moved to the sink. Marie washed her face and was just drying it when the clank of the door got her attention. She turned around, the towel still in her hands, and watched quietly as Eric walked into the cell.

"Good morning, Marie. How are you doing today?"

"You just stopping by for a friendly hello, or will you be joining me for breakfast?" she asked sarcastically.

"Yes and no," Eric replied, ignoring Marie's tone. "Yes, I stopped by, but no, not for breakfast."

A guard came in at that very moment and placed a plate of food on the bed.

"Once you're finished that, we're going for a walk," he said, then turned and left the cell.

Marie was instantly on guard. She did not trust Eric and automatically assumed he wanted something from her.

Twenty minutes later, the two of them walked down the hallway, escorted by two guards. Eric said, "You're not as feisty as you were when we brought you in. Is there a problem?"

Marie, not wanting to be baited, did not reply. Whatever this man wanted, Marie would not be pulled into it. She just kept walking, head up, hands clasped behind her back.

Eric, ignoring Marie's stony silence, continued, "Yesterday was your final scan. We've retrieved everything we need." He motioned Marie toward a door that slid open to a courtyard and let Marie enter the open area first. While Ann watched from the control room, the guards and Eric followed behind at a discreet distance. Marie stepped through the door and stopped momentarily to take in a breath of air. The smell of fresh earth, combined with the sweet smells emanating from the flowerbeds, was a welcome change from the recirculated air she had been breathing in. She exhaled and then walked to the centre of the yard, daring to stretch out her arms and feel the warmth of the sun. Its rays on her skin made her face tingle as they touched it. She closed her eyes and tilted her head up, enjoying even this little bit of freedom.

Eric approached her from behind and spoke quietly into her ear. "Feels good after being cooped up in cells twenty-four hours a day, doesn't it?"

Marie did not flinch but thought wryly that this is where Eric would undoubtedly begin a pitch for her cooperation. *Let the games begin,* she said to herself.

Eric watched her closely, letting her soak in the freedom she felt. He broke into Marie's silence. "Marie, we need you. As a matter of fact, I wish I had more like you and Johnson." Not waiting for any kind of reply, he motioned for Marie to follow him, and the two began to walk around the courtyard.

Marie was willing to keep this going for as long as possible. *Anything to stay away from that cell,* she thought and decided to play along.

"What did you have in mind?"

"Let's talk about your future first. You don't have many options now, do you? In fact, you have only two. You either volunteer to work with us, or we wash your memories clean and give you new ones, after which you sit in a facility that's a lot worse than this place for the next thirty years. Your choice."

Marie gave nothing away but knew that neither of those choices was acceptable. "When do you need an answer?"

"Tomorrow."

"You'll have it."

Eric motioned to one of the guards that he was ready to leave and ordered him to join them. Just before they arrived at the door, Eric said, "You can have a few more minutes out here, but l need to get going. I want you to think hard about what I said. Thirty years is a long, long time. You can give your answer to Ann tomorrow. I hope you make the right decision."

Marie nodded her head as Eric stepped into the doorway, slid the door shut and walked down the hall. Marie waited only a fraction of a second before she turned her back to the guard facing her at the door and, in one motion, slipped her finger between the band and her wrist. The band released, falling to the ground as she turned and punched the man viciously in the throat. The man gasped for breath and fell to his knees as Marie side kicked him in the head, knocking him unconscious. She then wedged the door shut from the outside and sprinted for the open ground.

Eric stood with the other guard in the hallway, peering out the window. As he watched Marie run, he spoke firmly to the guard. "You're on. Give her something to remember us by, but don't kill her." The guard nodded and then cracked the door open with a single heave.

Marie was pushing herself forward hard, teeth clenched, arms and legs pumping forward as she sprinted through the field. *One hundred metres more and I'll be there*, she thought.

Behind her, the second guard burst through the door, yelling orders and calling for her to stop before she would be shot. She ignored him, pushing harder and zigzagging as she ran, thinking that the point must be close. The first blast tore into the side of her leg, making her stumble. She cried out in pain, fighting to keep her balance, but she could see a portal opening ahead of her. Another blast seared into her right arm, feeling like a red hot poker jamming into her. She knew the next shot would be between her shoulder blades. Pushing hard with every ounce of her strength, lungs ready to explode, she gave a final, desperate cry, leaped into the light in front of her and was gone.

Eric attended to the injured guard. "Thanks for taking this on. Medical is here. They'll have you up in no time."

Ann walked through the door. "She didn't disappoint me," she muttered to Eric. The medics helped the injured guard to his feet as the other man came back over to them. Eric smiled grimly at him. "Nice shooting."

Marie was moved four more times in quick succession. Each move intensified the pain from her injuries, the last drawing a final scream of anguish from her throat. After what seemed to be an eternity of swirling light and pain, she found herself falling onto her knees to a cold floor. Her body collapsed, and she fell forward onto her hands, gasping for breath and trying to stop the spinning in her brain. She felt, rather than saw, someone walking toward her. He reached down, grabbed her by the collar and then heaved her to her feet. Instinctively, she slipped the hold and put the man into a position to break his neck. Applying force, she could feel the vertebrae start to separate. Just a millimetre more and his days would be done. She whispered fiercely into his ear, "Who the fuck are you?"

"Marie, let him go," a voice above her commanded.

Recognizing the voice, she looked up. "Nice reception, Bill," she shouted, still maintaining her hold on the man. His eyes were beginning to bulge, the lids half closed as he struggled for air.

Bill sighed tiredly. "Marie, we have rules. Let him go."

She released him, and the man fell to the ground with a thud, groaning softly. Marie bent over him, slapping him across the face. "Time to wake up, sweetheart."

A loud, harsh gasp pulled air into the man's lungs as he fought to bring oxygen into his body. Marie stood impassively, watching him, and then smiled up at Bill. "Thanks for the pickup. I need a patch on my leg and arm."

Ann and Eric walked into the Intelligence Section toward an open area that housed a hologram map of the world. A man standing beside one of the consoles asked Ann, "Who are you looking for, ma'am?"

"Rebel number 1173," she replied.

The man punched the request into the computer. "Should be up in a second," he said, looking up at the hologram.

A second later, a pinpoint shone brightly in a location thousands of kilometres away from them. Ann manipulated the hologram and zoomed into the area. She looked at Eric. "They did a good job of picking her up and moving her." She continued zooming in and stopped at the 400-metre mark above the building. "I think that's close enough."

Eric agreed. "Good work. Everything appears to be functional. Keep a close eye on her for the next few months."

Ann looked over her shoulder at him. "Of course, sir."

"I'm curious to see what they do with her," Eric said as he left the room.

Ann finished her work at the hologram and then walked out to her vector, deep in thought. She remembered the rhyme well but would never tell Stanton or anyone else. It was something her father would sing to the two girls when they were younger. He had told them they could hide all their secrets behind the words, and no one would ever find them. Ann was too young and didn't understand, but Marie did. Stepping into the vector, she found herself humming and then singing the childish rhyme over and over again. *Herbs for healing when medicine in need, berries and spice to flavour your mead.*

CHAPTER 45

Johnson lay in his bed, unwilling to leave it. His body felt like it had been run through a spin cycle on the washing machine. His mind was going over and over his encounter with Reilly and the finger he'd cut off. He'd played close to that line before but had never crossed it until that moment. What scared him was not knowing how far he might go the next time.

He reluctantly pried his eyes open and checked the time on his watch. It was late afternoon, and he had been asleep for nine hours. With a sigh, he swung his feet out from under the covers and onto the floor, easing himself painfully upright. He made the bed and then looked down at the dark blue bruising around his torso. He had seen worse, he thought wryly and made his way to the washroom. Johnson was pleasantly surprised to see no blood in his urine. *That's a good sign*, he said to himself. *No damage to the kidneys.* He started the shower, ensuring it was hot enough to loosen his tight and bruised muscles. Johnson gently pushed and probed around his ribs with his fingers. The brace they'd sent from Midgard had worked out fine, but he was still slightly sore. Finishing the shower, he dried off, got dressed and walked out the door to find a cab.

He found one sitting idle a short distance away and slid slowly into the back seat. The driver looked at him closely. "Rough night?" Johnson gave the driver only a cursory glance. He ignored the question, giving him directions and then turned his face to the window. The driver, accustomed to being ignored, went back to his steering wheel, pulled out and drove him to a location a few blocks from his brother's house. Shortly after, with his leg muscles just beginning to stretch out and relax, he found himself walking up the path to his Dave's home and knocked on the door. He was surprised to see Betty open it, a smile on her face.

"Hi, stranger," she said, letting him in. "How are you feeling?"

"I'm fine, just a little sore. How about you? I was worried. Wasn't expecting you to be up this morning."

"I'm a lot tougher than you think, and the heavy-duty brace worked well."

The two of them walked into the kitchen, where they found his brother doing up the dishes.

Dave caught sight of Johnson and said brightly, "Hi there. Would you like a coffee?"

"That would be nice," Johnson replied. He looked quizzically at his brother and then at Betty. "He looks different. What did you do to him?"

Betty laughed softly and picked up her coffee. "We got to talking last night, and he offered me a place to stay. We made a deal. Dave picked up my communicator from the apartment, and I sent a friend of mine his cancer prognosis. He sent me what we needed, and now he's on the mend. A few more months, and he should be clear."

Johnson stopped short and gaped at Dave. "Really? That's great!" He strode over to him and enveloped him in a hug. Dave laughed and said, "Sure is. I had one treatment this morning, and the headache was cut in half. That's a good first sign. Betty tells me I have a few more weeks before the tumour disappears completely."

Johnson turned gratefully to Betty. "You have a lot of good friends. Would you thank them for me?"

Betty slid a piece of paper over to him. "I do, and I will. I received this a few hours ago, by the way. It looks like you're finished here."

Johnson read the message explaining that the protocols HQ had run after his visit to Reilly had received satisfactory results. "You're right. It looks like everything's about over. Stanton's crew will take it from here. But I do have to see Sally tonight. She's got a meeting with a potential investor. She wanted me there, just to listen."

"Of course," Betty said. "You can't just disappear from her life without a word."

"Betty, I need to talk to you about staying here. You know how quickly you're going to age," Johnson started.

"You haven't figured it out yet?" Betty interrupted. "Some sixty years ago, Midgard had just started their travels to Earth. The process was in its infancy and wasn't as exact as it is now. A Traveller was sent, but he materialized in the middle of a battle in Britain sometime in the 1400s. My father saved his life that day, but the villagers thought the Traveller was a witch and burned down our home, killing my mother and father. I was five years old at the time. The Traveller couldn't just leave me there, I was injured, and they would have killed me, too. He took me back to Midgard against orders. No one other than the Director and immediate technicians knew that he had brought me back. He and the agency became my family. I grew up in Midgard, but I'm from Earth." She raised an eyebrow at him and teasingly added, "I most certainly have not aged since I came here, and you better not say I'm looking older."

Johnson couldn't reply. It all began to make sense now. Why she had so many contacts in the agency, why she had been sent here with him and why she hadn't aged. He finally asked, "Why didn't you tell me?"

"You didn't need to know, and it didn't seem important at the time. Now it does."

"So, I don't need to worry about you?"

"That's right. I'll be fine. I'll make this my home now. Home isn't one place when you're soldiers like us. You know that. Home is where you decide it to be."

Johnson felt like a huge weight had just been lifted off his shoulders. The outcome would be positive. His brother was on the way to health, Betty would survive these injuries, and she would still live a long life. They talked at length for another hour, discussing her plans for the future. He finished his coffee and left the two of them soon after.

Johnson had been walking for almost an hour when he recognized the scent of a fast-food hamburger joint. His stomach began growling automatically, reminding him that he hadn't eaten in over 24 hours. Stomach leading the way, he found himself reaching for the door and stepping inside the restaurant. The place was scarcely occupied but was overrun with the smell of fresh french fries and burgers on the grill. He ordered two double burger meals and inhaled them both, wiped his face with a satisfied smile and went on his way. *Midgard*, he reflected, *would never be able to replicate fast food.*

Fifteen minutes later, Johnson turned the corner onto 13th Avenue, arriving at the coffee shop. The sign above the door was unlit, and the restaurant appeared at first to be closed for business. The lights, however, were on, and a few people were gathered around a table. Johnson tapped lightly on one of the windows. Sally looked up and beamed when she recognized his face. She rushed to the door and opened it. "Glad you could make it," she said.

"Thanks for asking me."

She lifted her hand up to his face, running her finger above the scab on his cheek. "What happened here?"

"Embarrassing accident. I wasn't paying attention while I was out running and caught a branch on the side of my face," Johnson answered with a shrug. "Not to worry. I heal fast."

"I never knew running to be a contact sport," she replied skeptically. "Come on in and take a seat. We've just begun." She introduced him to the group and then opened her presentation. She was a natural at speaking, and her passion for the subject was contagious. An hour later, the pitch ended, and they broke up into smaller groups. Johnson helped himself to a cup of coffee and then stood off to the side. Forty minutes later, Sally walked over to him and said, "Thanks for waiting."

"No problem," he smiled. "You did a good job up there."

"You think so? I'll see just how good over the next few days, I suppose."

"Can I walk you home?"

Sally's smile turned to the floor, then back at him. "I'd like that, but Ian," she said, nodding over to a tall, slim man, "and I are going out for a bite to eat. I'd ask you to join us, but..." Johnson cut her off with a grin.

"Woah, Sally, that's okay! I'll drop by and see you tomorrow." As he walked away, he heard her call his name. "Steve! I almost forgot to tell you, I got a rather unusual letter from my dad this morning."

"Unusual? In what way?"

"Well, it was unusual for him. I didn't think he was even aware I was back working on the project. In any case, he wished me luck. I don't know why he had such a change of heart, but I'll take it."

"The little wins add up to big ones. It appears things are really looking up for you. You deserve it. I'll see you tomorrow."

Walking out the door, he looked back through the window and saw Sally and Ian standing close to one another and talking. *Good job,* he said to himself. *That girl is going to be okay.* Satisfied, he turned his head back to the street and strode confidently back to the apartment.

Marie sat across from Bill and said, "I know they put something in me and are tracking me at this moment. We can't find anything, so I'm assuming it's organic."

"I have a solution for that," he said coolly. "We're going to leave you out here on the outer fringes. Let them and our people get a little less interested in you."

She sat there for a moment, shocked. "Bill, there's nothing out here."

"I know. That's why I'm leaving you here. For a year, maybe a bit longer. We can bring you back slowly once we find a way to either take it out or counter it."

Marie was frustrated but betrayed nothing to Bill. She would go along with everything he said but had no intention of actually following through with his enforced detention. *A fucking year*, she thought. *I'm not staying here for a year.* She calmly replied, "I don't like it, but I understand, and it's better than sitting in an agency cell."

Bill, suspicious of her immediate acceptance of the circumstances, continued with cynical eyes. "Yes, it is. Besides, there's something you can be thinking about for the next while. Do you remember Jack?"

"Of course, why?"

"After you were captured, I reread all the private messages you'd sent me. There were too many inconsistencies with the information I was receiving from other sources. The only conclusion was that Sonia was working for Jack behind your back. It became obvious when I noticed your message about having Johnson and Sharpe under your control. Jack didn't know about that, did he?"

Marie said, "No, I only told you and, of course, Sonia knew. I was going to tell Jack after it was done because his original orders were to take Johnson out."

"I figure Sonia contacted him once she found out about Sharpe, and Jack, seeing an opportunity, wanted her sent back to Midgard. He could have used her for his own personal gain as a bargaining tool with the agency."

Marie walked around the sparsely furnished room, stopping at the window. She watched the dust devils gather out on the open prairie, twisting themselves into a frenzy as they spun across the plain. "You know when that little voice in your head tells you that something is fucked up, but you refuse to listen to it? It keeps repeating itself, warning you, but you ignore it, and then shit happens. That's what I did. I knew something was up but ignored my gut feeling, and this is where it gets me."

Bill said, "It happens to everyone. Not all the time, but it happens."

She turned and walked back to the table. "I've got something to keep me going now. Tell Jack I'm making a list and he's at the top of it. Once I'm done, there'll be plenty of room for promotions."

Bill walked to the corner of the room as the air started to stir, and a crack of light appeared. "I may have already mentioned that to him," he said, walking up to the portal as it stabilized. "We'll keep in touch." He took another step and was gone.

Johnson had just arrived at the entrance to his apartment when a message came through the wallet. *"Waiting for you in your apartment. Ann."* He opened the door and found her there, sitting on the sofa. "This is a nice surprise," he said, closing the door behind him and smiling at her.

"I came here to say goodbye to Betty and explain to her why I needed Marie alive."

"Betty was angry. She couldn't understand why the GIA wanted her back."

"Betty was only concerned with revenge, and that's not healthy for her. Marie is of more use to the GIA alive. She can possibly lead us to the Rebel HQ."

"You're not worried about ageing while you're here?"

"I'll be leaving tomorrow. The effects will be negligible."

"That's good," Johnson said, walking over to the fridge, taking out a couple of beers and opening them. He handed her one. "Is there anything else you wanted to be done here?"

"No, the results look good, and everything seems to be lining up."

"Even with her father?"

"That was interesting, actually. Initially, we weren't happy with the outcome that was predicted. There appeared to be a real chance that he would continue to try and stop her. Your meeting with him seems to have changed that outcome and turned it in our favour." She paused and looked at him curiously. "What could that have been about?"

"In my experience, sometimes people like him need to be convinced differently." Reaching into his pocket, he pulled out the severed finger and tossed it onto the coffee table. "My discussion with him showed him I was serious."

Ann's eyebrows lifted slightly. She lifted the bottle to her mouth and downed half of it before placing it on the table. "I see. Can I get another one of these, please? It tastes just like our mead. And throw that thing in the garbage."

Johnson took the loose digit to the washroom, where he flushed it down the toilet. On his return, he walked over to the fridge and took out two more beers, opened them and handed her one. She commented no further on Johnson's methodology, although he was well aware of her reservations. "You can start the cleanup and then come back to Midgard," she said instead.

"I'll do that," he said. "Your sister...I had no choice. She's a tough woman and put up one hell of a fight."

"I can see that by the marks on your face. She said she almost had you."

"It was touch and go for a few seconds. I was trying to be a gentleman."

She laughed sharply. "A gentleman! Don't bother. She would have served you up on a platter if she had the chance." Ann reached for the beer and took a long swig. "She escaped the other day, by the way, just after we placed a tracker in her."

Johnson glanced at Ann, the corner of his mouth lifting into a small smile. "She escaped just after you put a tracker in her? What a coincidence."

"Hmm," she said, "it certainly is, isn't it? That's all I know. It's unfortunate."

She drank her beer and watched Johnson processing what she'd just told him. He finally asked, "There's a lot you haven't told me. Why did Marie start working with the Rebels? How did two sisters end up on opposite sides of the war?"

"All good questions," she answered philosophically. "I suppose it all boils down to our father and how we reacted to his death. He was a GIA scientist who developed the scanner we use for memory retrieval. It was a huge undertaking at the time, and it allowed the agency a monumental breakthrough in Intelligence gathering. I don't remember much about it. I was very young at the time, but Marie was ten years older than I was, and she was very close to our father. I remember he would become furious at how his invention was used and who it was used on. My father was a brilliant scientist but fanatical in his belief that people were entitled to memories and thoughts of their own. I remember he was away from home a lot after that. It wasn't until I was much older that I realized he had affiliated himself with a Rebel Faction and had taken Marie with him. He died during a GIA raid on a Rebel facility when I was six years old, and Marie was sixteen. She never recovered and, of course, blamed his death on the GIA. Marie ran away from home just after the funeral but not before bombing the GIA laboratory where my father used to work. She'd come home maybe once a year in the beginning, but after Mom remarried, she stayed away. My stepfather worked with the government. It would have been dangerous for her to return."

"And you?"

"My stepfather was a good man who loved my mother. He treated me with respect, and I grew to love him as well. I joined the GIA partially because of his influence, but mostly because the Rebels are corrupt and believe the only solution to our social problems is through violence. Marie and I are on completely opposite sides of the spectrum now, but she's aware of her choices, and she's aware of the consequences."

Johnson regarded her quietly and then asked, "You don't have problems with the GIA scanning your peoples' thoughts?"

"If we can stop one innocent death, then I'm okay with it." Ann lapsed into silence. She had almost told him of her suspicions about Marie being able to circumvent the scanner but decided she had said enough.

Johnson walked over to the radio and turned it on to CJME 1300, the only decent rock station on the prairies. There was a lot more to the Marie situation than what Ann had just said, but he didn't really care. When she was ready to confide in him, she would.

He wasn't in a hurry.

"The Rebels' transponders you sent back," Ann continued, "we reversed engineered it and tracked it back to its originating point. We were able to find their Destination Machine and did a hit on the facility yesterday. Thanks to you, they can no longer travel to Earth or any other planet."

"They only had one machine?"

"Yes, only one. The Rebels may be able to build their own in time, but we'll try to keep ahead of them."

"So, Sally will be safe?"

"Yes, and everyone else on Earth."

He slid in close beside her, taking a sip of beer and looking wordlessly out the window across from them. They sat in comfortable silence before Johnson finished his bottle, placed the empty on the table to his front, and turned into her smiling face.

CHAPTER 46

*T*he next morning, Johnson got up, dressed and was out the door before Ann woke. He stopped in at a local convenience store and bought a coffee before walking to the park across the street. This is what he missed, he thought — mornings on the prairies. The brisk air and the vast blue sky surrounding him always filled him with life. He found a bench and sat down, thinking about this second chance that he had been given. He knew it was now time to see his wife and say goodbye. He had loved Elly; he still did. She had been given twenty years to mourn him and move on with her life. He had been given a fraction of that time. He needed the chance to say goodbye. The agency may not be happy with his decision, but it wasn't any of their business. Johnson felt a pang of nagging guilt about his night with Ann but knew that time had moved on for both Elly and him.

The coffee finished, and his mind made up, Johnson walked back to the apartment. He opened the door and heard Ann and Betty talking. When he entered, Ann turned and waved him in as Betty finished off. "I understand. I don't like it, but I understand. And it's time for me to let go. I'm tired of the hunt and always looking over my shoulder."

Ann took Betty's hand without comment and then looked up at Johnson. "Betty brought us some muffins. You out for a walk?"

"Yeah, just something to get the blood moving," he replied, taking a seat beside them at the table and helping himself to the muffins.

"I never had a chance to ask you something," Betty announced. "Since I'm staying, I want to ask you if you'd be interested in taking over my home in Midgard."

Johnson turned to look closely at her. Surprised, he asked,

"Are you sure you want to do that?"

"I'm sure you'll take good care of it," she said quietly. "Ann will set up all the security protocols so you can get in." She looked away and then said softly, "I certainly loved that little place. Ann will also contact my son. It will be hard for him, but he'll understand. You'll probably meet him. There are some things left in the house that I want him to have."

"Thank you, Betty. It's beyond generous of you to do this. I'll take good care of the place, and I'm looking forward to meeting your son." Johnson leaned forward and enveloped her in a hug, aware that she was closing off a chapter in her life and starting a new one in a new world.

Ann spoke up. "We'll look after all the details for you, Betty."

Betty pulled back slightly from Johnson but held onto his arms. "I liked you from the moment I laid eyes on you, lying on that hospital platform. Sometimes you can tell by just looking at people if they can do the job or not. I knew you could, and you proved it." She moved away from him. "Enough of this. Life is funny, isn't it? So many twists and turns." She patted his knee fondly. "Your brother is a fine man, and I believe I'll be very happy here. Will we see you before you go?"

Johnson nodded. "I'll clear things up with Sally and drop by to see both of you before I leave."

They walked Betty out of the apartment to the front steps, where Ann hugged her goodbye. As they watched her walk down the street, Ann leaned into Johnson and said, "I'll truly miss her. She is quite the legend." Her hand dropped down, searching for his, and, finding it, gripped it tightly. They waited there and watched as Betty finally disappeared around the corner before walking back up the steps to his apartment.

"There's one last thing I need to look after before going back to Midgard," Johnson said.

"Are you sure you want to go back? This is your home."

"It was my home. Too much time has passed, and there's

nothing left for me here. I have a new future that I want to explore. But I still need to visit my wife. There was never an opportunity for either one of us to say goodbye, and it's important to me."

"I don't see why not. The threat is gone. We'll fix the drop-off point for your insertion, and once you're ready to come back, you can send us a message." She leaned against the kitchen counter and asked, "How long do you think you'll need?"

"Three days should do it."

"I'll see you then. It's time for me to get going." Ann leaned in and kissed him on the cheek.

Johnson wrapped his arms around her and kissed her gently on the lips. "I'll see you at home," he finally said. They donned sunglasses and stood quietly, wrapped in each other's arms as the crack of light appeared and grew steadily larger and brighter. As it reached its peak, Ann gave Johnson a final, lingering kiss. She then separated from him, stepping into the portal and disappearing.

Sally stood behind the counter, a dishcloth in her hand, picking up each individual cup, wiping and then inspecting for spots before placing it back down. She heard the front door open and, seeing Johnson, dropped her cloth and poured him a cup of coffee.

"Service with a smile," Johnson said, grinning at her. He paid for his coffee despite a protest from her. "When's your break?"

She glanced around the room and then at the clock on the wall. The rush was over, and the shop was thinning out. "I suppose I can take it now."

She poured herself a coffee and followed him over to a table by the window where they took a seat. "You were more than welcome to join us yesterday, you know," she said.

"I would have been the third wheel. I checked out the way he was looking at you, Sally. He's very interested. I hope you had a good time."

"I did," she said, blushing. "Ian's a really nice guy."

"See? I'm glad it worked out."

"I didn't want you to feel like I left you hanging."

"Not at all. Besides, I had some other business to look after." He decided he had no choice but to tell her his plans as soon as possible. "I have to let you know that my university stay has to be postponed, at least for the short term. Something came up at home, and I have to go back. My family needs me," he began, his story already worked out well ahead of time.

Sally's eyes lifted compassionately into his, and she placed her hand over his arm. "Oh, no! What's happened? Is there anything I can do to help out?"

"There's nothing you can do, but thank you. Mom's been sick for a while now. It wasn't particularly serious, and Dad had no problems looking after her. Unfortunately, he's developed a heart condition and needs help. I was only going to go home for a month and see what I could do, you know, just sort some things out. But after I talked with the doctor, I found out this will be long term. At first, they didn't want me to come home. Mom and dad wanted me to stay here and go to university, but I can't in all good conscience."

"I'm so sorry," she said, disheartened. "Will you have to leave soon?"

"Tomorrow afternoon. I'll close everything at the university today and then pack up the apartment. It shouldn't take too long." They sat in silence as Johnson drank his coffee, and Sally watched him, biting her lip. She took another look around the cafe; it was now empty. "Give me a minute," she announced and got up and went into the back kitchen. Johnson stayed obligingly in his seat, awaiting her return. She came back wearing a light jacket and motioned for him to go outside with her. "Come walk with me. The boss says I have half an hour." He joined her, walking out the door and up to Albert Street, where they then headed south.

The two walked in silence for only a minute. Sally suddenly

reached for his arm, pulled him around, and asked, "So, what's really going on?"

Johnson maintained a steady gaze into her face as he replied, "I've already told you."

"No," she said fiercely. "Right from the beginning, you gave me a name and told me a story. I'm no fool. I've checked you out. On the surface, it all looked good, but that's the trouble. There's a surface story and nothing more. No details whatsoever. I explored every avenue on the internet, and it always seemed to end up at a dead end. So I'm asking you again. What's really going on — who are you and where do you come from?" Her voice remained calm, but Johnson could see a steely determination behind it that he could not help but admire. She forged ahead with her observations. "I need to know who it is I've been dealing with. You appear to be a very young man, but your reactions and words are those of someone twice your age. Do you think I haven't been aware of how you've been guiding me? How things have fallen into place since you've been here?"

Johnson placed his hand gently on her waist and said, "Let's keep walking, shall we, and I'll try to explain as much as I can." Sally grudgingly obliged him, and, after a few seconds, he began to speak again. "My name is Steve Johnson, and that much is the truth. Some of the other details, I may have taken some liberties with."

She smiled slightly. "Keep talking. You owe me some details."

"I was born and raised here, but now I work for an agency that watches people like you, people with your talents. They identified you, your colleagues and that machine you're about to design as a way to move into a brighter future. They became aware of how your father had halted your progress, and I was simply brought in to help turn that around."

Sally glanced at him with disbelief and said, "You've given me another convenient half-truth, Steve, and managed to brush over the specifics."

"I'm sorry. That's all I can say. You'll just have to believe me when I tell you there would be concerns if I gave you any more information. Believe it or not, that machine you're designing will change the world."

"Concerns? Perhaps one day, you'll be able to tell me. I'll have to be content with that for now, but...can you tell me...why me? How can they be so sure that I can make this work?"

Johnson smiled. "The people I work for know you can do this. I can see why they came to that conclusion. You're bright, your mind takes on a problem and finds solutions other people can't see. Sally, just keep doing what you're doing. Some days may be tough, but in the end, it will all work out. The future looks good, and I know you'll be fine."

They had come full circle in their walk and were now back at the coffee shop. Sally had not given up in her attempts to understand exactly what Johnson was doing there. She kept asking questions until he finally turned, wrapped his arms around her and said, "I can't, Sally. Enough."

She sighed tiredly into his chest. "Can I see you before you leave?"

He nodded, and they made plans to see each other one last time at his apartment before he left.

The next day, he dropped over to see his brother and Betty. He was immediately both thankful and delighted by the physical changes he saw in Dave. Johnson watched with a broad smile as his brother walked into the house from the garden. He was visibly healthier; his movements were steady and no longer shaky.

Dave caught the look of astonishment on Johnson's face and said with a grin, "I don't know what Betty did, but whatever it was, it worked. At my checkup this morning, the doctor was shocked. The tumour is considerably smaller, and the numbers in my blood work were close to normal. They had to recheck my records."

"That's great news," Johnson said, wrapping his arms around his brother.

Betty came into the room with a plate of cookies. The next hour was spent with the three of them sitting and talking, reminiscing about the past and discussing Dave and Betty's plans for the future. He left them with an ache in his heart, knowing that, in all probability, he would never see them again. "You two look after yourselves," he said, kissing Betty on the cheek.

"Things couldn't have worked out better," she whispered to him. "And I'll take good care of your brother."

The two men hugged each other one last time. Dave embraced Johnson roughly before quietly promising, "Your secret is safe with me." Johnson looked into his brother's face for a long moment before smiling. With a final wave to both of them, he turned and walked out the door.

His last stop was the cemetery. He strode up to the bench he had first seen his brother sitting on and sat down, gazing silently at the tombstones. Words left unspoken, time with his family he would never get back, and memories of happier days long ago flooded through him. He knew, however, that he had only one choice and that was to go forward. Finally, getting up, he placed a single yellow rose on each of the graves before turning and walking away.

Back at the apartment, he confirmed a departure time with Midgard and then wiped down the room when the front door buzzer announced Sally's arrival. "Glad you could make it," he said, opening the door when he heard her knock.

"Of course. I had to see you one last time," she said.

He invited her in, and Johnson immediately pointed around the room. "If you want any of this stuff, help yourself. I'm leaving everything here."

They wandered around the apartment, and she examined everything he was leaving behind. "You're not taking anything back with you?"

"I travel light."

Sally stopped at his bedroom door when she saw the backpack. "You're already packed?"

"I had some time this afternoon."

"Are you sure you have to go? I could always use an extra set of eyes."

"I'm sure. Besides, you have to do this on your own."

He held out his arms, and she slipped into the embrace, not saying a word. She knew her work would continue, with or without him.

Johnson said, "Let me show you one more piece of the puzzle."

She frowned slightly but nodded, saying, "Okay," as he got up and handed her a pair of sunglasses. They walked into the bedroom, where he pulled down the window blinds before turning back to her.

"You need to know that they searched this entire world and chose you. Believe me when I say the results of your work will ensure that your future and the future of the world, will be spectacular." He picked up his pack, hoisted it on and said, grinning, "Now keep what you're about to see to yourself. Earth isn't quite ready for it yet."

Puzzled, she started to protest, when from the corner of the bedroom, a small, brilliant ball of light appeared. The portal expanded quickly, and she shielded her eyes in wonder as the tear finally stabilized, encompassing almost the entire portion of the wall.

"Till we meet again," Johnson said and walked into the opening. He heard her call his name, and he turned to look at her.

"That's what I call an exit! Thank you!" Sally said in wonder.

He grinned and then disappeared, the light vanishing with him. Sally stood riveted in place for a moment and then walked over to where Johnson had been. She pushed the sunglasses to the top of her head, her scientist's mind already trying to dissect and understand what it was she had just witnessed. *Quite the exit, indeed*, she thought. "Next time," she muttered to herself, "he's taking me with him."

She turned and began to walk out of the apartment but then stopped and moved back to the kitchen. Scooping up a toaster with some satisfaction, she thought, *I don't suppose he'll be needing this.*

CHAPTER 47

Johnson stepped out of the tear and found himself on a damp asphalt road behind a large building in Collingwood, Ontario. He was relieved to find that his body was adapting to the jumps, and his eyes and equilibrium adjusted themselves after only a few moments. He walked from behind the building to Main Street and oriented himself. In the distance, he could make out the blinking neon light of a motel with a flashing vacancy sign. He made his way up to the motel and surveyed it carefully. It appeared to be well maintained and clean, even though it was an older style establishment. Its office was sitting front and centre, and the rows of rooms extended to its left and right. My kind of place, Johnson thought, as he walked across the street and down one side before returning and opening the door into the office. The warm air felt good, a respite from the coolness of the night. A woman stood behind the counter, looking at him with suspicious eyes.

She stood barely over five feet tall and was well past middle age. She should be at home and retired, he thought, not running a motel. "Saw you walking around back," she muttered. "Find everything to your liking?"

Johnson replied with a nod and said, "Everything looks just fine, ma'am, I like quiet places."

"Oh, it's quiet," she said, "and if it's not, we'll make it quiet, with no refund. How long were you looking at staying?"

"I'll be here until Sunday morning. Would rooms two, three, or four be available?"

"Room two is empty, but it's very close to the front office. Is that okay?"

"That'll be fine," he said.

"You've got room two till Sunday. The checkout is at eleven

in the morning. No loud music or partying. Keep the place neat and tidy."

Johnson grinned at the all too familiar lines and said, "I'll do that." He paid in advance, picked up his key and walked to his room. Opening the door, he turned on the light switch before dropping the backpack on the chair and making his way to the bathroom. He stripped down and threw his clothing into a jumbled pile on the floor, turned on the shower and stepped inside. The steamy, hot water rained down hard on his body, and he stood motionless for several minutes before heaving a tired sigh of relief. He lathered up, rinsed himself off and, reluctantly, turned the shower off. Wrapping a fresh towel around his waist, he stepped out and wiped the steam from the mirror.

The bruising on his face was fading and had almost returned to its regular colouring. His eyes, however, looked tired and bloodshot. He finished towelling off and walked gratefully over to the bed, lying down and closing his eyes. His body sunk deeply into the well-used mattress, and he could feel a dent down its centre that had been put there by a thousand other bodies. His breathing slowed as soon as his head hit the pillow, and he drifted off into a deep, dreamless sleep, not waking until the next morning.

Johnson rolled over in the bed and turned his eyes to the old clock radio, waiting sleepily until the numbers came into focus. It was a little past nine o'clock, and he had slept longer than he wanted to. Rolling out of bed and shaking off the last of his drowsiness, he was almost dressed when his wallet started to vibrate. The message was from Ann, who reported that his wife would be at a coffee shop just down the street at 10:30. This would be his only window of opportunity to meet with her. *One chance*, he thought. *I'll take it.*

He found himself just outside the cafe by 10:25 and instinctively scanned the faces of the people sitting out front. Not recognizing anyone, he walked into the shop and looked around but did not find who he was looking for. He ordered a coffee and sat down at the only available table. It wasn't close to the entrance, and he had to turn his chair to look through the crowd and see the door. Johnson settled himself into his seat, glancing impatiently at the clock on the wall that was now showing 10:45. *He'd wait at least another hour*, he thought. *Just be patient.* His thoughts were interrupted by the sound of a familiar voice, and he turned his head slowly back to the door. The woman was older; her once brunette locks were now silver and pulled back into a bun that emphasized her still elegant, familiar face. She had arrived with another woman who was obviously a friend, and the two of them began making their way to an empty table. Her blue eyes still dazzled from a distance, the creases of time seen creeping in on them, not lessening her beauty. She'd weathered the years well; her frame was still tall and slim, her movements graceful. They drew closer and, just as they were ready to pass Johnson's table, their eyes met. She stopped short. His eyes remained steady on hers, while hers began to fill with confusion. He could almost see the thought process she was going through as her mind muddled through a myriad of possibilities and questions.

Elly turned to her friend and whispered a few soft words. Her friend frowned slightly with worry but then nodded and continued on by herself. Elly looked once more at him, bewildered, before turning and walking quickly to the door and out into the street. Johnson immediately got up, dropped some change on the table and went after her. By the time he stepped out the door, he had lost sight of her. On the sidewalk, he looked up and down for several seconds before he caught a glimpse of her walking briskly away. He broke into a jog until he had almost caught up and called out gently, "Elly, please stop."

She kept walking with her head down, and her hands jammed firmly into her jacket pockets.

"Elly, please, please stop. It's me."

She shuttered and ground to a halt but still didn't look at him, her eyes firmly glued to the ground ahead of her. "This can't be happening. How can you be here? I can't believe this is happening," she said raggedly, choking back tears.

"Just let me explain. You deserve that. Once I'm done, if you want me to leave, I will."

She brought her head up slowly, her face questioning, as tears began to slide down her cheeks. "I don't understand," she said slowly, shaking her head. "Your brother called me saying something about you being here, but I thought his cancer was making him see things."

Johnson moved closer but still kept a distance between them. "No, I think Dave was just trying to give you a heads-up. It's really me." A moment passed, then two, their eyes not leaving one another. Finally, she unclenched her hands and moved her right hand up to his face, touching him gently with her fingers.

"It really is you, isn't it?" she said, stunned.

"It is." He let the words sink in and then asked, "Can we walk?"

She hesitated slightly and then said, "Yes. I don't understand. You're so young. How could that happen?"

"It's a long story," he countered. "Let's take that walk now. We've got a lot to talk about, and I've lost a lifetime with you."

Elly, trying to dry her tears, turned and began walking and talking with him. Their conversation, awkward at first, slowly transitioned into a running commentary on what had happened to both of them.

It was painful to tear open the old wounds again, but she talked calmly about her initial shock and the heartache. She had received a visit from the Military padre, who informed her of his Missing in Action status. A year later, his status changed from Missing in Action to Presumed Dead. She wanted only a plaque at the National Military Cemetery. The family, however, insisted on burial and a gravesite in Regina. She attended the funeral reluctantly but had never returned, not because she didn't miss him but because he wasn't there. Their plan had been to spend the rest of their days together, growing old with each other. That plan was shattered with his disappearance but eventually, she said, it had been time for her to move on. She was lonely living with just memories, but after some time, she had found someone else. "He's a good man," she said, with a sad smile on her face. "He loves me, and we have a good life now. We adopted two beautiful girls who have done well and are on their own now. My husband will be retiring next year. I'm happy, Steve."

It was now Johnson's turn to explain everything he'd been through. He recounted all that he could, the firefight, his rescue, arrival on another planet light-years away, his rejuvenation and his return to Earth. Throughout his explanation, her expressive face went through a myriad of emotions, from disbelief to amazement.

"But why are you here now?"

"That's difficult to explain. I suppose it's just easier to say that the people who healed me asked me to return to help someone out."

"Classified info, I suppose?"

He chuckled. "Nothing really changes, does it?"

"Not really," she said. "Especially with you. I never knew exactly what you were doing. But I always figured that the less I knew, the safer I was."

"And I'll always keep you safe, Elly."

She nodded and said, "I know."

They had walked and talked until late afternoon, stopping only for a hot dog and soft drink at a sidewalk caterer. They finally ended back at the cafe where they had started.

"I can stay for two more days if you'd like," he said.

"I'd like that very much. Two days will go by fast. I can pick you up at your hotel tomorrow morning, at 10 o'clock." She gave a wave goodbye, and Johnson watched her leave with conflicting emotions battling inside him. His love for this woman was confusing. Time had flown by for both of them, and she now had an entire lifetime of new memories with someone else.

The next morning, they pulled up to the bottom of a ski hill on the outskirts of the town. Getting out of the car, they looked up to the top of the rise, and Elly remarked, "It'll be a bit tough, but the view will be worth it." They found a path that wound its way through gullies and creases in the hills up to the top. Johnson took the lead but kept the pace slow and steady. Three-quarters of the way up, he stopped and turned back, watching her as she closed the gap between them. He took her hand to help her over a small rocky patch, and she smiled at him. Sweat ran down her tanned forehead, the activity making her face flush, but she had maintained a strong, measured step. At 20 metres from the top, they again stopped and joined hands as they walked the rest of the way together. Sitting down on a skier's bench overlooking the Bay, Johnson opened his water bottle and handed it to her. She took a long, grateful swallow and returned the bottle to him. They gazed silently at the sight of Lake Huron stretching out in front of them. After a moment, he said, "You could come back with me. We could get a place and live happily ever after."

She laughed at him then. "You always did like happy endings." Shaking her head, she continued, "I could never go. I could never leave what I have now. Besides, we've both changed — our lives have changed. I loved you, and I needed you, but that was a lifetime ago."

Looking straight ahead of her, she said, "You'll go back and do what you do because that's who you are. And I'll stay here, living my life."

"I had to ask," he said, putting his arm around her shoulder.

"Thank you." She leaned her head into him, and they settled into a comfortable silence.

Ten minutes later, she sighed, patted his knee and said, "It's getting late. Join me for supper, and you can stay the night in the spare bedroom."

"You sure?"

"I hate eating alone."

"Sounds good, then," Johnson said, and the two of them got up from the bench and followed the same path back down the slope to the car.

She dropped him off at the motel, where he packed his gear and checked out before walking to Elly's home on the waterfront. She was living in a six-story condo complex, each unit with its own long, extended balcony overlooking the water. He could see her standing on a balcony on the top floor. When she spotted him, she gave a short wave of welcome and disappeared into the condo. He made his way inside, got into the elevator, and arrived directly in front of her door. "Nice place," he said when she opened it and let him in.

"It is. A bit noisy in the summer when the vacationers come into town but not too bad otherwise," she said as she welcomed him in and offered him a drink. Elly took him on a quick tour. It had a light, open and stylishly furnished main living area, three bedrooms and two baths. They returned to the living room, where he spotted pictures on the mantel of the wood-burning fireplace. One photo immediately caught his attention. There were four people in it, Elly, her husband and two girls. *This could have been my life*, he thought, fighting the twinge of envy threatening to encompass him.

"Nice looking family," he finally said to her, picking up the photo and examining it.

She flushed slightly and said, "Thanks." Elly interrupted his thoughts by saying, "I thought we'd just have pizza. I remember you always enjoyed it."

"You remember right," he said, just as the door buzzer rang. "I've missed a good feed of pizza."

They settled themselves into the front room with pizza and a bottle of cold white wine, talking and reminiscing as the night grew on. There was still a connection between them, but it was no longer solid. Time, distance, and consequences were too great. It had worn away the intimate threads that made a relationship complete. It left them feeling like two old friends who had finally gotten together after many years. They had once been two people who were in love and had wanted to spend their lives together. Their lives, however, had been tragically torn apart. A part of him desperately wanted to hang on to his memory of their connection, but he knew that, for her sake, he had to let it go.

"I don't think I should stay."

"This will be the last time I'll ever see you. And I don't want you to spend it in a hotel by yourself. Your coming back has given me the kind of closure that no one ever gets. Seeing you again, alive and well...Steve, you've been given a second chance, and I've been given a chance to say goodbye. I'll always love you for that." With that said, she abruptly got up, picked up the dishes and put them into the sink before scolding him in a friendly manner. "So, you're not going anywhere tonight. You're going to spend at least another hour with this old lady and keep her company. You can leave tomorrow morning."

He laughed as he got up and helped her with the dishes. "You'll never be old to me, Elly."

Elly, true to her word, wished Johnson a good night after about an hour and went into her bedroom. Johnson took one last look at the family pictures on the mantle. This is what he'd wanted with her years ago, but now it was too late, and everything had changed. He finally had the chance to say goodbye, and it was now time for him to leave.

The next morning, Johnson got out of bed and looked out across the water. He called Elly's name, but there was no answer. He showered, shaved, put on clean clothes and walked out to the kitchen where he found a pot of freshly brewed coffee, a plate of cut fruit and cheese and a note that had been left on the counter saying, "Out for a run." Johnson had just poured himself a cup of coffee when he heard the door open.

'Hey, you up yet?" she called out from the door.

"I am. Thanks for the coffee," he said. "How was the run?"

"I'm a lot slower than I used to be, but I'm still moving, so it's all good."

Johnson already had his pack sitting in the front room. Picking up a pen from the telephone table, he wrote, "Clear to extract," on a piece of paper. He looked at Elly, taking in her flushed, healthy cheeks and tousled hair. "Would you mind if I drop by again to meet your family one day?"

She laughed. "And who will I introduce you as?"

"Ummm, your great-nephew?"

"Ouch, you're killing me."

Johnson smiled, opening his arms and enveloping her into him. He whispered into her ear, "I'll always love you."

"I'll always love you too, Steve," she sighed.

He pushed back gently and looked at her before leaning in and kissing her on the forehead. "Thank you for spending this time with me, Elly."

She kissed him on the cheek before holding his face in her hands and said, "I never gave up. You'll always be in my heart."

They gazed quietly at each other, Johnson seeing the young woman he had lost years ago, Elly seeing the man she had loved with such youthful passion. Johnson broke the moment by reaching around to his back pocket, taking out his wallet and placing the slip of paper into it. He then walked over to the drapes and closed them, saying, "It's going to get pretty bright in here." He picked up her sunglasses and offered them to her. "Better put these on."

He had no sooner finished his sentence when a brilliant light appeared in the centre of the room. The crack of light widened steadily, becoming broader and brighter until it reached its full height. Johnson secured his backpack and strode toward it before turning to her one last time. He wanted to say something, but everything had already been said. She understood and nodded silently. He did not take his eyes off her as he made his final steps into the portal. She lifted a hand in farewell as he lifted his, and then he was gone. The tears she had held in while he was with her now flowed soundlessly down her cheeks.

CHAPTER 48

Johnson felt himself being sucked and pushed into the void, rushing back to Midgard. The trip was better only because he knew what to expect, and he forced himself to relax and let Destination do the driving. Finally, the space around him began to slow, the atmosphere getting quieter as the darkness faded. An instant later, he found himself dropping clumsily onto the floor in the glass enclosure of the Destination Room.

"Welcome home," the man behind the console said.

"Thanks," Johnson replied, his stomach lurching and his head spinning. "My landings need work."

"You're scheduled for a quick debrief with HQ staff in Miss Petrov's office as soon as you're ready."

"Give me five," he said as he heaved himself up and walked out in search of water.

Five minutes later, the door to her office slid open as he approached it.

"Welcome back," Ann said, getting up from behind her desk and holding out her hand to him.

Johnson took her hand, shaking it while smiling. "Good to be back." He acknowledged the others in the room and took a seat.

Ann continued. "A quick debrief, and then we can let you have some time off."

The meeting started and went on for a couple of hours before Eric called for its adjournment. Ten minutes later, Ann and Johnson were alone in the office.

He asked, "How do I get into Betty's old place?"

"I'll take you through all the security protocols. We're free to leave now. Setup will only take a few moments." The two of them left the office and got into Ann's vector. When they arrived at

Betty's home, the front door opened automatically. Betty's recorded voice could be heard. "Welcome home."

He stopped momentarily. "I thought you needed to set up the security code?"

"I lied. You're already in the system. Just needed to get you alone," Ann said as she put her arms around him.

Over the next few days, Johnson slowly made Betty's place his own. Unpacking his backpack, he'd opened the closet to find his old uniform in the box that Betty had packed it in. The last thing she'd given him on Earth was a scarf, which she had wanted to be hung outside the back door. He tied it up carefully and then stepped back, watching it slowly catch the morning wind and wave its colours. A small piece of her would now always be there. He smiled, recalling the affectionate glances Betty and his brother had given each other when last he saw them. They would be good for each other.

Johnson asked Ann for the location of the best fresh produce within the travel distance of the vector. He made plans to go to one of them, a town located two hundred kilometres from his home. Getting into the vector, he set his coordinates and settled in for the short ride. Fifteen minutes later, he landed and was walking down the street of a quaint village. It had an oddly familiar feel to it, sporting symbols and architecture with a Scandinavian feel. The streets were crowded, and there was a celebration of some sort going on. In the centre of town was a park with roads running from it like the spokes of a wheel. Kiosks were spread throughout and had the enticing odours of barbecued meats emanating from them. Vendors were calling out for people to try their goods.

Spying a man selling pints of mead, Johnson made his way through the people to order. He found himself at the end of a short line, waiting for his turn. Johnson finally came up to the bartender, who said, "Good afternoon! What can I get for you today?"

He replied, "a pint of dark mead, please."

"Make that two," said a voice from behind him. "My treat," the stranger continued and threw some money onto the counter.

Johnson turned and looked carefully at the man. He was, Johnson thought, perhaps in his early forties with short black hair and a receding hairline. He sported a small paunch that indicated he may not possibly be in the best of shape. The man's smile seemed genuine and open. "Thanks. You didn't have to do that."

The man accepted the pints when they appeared and handed one to Johnson. "The name's Bill. Skol," he said as the two clanked their glasses together and took a long drink.

Johnson introduced himself. "My name's Steve."

Bill brought down the glass from his lips, wiped his mouth with his sleeve and said, "I know. You're younger than I thought you'd be."

"What would make you say that?" Johnson said, surprised. He automatically stepped back to create distance between the two of them. His hand went down to search for his weapon before he remembered he was not carrying that day. *Shit*, he thought.

"Don't worry about it, Johnson." Bill's tone remained quiet and cordial. "This is a public place. Nothing is going to happen here. I just wanted to meet you in the flesh and say hello. Marie has told me a lot about you. It seems like you gave her quite the challenge. That says a lot about your skills." He tilted the pint up to his lips again and downed the entire glass before giving Johnson a mocking salute. "If you ever get tired of the GIA, let me know. I've got a job for you." Bill turned abruptly and walked swiftly away from Johnson, seeming to melt back into the crowd as if he was never there.

Johnson calmly finished his mead, tilting the last of the pint's potent contents into his mouth and placing it back on the counter. A smile slowly crept across his face. *Life here is going to be interesting. I'm looking forward to it.*

The End